T0279378

BURNING CROWNS

Also by Catherine Doyle and Katherine Webber

Twin Crowns

Cursed Crowns

BURNING CROWNS

CATHERINE DOYLE & KATHERINE WEBBER

BALZER + BRAY

An Imprint of HarperCollinsPublishers

Balzer + Bray is an imprint of HarperCollins Publishers.

Burning Crowns
Copyright © 2024 by Catherine Doyle and Katherine Webber

Library of Congress Control Number: 2023943298
ISBN 978-0-06-332643-9

Typography by Chris Kwon
24 25 26 27 28 LBC 5 4 3 2 1

First Edition

For Grace Doyle, Louisa Tsang, and Virginia Webber—a trio of wonderful mothers

Beware the curse at last set free,

Death lurks beneath a burning tree. . . .

1

WREN

Wren Greenrock stood at her bedroom window in the west tower of Anadawn Palace, watching the moon rise above the distant trees. The sky was inky blue and pinpricked with a scattering of stars. It was a peaceful night and yet Wren felt strangely disquieted, as though the kingdom of Eana was not at rest but rather only holding its breath.

"When you're done gazing wistfully at the moon, I could use a little help over here!" Rose's voice cut through the stillness from across the room, where she was riffling in her wardrobe. "Truly, I've never seen such disarray."

Their royal tour had come to an end only hours ago, and Wren had arrived back at the palace to find that her bedroom renovations had at last been completed. Now she finally had a place that was all her own.

Of course, Rose had insisted on inspecting it at once.

The stone walls were hung with colorful tapestries, depicting the witch queens and kings of old, and the floor had been covered with a sprawling rug. A grand oak-wood bed with a gauzy canopy occupied the center of the room, while a looming wardrobe spanned the entire wall nearest the door. There was an ornate dresser by the adjacent bathing chamber, the drawers of which were already filled with various pots of creams and colorful shadows, all manner of blushes and brushes, and enough jewelry to sink a small ship.

Wren had been looking forward to an early night in her new bedroom, but energized from the success of their first royal tour, Rose was too restless to retire. So she had taken on another project at once—the complete reorganization of Wren's palace wardrobe. Every so often, a rogue pair of trousers or a scuffed boot would soar through the air.

"Why don't we do this tomorrow?" Wren suggested for the third time. "Or maybe never?"

"No, no, no," muttered Rose, wrinkling her nose at a muddy gown. "Trust me, you'll be glad when it's done. Wren, truly, *how* have you managed to get mud on everything already? You haven't even worn this dress yet!"

Wren recalled with fleeting fondness the evening on tour when, in a fit of boredom, she had hidden inside her traveling trunk to jump out and scare Rose, her sister shrieking so loudly the guards had come running. Perhaps she should have taken off her traveling boots first and saved all those beautiful, unworn dresses. But she didn't mind mud or sand, or mess. Sometimes, amid the royal grandeur of the palace, she found herself missing the untamed beaches of Ortha, the tang of brine floating on the breeze, the satisfying squelch of mulch in the surrounding forest, and the scratch of tree bark against her fingers as she climbed the trees up and up and up until the canopies broke and she could see all the way to the horizon.

Rose sighed as she surveyed another stained dress, then shot her sister a pointed look.

For a passing moment, Wren considered crawling out the window, clambering down the tower and escaping to the desert, but her feet were aching, and it wouldn't be worth the ire she would face upon her return. So instead she pouted at the moon like a sulking child.

A rogue wind whipped up, casting a chill in the air. As she reached out to close the window she caught sight of her reflection in the glass. She winced, hating the paleness of her face, the hollows in her cheeks, the new silver streak in her hair. It was a sign of her grief at losing Banba and a stark reminder that the world she had grown up in, sheltered and guided by her steadfast grandmother, was no longer the one in which she lived. It was a reminder of the crack in her heart.

And yet the world around Wren had already moved on. Over two moons had passed since the Battle of Anadawn, where the twins had fought the rebels who'd sought to overthrow them. Wren had broken the ancient curse that had once split their five strands of magic: tempest, enchantment, warrior, healing, and seeing. This had allowed all the witches of Eana to have control over each strand, as they once did before those powers were taken from them, splintered by their evil ancestor Oonagh Starcrest during a fight against her benevolent twin sister, Ortha, over a thousand years ago. Together, Wren and Rose had defended their throne. After, they had chosen to show mercy toward those who had risen up in fear of them and their fellow witches so they could remake the kingdom as a peaceful nation.

It was going well, so far. But deep down, Wren did not feel peaceful.

"This is entirely useless," Rose announced. She was on her feet now, glaring at Wren's wardrobe as though it had personally offended her. "First order of new business: now that we're back, you need your own seamstress."

"Fine by me," said Wren, slamming the window shut.

"Fortunately, I know just the one," Rose went on. "Do you know, she made the very gown I'm wearing?" She twirled to show it off. Even now, after an exhausting tour, Rose looked just like a princess should, in a pink corseted gown inlaid with golden brocade. Her hair hung in perfect chestnut curls that were pulled away from her face by a rose pin still in bloom. Her green eyes were as bright as emeralds, her cheeks rosy from her efforts at organizing Wren's clothes.

Wren tucked her silver streak behind her ear and looked down at her own crumpled blue dress, wishing she looked as put together as her twin. Wishing she felt the same sense of peace and confidence about the future. "I don't know what I'd do without you."

"Luckily, we won't ever find out." Rose kicked a rogue boot aside as she came toward Wren. "And anyway, this is what sisters are for. We take care of each other." She threw her arms around Wren, the warmth of her embrace chasing Wren's coldness away. When she pulled back, Rose studied Wren's face and pursed her lips. "Oh, Wren, you look absolutely exhausted. You really should get some rest. You need it. Now that we're back, there is a lot to do."

"Can't wait," said Wren, trying to summon a smidgeon of enthusiasm.

Rose laughed at her attempt. "Sleep well, Wren. Tomorrow, the real work of ruling Eana begins!" Then she skipped out of the room, humming as she went. When the door closed behind Rose and the room fell silent once more, Wren collapsed onto her bed, where a familiar fur-lined dress lay crumpled in a heap. Rose must have chucked it across the room during her excavation.

Wren pressed her face into the gown, inhaling the scent of wild pine and fresh snow. Her thoughts flitted, as they often did, to Gevra. To King Alarik. To Tor and Elske. And then, like milk curdling, her mind turned to Oonagh, who, after a thousand years, had broken free of her icy tomb on the northern continent and was now hiding somewhere in its wilderness.

Wren's time in Gevra had changed her, though she was careful not to show it around Rose. But now that she was finally alone, she could no longer ignore the faint stinging in her wrist. She rolled her sleeve back, revealing the jagged silver scar that had appeared not long after the Battle of Anadawn. She traced it with her thumb, setting loose a plume of nausea inside her.

She lay back and closed her eyes, willing sleep to find her so she could forget the terrible blood spell she and Alarik had performed in Gevra. So she could forget the ancient witch queen she had accidentally awoken and the strange scar that was part of her now.

After a while, the nausea subsided but a deep feeling of unease remained.

2

ROSE

Rose Valhart smiled as she strolled through the Anadawn orchards. This morning, she wore a pale pink day dress the color of spring blossoms that swished around her ankles, and her hair was pulled back in a simple braid. The sound of children's laughter echoed through the trees, and Rose spotted a glimpse of Tilda, a spirited young witch from Ortha, leading a group of other young witches deeper into the orchard. They were giggling and shouting as they pulled plums off the trees, and the sound of their merriment was so joyful, Rose couldn't bring herself to tell them that they were wasting perfectly good fruit.

It was good to be home. Even better than that, it was good to be home as queen. To know that she and Wren were making steps toward building the kind of country their people deserved. One that was prosperous and bountiful, and welcoming to all. One that was safe.

Rose stumbled on a tree root, her smile slipping. The morning breeze was cooler than she was expecting, and as she rubbed the chill from her arms, she regretted not bringing her shawl with her. The coldness in the air turned her thoughts. She had not forgotten the shared vision she and Wren had seen several weeks ago: that terrifying glimpse of their wicked ancestor Oonagh stalking through the wilds of Gevra.

The twins had not discussed it since, and Rose thanked the stars that she had not been plagued by any further visions. But on tour there had been times when she'd heard Wren cry out in her sleep or seen her wake suddenly, trembling. Rose knew in her heart that the safety she felt—for herself, for her sister, for their people—was only temporary. But, she reasoned with herself, there would always be something threatening them. There was no use in fretting about the unknown.

All she could do was prepare as best as she could. Fortify their army. Strengthen their relationships with their allies. Mend her own broken country. Show the people that she and Wren were rulers to be trusted, rulers who would do anything for Eana.

Because Eana was Rose's own beating heart. She knew that her country was her purpose. And while she loved the trappings of being queen—her crown was divine, her wardrobe spectacular, and her castle magnificent—most of all she loved that sense of purpose, of knowing that she and Wren would do anything to protect and defend their beloved kingdom.

The distant screech of a raven startled Rose from her thoughts. She had been so caught up in thinking about the future and what dangers it might hold that she had lost sight of the children playing through the trees. She shook her head, scolding herself. She would not let the specter of Oonagh Starcrest ruin everything she had worked for.

As the young witches' giddy laughter drifted across the orchard, Rose heard the unmistakable wail of an upset child. She picked up her skirts and hurried toward the sound. At the south end of the orchard, Tilda was standing with her back to the fence, looking sheepish. Next to her, Marie, a shy young witch, was snuffling as she held her red-dened cheek. The others crowded around them, and Rose noted they all had plums in their hands.

"What happened?" said Rose, trying to untangle the upset.

"She threw a plum at me!" Marie pointed an accusing finger toward Tilda.

"It was an accident," said Tilda, rolling her eyes. "I said, 'Catch.' And she didn't catch. What kind of witch can't catch a plum?"

"You used tempest magic!" said Marie.

"Of course I did! And you should have used your own magic to send it back to me. We told you that you were too little to play and now you've proved it," retorted Tilda, which only made Marie cry harder.

"There, there," said Rose, kneeling next to Marie and rubbing her back. She offered a quick burst of healing magic to help mend the bruise blooming on her cheek. "We shouldn't use our magic against each other." She gave Tilda a stern look. "Magic is for making things better, remember?"

"What about warrior magic?" said a young boy of around twelve. "That's fighting magic."

"It's protective magic," Rose corrected him. "You can use your warrior strand for all sorts of things other than fighting. It gives you better balance and agility, certainly better rhythm. Did you know that warrior witches make wonderful dancers?"

The boy harrumphed.

Rose sighed. "And you shouldn't be throwing perfectly good plums, anyway," she said, returning her admonishing gaze to Tilda. "You know better than that."

"When is Shen coming back?" said Tilda petulantly.

"I don't know," Rose admitted. "He's busy ruling the Sunkissed Kingdom, you know that."

Tilda pouted, and Rose felt her heart go out to the child. She knew that Shen was Tilda's favorite of all the witches, as he had been the one to teach her how to master her warrior strand. Rose didn't blame her for missing Shen. Rose missed him, too.

"He's way more fun than you. So is Wren," Tilda said, folding her arms. One of the other children gasped at her rudeness. "Wren would never tell us to stop throwing plums. She'd throw them, too."

Rose bit the inside of her cheek, trying to let the insult wash over her. Tilda was still a child, after all, and a particularly headstrong one. And as much as Rose hated to admit it, Tilda wasn't wrong either. Wren would have been throwing plums harder and faster than anyone.

"That may be," she said calmly. "But *I* can tell you all that Cam has made the most delicious chocolate cake. And if you tell him that I sent you and bring him some of these lovely plums for him to make jam, I'm sure he'll let you have a slice. Even before supper." She smiled as the children perked up in excitement. Even Marie seemed to have forgotten her upset. "You may say it is a royal decree from Queen Rose."

"Thank you, Queen Rose," said Tilda, who seemed to be regretting her earlier petulance.

"And you must apologize to Marie," Rose added.

"Sorry, Marie," said Tilda, crouching next to her. "Next time I'll show you how to send the plum back to me, okay? I bet you'll be able to hit me with them in no time!"

Rose groaned. "Tilda, that's not at all what I meant." But Tilda wasn't listening. She was taking Marie by the hand and running with her back to the palace.

"Come on!" Tilda cried over her shoulder. "Let's go and get some cake!"

"You forgot the plums!" Rose called after them, but they were already off and running, their laughter ringing through the air, plums and tears already forgotten.

Rose shook her head and smiled as she picked up a discarded plum. It was ripe and soft in her hands, and she had a sudden, irresistible urge to take a bite. She closed her lips around it, anticipating a burst of juicy sweetness, but as her teeth sank into the purple flesh, a sour taste filled her mouth.

"Oh!" she spat, and looked down at what she had thought was a perfect plum.

It was rotten and mealy in her hand. A maggot wriggled at her. Rose spat again and threw the plum as far as she could. A shudder rushed through her, but she shook it off. The plum had been on the ground. That was why it was rotten.

With a trembling hand, she plucked another from the nearest tree. Though it looked beautiful and ripe, she knew as soon as the plum touched her lips that it was rotten, too. She dropped it, a feeling of great dismay coming over her. As Rose stood in the orchard, trying to make sense of this sudden and strange decay, it began to rain. Slowly at first, the droplets heavy and hard as they hit her skin. Rose hurried back to the palace, the shower becoming a downpour, until she was utterly soaked to the bone.

She tried to tell herself it was nothing, that it was only two rotten plums and an unexpected spring shower. It wasn't a sign, it was spoiled fruit and rain and nothing more.

Be reasonable, she told herself, as she ducked into the shelter of the palace. *Do not fear something as silly as this.*

But even after she returned to her bedchamber and took a scalding hot bath, she could not stop shivering, and the sour taste in her mouth still lingered.

WREN

Wren stood on the banks of Lake Carranam, trying to rub the goose bumps from her arms. The water rippled amber and gold, illuminated by the sun's dying rays. Even though it was the first day of spring, there was a chill in the wind. There was a chill in Wren's bones, too. But that had been there long before today.

"Tonight will be perfect," said Rose, squeezing Wren's arm. Rose stood beside her, looking beautiful in her new gown. It was pale green and embroidered with fine lace flowers to reflect the coming of spring. Agnes had threaded daisies through Rose's hair, which hung in loose curls down her back. "Our ancestors are smiling down on us. I just know it."

Wren's gown was a simple sheath of midnight blue, cinched at the waist. Around her neck, she wore a sapphire gemstone that had once belonged to her mother, and in her braid, a vine of delicate winter flowers still pricked with thorns. She had told her sister she wanted to represent the passing of winter, but as she had threaded those fine white flowers through her hair that morning, she couldn't help picturing the kingdom of Gevra in her mind and the proud spires of Grinstad Palace jutting up from the snowy mountains.

Rose had approved of the symbolism in her sister's choice. Winter was behind them now, and with it, the terrible rebellion that had once threatened Eana's future.

Since their return home, Wren and Rose had held several royal audiences, throwing open the golden gates of Anadawn Palace to their subjects. The town of Eshlinn had been rebuilt, the surrounding forest planted with thousands of saplings. The Anadawn Royal Fleet had been purged of traitors and reformed with willing young soldiers, grain stores across the country were now refilled, farmland had been redistributed, and thirty-seven new infirmaries were now open. With more healers than ever, the witches of Ortha found themselves in high demand. In the last few months, many had spread out, some traveling as far as Norbrook to settle, while others journeyed south, to where the Amarach Towers were thrumming with new apprentices itching to read the secrets of the sky.

Slowly but surely, the twins were establishing themselves as true leaders. Witches who were respected in their own country, not feared. Queens who intended to usher the kingdom into an era of peace and prosperity. A new dawn had come. Tonight, they were marking it by celebrating the Festival of Imbolg a few miles east of Anadawn Palace on the banks of the oldest lake in Eana.

At the palace's invitation, thousands of people had gathered at Lake Carranam to celebrate the festival. Under the watchful guard of Anadawn's soldiers, they reveled in the swell of music. Some danced under the setting sun while others congregated by the serving tables, drinking wine and feasting on the treats that Cam and his team of cooks had prepared for the occasion. Celeste, Rose's best friend, had already gone back for seconds. There were crispy potato croquettes, roasted lamb bites, figs with goat cheese and honey, pear and almond tartlets, spiced carrot cake, and chocolate stars.

The twins stood apart from the revelry, watching their kingdom celebrate. Rose giggled at the sight of Shen Lo dancing with Grandmother Lu, the old witch cackling as he spun her far too fast. Although it was a long way to travel, the newly crowned king of the Sunkissed Kingdom wouldn't dream of passing up an invitation from the queens of Eana.

He was, after all, hopelessly in love with one of them.

Wren glanced sidelong at Rose. "Aren't you going to dance with Shen?" she asked, amused and secretly pleased by the ongoing mutual fawning between her sister and her oldest friend.

Rose smiled coyly. "Once he asks me."

"Why don't you ask him?"

Rose wrinkled her nose. "Because *I* am the prize, Wren."

"He hasn't been able to take his eyes off you all night," Wren pointed out. "Maybe he's nervous."

"I've never known Shen Lo to be nervous about anything," said Rose, a note of warmth creeping into her voice. "Although I will admit my dress *is* particularly fine this evening."

A cold breeze swept through the clearing. The lake rippled and Wren looked down, scowling at her own reflection.

"Stop admiring yourself," said Rose. "Vanity is unbecoming of a queen."

Wren snorted. "You spend hours looking in the mirror."

"Yes, but *never* in public. Or at least not so obviously."

Wren didn't know how to tell Rose that she wasn't looking at herself. When she peered into the waters of Lake Carranam, she swore she saw Oonagh Starcrest looking back at her. The twins never spoke of their ancestor—who was still hiding in the wilds of Gevra, likely gathering her strength—but with each passing day, Wren saw more of Oonagh in her own haunted eyes. A strange emptiness yawned inside her, reminding her of everything she had given up in pursuit of blood magic: the healing strand of her magic and therefore her peace of mind.

Rose still didn't know about any of that.

Wren didn't know how to tell her.

"Are you ready?" said Rose, reaching for her sister's hand. "It's almost time for our performance."

Wren pulled her gaze from the lake. "I'm ready."

Rose made a gesture at the minstrels. The music quieted. Shen Lo fell out of his dance, smiling as he turned toward the twins. The rest of the revelers followed suit, looking eagerly to their queens. Even the wind stopped, as though to listen.

Lanterns flickered all around the lake, casting Wren and Rose in their glow.

"Welcome to the Festival of Imbolg," Rose called out. "It is our honor to mark with you the end of this long winter and to welcome the beginning of spring. This season is a time for new blessings. And so we celebrate together, with rousing music and delicious food, and of course, magic."

The crowd cheered.

Rose nodded at Wren, giving the signal.

Wren raised her free hand, summoning the tempest magic inside her. Aside from her native enchantment, her tempest strand came the easiest to her now. It was Banba's legacy, after all. Although Banba had passed on, Wren's grandmother was still close to her heart. Wren thought of her every time she glimpsed the new silver streak in her hair, felt her strength whenever she reached for her tempest magic, and heard her voice in the rumble of every storm.

Whipping up a new wind, Wren raised a river of water from the lake. As it swelled, it became a storm cloud. She exhaled through her nose, concentrating as she moved the cloud directly over the lake. Power buzzed in her bloodstream and rattled in her teeth.

"Tonight, we say goodbye to the fear and dissent of the past," Rose proclaimed. "We banish all memory of war and bloodshed."

Wren released her grip on the storm just as Rose raised her free hand, shearing the storm cloud in two. There was an almighty thunderclap. The crowd cheered as lightning flashed all around them. Rain fell in a great gushing waterfall, pummeling the lake. And then, all at once, the deluge stopped. The sky was clear once more.

A sudden shock of pain tore through Wren. She ground her teeth, forcing a smile, but her hands were trembling and her knees were growing weak.

"Today, we welcome a brighter future for Eana," said Rose, her voice loud and clear, smile broad and sure. "We welcome new life. New growth. New hope."

She squeezed Wren's hand. It was time for their enchantment. The twins knelt and each picked up a fistful of silt from the lakeshore. The fresh earth in Wren's hand strengthened her as she stood. If Rose noticed her sister's sudden exhaustion, she didn't show it.

The twins' voices arced as they recited their enchantment, the spell ringing out like a song.

"From earth to dust, with flames so bright, we welcome spring and its new light."

Just like they had been practicing all week, Wren and Rose cast their earth and conjured a magnificent oak tree made of flame. It hovered on the surface of the lake like a great burning statue. The crowd erupted in applause.

"People of Eana, we invite all of you to join us," cried Rose. "Those without magic, take a candle from one of our stewards and raise it to the sky, joining your light with ours. Witches, lend your magic to our spell. With this symbolic Tree of Light, help us to cast new blessings on this ancient land."

All across the clearing, candles were lit and raised. Witches knelt to gather dirt before casting their own enchantments, adding whips of flame to the great burning tree until it sprawled across the entire lake, its branches twisting up toward the sky. The clearing flared amber and gold, no longer lit by the dying sun but by the Tree of Light. The symbol of Imbolg.

Everyone looked up, marveling at such a feat of power.

Rose's laughter rang out, merry as a song. "Oh, Wren, isn't it wonderful?"

The great tree burned tears in Wren's eyes, and for a brief, perfect moment, she felt invigorated, filled with a hope she had thought was lost to her.

Then the smoke came. It stole up from the base of the tree, hissing as it swallowed the flames.

"Oh no!" Rose kept her voice low, but Wren heard the panic in it. "What's happening?"

Wren winced as fresh pain lanced up her arm. She dropped her hand, letting her magic go out, but it was too late. The spell had twisted. The smoke was getting thicker, blacker. It traveled along the branches of the tree, stealing every flicker of light. Then it billowed across the lake, smothering the candles in a choking cloud of ash.

The crowd screamed as darkness fell.

"Wren! Something's wrong!" hissed Rose, grabbing her hand.

Before Wren could say another word, an eerie laugh rang out. It seemed to echo all around her, finding its breath in the smoke. Wren froze. Suddenly, she knew—not what was wrong but *who*. Somehow, Oonagh Starcrest was here. Wren dropped Rose's hand and fled.

4

ROSE

Rose hated feeling afraid. She had spent her entire childhood learning how to live with fear. How to bear it; how to try to outrun it. She had promised herself that as soon as she was queen, she would never be afraid again.

But standing on the banks of Lake Carranam with thick, billowing smoke stinging her eyes and choking her, with the screams of her people ringing in her ears and with her sister suddenly ripped from her side, true fear coursed through Rose.

It was so potent that for a moment she thought she was frozen. But Rose had learned not to let fear rule her. And she certainly wasn't going to let it consume her now. She was no longer a frightened child or a naive princess, a puppet to be used for someone else's gain. She was a queen. A witch. A leader.

And something, or someone, was threatening her people. Her sister. Her celebration!

She would not stand for it. Rose's terror was swiftly replaced with a hot and righteous anger. She strode into the darkness, ready to take control. But first, she had to clear this wretched smoke. She couldn't see a thing, including her own sister, who had been standing here just a moment ago.

"Wren, where are you?" she hissed.

There was no response. Rose pushed down her rising worry and focused on the task at hand. *One step at a time*, she told herself. That was how anything got done. First clear the smoke, then calm the crowd, and then . . . then she would find Wren. And try not to throttle her.

Of the five strands of magic, the tempest strand was the one Rose struggled with the most. The wildness of it felt fierce and unfamiliar, but she focused her energy now and cast her magic out, searching for a wisp of wind that she could bend to her will. *There.* She found one and managed to turn it into a weak gust, blowing away a plume of smoke and dispersing it out over the lake.

As some of the darkness began to dissipate, Rose saw a handful of terrified faces staring back at her. Those without magic held their candles uncertainly, only a few still flickering, while the witches were standing to attention, waiting for instruction.

Wren was nowhere to be seen.

She's fine, Rose told herself as she plastered on her brightest smile. *Everything is fine.*

But she needed help.

She caught Rowena's eye, and desperately hoped the witch would hear her silent plea. Rowena was the strongest tempest she knew. And even if she didn't like Rose very much, surely she would help her clear the darkening fog.

Rowena caught Rose's gaze and dipped her chin, squaring herself to the task. Moments later, a brisk wind picked up and blew the remaining smoke across the lake. Rose lifted her hands, pretending she was clearing the air. "And no matter what darkness may fall on us, together we may banish it," she cried in a rallying voice. "And we will burn even brighter than before."

Rose could have sworn she heard Tilda snickering nearby, but Rose kept her smile in place as she solemnly bowed her head, and then, feeling quite out of ideas about how to get the festival back on course, she briskly clapped her hands three times.

"And now it is time for the . . . ceremonial flower gathering! Everyone must pick a wildflower and . . ." She trailed off and did an elaborate twirl, desperately trying to think of a clever distraction. "And weave it in their hair! Yes, that's right. A flower from the banks of Lake Carranam is known to bring good fortune indeed." Rose feigned a chuckle. "And we are all deserving of that."

There was an agonizing moment of silence. And then Tilda, who always loved to cause a commotion, let out a whoop of excitement. "I bet I can find a water lily to wear like a hat!" she crowed. "That will be the luckiest flower of them all!" With that, a chorus of laughter broke out, and to Rose's overwhelming relief, everyone knelt down and began to pick their flowers.

Rose beamed. "And of course, after the ceremonial flower gathering there will be more treats for all! And more wine!" Goodness, she hoped Cam had brought extra cake. "And dancing! To show off our flowers!"

Once everyone was duly distracted, Rose turned on her heel and crashed straight into the person behind her, nearly falling over.

Strong hands steadied her. They were warm and familiar.

For the briefest of moments, Rose let herself be held. She inhaled

Shen's intoxicating scent, enjoying the feel of his body pressed against hers. Then she pulled away. It would not do for her to look weak, as if she could not stand on her own. Even if she wished she could steal away to a hidden clearing and sink into his arms again.

"Ceremonial wildflower gathering?" he said, raising a dark brow. "How come I've never heard of that?"

"It's a time of new traditions," said Rose, her lips twitching. Despite the disastrous turn the festival had taken, seeing Shen Lo still made her smile. At least for a moment.

His face grew serious then, mirroring her own. "What just happened?"

Before she could reply, Rowena barreled toward them, practically shoving people out of her way. "*Hissing hell*, Valhart, what was that? You're lucky I was here to help."

Rose hushed her. "Please lower your voice!"

Rowena carried on as if she hadn't heard her. "And where is Wren? She could have blown all that smoke away with ease."

Rose smiled through clenched teeth, all too aware of a nearby cluster of townsfolk leaning in to eavesdrop. "Rowena, I think I saw a lovely patch of bluebells over by the trees. They would look especially splendid in your hair. Shall we go and look together?" She linked arms with the scowling tempest witch, who rolled her eyes but gamely walked with Rose away from the crowd.

Shen followed a few steps behind.

"Well?" Rowena prodded. "Where's Wren?"

"I don't know. She disappeared when the fire tree went up in smoke."

Rowena gaped at Rose. "And you're just pretending like everything is fine? Like all that choking smoke was part of your little act?"

"What would you have me do?" Rose challenged her. "Cause a panic? Terrify everyone? No. I did what I needed to do."

Rowena narrowed her eyes, and Rose knew she wasn't imagining the wind picking up again. "And now you're sending everyone on a fool's errand looking for wildflowers? How is *that* helpful?"

"It's far better than announcing I have no idea what just happened *or* where Wren has gone!" Rose's voice came out shriller than she'd intended. She winced at the sound of her own panic. She forced herself to breathe slowly and deeply. "The enchantment was likely too big. It must have crumbled . . . or . . . something."

Rowena scoffed. "That's not how magic works. You would know that if you were a real witch."

"I am a real witch!" Rose felt her temper rising. "Just because I didn't grow up in Ortha doesn't mean I'm not a witch."

Behind them, Shen Lo chuckled. "I never thought I'd hear you claim your heritage so adamantly."

"This is not helping." Rose rubbed her temples. "Can we please focus on finding Wren?" Just as she said it, she stepped on something hard. She looked down to find a piece of metal glowing dimly in the dark. "It's Wren's crown." Rose bent down to pick it up. "She must be around here somewhere."

Shen suddenly went very still. His gaze sharpened as he scanned the shadows in the trees. "I think she's in the woods."

Relief flooded Rose. She had thought for a moment the worst: that something, or someone, had stolen Wren in the smoke. She picked up her skirts and stepped over the tree line, only pausing when she noticed

Rowena was following them. "I think the bluebells are actually in that direction," she said pointedly. "Back toward the lake."

Rowena caught her meaning and glared at Rose. "Eat your bluebells, Valhart. I'll go and find Tilda and make sure she doesn't drown while searching for some pointless water lily." She turned on her heel, raising a finger in warning. "Just make sure Wren is all right. It's not like her to go missing like that."

"Of course," said Rose brusquely, even though she knew it was *exactly* like Wren to disappear.

5

WREN

Wren stumbled through the smoke, trying to outrun the shrillness of Oonagh Starcrest's laugh, but the piercing sound echoed in her ears. She wasn't sure which was more terrifying: the idea that her ancestor might be at Lake Carranam or that she alone was hearing Oonagh's voice in her head.

People jostled Wren as she ran, their screams joining the chorus of panic around them. Wren didn't dare stop. Soon, the smoke would clear and they would all see their queen for what she really was: weak. Frightened. Tainted by forbidden blood magic.

She couldn't let her people see her this way. She couldn't let Rose see her this way.

Up ahead, the ancient trees that surrounded Lake Carranam swayed in the smoke. Wren made for the forest as nausea roiled in her gut. She tore her crown off and tossed it in the long grass, searching for some relief. None came. Her magic was twisting and writhing inside her, like an injured animal.

When she reached the first of the trees, she braced her hand against it. The bark was rough against her skin, grounding her.

Breathe, she told herself.

This feeling will pass.

After all, this wasn't the first time her magic had acted up in the last three months. And it wasn't the first time she had heard that awful, screeching laugh. She often dreamed of Oonagh wandering through the snowcapped mountains of Gevra, smiling at her with blood in her teeth. Sometimes when she woke, Wren could still hear her ancestor's voice in her head, taunting her.

You are tainted like me, broken bird.

There is no going back now.

Wren lumbered to the second tree and then the third. She wound her way deeper into the forest as the smoke cleared behind her. The screaming stopped. Somewhere in the distance, Rose's voice filled the strained silence. Wren blew out a breath of relief. Her sister was taking charge, soothing their subjects with steady words, a careful laugh. Not for the first time, Wren thanked the stars for Rose. She was the queen that Eana truly deserved. Ever since Wren had returned from Gevra, she felt more and more like she was hanging on by her fingernails. Not just to the throne but to herself.

After a moment, the laughter in Wren's head began to fade. She became aware of her surroundings, the trees looming in the darkness, the solemn song of a nightingale perched somewhere overhead.

Wren was suddenly conscious of the pain flaring in her wrist. It felt as if her scar was on fire, as though a cattle brand had been seared into her skin and it was burning through flesh and bone.

She pitched forward, vomiting on the forest floor. The terrible heat remained.

"*Hissing seaweed.*"

She rolled her sleeve to her elbow, inspecting the jagged silver crescent. It glowed softly in the fractured moonlight, the pale skin around it reddening as it burned.

Wren cursed again. This was not the first time the scar had caused her pain, but it had never been this bad before. She grabbed a fistful of dirt and smeared it on her wrist to cool her skin. Her stomach lurched and she vomited again.

She crawled to a nearby tree, pressing her forehead to the trunk to ground herself.

Help me, Eana, first witch of this land.

Let this horror pass.

Wren didn't know how much time went by as she knelt by the tree or how many breaths it took to calm the poker-hot pain in her arm, but after a while, the leaves around her rustled and a familiar voice rang out.

"Wren? What's going on?" Shen Lo came through the trees like a brisk wind, making no sound at all. A determined *crunch* announced the presence of Rose, who was following close behind.

"Wren! Oh, thank the stars, you're safe. I was afraid . . ." Rose's voice wobbled as she held up Wren's crown, which she must have plucked from the grass. Now that she could see her sister was all right, Rose's concern quickly turned to anger. "What are you doing hiding in here? You completely abandoned me out there!"

"Sorry," said Wren, pulling herself to her feet. "I . . . needed a minute."

Rose folded her arms, glaring at her sister. "Well, I needed *you*. And you disappeared. Again."

Wren knew Rose still hadn't forgiven her for sneaking off to Gevra in the dead of night all those months ago. And she didn't know the half of what had happened there.

"She's been sick," said Shen, coming to Wren. His eyes were filled with concern. "You don't look well."

"I'm all right." Wren wished her hair was loose so she could pull it around her face. Shen was doing that annoying thing again where he saw right through her. "It was Cam's chocolate stars. They were so rich."

Rose wrinkled her nose. "I did say you'd regret eating seven in a row."

Wren forced a chuckle. "Banba always said my eyes were bigger than my stomach."

Shen was still frowning. Wren wanted to shoo him away and tell him to mind his own damned business. He was too nosy for his own good, and it didn't help that as her best friend, he knew Wren better than anyone. He knew the cadence of her lies, the sound of the truth in her mouth.

He knew she was lying now.

"What about the crowd?" said Wren, quickly changing the subject. "Did you manage to calm them?"

"Once the smoke cleared," said Rose with a sigh. "I had to ask Rowena to help. You know how I struggle to harness the wind." Wren heard the unsaid accusation in her sister's voice: that if she had been there, she could have helped Rose banish the smoke. "But we got through it."

"Good," said Wren, looking everywhere but at Shen.

Rose frowned as she went on. "The spell must have grown too big. It became unwieldy."

"That must be it," said Wren, trying to keep the guilt from her voice.

"But it was brilliant, wasn't it?" said Rose, with an uncertain smile. "At least for a while."

"It really was," said Wren, relieved to have found a kernel of truth in this moment.

Rose was finally softening, but much to Wren's annoyance, Shen was growing more suspicious. "Uh-huh," he muttered, his gaze falling to the scar on her wrist. Wren tugged her sleeve down but it was too late. He opened his mouth to speak.

"Don't," she hissed. "Not here."

"Wren," said Shen sternly.

"What is it?" asked Rose, coming over.

Wren grabbed Shen's shoulders and turned him around. "Hey, do you hear that?" She gestured back toward the lake. "The minstrels have started playing again. You *love* this tune, Rose. If only you had someone to dance with."

Shen scowled at Wren. "I know what you're doing."

Rose misread his annoyance, and her cheeks flushed with embarrassment. "I think you will both find that I have *many* people to dance with." She picked up her skirts and spun on her heel. "Now if you'll excuse me, at least one of us should be getting back to the festival."

She strode off, her skirts swishing back and forth behind her.

"Rose! Wait!" Shen hurried after her, but not before tossing a knowing glance over his shoulder.

Wren knew that look well.

This isn't over, Greenrock.

No, she thought as she refixed the button on her sleeve. *It* isn't *over. Whatever this trouble is it has only just begun.*

But Wren would worry about that tomorrow.

For now, she needed to dance with her sister and welcome the spring.

6

ROSE

The festival lasted long into the night.

Rose kept a close watch on Wren, half expecting her sister to disappear again, but she seemed to have recovered from her mystery ailment and appeared determined to make the most of the evening. And that was exactly what Rose needed from her sister tonight: a brave face and a rallying spirit.

Even though Rose couldn't shake the fear she'd felt when their tree had gone up in flames, and worse, when Wren had vanished, she knew how important tonight was. They could not afford to show fear in front of their people. And so, as Wren rose to the importance of the occasion, so did she.

The sisters danced together until Rose was dizzy and stumbling with laughter, but Wren kept going. She drank goblet after goblet of fruit wine, despite Rose's warnings that it would make her feel ill again. Wren even went back for more of Cam's chocolate stars, joining Celeste and Shen at the dessert table. Then she danced with the Ortha witches, spinning from one to another, her eyes shining until she looked as if she was lit from within.

Rose watched the Ortha witches beaming at Wren and wondered if they would ever look at *her* so fondly or if they still secretly thought of Wren as their one true queen. The ruler they had long planned would sit on the throne.

No. Rose banished the thought. She and Wren were meant to rule together. She knew that in her heart, in her bones. And after the Battle of Anadawn, she hoped the other witches did, too. After all, they had stood together to embrace the fullness of their power and defend Anadawn. She hoped that wouldn't soon be forgotten.

And yet something close to envy bloomed inside Rose as she watched her sister charm the other revelers, flitting from a group of chatty Eshlinn seamstresses to their new Captain of the Guard, who she easily cajoled into dancing with her.

Even Chapman, the uptight Anadawn steward, joined Wren in a jig around the bonfire, which thankfully didn't turn into another accidental inferno. Rose didn't think she could handle any more mishaps, magical or otherwise, tonight.

Rose took a deep, calming breath and studied her sister. Tonight, Wren didn't need any enchantments to cast her spell on people. When she smiled, *truly* smiled, it felt as if she was about to confide a delicious secret or entice you on a thrilling adventure.

Rose knew she herself was charming in her own poised and practiced kind of way. She had spent her whole life perfecting it, after all. Her warmth and affection for her people was genuine, of course. But Wren, for all her fierceness, burned with the kind of brightness that drew people to her, no matter how contrary she might be.

She had even thawed the icy heart of at least one Gevran.

Not that Rose had any details about *exactly* what had happened between Wren and Captain Tor Iversen in Grinstad. While Wren teased Rose mercilessly about Shen, nothing made Wren clam up as fast as Rose mentioning the handsome soldier.

Or anything to do with Gevra, really.

Deep down, Rose knew her sister was still healing from everything she had endured there. She was reminded of it every time she saw the silver streak in her sister's hair, the strand of Wren's grief for Banba plain for all to see. And so in the end, beneath her jealousy and uncertainty, Rose was glad to see Wren enjoying herself, even if it was just for an evening.

By the time the queens finally left for the palace, it was well after midnight. Once they were seated in their carriage, Wren kicked off her muddy shoes and yawned. "I'd say that was a success, wouldn't you?"

"It was in the end," Rose admitted, frowning at her sister's muddy shoes. "You certainly perked up."

"That's what you wanted, wasn't it? For us to act as if everything is merry. To set aside our worries and put everyone else at ease." Wren's voice slurred as she yawned again, before resting her head on her sister's shoulder. "Wake me when we're home."

Back at Anadawn, once her sister was fast asleep in her own bed, Rose found herself feeling restless. She paced her room, still in her festival gown. It reeked of smoke and the hem was torn, but she couldn't bring herself to take it off just yet. Partly because she was so cold. She'd caught a strange chill down by the lake that she couldn't seem to shake.

What she really wanted was a bath. Yes, that was it. A hot bath always helped.

But as she waited for the nightmaids to arrive, Rose found herself thinking of those rotting plums in the orchard. Odd, that they would come to her mind now. She hadn't even mentioned them to Wren. Because it was a silly preoccupation, she reminded herself. The future of an entire kingdom could not be divined from a few rotting plums. Everything was fine. Tonight had been strange, but it had ended well. Rose told herself this over and over, refusing to be afraid.

Refusing to peer a little closer at what there was to fear.

When the maids arrived with pitchers of warm water, Rose decided that something else was missing. "Florence, could you please bring me some hot chocolate from the kitchens? It might help to banish this awful chill."

The maid dipped her chin. "Of course, Your Majesty. Is there anything else?"

"That's all, thank you."

Florence nodded and scurried down the stairs after the others. Back in her bathing chamber, Rose enchanted a ring of flickering everlights around her claw-foot tub before fetching her favorite jasmine soap and pouring until the bubbles reached the rim.

When the tub was full, she peeled off her gown and stepped in, luxuriating in the warm water gently lapping against her skin. And *oh*—the scent was truly divine. Far better than the awful smoke that had followed her home.

She smiled as she laid her head back, listening to the bubbles crackle in her ears. These days, baths reminded her of her time in the desert with Shen Lo and the secret hot spring they had found together. And that was a welcome thought indeed.

Rose sighed with pleasure as she sank into the bubbles. Yes, a hot bath was just what she needed. Tomorrow, she would wake up refreshed and ready to face the day. In fact, she was so relaxed already, she thought she might just drift off. . . .

She closed her eyes and—

There came a knock at her door.

"Come in!" Rose called. The bedroom door creaked open. "I'm already in the bath, but you can leave the hot chocolate on the table by the bedside!"

A moment later, she heard the bedroom door shut.

"I'm afraid I didn't bring you any hot chocolate."

Rose's eyes flew open at the familiar voice.

Leaning against the doorframe to her bathing chambers, still dressed in his festival clothes and wearing a rakish grin, was Shen Lo.

"Shen! I'm in the bath!" Rose ducked in the water, peering out from behind a mountain of bubbles.

"I heard," he said in a low voice. "Why else do you think I came in?"

In the flickering candlelight, with his strong jaw and chiseled cheekbones, he looked as if he'd been carved from stone. Rose couldn't help the sigh that escaped her lips as she gazed at him. He gazed back, his eyes darkening as he drank in the sight of her in the tub.

Rose felt the sudden urge to fan herself.

Goodness, Rose. Get a hold of yourself!

And anyway, she was still irritated at Shen, handsome as he might be.

She cleared her throat. "What are you doing in my bedchamber this late? Or at all, come to think of it? Rather presumptuous of you, especially considering you didn't want to dance with me at the festival."

"Of course I wanted to dance with you," he said with some surprise. "You were the one avoiding me."

"I certainly was not!" She scowled at him. "I had important business to discuss."

He raised a dark brow. "Were you truly that desperate to find out what kind of bait the fisherfolk at Wishbone Bay use?"

Rose's traitorous lips twitched. "Rude of you to eavesdrop."

"It's my specialty," he said unapologetically.

"And yes," she went on, "a queen must take an interest in these types of things." At his look of utter bemusement, she sighed. "Fine. I was avoiding you. But only because you embarrassed me by not asking me to dance!"

"I was waiting for the right signal. A lingering look. A seductive wink." He winked at her. "It's not that difficult surely."

Rose considered throwing a fistful of bubbles at him.

"But you were busy doing . . ." He waved his hand around. "Queenly things. Far be it from me to take you away from a scintillating conversation about fish bait. I didn't want to distract you."

"Shen Lo, you are entirely too vain," Rose huffed. "I would never let you distract me from my duty."

"Is that so?" he said, finally taking a step forward.

Rose felt her heart skip. "Never," she breathed.

Another step. "That sounds like my kind of challenge." He was close now. So close that if she dared, Rose could reach out and touch him.

He leaned down and her breath caught in her throat. His fingers brushed against her temple. "You still have a flower in your hair." He gently pulled the daisy from where it had become tangled behind her ear.

"And where is *your* Lake Carranam flower, Shen Lo?" she said in a whisper. "Do you not wish for luck this coming spring?"

He chuckled, the sound low and full of promise. "Do you have to ask? You are my flower, Rose." He leaned closer, tracing her jaw with the pad of his thumb, then brushing it along her bottom lip. "And all the luck I need."

Rose arched upward, closing the distance between them. His cheeks flushed as the bubbles gave way around her. Suddenly, he was speechless. Rose smiled as she wrapped her arms around his neck, no longer caring about propriety.

"I am still very, very angry at you," she whispered against his lips. "You are going to have to try *very* hard to make it up to me."

Shen groaned, opening his mouth to her own. The kiss deepened as he slid his hand up the back of her neck and tangled it in her hair.

Rose tugged him closer. Water sloshed over the side of the tub, soaking his chest, his arms.

"Oh!" she said, pulling back. "Your clothes!"

"They'll dry," he said, leaning in to kiss her again.

"Or . . ." Rose's heart pounded as she willed herself to say what she was thinking, what she desperately wanted. "You could always . . . hang them up. For now."

Shen blinked in surprise. "Queen Rose, are you suggesting I take off my clothes?"

Rose flushed. "Your shirt is made from such fine linen. . . . I would hate for it to get damaged. . . ."

Shen was already on his feet. As he pulled his shirt over his head, there came a light knock at the door to Rose's bedchamber. Then, to Rose's horror, it creaked open.

"Your Majesty?" called Florence. "I've brought your hot chocolate."

Shen froze, laughter dancing in his eyes.

"Thank you!" Rose cried out in a strained voice. "Please leave it by the bed! On the table!"

"Certainly," said Florence, and there came the sound of a cup being set down. "Will there be anything else, Your Majesty?"

"No! No! That's all! Thank you!"

The door closed and Rose exhaled in relief. She sank back into the tub, which was now decidedly tepid.

"Well," she said, blowing a bubble from the tip of her nose. "That was rather poorly timed. Would you . . . like some hot chocolate?"

Much to Rose's disappointment, Shen was already shrugging his shirt back on. "As nice as that sounds, I should be going. I came by because I wanted to say goodbye before I left."

"Goodbye?" Rose frowned. "It's the middle of the night!"

"You know that's the best time to travel through the desert."

"But you've only just arrived," she said crestfallen. "I hardly get to see you anymore."

"I wish I could stay longer. But I have to get back to the Sunkissed Kingdom. There's still much to be done." Shen ran his hand through his hair, the stress of these past few months written in the lines on his brow. "You've spent your whole life preparing to rule, Rose. I'm still learning how to be king to a kingdom of people who barely know me. My place is with them, now more than ever. You must understand that."

Rose looked away so he wouldn't see her bottom lip tremble. She hated that she cared so much.

"Rose?"

"Of course I understand. I wouldn't want to distract you from your duty."

His voice softened. "The truth is, even when I'm not with you, you are a distraction. You're never far from my mind, Rose."

She turned back to him. "And you really must leave right this very moment?"

"Lei Fan and the others will be waiting for me. I was meant to be at the gates an hour ago." He chuckled. "I wasn't expecting to find you in the bath and to get so . . ."

"Distracted?"

"Exactly."

For a beat, they smiled at each other.

Then Rose pouted. "Why don't you send them on without you? You can catch up. Storm is the fastest horse in all of Eana. . . ." She trailed off.

"Don't tempt me," said Shen, his night-dark eyes burning with desire. "You know I would if I could."

Rose did know that. But it didn't make it any easier.

Sometimes, she secretly longed for the time before Shen knew he was the lost heir of the Sunkissed Kingdom. When he was still a bandit and his time was his own.

Now he had other responsibilities.

Other duties.

"Fine," she said, rising from the bath. "Then at least pass me my robe."

His gaze roamed, and for a moment, he looked as if his resolve would crumble. Then he sighed, turning from her to fetch the robe. "Of course."

Shen left shortly after that, pressing a kiss to Rose's lips and whispering a promise that he'd be back soon to join her in that bath.

Rose watched from the window as he rappelled down her tower.

"You do know that you can take the stairs now?" she called after him. "The guards all know you."

His laugh echoed in the dark. "Where's the fun in that?"

She shook her head and laughed just the same. "Good night, Shen. Give my love to Storm."

"Lucky horse."

WREN

Wren pulled her cloak tighter as she trudged through the deep snow. Her fur collar feathered her cheeks as she blew a breath through her hands, desperately trying to warm her numb fingers. It was no use. The wind howled, sending a shiver rippling up her spine and chattering through her teeth.

Hissing hell.

All around her, the air was hazy and white. She squinted through the fog, pushing farther into the unknown. She was lost in the damned mountains again, trying to outrun that terrible screeching laugh. It always came with the wind.

Oonagh Starcrest was taunting her.

Run, run, broken bird.

You cannot hide from me.

"Hush!" yelled Wren. "Leave me alone!"

She stumbled on, through snow so deep it reached her knees. The wind whipped her cheeks and stung her eyes, mocking her. Every breath was a struggle.

Dimly, Wren was aware that she must be dreaming, but the cold was so *real*. The panic was, too.

The scar on her arm began to burn. She fumbled with the buttons on her sleeve, rolling it up to her elbow. Her wrist was a deep, bubbling red, the silver crescent brighter than she'd ever seen it.

She let out a hiss of pain.

Oonagh's laugh grew shriller. It soared on the rising wind, echoing through the mountain pass.

Wren grabbed a fistful of snow and smeared it across her wrist. It helped, but now she was even more aware of the blistering cold. She couldn't feel her toes anymore. She stumbled on, desperately looking for a way out.

The blizzard roared as it grew.

A shadow appeared up ahead. Wren frowned. In all the times she had found herself trapped in this nightmare over the last three months, she had always been alone.

"Who's there?" she called out.

The shadow lurched, falling forward.

Wren charged, spurred on by the appearance of the figure. "Oonagh? Show yourself!"

Instinctively, her hand went to her hip, reaching for her dagger. But she was always weaponless in this place. The snow parted as Wren pushed through it.

Up ahead, the figure was on its knees.

"Speak!" she called out. "Who are you?"

The figure groaned.

Wren saw it then, a glimpse of blond hair streaked with an ink-black line.

She froze. "Alarik?"

The king of Gevra groaned again. *"Help me."*

Wren came to her knees before him. "What the hell are you doing here?"

In my nightmare.

In my mind.

With great effort, Alarik Felsing raised his head. His icy blue eyes were bloodshot, his skin so pale he looked ill. "I was about to ask you the same thing," he said through his teeth. "This is *my* hell."

"This isn't real," whispered Wren. "You're not here."

Alarik pitched forward. He fisted the snow, searching for breath. "It's killing me," he heaved. "*She's* killing me."

The wind began to laugh again. The blizzard kicked up, spitting snow in Wren's face. She reached for the king, but the world was spinning, turning everything to bright, blinding white. "Alarik?"

Far away, along the jagged mountaintops, there came a distant thud.

Thunk.

Thunk.

Thunk.

An avalanche was brewing. Wren screamed, but the sound died in her throat. The world blinked, from white to black, until only that sound remained.

Thunk.

Thunk.

Thunk.

Wren shot upright in bed, blinking the sleep from her eyes. Slowly, mercifully, reality filtered in: the first wisps of dawn creeping through the window, the feather-softness of her pillow, and the canopy around her four-poster bed gently rippling.

The nightmare was over. She was back in her bedroom in the west tower of Anadawn. Safe. Last night she had played the part of the joyful queen, welcoming spring with all the cheer she could muster. The act, and the entire evening, had so exhausted Wren that she'd fallen asleep in the carriage and couldn't even remember climbing into her own bed.

She should have felt relieved that it was only a nightmare.

And yet, her stomach was in knots. Her forehead was clammy, and the scar on her wrist was stinging. And that laugh was still echoing in her head. The same one that had rung out during the ceremony.

She reached for the pitcher on her nightstand and swallowed a mouthful of water in a bid to chase away the heat inside her.

Thunk.

Thunk.

Thunk.

That sound again!

Wren whipped her head around. "What in hissing hell—"

There was a nighthawk tapping on her window. A Gevran messenger. Wren leaped out of bed and swung the pane open, reaching for the scroll tied to the bird's foot. She unrolled it, her heart hitching as she glimpsed the signature at the bottom.

It was from Tor.

Dear Wren,

These past few months have felt longer and colder than most. I've thought of you often: on clear nights when the sky is bright with stars, at dawn when Elske and I walk along the frozen lake, and when the wind sings through the Fovarr Mountains.

I've tried to write to you a hundred times, but I've been afraid to say the wrong thing. To expect anything after our goodbye. To imagine a future where we will see each other again. I don't know how to tell you that I've missed you without making it worse. It feels selfish to share this pain with you and to hope, deep down, that you might feel the same way.

And yet, I find myself compelled to write. Not for myself but for my kingdom, and for yours. There have been strange stirrings across Gevra. A shadow creeps across our land. The animals have grown dangerous and the king's beasts have turned feral. They howl at the mountains as if they can sense a badness there.

Over recent weeks the fields south of Grinstad have been disturbed. The graves of our beasts lie empty, the barren earth cracked open. Could this be the work of the Starcrest witch who wears your face? Is Eana suffering the same strangeness?

And there is worse news still. The king is not well. He has requested an urgent meeting with you, although he will not say why.

Can you come to us, Wren?

We have to get to the bottom of the curse that plagues our kingdom. I can only hope it has not yet breached the shores of Eana.

I await your answer.

Yours,

Tor

(and Elske)

Wren's gaze lingered on the small inking of a paw scribbled beside Elske's name. She smiled, fleetingly, before returning her attention to the words above it.

These were grim tidings indeed. Badness was stirring in the north. It stirred in Wren, too. She couldn't shake the uneasy feeling that Oonagh Starcrest was on the move. Her strength likely regained, their ancestor was finally coming out of hiding.

Wren looked to the tapestries that hung on her bedroom walls, finding among them the portrait of Ortha Starcrest, the bravehearted witch queen who had ruled Eana alongside Oonagh a thousand years ago. The witch who had tried to stop her sister, Oonagh, even as she cursed her on the banks of the Silvertongue, ruining their magic and destroying their reign. Ortha had died defending her kingdom, and even now, in the quiet dawn, her green eyes seemed to shine with that same unfailing loyalty.

Wren met that gaze—so like her own—and wished Ortha Starcrest could help her.

What is your sister up to, Ortha?

And more important still: *How can we stop her?*

With a sigh, Wren returned her attention to Tor's letter, worrying for Gevra and its king.

Seeing Alarik in her nightmare was no coincidence. Whatever affliction was bothering her must have reached him, too. Why else would he be seeking her out?

While the nighthawk waited on the windowsill, Wren went to her desk to scribble her reply. There was so much she wished to say to Tor, a hundred thoughts and fears and feelings, but this letter was not the place, and time, now, was of the essence. So she wrote, simply:

> Tor,
> Meet me at Sharkfin Point at sundown tomorrow.
> Yours,
> Wren

Wren fastened the note to the nighthawk's foot.

"Fly fast," she urged as it flew out into the dawning sky.

A flock of starcrests peered down at Wren from the castle roof. Since the breaking of the witches' curse, starcrests visited Anadawn almost every night. They lined the west turret now, watching the hawk as it soared up and away, into the morning clouds. Then they looked back at Wren, as though they had something they wished to tell her. But night had passed and despite the return of her full magic, Wren had proven to be a woeful seer. She wasn't patient enough to watch the skies at night, and more than anything, the starcrests' patterns confused her.

And besides, there was nothing the skies could tell her that she didn't already know. Trouble was brewing across the Sunless Sea.

Wren reeled back into her bedroom and shut the window. She slid to the floor and read Tor's letter again. And again. And again. A terrible truth was crystallizing. Gevra was suffering, and soon, Eana would be, too. After all, this was Oonagh's kingdom. It would not be long before the ruthless queen returned to it.

The pain in Wren's scar flared, as though in agreement.

She was reminded of her dream, of King Alarik kneeling in the snow with the same pain etched across his face. She vowed to find out what that vision meant.

For both of them.

When morning broke in earnest, and the room was bathed in soft golden light, Wren got to her feet. She grabbed a robe from her closet and shrugged it on, preparing to face another unavoidable truth.

Soon, she would have to tell Rose everything.

8

ROSE

Rose woke with a smile on her face, dreams of Shen still dancing in her head. She hoped she would see him again soon. And when she did, perhaps they would finally seize their courage and figure out a way to be together. She couldn't bear any more goodbyes.

But, *goodness*. How on earth did one navigate such a thing? Did Rose need to send out a proclamation that her heart was taken? Or should she forsake love for duty and continue to entertain foreign suitors in pursuit of bettering Eana's relations with other countries?

Hmm. Of course, there were still Wren's romantic prospects to consider. . . .

The thought of Wren marrying strategically made Rose snort. No, Wren had made it clear she would not even contemplate an arranged marriage, no matter the suitor. Whenever Chapman dared to broach the topic, Wren reminded everyone of poor Prince Ansel. A cautionary tale indeed.

Thinking of Ansel always made Rose's heart ache. Even though she hadn't wanted to marry King Alarik's younger brother, she desperately wished he had lived to find his own happiness. At least he was at rest now. In the end, with the help of her healing magic, she had been able to grant him the peace he deserved.

A shiver rippled down Rose's spine as she sat up in bed. She didn't like to think about what had happened in Gevra all those months ago. About the blood spell her sister had attempted. About Oonagh.

Rose supposed she should be grateful that her undead ancestor was far away across the Sunless Sea, but deep down, she had a prickling feeling that Oonagh wouldn't stay hidden forever.

Rose clambered out of bed and threw open the curtains, suddenly desperate to see the sun. Morning light flooded her bedroom, washing away her worries. She stood in its warmth and reminded herself that there was no point in fretting about the unknown. But even so, her gaze flitted to the orchards, and she frowned. She made a note to herself to ask the gardeners if they had noticed anything strange about the fruit recently.

A knock at the door made her jolt.

"Rose?" called Celeste. "Are you awake?"

Rose hurried to open it, beaming at the sight of her oldest and dearest friend. Celeste was dressed in a violet day dress, her black curls piled high on top of her head. "You're looking surprisingly fresh this morning," said Rose. "As I recall, you were still dancing with Grandmother Lu when Wren and I left the festival."

Celeste stepped into her room and closed the door behind her.

"Don't be fooled," she said wearily. "I've barely slept."

"You must tell me all about your night," said Rose, pulling Celeste over to the window seat. "Have you had breakfast yet? I was about to call down for bread with jam and honey...." She trailed off at the sight of Celeste's somber expression. "Oh dear. What is it?"

Celeste took Rose's hands in her own. "I need to talk to you."

Rose's mouth went dry. "Is it about Wren?"

"No," said Celeste quickly. "I had a vision last night."

"Of what?" said Rose, a touch too shrilly. But Celeste's words and the haunted look in her eyes had set her on edge. First the tree had gone up in smoke, then Wren had disappeared into the forest, and now this: a vision from Celeste. Rose's stomach clenched with worry.

"I think it was your ancestor," said Celeste, worsening the knot in Rose's stomach. "At first, I thought it was you. Then Wren. But this other woman . . . Her gaze is hollow. And her smile . . . it's cruel."

"Oonagh?" Even uttering the name cast goose bumps across Rose's arms. "Are you sure?" she said, trying to will it away. If she didn't accept this vision Celeste was bringing to light, perhaps it would never happen.

"I'm not sure of anything," said Celeste, more to herself than to Rose. "But I know she's not of this world. Of this time. And last night, when I glimpsed her, she was surrounded by . . ." She frowned, as though she was still trying to make sense of it. "Dead animals." She shuddered, then corrected herself. "Only, they weren't all the way dead."

Bile pooled in Rose's throat. "I don't understand," she said weakly. "How can something be dead and not dead?"

Celeste's gaze darted. "Like how Ansel was," she whispered. "Her hands . . ." Celeste closed her eyes, a dent appearing between her brows. "They were crusted with blood. As if she had been soaking them in it. And she was laughing, Rose. I've never heard such an awful sound. For a moment, I swear it felt as if . . . as if . . ."

"What?" Rose held her breath without meaning to.

Celeste's eyes flew open. "As if she's getting closer, Rose. Too close."

Rose leaped to her feet. "We need to tell Wren."

Celeste pulled her back. "Wait."

"For what?" said Rose impatiently.

"There's something off with Wren. I can't put my finger on it, but lately I feel as if she's been hiding something."

Rose let out an impatient snort. "Like what? Our undead ancestor?"

"I don't know. Maybe."

"Oh, Celeste!" Rose almost laughed. "Don't be so ridiculous. You've never fully trusted Wren, that's all."

Celeste glowered at her. "I'm not being ridiculous. I'm being wary. And you should be, too. I understand Wren is your sister, but we both know she hasn't always been the most forthright."

"I trust Wren completely," said Rose firmly. She *needed* to trust Wren. If she couldn't trust her own sister, then who could she trust? And Wren had told her everything that had happened in Gevra. Hadn't she? It was the stress of it all—the loss of Banba and the battle that had followed—that was causing Wren to act strangely these past few months. That was all.

"Just because you want something to be a certain way doesn't mean you can make it happen by sheer force of will," said Celeste pointedly.

"I can certainly try," said Rose.

Celeste laughed uneasily. "Well, I suppose if anyone can, you can."

Rose smiled at her friend. "We can trust Wren, Celeste. In fact, I'd wager my life on it."

Celeste sighed. "I wish you wouldn't."

"Now," said Rose, as if she hadn't heard her, "what shall we have for breakfast?"

After breakfast, Rose met with Chapman in the throne room to discuss the day's agenda. She yawned as she pored over the stack of papers the steward had prepared for her, only brightening when she saw that one of the items was to be the establishment of new schoolhouses throughout Eana.

Rose and Wren both felt that, while displays of magic were certainly one way to win over the people of Eana, the best approach was for the children to learn about magic and where it came from. That way, they wouldn't grow up to fear it.

"Fetch me a map," said Rose to Chapman. "We can decide where the new schoolhouses should be and allocate funding accordingly."

Chapman sighed. "Your Majesty, that particular topic is fourth on today's agenda. We have much to discuss before that."

"Chapman, I am the queen," Rose reminded him impatiently. "I am not beholden to any agenda. I may skip to whatever items I like."

Chapman cleared his throat. "But, Your Majesty, we first need to go over the finances. Only then can we know how much coin we have to allocate. To do that, we must meet with the keeper of the treasury, and they aren't arriving until noon." He huffed a sigh. "And before that, we must discuss the trade requests from neighboring nations so we know what kind of position we are in when we meet with the keeper of the treasury."

Rose rubbed her temples, wondering when her wayward sister would show her face. Wren had an uncanny ability for wriggling her way out of meetings. "Very well. We'll save the map for later." She took a large sip of coffee, grateful it was still hot. "Shall we go through the recent trade requests? Now that magic is being celebrated in Eana, it's pleasing to see more interest in our kingdom."

"Indeed," said Chapman, with no small amount of satisfaction. "While magic isn't something that can be traded, our neighbors are certainly eager to remain on the good side of a country that can now control the wind, among other things."

Rose gave him a sly smile. "I never imagined our tempests would be what impressed you the most, Chapman."

The steward chuckled. "You forget I encounter Rowena every day. Her temper is a mighty thing to behold. And the storms she brews even more so."

Rose laughed. "Chapman, do you fancy Rowena?"

Chapman flushed. "Certainly not! But one cannot deny that she is very noticeable." His mustache twitched, giving him away, but he plowed on determinedly. "Now. Speaking of trade requests, and erm . . . fancying people . . ."

Rose smiled. "Yes?"

"Well, Caro has sent an ambassador to discuss their most recent trade request."

"And you fancy the ambassador?"

Chapman's blush deepened. "No, no, no, Your Majesty. Nothing of the sort!" He cleared his throat. "Well, what I mean is, it doesn't concern me, and he isn't *strictly* an ambassador or . . . well, I suppose he insists he is, but the trouble is, he's also, well, hmm—"

"Chapman, I've never known you to be so muddled with your words," said Rose, with mounting exasperation. "Please speak some sense."

There came a sudden, loud trumpeting from outside the throne room.

Chapman glanced at his pocket watch. "Oh dear. He's early. But I suppose that's a good sign." He was beginning to sweat. "Better early than late."

"Really, Chapman. What are you blundering on about? And where is that infernal trumpeting coming from?" Rose flinched at the racket. "Has Wren secretly planned another concert I don't know about?"

"Your Majesty, now please remember, I want only the best for you. And for this country, of course." Chapman stood up and offered his arm. "If I may escort you to the balcony?"

"The balcony?" Rose blinked in confusion. "Whatever for? I thought we were on a schedule."

"This *is* part of the schedule." He tried to smile but his mustache trembled, and Rose had the sudden sense that the steward was nervous. "It will all make sense shortly."

She stood, shaking out her skirts. "I certainly hope so."

Chapman led her to the balcony, where not long ago, Rose and Wren had stood after their coronation, waving to their adoring subjects. As Chapman opened the doors, the trumpeting grew louder. Beneath the thunderous melody, Rose heard the braying of horses.

What on earth . . . ?

She strode out into the sunlight, shielding her eyes as she tried to see where the commotion was coming from. She took one look over the balustrade and gasped.

She whirled to face Chapman. "Pray tell why the Crown Prince of

Caro is standing in my garden, surrounded by a dozen horses, six minstrels, two very large trunks, and what looks to be *an entire forest* of olive trees?"

Chapman gulped. "He must have heard what happened to the olive tree his mother sent," he said. Queen Eliziana's coronation gift had gone up in flames during one of the Arrows' early attacks.

"And how do you explain everything else?" Rose hissed before risking another glance over the balustrade. "The horses are dancing!"

All at once, the trumpeting stopped.

"At least now I can hear myself think," said Rose, but then she heard the strumming of a lute. Her eyes went wide.

Somewhere down below, the Prince of Caro began to sing.

Rose could not resist returning to the balustrade to watch the spectacle unfold. The prince had thick dark hair cut into the typical Caro style: heavy bangs and long sides that ended bluntly at his jawline. He was wearing a magnificent red cape that billowed out behind him. His trousers were red, too, and his pristine white shirt sported a rather enormous collar.

Rose noted a ring on every finger, each with a gemstone that glittered in the sunlight. She felt as if they were winking at her.

The prince's song drifted up to the balustrade, his dark unblinking gaze never once leaving her face.

"Queen Rose, your beauty is known by all,
Queen Rose, I cannot resist your call,
With magic in your fingertips, and goodness in your heart,
I hope that today will be the start . . ."

He broke off into a lengthy finger solo, before finishing with gusto:

"Of something new! Between me and youuuuu!"

"Is he . . . serenading me?" whispered Rose in astonishment. "I don't even remember his name. We met once as children, a long time ago."

"His name is Prince Felix," Chapman whispered back. "I did mention you enjoyed romantic gestures, but I wasn't expecting something quite so . . . grand."

"And why exactly have you been in contact with the Crown Prince of Caro, Chapman?" said Rose through a clenched smile. Underneath his regalia, the warbling prince was quite handsome, she had to admit, even while strumming a tiny lute and singing a *ridiculous* song. "Surely those are conversations I should have been involved in."

"I never spoke to Prince Felix directly!" said Chapman, hurriedly mounting his defense. "I only mentioned the possibility of a love match to his adviser, Andrea, in my letters. See. She's that one there, over by the horses."

"Ah yes," said Rose, spotting the petite dark-haired woman. "I didn't notice her standing behind the *twelve dancing horses* in my garden!"

Prince Felix was still happily crooning away, and showing no sign of stopping.

"He does have a nice voice," Chapman said meekly.

"Thank the stars for that small mercy," said Rose. "I suppose we should invite him in. I can only hope you told Cam about our surprise guest so the cooks are at least prepared to make a lunch suitable for visiting royalty."

She could tell by the look of abject horror on Chapman's face that he had done no such thing.

Rose sighed. "Oh, Chapman."

Several hours later, Rose sat across from Prince Felix in the royal dining room. Thea sat beside him, while Wren occupied the chair next to Rose, looking more out of sorts than usual. Rose didn't miss the way she wrung her hands on her lap, or how her gaze kept flitting to the door as though she wanted to bolt through it.

"I need to talk to you," Wren hissed once they had sat down to eat, but Rose had gently hushed her.

"After dinner. We have a guest."

Thankfully, Cam had risen to the occasion, preparing a spectacular feast of two whole red snappers cooked in Caro spices and served on a bed of tomatoes and peppers, accompanied by lightly fried potatoes and charred asparagus. As she ate, Rose felt as if the eye of the fish was watching her. She avoided looking at it and instead smiled at the prince.

"You are most welcome to Eana, Prince Felix. It is our pleasure to host you."

"The pleasure is mine," said Prince Felix in a lilting Caro accent. "I have long wanted to return to your breathtaking country, which is graced with the most beautiful people." He winked seductively at Rose, and Wren nearly choked on a piece of asparagus. "And the most beautiful magic! Truly, Eana is blessed."

"It is indeed," said Rose, holding her smile as she pinched her sister under the table. "Just as your country is special in its way. Caro silk is famed for its bright colors, and we often enjoy your wine here in Eana. And of course, many of my favorite spices hail from your beautiful country."

"And yet, alas, we do not enjoy the spoils of magic," said Prince

Felix with a pout. "But we are not afraid of it," he added quickly. "In fact, we would welcome it on our shores. Indeed, I wonder if . . ." He trailed off, stroking his chin as if an idea had only just occurred to him.

"If?" prompted Wren warily.

"If an Eanan flower planted somewhere else . . . say, somewhere warmer . . . would bloom as well as it does in its native soil." He gazed intently at Rose. "Excuse me for speaking so directly, but we are a direct people."

Wren snorted. "You don't say."

"What I am trying to ask is this, Queen Rose. If you and I were to have children, they would most certainly be beautiful, but they would also be magical, would they not?" This time it was Rose who nearly choked on her food. Prince Felix seemed not to notice. "Is it possible to spread the magic of your country to another?"

"The closer we are to the source of our magic, which is the land of Eana itself, the stronger our magic is," said Thea politely, as if the Prince of Caro had asked her about the potatoes they were eating rather than the possibility of Rose bearing magic children for him. "Prince Felix, I must say, the horses you brought with you are very fine. I was admiring them this morning."

Rose offered the Queensbreath a grateful smile.

"Ah!" Felix's eyes lit up. "Those are our very finest Caro stallions. They are a wonder unto themselves."

"Then perhaps you should mate with one of them instead," said Wren under her breath.

"They are a gift to the queens," he went on with great excitement. "Six for each sister. You'll find the Illonian breed are the fastest horses anywhere on this earth. I'd bet my castle on it."

"Then I'm afraid you would lose it, Prince Felix. As they could not possibly be as fast as our desert horses," said Rose sweetly.

Felix leaned forward. "Is that a challenge, Queen Rose? And if it is, what would you wager on it?" He leered at her. "Will I win your hand in marriage if one of my horses beats your own?"

Wren looked between them. "This is either the best or worst proposal I've ever heard."

"Prince Felix, you are far too kind," said Rose between sips of wine. "We cannot accept such generous gifts."

"But we'll keep the olive trees," said Wren, swishing her fork around.

"The trees are from my mother," said Felix. "But the horses and the jewels"—he smiled widely at Rose—"those are gifts from me. Hand chosen for the most beautiful maiden in Eana. This is but a small measure of the kind of treatment you can expect as a bride of Caro."

"Rose is queen of Eana," said Wren pointedly. "This is the kind of treatment she already deserves."

"And I am not yet anyone's bride," said Rose, keeping a tight leash on her temper. She had done this song and dance once before, and it had ended in tragedy. She was not interested in being bartered again, and certainly not to Prince Felix of Caro.

He held up his hands in supplication. "Apologies," he said with a toothy smile. "I meant no offense. Indeed, I seek only to please you." He waggled his brows. "And you should know, I take pleasing women very seriously. In Caro, it is an art."

"Oh my," said Thea quietly.

Wren wheezed into her napkin.

Rose's cheeks flamed. "Prince Felix, we hope to have a long and prosperous alliance with Caro. But I'm afraid I simply cannot accept *anything* from you at the present moment."

Prince Felix frowned. He looked, almost reluctantly, to Wren. He cleared his throat. "Queen Wren—"

"Don't bother," said Wren, cutting him off. "I'm afraid it's a no from me, too." She skewered the fish eye with her fork. "In fact, make that a *never.*"

"Very well," said Felix, taking a large slug of wine. "Queen Rose, you will see I am both a very patient and very persistent man."

Rose steadied her voice. "What *admirable* qualities."

Felix grinned over the rim of his goblet. "I look forward to showing you the rest of them in due time."

Stars above, thought Rose, reaching for her own cup of wine. Maintaining trade relations with their closest allies was going to be *much* more complicated than she had anticipated.

WREN

After dinner, Wren followed Rose back to her bedroom, where her sister slumped onto the end of her bed and kicked off her shoes.

"That odious prince," Rose huffed. Her hands flew to her temples, massaging the ache there. "For such fine food, I've never enjoyed a dinner less."

"I'm only sorry I missed the grand serenade earlier," said Wren. Indeed, she had spent the day preparing for her imminent trip to Sharkfin Point, sending word to Celeste's brother, Marino, the dauntless captain of the *Siren's Secret*, to be ready for her, and secretly arranging for a carriage to take her to Wishbone Bay this very night. Her satchel was packed and ready. Now all she had to do was tell her sister.

Rose's hand shot out. "Help me soothe this awful headache," she said, reaching for Wren's hand.

Wren stiffened. "I can't."

Rose frowned. "What's got into you?"

"You know my healing strand is poor."

"It's just a headache," she said impatiently. "Can't you at least try?"

"I'm too tired," said Wren, a bolt of panic running through her. This was not the way she wished for Rose to find out she had no healing strand. "Prince Felix drove me to exhaustion."

Rose did not relent. "Why are you being so difficult?" she said, coming to her feet. "Even at dinner tonight. You were so distracted, so . . . so disagreeable."

Wren recoiled, hating how the words wounded her. Only because they were the truth. "Maybe I have other things to think about," she snapped. "I don't have time to swan around all day, obsessing about being queenly or whatever it is you spend all of your time thinking of."

Rose bristled at the barb, and Wren regretted it at once.

"I do not think about being queenly. I *am* queenly," Rose shot back. "And at least I care about Eana! These days, I feel as if I have to drag you everywhere against your will. I don't know what you care about anymore, Wren. You're too selfish to even bother healing your own sister."

Something inside Wren crumpled.

Rose stilled at the pain in her eyes. "I'm sorry," she said quickly. "I shouldn't have said that."

Wren tried to blink away her tears, but her eyes were welling up and so, too, was another more terrible truth. "I'm sorry, Rose. I want to help," she confessed in a small voice. "But . . . I can't. My healing strand is broken. There's something wrong with me."

Rose came toward her, her face tight with worry. "What are you talking about?"

"This." With little ceremony, Wren rolled up the sleeve of her gown, revealing the angry silver scar that had been haunting her for weeks now. "It's hurting me, Rose. It's hurting my magic."

A gasp stuck in Rose's throat. "Stars," she muttered, looking more closely at the mark. "How did I miss this?"

"I've been hiding it from you," Wren admitted.

Rose jerked her head up. "Why would you do that?" she said, a bite of anger in her voice.

"Because of the way you're looking at me right now."

Rose glared at her sister, fear and betrayal warring in her eyes. "How exactly am I looking at you?" she said crisply.

Wren pulled her arm back. "Like I'm Oonagh Starcrest."

There was a beat of silence. Of more bitter truth.

Then Rose shook it off. "Show me the scar again," she said, reaching for Wren's wrist.

Wren flinched as Rose traced the jagged mark with the pad of her thumb.

"I can't believe you hid this from me for *months*. Goodness, Wren. What were you thinking?"

"It's *barely* noticeable."

Rose's nostrils flared. "You clearly didn't want me to scold you."

"That may have been part of it," Wren admitted. "I thought if I ignored it, it might go away."

Rose lowered her voice. "What happened in Gevra—with Ansel, with that blood spell—it wounded you." She returned her gaze to the scar, her frown deepening. "We have to fix this."

"You mean fix *me*," muttered Wren. She couldn't help the sour taste—the sour feeling—in her heart. All she had ever done was try to help Prince Ansel and rescue Banba, but the blood spell she had performed with King Alarik had twisted something inside her. Not only had she accidentally woken Oonagh Starcrest, but she had woken something inside herself, too. A dark and angry creature that refused to go back to sleep.

Every time the pain in Wren's scar flared, she was reminded of her mistake. Her own searing stupidity. And worse still, it had all been for nothing. Prince Ansel was dead and so was Banba. Wren's grandmother had never made it out of the Gevran mountains. Instead, it was Oonagh who'd escaped.

She blinked again, determined not to cry. "What if I can't be fixed, Rose?" she said, voicing her deepest fear aloud for the first time.

Rose's voice softened. "Hush now," she said gently. "Let me try to heal the wound."

She laid her hand on Wren's scar, her fingers circling her wrist. She closed her eyes, and a dent appeared between her brows. Wren closed her eyes, too. Her wrist began to tingle. She could feel Rose's magic brushing against her own, like a breath of warm wind. Searching, careful.

"Hmm," said Rose after a moment. "It's not a flesh wound. It feels . . . *deeper* than that. . . ."

Wren felt a strange pressure. Rose was beginning to prod, making her magic go deeper. Under the surface of Wren's skin. Under blood and bone. And still, she prodded.

The pain in Wren's wrist flared. *"Rose."*

"I can see your magic," Rose murmured. "There's something wrong . . . *something* . . ."

The pain flared again, only it was worse now. Wren's breath grew shallow in her chest and her head began to spin. Something inside her was bucking, trying to push Rose away, but Rose held her wrist in a viselike grip, refusing to let go.

Wren slumped to the floor, pulling Rose with her. The pain was becoming unbearable. Rose's magic had burrowed deep inside her. Now it felt as if it was plucking at the strings of her soul, trying to find the broken one.

"*Stop*," Wren begged.

Rose's breathing grew labored, and she began to sway. "I almost have it...." She gasped suddenly, her grip tightening. "*There.*"

Wren lurched. Blinding heat tore through her body, wrenching a scream from her.

"*No!*" cried Rose.

Wren snapped her eyes open.

Rose's mouth slackened in horror as she watched a plume of smoke seep from the scar on Wren's wrist. "It's *poison*," she gasped as tears streamed down her face. "I have to get it out."

Words had deserted Wren. She could only watch in utter dread as the smoke twisted between them, growing thicker, darker. She heard Oonagh's terrible laugh in her head.

Rose whimpered, and Wren knew she could hear it, too.

The smoke kept rising. Wren could feel it swelling between her rib cage now, pushing her breath from her lungs. There was too much poisoned magic to extract. Too much to heal. It was already hurting Rose. She was trembling on the floor. Her lids were heavy, her breathing, too. "I c-can't. I ... *I* ..."

"Stop," Wren managed to grit out. "*Let go.*"

Rose's hand fell away as she lost consciousness. She collapsed, her head falling against Wren's shoulder. Without the pull of her healing magic, the smoke had nowhere to go. It hissed as it rushed back inside Wren.

The pain tore another strangled scream from Wren. She felt as if someone was stabbing her with a white-hot poker, skewering the deepest, darkest part of her soul. And then everything went black, a familiar darkness crowding in on her and whisking her far, far away.

This time, she welcomed it.

Wren blinked to find herself in a cold, cavernous room. It echoed with growling beasts. All around her, huge white pillars climbed toward a domed ceiling. The hall was dark and full of shadows, but she knew where she was. She had been here before. Grinstad Palace.

She saw the empty throne sitting high on the dais before she spotted the king on his knees in front of it. Alarik was slumped against the marble steps, fisting his hair in his hands.

Wren heard him cry out.

She ran for the dais but with every step she got farther away. The throne room grew bigger and wider, the king's scream echoing from every alcove. The floor cracked at Wren's feet, a chasm opening beneath her. She fell before she could jump, spiraling down, down, down, into a pit of choking dark smoke.

"WREN! WAKE UP!"

Wren gasped herself awake to find Rose's tearstained face inches from her own. "You passed out." Rose's eyes were glassy, her bottom lip trembling. "We both did."

There was a sharp knock at her bedroom door, but Rose shouted back, sending away the guards who had come to check on them.

"That awful smoke . . . there was so much of it. . . ." she said, dropping her voice. "I was scared of it. My *magic* was scared of it. I couldn't do it. . . . I wasn't strong enough. . . ."

Wren swallowed against the scorched dryness of her throat. "What did you see when you passed out?"

"Just . . . nothingness." Rose frowned, her voice turning cautious. "Why?"

"Because I saw something. Someone." Wren sat up and laid her head back against the wall, coming at last to the point of her visit. "Promise you won't be angry at me. . . ."

"I'll promise nothing of the sort," said Rose at once. "Now do go on."

So Wren did, confiding in her sister about the king of Gevra and her strange visions. "I need answers about what's going on with me," she said then.

"We certainly do," Rose murmured.

Wren blew out a breath. "So I'm going to Sharkfin Point. To see King Alarik."

Rose snapped her chin up. "What? When?"

"Tonight." At her sister's look of abject horror, Wren added, "Don't worry, I'll be quick. And careful."

Rose huffed a mirthless laugh. "You don't know the meaning of careful. And for that matter, neither does Alarik Felsing."

Wren was silent then. Her sister was right.

There was nothing careful about Alarik Felsing.

A short while later, they embraced in the courtyard under the midnight moon, Rose stiffening as Wren threw her arms around her.

"Please don't be like this," said Wren, only squeezing her harder. "I'll be back before you know it."

"It just feels all too familiar." Rose's eyes prickled as she traced the streak of silver in her sister's hair. "The last time you took to the Sunless Sea, I almost lost you."

"It's different this time. I'm only going as far as Sharkfin Point."

Rose wriggled out of Wren's grasp. "I just don't understand why you think someone like Alarik Felsing will have answers for you."

"Neither do I," confessed Wren. But the king of Gevra had fallen into her dreams for a reason and she intended to find out why. "At least you won't be bored without me," she went on at Rose's scowling face. "You'll have your charming Caro prince to keep you company."

"That is *not* funny."

Wren chuckled. "That poor wretch is probably already in love with you."

Rose smirked a little at the compliment. "All these proposals are frankly *exhausting*."

"If only I could relate."

"You'd better not." Rose raised a warning finger.

They embraced again.

This time, Rose hugged her back. "Be safe, Wren."

"You too, Rose."

It was almost dawn when Wren arrived at the *Siren's Secret*, one of the sleekest merchant vessels in all of Eana. She had traveled undercover to Wishbone Bay, in an unadorned wooden carriage escorted by four royal soldiers dressed in plain clothing. She wore dark trousers and a loose-fitting shirt under a gray spun cloak with a large hood to cover her face. She pulled it tightly around her as she made her way across the gangway.

Captain Marino Pegasi was waiting for her on deck, his smile as wide and bright as ever. His dark curly hair was slightly longer now, and his jaw was lightly stubbled. He was dressed impeccably, in a magnificent sapphire frock coat with gold buttons, black fitted trousers, and matching laced boots. His black hat was trimmed in gold threading, mirroring the ornate handle of the sword at his hip. The sword had been a recent gift from Wren, to thank him for getting her safely home from Gevra some months before.

Since then, Marino had visited the palace several times as a favored guest of the queens.

"Welcome back to the roiling seas, Your Majesty," he said now, splaying his arms in welcome. "I trust you remember your way around my humble ship."

"This fancy ship is about as humble as you are, Marino," said Wren, taking his arm as they walked along the deck. "Although it is nice not to be a stowaway this time."

The crew of the *Siren's Secret* scurried around them like dutiful mice, preparing to set sail. Before long, they were pulling away from the dock. The bay turned amber and gold, reflecting the rising sun as they made for the open sea. The morning breeze was warm and gentle, feathering Wren's cheeks as she stood on the upper deck.

As much as she enjoyed Marino's company, she was hoping for a quick journey to Sharkfin Point, the towering white glacier that jutted up from the middle of the Sunless Sea. She might not have feared the king of Gevra, but she didn't want to keep him waiting either. She gripped the railings and leaned over the still water, trying to cast away her doubt. Her face stared up at her: pallid, nervous. Perhaps Rose was right—maybe this was a bad idea. After all, Wren didn't exactly have a history of making good decisions. And what *could* the king of Gevra possibly tell her about her own magic? He didn't possess any of his own.

"Are you angry at the sea?" Marino's voice interrupted her thoughts.

Wren snapped her chin up. "What?"

"It's just, well, you're looking at it kind of . . . murderously."

Wren frowned. "No. It's not that. I'm just . . ."

"Anxious?" guessed Marino. "You never did mention why we're taking this little morning excursion," he said conversationally. "When I asked Celeste about it, she told me to mind my own business."

Wren tugged on her sleeve self-consciously, suddenly afraid Marino could sense the scar burning underneath it. "The less you know about this meeting the better."

Marino chuckled. "I *knew* it."

Wren glanced at him over her shoulder. "What?"

He smirked. Somehow, it made him look even more handsome. "I had an inkling already, of course. I saw the way he looked at you the last time you sailed to meet him on the Sunless Sea. He was watching you so intently he wasn't even blinking!" He laughed again. "It was as if he was afraid he'd miss something if he did. He looked so . . . *thirsty*. And now this." Marino waggled his eyebrows. "A clandestine meeting . . . You hardly thought I wouldn't figure it out. I'm far too clever. Not to mention well versed in the art of romance."

Wren turned around. "What on earth are you talking about, Marino?"

"The Gevran king." Marino glanced side to side, then lowered his voice, making sure his crew was out of earshot. "It's obvious. You two are embroiled in a secret love affair."

Wren stared at Marino for a long moment, waiting for him to smile. His face grew only more serious.

"That's *absurd*," she said at last. "It's laughable."

He crooked a brow. "Then why aren't you laughing?"

"Because I'm traumatized by the mere suggestion!" said Wren, far too shrilly. Her cheeks blazed as she remembered her blizzard kiss with King Alarik. The devastating grief that had swept them both up, wrapping them in each other's arms for a brief moment of comfort. It had happened several months ago now, but every so often the memory of that kiss would explode in her mind like a wayward firework. It was a terrible mistake. And yet no matter how hard she tried, she couldn't seem to forget it.

"Consider me unconvinced," said Marino.

"I do not have feelings for Alarik Felsing."

"Fine. My mistake."

"It is," said Wren firmly.

"If you say so."

"Marino! Stop smirking at me!"

"I can't help it. It's just my face."

Wren scowled at him, then stomped away. The thud of Marino's boots told Wren that he was following her. She went to the prow, where the wooden mermaid peered over the water as if she were marveling at her own reflection. "If you want to talk about love affairs, let's discuss your mermaid," Wren challenged.

Marino's face fell. "Alas, I still haven't found her."

"Don't you think it's time you settled down with . . . oh, I don't know . . . someone with legs?"

"Such as who?"

Wren shrugged. "It's a pretty low bar, Marino. What about Rowena? She never shuts up about you."

Marino shook his head. "Too temperamental. She'd blow me away in a storm."

"She did uproot an apple tree last week when she lost a game of cards against Bryony," Wren conceded. "Well, you could have your pick of anyone."

"Why settle?" The captain folded his arms. "One day the sea will lead me to my true love."

"And if it doesn't?"

"Then I shall die alone. And rich. Very, very rich."

Wren snorted. "That is tragic."

"At least I'm not in love with a Gevran."

Wren raised a warning finger. "I am not in love with King Alarik."

"I didn't say the king this time," said Marino with a wink.

Wren was silent then. Her thoughts turned to Tor, the feel of his strong hands sliding up her back, the heady press of his lips against hers, desperate, searching. A new heat stole through her body, casting a blush in her cheeks. She couldn't deny her feelings for him. She wore them too plainly, thought of him too often to lie about it. And anyway, she didn't *want* to lie about him. He deserved better than that. Better than her.

Marino's brown eyes danced. "This is going to be a fun voyage."

"Speak for yourself," groaned Wren. "Can't you make this bloody ship go faster?"

"I can certainly try," he said with a grin. He raised his hands as though he were reaching for the moon. "Rowena's been helping me with my tempest magic."

Learning Marino Pegasi was a witch had come as a surprise to everyone at Anadawn, especially his sister, Celeste. Celeste had spent so many years denying her own seer abilities, which she had unknowingly inherited from her mother, that she never thought to find out whether her older brother might be a witch, too. Marino said he had been stargazing all his life, thinking nothing of the shapes that used to appear in the night sky out at sea. He considered himself a gifted sailor who could read the constellations, not a witch who could read the future.

But once the witches' curse had been broken and the five strands of power restored to every witch in Eana, Marino began to notice other things about himself. Other abilities.

Magic bloomed inside him, and he welcomed it.

He closed his eyes now and opened his fists, frowning as he concentrated. Wren watched him in silence, curious to see what he could do. A minute passed and then another. A rogue breeze whipped up, but it died almost as quickly. "Slippery little thing," Marino muttered. "I almost had it."

Wren cleared her throat. "Do you want me to—?"

"I can do it," he said. "I've done it before."

Wren doubted that but she wasn't going to argue with him in front of his crew. They were lingering nearby, watching him struggle. Some of the swabbies were laughing among themselves. Wren shooed them away with a glare.

She turned back to Marino. "Picture the storm in your mind. The clearer you see it, the quicker it will come."

"Wind is invisible," he huffed. "How am I supposed to *picture* it?"

"Don't think of the wind on its own. Think of what it *does*," urged Wren. "Imagine the mainsail full and straining. Or your fancy new hat flying off your head. Think of the waves slapping against the ship, spitting sea-foam in our faces."

Marino's shoulders relaxed, and his frown loosened.

"Once you conjure the image of what you need, your magic will know what to do," said Wren. "It just takes a little practice. Concentrate. And keep your palms open. Good. Just like that."

Marino smiled. "You're a good tutor."

"We'll see," said Wren.

After a minute, she felt the wind pick up. It yanked the hood from her face and sent her hair streaming through the air. "It's working!"

Marino laughed as his frock coat rippled behind him. "I can feel the storm inside me!"

The wind howled as if it were laughing, too. It punched the mainsail taut, sending the ship skittering along the waves. They were growing, slapping against the hull as if the wind was urging them faster. Before long, Wren had to grab on to the railings for balance.

"I think that's enough!" she called over the roaring sea.

"I could do this all night!" roared Marino gleefully.

Wren yelped as the ship veered to the left, heading for a cluster of sea rocks. "You might want to try steering now!"

Marino snapped his eyes open. "Good idea!" he yelled, sprinting for the wheel.

Wren ran after him, grabbing a rung to help him steady the ship. They narrowly avoided the rocks, adjusting the course four notches to the left, where the open sea was calling them. When Wren looked back, Wishbone Bay had disappeared. Eana was behind them, their voyage well and truly underway.

Wren stayed by Marino's side as the morning sun arced over them, and the sky changed from amber to blue. When her stomach began to grumble, she ventured belowdecks, where a bowl of fragrant fish stew was waiting for her in the captain's cabin. She devoured it in ten bites before collapsing into bed, grateful that Marino had offered her his cabin with all of its finery and luxurious comfort. The waves soon rocked her to sleep.

Mercifully, she was too tired to dream.

When Wren awoke, there was a chill in the air. The cabin was silent. The candles had dwindled to nothing. She could tell by the frost webbing the porthole and the eerie stillness of the ship that they had reached the Sunless Sea. The sun had set, a slant of graying evening light slipping through the window.

Wren washed and then dressed in her leathers before shrugging on a fur-lined cloak. She donned her sturdiest boots and the gloves Celeste had gifted her for Yulemas—as though she had known even then that Wren would be returning to the Sunless Sea. As Wren stood in front of the mirror, braiding her hair away from her face, she traced the silver streak self-consciously, trying not to linger on the shadows under her eyes.

Up on deck, Marino was bright-eyed and good-tempered, despite a full day of rough sailing. He was standing at the wheel, sipping on a mug of coffee.

"You look nice," he said by way of greeting. "Not that it matters, of course. Since this is definitely not a secret romantic meeting."

"Please don't start that again." Wren snatched the mug from him and took a long leisurely sip. The coffee zipped through her bloodstream, warming her fingers and toes. "How much longer?"

Marino nodded at something over her shoulder. "See for yourself."

Wren turned and squinted through the evening mist. And suddenly there it was: a towering white rock jutting up from the sea in the shape of a shark's fin. They had made it to the meeting point. It took her another moment to spot the warship floating just beyond the mighty rock, and the Gevran king's flag rippling atop the mast pole.

And there, below the flag, standing side by side, were King Alarik and his faithful captain. Wren couldn't help it. The moment she saw Tor, her face broke into a smile.

Alarik smiled back.

Behind Wren, Marino chuckled. "This is going to be fun."

10

ROSE

Rose would never admit it to Wren, but the morning after her sister left for Wishbone Bay, she climbed out onto the roof of Anadawn Palace and used Celeste's spyglass to watch the *Siren's Secret* set sail at first light.

Before Rose became queen, she and Celeste had often come here late at night or early in the day to watch Marino's boat come and go. Celeste always pretended she didn't worry about her brother, but Rose saw the way her best friend gripped that spyglass until her knuckles paled and knew that she did.

And now that she had her own sister to worry about, Rose truly understood the relief Celeste felt every time the *Siren's Secret* safely returned to Wishbone Bay.

As Rose watched the ship get smaller and smaller and then disappear from sight entirely, she closed her eyes and sent a wish to the stars that the journey would go well, that Wren would find the answers she was looking for and then return home, healed and happy.

Rose sighed. She couldn't stand here staring out the window until Wren returned, so with some reluctance, she clambered back inside the palace and went in search of distraction. She soon found herself wandering toward the library, looking for a cozy fairy tale or a sweeping adventure story to take her mind off her worries.

When Rose was a young girl, confined by Willem Rathborne to the palace for weeks on end, she had always turned to books. They had been her escape, her comfort, her greatest joy. The only question now was which story to pick. Something familiar and soothing, she decided. Perhaps even something with romance. She quickened her steps as she reached the library, the door closing behind her with a soft thud. She hummed to herself as she perused the stacks, trailing her fingers over the familiar gilded spines. She was so lost in thought that she didn't see the figure sitting in one of the window seats until she was nearly upon him.

"Oh! Prince Felix!" she said with a start. "I wasn't expecting to find anyone in here."

"Ah! Queen Rose!" he said, hastily shoving something behind his back. "What are you doing up so early?"

"Well, a dutiful queen must rise early to face the day." She frowned slightly, trying to peer over his shoulder. Something was winking in the sconce-light. "Now I'm looking for a book, which is, I believe, customary in a library. What, may I ask, are you doing here?"

"The very same thing!" he said quickly. "You have a lovely collection. I was hoping to find a book about . . ." He paused. In the short time that Rose had known Prince Felix, she had never seen him lost for words. And here, in the pale morning light, with his hair unkempt and shadows pooling under his eyes, he looked wretched. As though he hadn't slept a wink.

"A book about . . . ?" she prompted.

"Horses! A nice book about horses!"

"Prince Felix, what is that behind your back?" said Rose, peering over him to see what he was hiding.

"What is what?" Felix summoned a shaky grin. "Why, I am holding nothing but my great affection for you."

Rose didn't like to use magic against people if she could help it, but something about the way the prince was acting had set her on edge. She took a steadying breath and summoned her warrior strand, which granted her greater agility and precision.

"Perhaps I might take a look anyway?" She shot her arm out and grabbed Felix's wrist, twisting until he released what he had been gripping. He yelped as it fell to the floor with a clatter.

Rose looked down and gasped. It was her jeweled mirror. The one that she and Wren had used to communicate when they were apart from one another. One of the sapphires was still faintly shimmering.

"Ow!" said Felix, rubbing his wrist and glaring at her. "That wasn't very polite."

"Neither is taking people's things." Rose swiped the mirror from the floor just as the final sapphire winked out. "When were you in my bedchamber, Felix?"

"I was never in your bedchamber!" he said aghast. "I found the mirror right here in this very library when I was innocently perusing your historical records." He folded his arms and stared down his nose at Rose. "What a preposterous accusation!"

Rose narrowed her eyes. "I'm sure this mirror was on my dresser when I left my room before dawn. And even if you had indeed found it here, as you claim, why were you hiding it from me just now?"

"That wasn't my intention." Felix sighed and ran a hand through his hair. "If you must know, I found the mirror right here, on this shelf. And when I realized something so fine must of course belong to you, I thought it would give me a most perfect excuse to go to your chambers and return it to you later."

Rose felt a strange prickle of relief at his words. That certainly did sound like something Felix would do. And surely, he wouldn't have broken into her bedchamber . . . but then, who would have removed her mirror and put it all the way down here, in the library?

"Well, I have it now," she said, holding it to her chest. "So there is no need for you to trouble yourself by going all the way up to my chambers." Rose was frustrated by the encounter, but she didn't want to make too much of a fuss. She had enough to worry about without offending the Prince of Caro. "Especially as it is almost time for breakfast."

"Why, I would be *delighted* to break my fast with you, Queen Rose," said Felix, brightening at the prospect of dining with her. "Thank you for the invitation."

"Oh. Wonderful." With great effort, Rose summoned a practiced smile. "I'll see you in the morning room shortly." She turned to leave, and something crumpled under her foot. She bent to retrieve the balled-up piece of parchment at the same time Felix did, and they bumped heads.

Rose scowled at the dull thud of pain, her patience running out. "Please give that to me," she ordered.

"I cannot," said Felix, clutching the parchment in his fist. "It's far too embarrassing. You see, I'm writing you a poem. And it's not finished yet." His smile vibrated at the edges, his eyes wide and barbed with red. "I'll show you when it's complete, when it's as perfect as you are."

Rose sighed heavily. "I see. I suppose I cannot command you to stop writing poetry."

"That would be like asking the stars not to shine, the waves not to crash, the clouds . . ."

She held her hand up. "You have made your point. Well, take better care not to leave your poetry on the floor where anyone could find it and mistake it for rubbish."

Felix, for once, was surprised into silence.

Rose left the library in a hurry, unnerved by the strange exchange and eager to return her mirror to its rightful place.

That night, it took Rose a long time to fall asleep. Her dinner with Prince Felix had felt especially forced after their encounter in the library and his continuing strangeness throughout the day, and then when she'd finally been able to return to her bedroom, she found it unseasonably cold. Even with a roaring fire in the grate and an extra quilt, she couldn't get warm. Wrapped in her blankets and still shivering, Rose found herself thinking of Shen, wishing he were here to warm her. The thought of his strong arms wrapped around her and his body pressed up against hers filled her with a welcome flurry of heat. It was just enough to lull her to sleep, where her last thoughts were of the Sunkissed king and his perfect, dimpled smile.

But Rose didn't dream of Shen.

In the depths of her slumber, she found herself lost in a snow-swept tundra. The wind howled with an eerie laugh that felt both haunting and familiar. Rose stumbled through the snow, searching for a way out of her nightmare, only to find herself at the edge of an icy ravine.

A terrible wind whipped up, pressing cold hands against her back. They shoved her forward. She screamed as she fell down, down, down into the abyss. . . .

Rose woke with a start, a hand pressed to her pounding heart.

It was only a dream, she told herself. *A silly nightmare.*

She curled her hands into the bottom of her nightgown, grounding herself in its softness. There was nothing to be frightened of now that she was awake.

Her teeth began to chatter, her quickened breaths hanging clouds in the air. The fire in the grate had gone out and her room was even colder than before. Her blankets were tangled around her feet. Rose sat up to reach them and froze.

There was someone standing at the foot of her bed.

Rose bit back a scream.

"Shen?" she said quietly, hopefully. Perhaps she had summoned him with the strength of her desire.

The figure laughed. It was the same laugh from Rose's dream. It did not belong to Shen.

Rose began to tremble. "I'm still dreaming," she whispered to herself. "This is a dream within a dream." She pinched her arm, hard. "Wake up," she said desperately. *"Please."*

The figure stopped laughing, the air growing so cold it turned the water pitcher to ice.

"You are a gutless fool," said a low, mocking voice, and the sound of it scraped against Rose's bones. "Just like my sister was. I have come for the other one, the one who thinks like me. . . ."

Bile gathered in Rose's throat as she realized who was talking to her. Somehow, Oonagh Starcrest was here. In her room. In her head. She tried to find her voice—to tell her to leave—but fear had frozen her stiff. She could only stare in horror at the looming shadow.

It must be a trick of magic. An apparition. A night terror.

The shadow kept speaking. "But you are the one in my palace so *you* are the one who will heed my warning."

Rose slowly pushed herself backward, hitting the headboard. The shadow lunged. With lightning speed, Oonagh Starcrest scrambled across the bed until she was nose to nose with her.

Rose released a strangled cry. Wren had told her that Oonagh wore their face, but seeing it herself, so close and real and *cruel*, was a harrowing shock.

Oonagh's eyes were cold. Empty.

"*You* are the weak one," she sneered, her mouth so close to Rose, she could have kissed her. The stench of rot rolled off her breath, and for a moment, Rose thought she might be sick. "Look at you. You aren't even fighting me."

"This is a dream," Rose whispered, a frightened tear sliding down her cheek. "It's just a dream."

"Pathetic, wilting flower," hissed Oonagh. "You know who I am. Do not deny me." Her hand shot out, grabbing Rose by the neck. "I will return in one moon's time to take back what is mine. When I am at my full strength again, you and your sister will give me my crown and throne." Oonagh squeezed, choking the breath from Rose's windpipe. "If you refuse, I will take Anadawn by bloody force." She spat the words with such disdain, flecks of spittle landed on Rose's face. "And this country will face a war more brutal than any you could ever imagine."

A vision suddenly crashed into Rose's mind. Her people dying in a battlefield slick with blood. Children running and screaming, unable to find safe refuge in towns and villages consumed by flames. The land choking under great plumes of smoke, the dead rising from their graves, their teeth snapping like beasts as they ripped the living apart limb from limb.

Crops withered to dust—leaving behind barren fields of ash, all of Eana little more than a husk. And lording over it all, alone on the balcony of Anadawn Palace and laughing her terrible, screeching laugh, stood Oonagh. Power glowed in her eyes, growing with every drop of blood spilled, every death across the land.

Rose felt the terror of her dying kingdom as though it were her own, the agony of her people singing in her blood. She clawed at the blankets, a cry pouring from her as she tried to wrench herself free from this nightmare, this vision that felt so real, so *close*.

"Do you see?" hissed Oonagh. "Your kingdom will crumble to ash, and I will rebuild it as I like. All of Eana will belong to me."

The vision fell away, like ash in the wind, and Rose blinked to see her ancestor smiling before her, her teeth gray and rotting. But her eyes shone with that awful promise of power, and Rose knew this was no empty threat. "Do you understand?" Oonagh added.

Rose locked eyes with her ancestor, her response coming on a trembling breath. *"Yes."*

"Good." Oonagh dug her nails in, clawing Rose's skin as she released her.

Rose whimpered as warm blood dripped down her neck.

Oonagh stood up, towering over Rose like a terrible wraith. "I expect a warm welcome on my return." She stepped backward, dropped to the floor, and disappeared, leaving nothing behind but a wisp of smoke and the echo of her laugh.

Rose sat shivering in her bed, too frightened to move. Slowly, so slowly, she reached up to touch her neck. Her fingers came away slicked with blood. Still shaking, she forced herself to crawl out of bed.

Her curtains were open, but the window was shut. Her bedroom door was still locked. Rose turned on her heel, trying to make sense of the intrusion. Her heart stuttered at a glint of silver by the foot of the bed. There, on the floor, with smoke rising from it, was the bejeweled mirror she had taken from Felix in the library only hours ago. The mirror that had once belonged to Oonagh and Ortha Starcrest.

"Eana, first witch, please protect me," Rose whispered as she picked up the mirror. With trembling hands, she smashed it again and again against the nightstand until, at last, it shattered.

She stared at the pieces, her mind whirring. Was it purely a coincidence that she'd caught the Prince of Caro with the mirror the very day that Oonagh Starcrest rose out of it?

It *had* to be. Prince Felix had no magic. No link to Eana or knowledge of Oonagh Starcrest.

And yet, the timing was deeply unnerving. . . . *All of it* was unnerving.

Still shivering, Rose crawled into bed and buried herself under her blankets, willing morning to come swiftly. When dawn finally broke, she still hadn't slept. She was wide awake when she heard a shout of dismay from the courtyard. In a daze, she went to the window.

Even from her tower she could see the cause for alarm. Everything in the gardens was dead. The flowers had all withered. The ground was strewn with dead petals and the rosebushes had blackened from decay.

Rose closed her eyes, fighting tears. She raised her hand to her neck. The bleeding had stopped sometime in the night, but the graze was deep, and the wound was stinging.

The truth was undeniable.

It had not been a night terror after all.

Oonagh Starcrest was coming home to Anadawn.

WREN

With expert ease, Marino Pegasi brought the *Siren's Secret* to rest along-side the Gevran war boat until both ships drew level in the mist. The anchor whirred as it plunged down into the Sunless Sea, the sizable chain almost running out entirely until, at last, it settled on the ocean floor.

A gangway was erected between the ships. Wren stood at one end of it, waiting. Alarik stood at the other end, watching her.

"Well?" he called out. "Is there a reason you're stalling?"

"I was about to ask you the same thing," Wren called back. "Aren't you coming?"

The king laughed. "The meeting will be on my ship."

Wren folded her arms. "I'd prefer mine. It's fancier."

"This is actually *my* ship," hissed Marino, who was standing behind her.

"That's not the point," she hissed back.

"What *is* the point?" he whispered. "Why aren't you going over there?"

"Because Alarik Felsing needs to know that he cannot simply snap his fingers and expect me to jump for him."

Marino snorted.

"What are you two conspiring about over there?" shouted Alarik. Through the icy mist, Wren could see he had dressed well for their meeting. He was wearing a dark gray frock coat trimmed in silver ermine, with a high collar that brushed the underside of his jaw. Despite sailing aboard the king's official vessel, he had forgone his crown— or perhaps he had simply not yet replaced the one Oonagh Starcrest had stolen from him—making his wheat-blond hair look unusually unkempt. With the fog thickening between them, Wren couldn't see his face properly, but she could hear the scowl in his voice. "Stop these childish games, Wren Greenrock, and come aboard my ship. We have urgent matters to discuss."

"No. *You* come over here." Wren stood her ground, even though she knew it was indeed childish. She was as safe on Marino's boat as she would be a stone's throw across the water, but now that she was faced with the daunting prospect of sitting down with Alarik Felsing again, she couldn't help the sudden flurry of nerves. If she walked that gang-way, her knees might tremble. Her hands might sweat. And he would see her and know he had the upper hand. "I'm getting frostbite, Alarik! I've come all this way. This really is the least you could do!"

She heard him sigh, then mutter, "I don't remember her being this irritating. Do you?"

Marino sidled over to Wren. "Just so you know, this feels a lot like flirting to me."

"It's a power play," Wren corrected him. "I'm resetting the balance between us. Alarik Felsing needs to learn how to meet me half—"

Thud.

She paused at the sound of footsteps on the plank. Wren smirked. *"See?"*

The gangway creaked as it bore new weight, the footsteps drawing closer, and then the mist shifted, revealing the figure stalking across it. It was not Alarik.

It was Tor.

Wren peered up into the soldier's perfectly chiseled face and was suddenly all too aware of her heartbeat. Tor was impossibly tall and broad-shouldered, and dressed in his impeccable blue uniform. His tousled hair swept low across his storm-gray eyes. He raked it back to see her better, the hint of a smile softening the hard edge of his jaw.

Stars above.

Wren's mind whirred, desperately searching for something clever to say, a greeting so alluring and disarming, it would flood him with the same rush of longing she was feeling just then. "Um, hi."

"Smooth," whispered Marino.

Wren shoved him aside. "Hi," she said again. "It's good to see you."

"And you, Wren." Tor's voice was huskier than she remembered. "As ever."

Not for the first time, she found herself caught in the lightning of his gaze.

Tor paused on the edge of the gangway and offered his hand out to her. "Let me help you across."

Wren stared at it.

He misread her hesitance. "I won't let you fall."

"That's not why I don't want to come," she said, realizing she hadn't won the battle of wills after all. Alarik had simply sent Tor to fetch her. "I'm . . . well, I'm making a point."

"*Wren*," he said, his voice stern. "This is not the time." Wren glowered up at him, but his frown was sharper. "Trust me," he said, and in the gravel of his voice, she heard a plea. She saw the worry in his eyes. "Please."

She sighed, wavering.

"You shouldn't go over there by yourself," said Marino, his hand coming to the hilt of his sword. "I'd be happy to escort you."

Tor's jaw tensed. "She's in no danger."

"Even so," said Marino, stepping forward. "The queen should have an escort."

"I am her escort," said Tor, shooting Marino a warning look.

"I'm all right, Marino," said Wren, if only to quell the rising tension between them. "I'll be back within the hour."

Tor's gloves were made of leather, but Wren could still feel the warmth of his touch as he took her hand, curling it inside his own. She clambered up onto the wooden plank and let him lead her through the mist, to where the king of Gevra was waiting.

Tor leaped easily off the gangway, then turned back to her. Even though Wren was confident enough to make the jump by herself, she hesitated, letting him curl his arms around her waist, hold her tight against his body, if only for a fleeting moment. When he set her down, she found herself momentarily breathless.

"I knew you'd come for him." Alarik Felsing was leaning against the mainmast of his ship with his arms folded. His skin was almost as pale as his hair, but his eyes were bright. Focused. "It took you long enough."

Wren stalked toward him. "Tell me, Alarik, was it laziness or cowardice that kept you from my ship?"

"Call it stubbornness," he said mildly. "Speaking of which, thank you for surrendering yours."

"I didn't want to make a scene."

"How unlike you."

Wren looked him up and down, noting the hollows in his cheeks and the circles under his eyes. "You look dreadful."

He flashed his teeth. "If I wasn't such a gentleman, I'd say the same thing to you."

Tor cleared his throat, stepping into the space between them. "If you insist on greeting each other with these childish insults, can I suggest we do it belowdecks before you both freeze to death?"

"Fine by me," said Wren.

Alarik pushed off the mast and stumbled. Tor lunged, catching him by the arm.

"I'm all right," he snapped, shrugging him off. Alarik barged ahead, taking the stairs belowdecks. Wren didn't miss the way he held tightly to the banister, or how, when he finally released it, he veered a little to the left. The king was unsteady on his feet.

"Oh," she said quietly.

Tor glanced back at her, and she understood that worried look in his eyes then. And why Alarik wouldn't cross the gangway to Marino's ship. He couldn't trust himself not to fall. They followed the king downstairs into the captain's cabin, which was full of ornate furniture draped in lavish furs. Candlelight flickered along the walls, setting an eerie glow about the room.

Alarik collapsed in an armchair by the window. He looked exhausted already.

Wren perched against the dark wood dining table, unsure where to put herself, while Tor stood with his back against the door, guarding their privacy. Wren looked around for Elske, but there was no sign of the wolf.

"She's in the galley," said Tor, reading her thoughts. "Hunting for scraps."

"You should feed her better, then."

"I always give her the best cut of meat."

Wren looked back at him, catching his smile. "She's lucky you have such a soft spot for her."

Alarik was unusually quiet. He was looking out to sea, trying to hide his discomfort. Wren poured him a glass of water from the pitcher on the table and brought it to him. "Here."

He regarded the water as if it were poison.

"I know you're not well," said Wren. "Drink it."

Alarik opened his mouth to say something, then thought better of it. He took the water, draining it in three gulps. "Thank you," he said in a gruff voice.

Wren raised her eyebrows. With remarkable quickness, they had navigated the discomfort of seeing each other again and had arrived at civility. "You're welcome."

Looking brighter already, the king sat back in his chair and studied Wren. She fought the urge to tug her braid loose and hide her face. "It seems you are not well either."

"I've been better."

Alarik cocked his head, still watching her. "I've been dreaming of you, Wren Greenrock."

Wren saw Tor stiffen out of the corner of her eye, but she didn't tear her eyes from the king.

"In pain," Alarik added. "You're always in pain."

Wren felt a curious twinge in her heart, as though Alarik had pricked it with a pin. They had gone through so much together back in Gevra, and in many ways he had seen her more clearly these last few months than her own sister had. The thought of it made Wren want to cry. She bit down on her lip, waiting for the feeling to pass. "Yes," she said quietly. "I've seen you, too."

He didn't look surprised by her revelation. He jerked his chin up, looking past her. "Iversen, can you give us a moment?"

Although it was phrased as a question, it was plainly an order, and Tor didn't look remotely pleased about it. He glanced between them, then turned on his heel, shutting the door behind him with a thud.

Alarik chuckled to himself. "It takes some work to break Captain Iversen's composure."

"Was that necessary?" said Wren.

The king smirked. "I'm afraid I'll need your full attention."

"For what?"

"See for yourself." Alarik rolled up his sleeve.

When Wren saw the silver crescent scar on his wrist, a gasp caught in her throat. She sank to her knees. Without thinking—without asking—she traced her thumb across it.

Alarik shuddered.

"How is this possible?" she whispered.

At his look of confusion, she removed her glove and showed him her matching scar. He took her wrist, tracing it as she had done. Instead of pain, Wren felt a strange tingle of warmth. She closed her eyes, trying to make sense of it.

"Does it hurt?" he asked.

"Not now. But sometimes it does. Especially whenever I use my magic."

"I see."

"And yours?"

"At night, mostly. I think it's making me . . ." He trailed off.

"Ill?"

"Weak." Alarik's frown sharpened his cheekbones. In the flickering light, he looked a bit like a wolf. "I can't afford to be weak right now."

Wren realized his hand was still on her wrist. There was something soothing about his touch, about the nearness of his pain, so like her own. Then she thought of Tor, standing just outside the door.

She pulled her arm back and reached for her glove.

Alarik narrowed his eyes. "Whatever this thing is, it's affecting both of us."

"Yes," said Wren as she stood up. "Something must have happened when I was in Gevra to create this strange bond."

"I was thinking the same." Alarik cleared his throat. "Perhaps it was that day . . . after the mountain came down." Wren saw a memory spark in his eyes, heard the hunger in his voice. He was thinking of the blizzard, of the kiss that had swept them up. "When it began to snow—"

"No," she said quickly. She didn't want to think about that. "It wasn't the blizzard, Alarik. It was the blood spell. It must have happened when we raised Ansel from the dead."

Alarik frowned. "Oh."

Wren began to pace, building her theory. "It was your blood and my words. My magic. We messed with the dark side of power and did something unforgivable. And now we're paying the price. With this pain . . . this scar. There's something wrong."

"So make it right." Alarik stood up, the hardness returning to his voice. "You're the witch. Fix it."

"It's not that simple," said Wren. "I can't heal. I told you that."

"Your sister, then. She's a healer."

Wren shook her head. "Rose already tried to heal my scar. But it's made of something else. Something deeper than skin, deeper than blood and bone. I don't understand it myself."

"Figure it out, Wren." Alarik raked a hand through his hair, pulling at the strands around his temple. "My country is sick, too. My beasts are turning feral. My graveyards lie in ruins. Your ancestor stalks my kingdom. Day and night, my army has been searching for her. And finally, after months of searching, they spotted her on the cliffs of the Sundvik Shore two days ago."

Wren stilled. "You *found* her?"

"We didn't just find her, Wren. We tried to kill her." Alarik's face was grim. "We fired forty steel arrows. Half of them found their mark, and yet not one could pierce her. My soldiers charged with their swords, but she was impervious to those, too." He shook his head in disbelief. "Then she dived from the cliffs and let the sea swallow her whole. But she's not gone, Wren. I can still hear her laugh on the wind. I feel it rumbling in the mountains."

Wren curled her fists, trying to fight the sudden rush of her panic. "Do you mean she cannot be killed?"

Alarik's lips twisted. "Not by Gevran steel. Evidently."

"This is bad." Far worse than she'd thought.

He gave a mirthless huff. "I had hoped she would give up eventually, find another mountain to crawl inside and die."

Wren shook her head at the idea of her ancestor going anywhere quietly, of laying aside her claim to Eana, to power. "She must have been hiding all this time. Gathering her strength. Planning for what comes next."

His face tightened. "Which is?"

"I don't know," she said in a whisper. And that was the worst of it.

"Gevra needs a strong ruler now more than ever," said Alarik, a new bite in his voice. "I *cannot* be seen as weak, Wren."

"I'm not the one who made you weak."

"You're the one who cast the spell."

Wren bristled. Not this again. "You made me do it!"

"You messed it up!"

"Do you think *I* want to be like this? I'm supposed to be a witch and I can barely do magic. Whenever I cast a spell, it hurts me. It wounds my *soul*. I'm tired all the time. Distracted. Anxious." Her anger flared, the unfairness of it all crowding in on her. "And then at night, when I can finally stop pretending and be alone, I dream of *you*. I can't escape what we did at Grinstad. I cannot escape *you*."

Alarik threw his head back and scoffed. "I suppose you think I enjoy hearing you scream when I fall asleep? That I like chasing you through the snow, night after night, trapped in a hellish maze I can't escape?"

He glared at her. "You are the one haunting me, Wren."

Wren braced her hands on the table, glaring right back. "Can you stop arguing with me for one second?"

"Fine," he said. "Let's be practical. We need to free ourselves from that wretched blood spell, once and for all."

"Clearly," said Wren.

"I have a kingdom to run. And I don't have the luxury of a twin sister who will do that for me."

"What about Anika?"

Alarik threw her a withering look. "Do not jest at a time like this. My sister would eat your nation for breakfast. All it takes is one bad mood."

Wren slumped into a chair. "I don't have any answers for you, Alarik. I was hoping you'd have answers for me."

This time when Alarik laughed, Wren joined in. It suddenly felt so absurd, both of them stuck in the middle of the Sunless Sea, trying to muddle their way toward a miracle solution for something they didn't remotely understand. This scar. This pain. This strange bond.

"Maybe not an answer, but a direction will do. Isn't there someone we can speak to? One of your kind?"

Wren frowned. She had been hoping to avoid involving Thea in this, but she could see no way around it now. Whatever this thing that had taken root inside them was, it was damaging Wren's magic and Alarik's health. And it was getting worse. "My grandmother's wife has been a healer all her life," she said slowly. "She grew up in the Mish-nick Mountains, an ancient place of teaching and meditation. Thea learned from the very best. She lives at Anadawn Palace now. You'll have to come back there with me."

The king raised his brows. "Can't she come to me?"

Wren almost laughed in his face. "If you think I'm dragging my grandmother's widow across the Sunless Sea to the frostbitten country that killed her wife, then you're a lot sicker than I thought." Wren pointed to his wrist. "If you don't like my plan, then feel free to go back to Gevra and rub some snow on that. Frankly, it will be a miracle if she agrees to see you at all."

"What an enthusiastic invitation." His voice dripped with sarcasm. "How could I say no?"

Wren rolled her eyes.

"It will have to be a brief, clandestine visit," he went on. "And I warn you, Wren, if I travel all that way and you fail to help me, then—"

Wren flung a candlestick at him. It cracked against the wall. "For stars' sake, Alarik. Stop threatening me!"

He smiled sheepishly. "Sorry. Force of habit."

Wren blew out a breath. "So, it's decided, then. We can return on Marino's ship for secrecy."

He dragged a hand across his jaw. "I'll have to consult with Captain Iversen first."

Just then, the door flew open. Tor stood in the doorframe, looking between them. "Ready and willing, Your Majesty."

Wren's smile died on her lips. She groaned.

"What is it?" they chorused.

"Marino is going to be insufferable about this," she said with a sigh.

ROSE

Rose didn't tell anyone about her midnight encounter with Oonagh. She took the shattered pieces of the mirror and buried them deep in her garden, whispering an enchantment to keep them hidden.

Her beloved rose garden now mocked her with its decay. She overheard the palace gardeners speculating about what had happened. An early frost, said one. Locusts, said another. A magical curse, someone suggested, laughing at the very thought.

But Rose knew that was closest to the terrible truth. And the roses were only the start of it. The morning had been curiously absent of birdsong, and then at midday, there were thumps heard all across the palace as birds fell dead from the sky. Dozens of them. Mostly starcrests but dawnbirds and blackbirds and carrier pigeons, too. Rose wondered if birds were falling out of the sky across Eana or only over Anadawn. She hoped that some of the starcrests had flown away, that they had managed to find a safe haven somewhere. She ordered for the ones that had fallen to be picked up and burned, but she knew it would not be so easy to rid Anadawn—or indeed Eana—of Oonagh's lingering threat.

And as for her own injuries ... Rose wore her hair loose to hide the marks on her neck. She could not afford to be seen as weak, as injured. Not now. Or ever.

She crafted a careful veneer that allowed her to tolerate polite conversation with Prince Felix, who was at the breakfast table before her, a scroll of parchment in his hand. With dramatic flair, he recited a meandering romantic poem to Rose, seemingly oblivious to the state of the palace around him or indeed the queen upon whom he gazed with wide covetous eyes.

When Rose met with Chapman after breakfast as usual, the steward was mildly alarmed by the birds and the garden, but Rose mumbled something about the changing weather that he accepted. She knew she would soon have to prepare him, and all of Anadawn, for the inevitable return of Oonagh Starcrest, but to do that, she needed Wren at her side.

Rose even avoided both Thea and Celeste. Rose suspected the Queensbreath would see through her act, and with her impressive healing skills, might quickly sense something was deeply wrong.

As for Celeste, Rose had never lied to her best friend before, and she couldn't bear to start now. So, better not to see her at all, for the time being. Celeste was already having visions of Oonagh, and Rose knew if she met with her friend, she wouldn't be able to keep the truth from her.

She needed to tell Wren before anyone else. Then the two of them, together, could come up with a plan for what to do next. As Rose prepared for bed that night, she enchanted a row of everlights along her windowsill and built up the fire in the grate as high as it would go. She could not face the dark, not tonight. Not on her own.

Come home soon, Wren. I need you.

♛

When Rose awoke from a fitful slumber, the sun was already high in the sky. But the everlights on her windowsill still glowed and despite her fears, she hadn't received any more unexpected bedroom visitors.

Rose yawned as she dressed, trying to shake off her exhaustion. She chose a yellow day dress embroidered with white butterflies and a delicate lace scarf before brushing her hair to its fullest. She was just finishing applying her favorite lavender hand cream when she heard a commotion in the courtyard.

Goodness. Was it more dead birds? Or perhaps another erstwhile suitor? Or was Prince Felix preparing some other extravagant display of unwanted affection?

Rose sighed. She *really* did not have time to be wooed right now. Except perhaps by Shen, and he was far too busy with his own affairs in the desert, as she well knew. And besides, Shen never made a racket when he arrived at Anadawn. He preferred to slip inside, soundless as a breeze. That was part of the thrill of it.

When a familiar howl rose above the din, Rose's spirits lifted. Elske was at Anadawn! Which meant Wren had returned, just as she had promised. She must have convinced Captain Iversen to give her that wolf she loved so much. The thought broadened Rose's smile. While she would have never admitted it to Wren, she really did have a soft spot for Elske. And after Oonagh's midnight visit, they could certainly use the extra protection.

Rose raced down the tower stairwell and through the halls of Anadawn, breathlessly apologizing to a maidservant she nearly knocked over as she burst into the courtyard.

"Wren!" she cried, beaming at the sight of her sister. Now that she could see her in the flesh, she could admit the fear she hadn't dared to say out loud. The fear that this time, Wren might not come back at all. But she *was* back, which meant the two of them could figure out how to deal with the looming threat of Oonagh together.

Rose froze midstep as she saw who was standing on either side of Wren. Two towering Gevrans, looking entirely out of place. She blinked, sure it was an apparition, but the men remained. "Is that . . . ? *Oh no.*"

Alarik Felsing had the audacity to smirk at her. "That's hardly the right way to welcome a king."

For the second time that week, Rose found herself staring mouth agape at an unexpected royal visitor. She turned to her sister, who at least had the decency to look sheepish. "Am I to take it that King Alarik did not hold the answers you were looking for?" she asked crisply.

"Not exactly . . . ," admitted Wren.

Rose took a closer look at the Gevran king. He was paler than he had been before and despite his arrogant demeanor, his eyes were glassy. There was something else different about him. . . .

An all too familiar uneasiness prickled at Rose. It was as if her magic could sense the same wrongness in him she had found in Wren. But she needed to be sure. She strode over to him. "Let me see your wrist," she demanded.

Alarik folded his arms. "Hands to yourself, witch."

"Alarik," said Wren, with a long-suffering sigh. "She's trying to help."

"We didn't come here for her."

Wren tossed him a warning look. "You came here because I told you to."

Rose raised her brows at her sister's overfamiliarity with King Alarik but kept her thoughts to herself. There were far bigger things to worry about now.

"Fine." Alarik rolled up his sleeve with exaggerated slowness. He stepped close to Rose, his voice low. "But do take care. I don't wish to become idle gossip for your servants."

"You should have thought of that before you wore leather trousers to the Gevran feast," said Wren.

Captain Iversen coughed, stifling a laugh.

Rose turned the king's wrist to confirm what she suspected. There it was: a jagged silver scar in the shape of a crescent. Alarik hissed as she brushed her finger against it. Rose stilled, gently prodding the mark with her magic. Her stomach lurched as the same darkness she had felt in Wren's mark reared up against her. She withdrew her hand as if she'd been burned.

"It is the very same," she said, her eyes darting back and forth between them. They wore a matching look of uncertainty, of fear.

"That's why we're here," said Wren. "We need to talk to Thea."

"Wren, this isn't solving your problem; it's doubling it," said Rose anxiously. "Alarik's not even a witch."

"Does that matter?" said Tor, stepping into their circle. "Whatever this mark is, they both need healing from it."

Rose glanced at the towering soldier, her eyes narrowing. "Please don't tell me that you also bear this mark."

"I do not," said Tor stiffly.

"Well, at least that's one less thing to worry about," she muttered.

Alarik cleared his throat. "I realize we have significantly more

important things to be discussing, but I must ask . . . Why is your garden such a mess? Did every tempest in Anadawn throw a tantrum at
the same time?" He gestured, unnecessarily, to the mass of charred and
withered plants. "I remember it being in much better shape."

"I remember *you* being in much better shape," snapped Rose.

Wren was only now noticing the decimated garden. She pulled her
arms around herself as she drifted toward the garden. "What happened
here, Rose?"

Rose eyed Tor and Alarik warily. "Perhaps we should go inside."

"You can trust them," said Wren, reading her hesitation.

"Well, you can certainly trust Tor," said Alarik drolly. "As you'll
recall, Captain Iversen is more loyal to your sister than to his own
crown."

Tor bristled.

Wren glared at him. "Do you have to be like this?"

"Sorry," mumbled Alarik, and Rose thought he looked regretful
then. "Being back here . . . in the place where Ansel died . . . It brings up
bad memories. I'm sure you understand."

"You made the choice to return with Wren to Anadawn," said Rose.
"So I ask that you treat this place, and us, with the proper respect." Her
voice softened. "You know I too cared for Ansel."

Alarik held her gaze, and Rose saw a flicker of warmth in its cool-
ness. A crack in the ice. "I'll never forget what you did for him on the
Sunless Sea. How you gave him peace."

Rose's eyes welled with unexpected tears, and in that moment, she
decided Wren was right. Gevra had once been their ally, and they could
be so again. Perhaps this meeting would prove fortuitous after all.

She took a deep breath, turning back to her sister. "Something happened while you were away."

Quickly and quietly, Rose told them about Oonagh's midnight visit.

"It was a dream," Alarik interrupted, when Rose recounted the moment she realized who her midnight visitor was. "Your ancestor haunts dreams. She does it to me and to Wren and . . ."

He trailed off as Rose unwrapped her scarf, revealing the three bloodied scratches on her neck.

Wren recoiled. *"Hissing hell."*

"It was no dream," said Rose. "I wish it were. My flowers are dead, and the starcrests have deserted Anadawn. Even the dawnbirds have fled."

"Oonagh has left decay in her wake," said Tor grimly. "As she did in Gevra."

"The gardens aren't even the worst of it," said Rose, telling them of the threat Oonagh had made, the terrifying vision she had shown her. Her promise to return in one moon's time to reclaim her throne.

"Are you all right?" said Wren, stepping close to examine Rose's wound. "It looks painful."

"I'm fine," said Rose, trying to smile. "The wound will heal in time."

"I hope so," said Wren, frowning.

Alarik suddenly groaned. "You know what isn't healing? This *infernal* pain," he said, curling his fingers around his wrist. "Something must have aggravated it."

Rose was seized by a sense of urgency. "Come," she said, beckoning them to follow. "Thea will know what to do. We'll need you both at your strongest for what's to come."

13

WREN

Wren and Rose made their way to the throne room. There were too many prying eyes out in the courtyard, too many listening ears. Wren was still reeling from what her sister had told her about Oonagh. She couldn't believe their ancestor had used her magic to slip unnoticed into Rose's bedroom and threaten her while Wren was away.

After escaping the Gevran army, Oonagh Starcrest had managed to breach the golden gates of Anadawn with worrying ease, and left no trace of herself afterward, save for the marks on Rose's neck. As they walked through the winding hallways, Wren could tell her sister was trying to hold her nerve, but her hands were trembling at her sides, and she was being unusually quiet.

Tor and Alarik followed a few steps behind them, pretending not to notice the alarmed faces of the palace guards or the servants muttering as they passed. Elske padded at Tor's side, studying every shadow, ready to pounce. Oonagh might have disappeared, but it seemed the wolf could still scent her.

Wren couldn't stop staring at the marks on Rose's neck. "We should have Thea look at those."

Rose waved the suggestion away. "Nonsense. Your problem is far more pressing." She glanced over her shoulder at Alarik before dropping her voice. "Not to mention delicate. We don't want anyone here to get the wrong idea. Anadawn has had enough potential suitors for one week."

Alarik snorted. "I'd sooner marry Borvil. And that bear is half feral."

"Just like you, then," said Wren.

Tor chuckled. Alarik rolled his eyes. "Very mature."

"Well, I'm glad you're all finding this so amusing," said Rose, glaring back and forth between them. "For all we know, that terrible resurrection spell has done irreparable damage to both of you. And right at the very moment we need our wits about us!"

Wren bit her lip while the Gevrans cleared their throats, duly chastened. They walked on in silence. When they reached the throne room, Rose cleared every soldier and servant, closed all the windows, and shut the doors. Much to his dismay, even Chapman was turned away.

Then they sent for Thea.

While they waited for her to arrive, Alarik walked the perimeter of the room, taking in the corniced ceilings and lavish paintings as the syrupy spring sunlight poured through the arched windows. "Hmmph," he said, to no one in particular. "It's smaller than I expected."

Rose bristled.

"Don't take the bait," Wren warned her. "He's just trying to needle you."

Wren knelt by Elske and buried her face in her fur. "You truly are the only Gevran that doesn't find a way to unsettle me," she whispered.

Wren watched Tor's boots in her periphery, moving closer. He crouched down beside her, letting his arm brush against hers as he scratched under Elske's ears. "I think she's been missing you."

Wren looked up at him. "What makes you so sure?"

Tor held her gaze. "I know the feeling."

"Please do not touch the artwork!" snapped Rose from halfway across the room. "It is irreplaceable. My ancestor Thormund Valhart painted that landscape."

"Artistic talent clearly does not run in your family," said Alarik, tracing the gilt frame. "What are these supposed to be? *Deer?* The color palette on those trees is all wrong."

"I suppose you'd rather it was a big bloody battle scene on some kind of glacier," said Rose sourly.

"Well, that would be an improvement."

"So would your silence. How about we all stay quiet until Thea arrives?"

Wren giggled into Elske's fur. "He's going to get himself thrown out of Anadawn if he's not careful."

"This is the most fun he's had in months," said Tor.

"Me, too," said Wren. "Nobody here would dare talk to Rose like that. This is thoroughly entertaining."

Alarik sauntered over to the dais and sat in Rose's throne. At her look of utter annoyance, he flashed her a wolfish grin. "You don't mind, do you?"

She folded her arms but said nothing.

Alarik squirmed in her seat. "It's not even comfortable."

"Shall I get Cam to bring up a big block of ice for you to perch on?" Rose offered.

"That depends. Will your ancestor burst out of it again?"

Rose rolled her eyes. "Stars save us. I feel as if I'm in a nursery."

The bickering ceased when Thea arrived. She bustled through the door, her frown deepening as she surveyed the scene before her. The king of Gevra lounging on the throne of Eana under Rose's admonishing glare while Wren crouched at the other end of the room with his Captain of the Guard, laughing like a pair of guilty children.

"What exactly is going on in here?" said Thea.

Wren stood and went to her like a prisoner approaching the gallows. She rolled up her sleeve and told Thea everything. About the spell she and Alarik had cast all those months ago in Gevra; about the scar that had appeared on her wrist shortly afterward. The same one that he bore. She spoke of her harrowing nightmares, how Oonagh's laugh often rang in her ears, how Wren had begun to see Alarik in her dreams often doubled over in the same pain.

Thea listened in grave silence before summoning Alarik. He went to her willingly, revealing the matching scar on his wrist.

She brushed her thumb over it. "Goodness," she muttered.

"Can you heal it?" he asked anxiously.

"I'll do my best," she said, sounding unsure. She jerked her chin up then, shooing the others from the room. "Leave us."

"I'd rather stay," said Rose. "I want to learn how to heal this kind of ailment. And also . . . I don't trust Alarik."

Thea shook her head. "The king's privacy is as important as any other's, love."

"More important actually," said Alarik.

Wren rolled her eyes. "Come on," she said, tugging Rose away. Tor fell into step with her while Elske padded behind them. They closed the door to the throne room and waited on the other side of it.

"This is ridiculous," fumed Rose as she paced the corridor. "To be kicked out of my own throne room! By a foreign king!"

"It's better this way," said Wren quietly. "For everyone."

Tor leaned against the wall with his hands in his pockets. He looked her up and down. "Are you all right?"

"Me?" Wren didn't realize she was wringing her hands until she caught him looking at them. She scrunched them into fists. "Of course. I'm fine."

"Come here," he said, reaching for her.

Wren stepped into the heat of him and laid her cheek against his chest. She had almost forgotten how tall he was, how broad and sure. He curled his arm around her, bringing his chin to rest on the crown of her head. Elske settled at their feet, guarding this moment, this peace.

"It's going to be all right," Tor murmured.

Wren wasn't sure she believed him, but she felt a little better anyway.

The minutes passed in strained silence. Rose continued to pace. "It shouldn't be taking this long," she said, more to herself than to Wren. "Thea's the most skilled healer I know. She's quick. After all, she's had years of—"

Alarik screamed.

Rose froze.

The king's agony filled the hallway like a terrible aria. Wren turned into Tor's chest, trying to remember how to breathe. The scream felt close enough to be her own.

Tor tightened his embrace, holding her on her feet. But Wren could feel the sudden stiffness in his shoulders.

Then all at once, the scream stopped.

"Stars!" cried Rose. "What on earth is happening in there?"

Wren couldn't take it anymore. The screaming. The silence. The *not knowing*. She shoved through the doors and marched into the throne room. Alarik was on his knees with his head in his hands. An all too familiar sight. Thea was crouched beside him, rubbing his back.

She looked up at Wren, then shook her head. "I'm afraid the wound is too deep. I cannot heal it without killing him."

Wren waited for Alarik to raise his head and say something sharp or clever, but he just sat there in a daze.

Tor wordlessly lifted the king to his feet, easily shouldering his weight as he guided Alarik to the thrones. Rose and Wren went to Thea, helping her to her feet. She was breathing heavily, the lines in her face much deeper than before.

"Do you want to sit down?" said Rose anxiously. "I'll have someone fetch you a cup of tea. A biscuit, too. You look terribly pale." She glanced back at Alarik, who was slumped in her throne. "You both do."

Thea's smile was shaky. "That's a fine idea, love. But let's not wait for the servants. We don't want anyone getting wind of what's happening in here. Perhaps you might fetch the tea yourself?"

"Yes, yes, of course," said Rose in a bluster. "I'll go now. I won't be a moment!"

Rose scampered off with Elske in tow.

Thea waited until she was gone before turning back to Wren. "Show me your scar."

Wren hesitated. "I don't think that's a good—"

"Let me see it," said Thea, reaching for her arm. "Perhaps I can do for you what I could not do for him."

"You heard what happened when Rose tried to heal it," said Wren. "It was too much. And you're barely standing as it is."

Thea regarded Wren with uncharacteristic sternness. "I've been healing ever since I could walk, Wren Greenrock. I know my own limits. And besides, you are a witch, which means you are stronger than the king. You can withstand what he could not."

Wren wasn't convinced, but Thea wasn't taking no for an answer. Reluctantly, Wren rolled up her sleeve. Thea took her hand and closed her eye. Her brow furrowed, and Wren felt the first prick of heat in her arm.

She sucked in a breath, steeling herself as it grew sharper, deeper.

Thea began to mutter to herself.

Wren did her best not to scream, but the pain was like a burning poker searing through her flesh. "STOP!" she cried out.

Thea tightened her grip.

Wren's knees buckled. "LET GO!"

But Thea would not.

Somewhere in the distance, Wren heard the thrum of footsteps. Someone was running to her, calling her name, but she couldn't see beyond the pain. When her scar opened and the black smoke came, it wrenched a scream so agonizing from her that it scorched her throat.

This time, Thea cried out. She snapped her hand away and scrabbled backward, like the smoke was a beast come to devour her. The second she let go, it rushed back inside Wren, taking the pain with it.

Wren collapsed in a heap, listening to the echoes of her scream die away. The ceiling blurred in and out of focus.

Then Tor's face appeared above hers. He was pale as mountain snow, but his eyes were as dark as storm clouds. "Wren?" he said hoarsely.

Wren summoned a weak smile. "Well, that was embarrassing."

"Not to mention horrifying," croaked Alarik, from across the room. "What in freezing hell *was* that?"

It was Thea who answered them. She was sitting on the floor beside Wren. "That, Alarik Felsing, was a curse." She sighed heavily. "I'm afraid our worst fears have been confirmed."

Wren closed her eyes, trying to hide her anguish as Thea went on. "The blood spell you cast on Prince Ansel must have twisted. It didn't just curse the young prince. It cursed you, too." She looked to Alarik. "Both of you."

The king swore under his breath.

Wren reached for Thea, but the old healer looked frightened now. Of the curse. Of Wren. She wouldn't take her hand. Wren's eyes pricked with tears. Her own family was afraid of her. Now that she had glimpsed the thing inside her, she was afraid of herself.

Tor tried to help Wren up, but she pushed him away. "I'm all right. Help Thea."

Wren staggered to her feet and made her way to her throne. Alarik watched her stumble toward him with the same haunted look on his face. When she sat down, he leaned over. "I take it back. Maybe this velvet isn't so bad after all."

Wren was too worried to laugh.

"Speak plainly, healer," said Alarik. "Are we lost causes?"

Thea worried the edge of her eye patch, taking a long time to answer. "There is another place you can try," she said at last. "The Mishnick Mountains in the north were once home to Eana, the first witch. Eana was the founder of this kingdom, the maker of this island." She looked to Wren, confirming what she already suspected. That true help waited far beyond the gates of Anadawn. "The waters there are blessed by the first witch," Thea went on, for Alarik's benefit. "Their healing properties are unmatched. As is the magic of the Healer on High, who oversees the mountains and knows best their secrets . . . their power. If there is a way to break this curse, the Healer on High will know it."

"Just what I wanted to hear," muttered Alarik. "Another journey."

"When you reach the mountains, look for bloom and birdsong, and the opening will reveal itself to you. But you must go in secret." Thea's gaze darkened and so, too, did her voice. "No one must know about the curse. It would threaten the very fabric of this kingdom." She turned on Alarik. "And yours."

Alarik's lips twisted as he tasted her words.

Wren turned to him. "What's your answer?"

He frowned, seemingly weighing his response.

"There is only one answer," said Tor decisively. "If there's a way to break this curse, then we will go to the ends of the earth to do it."

Wren thought he was speaking for his king, but when she looked up, he was staring at her. Worry strained the hard line of his jaw, and in his eyes she saw her own pain reflected back. She understood what he was saying. He would go to the ends of the earth for her. And she would go, too, so long as he was there.

"Very well," said Alarik, giving in to reason.

"Then it's decided," said Wren, squaring herself to the task. Her face fell as something else occurred to her. "Ugh. Rose is going to hate this."

Just then, the throne room doors creaked open, and Rose tiptoed in, struggling to balance a tray of macarons and several wobbly cups of tea.

"Hate what?" she said, brows furrowed in suspicion.

Alarik chuckled under his breath. "This honor is all yours, Wren."

14

ROSE

When Wren told Rose about Thea's proposed trip to the Mishnick Mountains, Rose nearly dropped the tea tray.

"Absolutely not," she said, setting it down with a clatter. "I won't allow it." She crossed her arms and moved to the doorway of the throne room, as if she could physically bar them from leaving. "And that's that."

"You have no authority over me," said Alarik, with a derisive snort. "But it's charming that you think you do."

Rose glowered at him. "Do not test me, King Alarik. I'll quite happily enchant these doors to keep you locked in here forever if it means keeping my sister safe."

"I think that's a tad beyond your capabilities," muttered Wren.

"Don't *you* test me either!" snapped Rose. "You clearly don't know what's best for you if you think disappearing into the Mishnick Mountains with these two is a good idea!"

"Rose, love, traveling to the Mishnick Mountains is the only thing that can help Wren now," said Thea gently. "You know as well as I do that whatever has infected Wren and the king has burrowed deep inside them. Only the most practiced healers will be able to cure them."

"Then send for them! Let them come here. Wren doesn't need to risk the journey." Rose offered a brittle smile. "See! Problem solved."

Thea laid a calming hand on Rose's arm. "It's not only the healers, Rose, but the mountains themselves that have the power to heal. If there was any other way you know I wouldn't suggest this. But I believe they *must* journey there, and do so soon."

"Well then, I'm going with you! I won't let you disappear again." Rose could hear hysteria creeping into her voice, but she couldn't help it. Everything was falling apart. "We're supposed to be ruling together. Everything is supposed to be going well." She raked her hands through her hair. "How many bloody curses do we need to break before we can get on with our lives?"

Wren went to her sister and put her arms around her. Rose stood stiffly for a moment and then relaxed into her embrace. "I promise I'll be fine, Rose. Better than fine. My magic will be fixed. *I'll* be fixed."

"You keep saying that!" said Rose shrilly. "And then the next thing I know, King Alarik is in my throne room insulting the decor! And we suddenly have bigger problems!"

Wren let out a strained laugh. "This time it will be true. Have a little faith."

"Forget faith. I'm coming with you," said Rose adamantly.

Wren pulled back from her sister and squeezed her shoulders, as though to strengthen her. "Rose, I need you to do what you do best and protect our kingdom. You can't do that if you're in the mountains with me. One of us must be strong now. One of us must stay here and rule."

Rose sniffled. "How am I supposed to protect Eana from our powerful undead ancestor who knows this country as well as we do? Probably better than I do!" She tried to shake off the memory of Oonagh's midnight visit, but it knotted in her stomach, making her feel ill. And worse, hopeless. "Can she even be killed?"

"Not with Gevran steel," said Alarik darkly. "Despite our best efforts."

At Rose's look of alarm, the king went on, telling her and Thea about what had happened on the Sundvik Shore only days ago. How Oonagh had been fired upon, only to survive, seemingly unscathed.

"Stars," whispered Rose. "So she truly cannot be killed."

"Nonsense. No witch, no matter how ancient they are, is ever truly invulnerable." Thea let out a disgruntled huff. "If Oonagh Starcrest cannot be felled by Gevran steel, then we must use our own weapons to bring her down. Something witch-made will do it. The older the better." Her dark eye glowed with certainly, the sureness in her voice commanding the room. "There is power in age."

"Finally, a morsel of good news," remarked Alarik.

"Hardly," said Rose, in a panic. "Where are we supposed to find an ancient witch-made weapon?" Her gaze darted between Wren and Thea. "You both know as well as I do that the Great Protector rid this country of anything to do with witches long ago!"

"No one is that thorough," said Wren. "There are places even in Anadawn that the Great Protector didn't know about. The tunnels here still burn with ancient everlights."

Something else suddenly occurred to Rose. "The Sunkissed Kingdom!" she burst out. "Their armory is full of witch-made weapons. If we can't find anything here in Anadawn, then surely there will be something in the desert that can be used against Oonagh."

"Speaking of the Sunkissed Kingdom, we need to tell Shen what's happening," said Wren. "Oonagh is a threat to every single witch in this land. We'll need all the help we can get to stand against her."

"Yes," muttered Rose. "We must warn Shen. We can't risk putting such sensitive information into a letter. If the bird falls from the sky, if word gets out, the kingdom will fall into a state of hysteria. I'll go and speak to him myself. I'll be as quick as I can. . . . There and back in a couple of days."

"A much better endeavor than hiking into the mountains with your poorly sister for who knows how long," said Wren, with a weak laugh. "You have far more important things to do."

Rose gripped her sister's hand. "Nothing is more important than making sure you are all right."

"She will be all right," said Tor gruffly, and Rose didn't miss the blush that stole across Wren's cheeks. "You may surrender your worry to me, Queen Rose."

"I always worry," said Rose, with a small laugh. "But in this instance, I will put my faith in you, Captain Iversen."

Alarik cleared his throat pointedly. "What about me?"

"And me?" added Wren.

"Must everything be a competition with you two?" Rose chastised. Then she straightened her skirts. "Now, if you'll excuse me, I'm going to go down to the tunnels to see if our ancestors have hidden anything useful down there. Tomorrow, I'll leave for the Sunkissed Kingdom."

"And we'll leave for the north mountains," said Wren.

Rose turned to Thea. "Will you look after things at Anadawn while we're both away?"

"Of course, love," she said at once. "That's what I'm here for."

Rose gave her a grateful smile.

"And just think, when I'm back and feeling better," Wren went on, "and we've dealt with Oonagh once and for all, we can throw the most extravagant ball this country has ever seen."

"I would very much like to have a ball." The thought alone helped brighten Rose's mood. "A ball where nothing goes wrong and everything is perfect." She looked up at Tor and Alarik. "I'll even invite the two of you, and Princess Anika, too. Celeste certainly seems to have a soft spot for her."

Alarik stood up. "If your magical mountain healer can cure me of this cursed affliction, I will attend whatever event you like so I can loudly toast your excellence."

"Just make sure you put on a shirt this time," teased Wren.

"And disappoint the masses?" he said, with a wicked smirk.

Tor chuckled. "I'll admit I greatly enjoyed the last ball I attended here at Anadawn."

Alarik frowned. "I can't imagine why, Iversen. You were working."

"It had its moments," said Tor, with a lingering look at Wren.

"It certainly did," she murmured.

Rose cleared her throat. *Goodness.* Was it really a good idea to send these three into the wilderness together? "Well, the next ball will be even better," she said, brightening at the thought of it. "I must say, now I am well and truly motivated to find a suitable weapon."

"Do you want me to go with you to the tunnels?" said Wren.

Rose shook her head. "No. You get your rest. You'll need it for the journey ahead."

"Ask Rowena, then. She has a good nose for magic. And snooping."

Rose's lips twisted. "You know Rowena doesn't like me."

"Oh, she likes you fine. That's just how she shows her affection. With insults and threats."

"Are you sure she's not Gevran?" remarked Alarik.

"Fine." Rose sighed. "I'll take Rowena to the tunnels. I'm assuming we can trust her with the delicate news about Oonagh's impending return?"

"Of course," said Wren at once. "She's an Ortha witch. Loyal to her core."

Loyal to whom? Rose wanted to ask, but she simply nodded.

Rose would have never admitted it to her sister, but she didn't like the tunnels underneath Anadawn. Wren said they made her feel connected to the witch queens and kings of old, but Rose found them damp and eerie. To her, they felt haunted.

The everlights flickered companionably as Rose and Rowena journeyed deeper beneath the palace. While the biggest tunnel led to the banks of the Silvertongue River, they were exploring less-trodden, narrower passages that Rose had never been in.

"Thank you for coming with me," she said, with a glance back at Rowena.

The fair-haired witch snorted. "Not like I had much of a choice. You called it a royal summons."

"Well, I appreciate it all the same," said Rose, trailing her fingers along the ancient stone walls. "Do you . . . sense any magical items down here?"

Rowena barked a laugh. "How exactly do you think magic works? That we can just smell it on the wind when it's close by?"

"Oh, I don't know!" said Rose with a huff. "Wren implied it would be easy."

"I imagine the witches took their weapons with them when they left Anadawn," said Rowena, peering into a gap between two large stones. "It's a fool's errand, poking around here in the dark."

"Well, we had to at least look," said Rose defensively. "There might have been something stashed away down here." She stopped at another gap in the stonework, only to quail at the giant river spider peering out of it. "And there still might be. We haven't even reached the end of this tunnel."

Rowena twirled a finger and gusted the spider back into its hole. "So, what's the plan, then? Find a fancy weapon and run big bad Oonagh through with it?"

"Yes, I suppose that *is* the general idea," said Rose, wrinkling her nose. Then a glint in the wall up ahead caught her eye. She rushed to inspect it. "Oh! Now what's this?" It was not a weapon; that much was clear. It was a cloudy-blue gemstone, wedged in between the stones. Rose crouched to get a better look at it. "Do you think I can pull it out?"

"And do what with it exactly?" said Rowena, peering down at it. "Put it in a slingshot and knock out one of Oonagh's eyes?" She sighed. "Why must we fight her anyway?"

"Excuse me?" said Rose, standing so quickly she nearly knocked into her.

In the stony silence, Rowena chewed on her lip. "I just mean, well, maybe it's not such a bad thing that she's back. She's a witch like us. A queen, like you. Have you or Wren thought about what she could do for this kingdom? No offense but—"

"I'm already offended," Rose interjected.

"Maybe Oonagh is a better fit for the throne," Rowena went on. "Maybe she's the true witch queen we've been waiting for."

"Rowena," said Rose, her voice steady but stern. "Oonagh Starcrest tried to murder her own sister. She turned on her people for power and splintered our magic into five weak strands for over a thousand years. We nearly lost this land because of her. She is *not* coming back to save this kingdom. She is coming back to bend it—and us—to her will. She is not to be trusted."

"Maybe she's changed," said Rowena uncertainly. "A thousand years or so frozen in an ice tomb can do that to a person. . . ."

Rose shook her head. "She will destroy Eana. And its people."

"This country has a lot to answer for, Rose. Don't forget what it did to our ancestors," said Rowena with uncharacteristic seriousness. "As long as she protects the witches . . ."

"Rowena." Rose glared at her. "Our ancestors' anger is not our own. The time of war and bloodshed is behind us. Peace is what matters now. Forgiveness. Harmony. Only then will there be true prosperity in this kingdom. We are a united Eana now, you know that."

Rowena stirred a gust of wind, making the everlights along the tunnel flicker higher. "When Banba used to talk about the witches returning to power, she never mentioned peace. She spoke about the witches taking their rightful place and turning the rivers red with the blood of all those who stood in our way." The everlights flared, casting away the darkness. "We've hidden in the shadows long enough."

Rose shuddered at the sudden chill in the tunnel. She knew Wren loved Banba and mourned her deeply. Rose mourned her, too, in her own way, but sometimes how the Ortha witches spoke about Banba, about her vision and her vengeance, frightened Rose. "Anger is a powerful force, Rowena. Sometimes it can be big enough and dark enough to cloud even the brightest horizon."

Rowena nodded as though in reluctant agreement.

"Banba had her own vision for this kingdom, but you can't carve a future out of vengeance. You can only tear it down and live in its ruins." Rose drew a breath, readying another uncomfortable truth that had got lost in the ire of their conversation. "My grandmother is no longer with us, Rowena. We don't know truly what she would have wanted now that we're here. And that is because Oonagh Starcrest killed her." She held Rowena's gaze, fire meeting fire. "I urge you not to lose sight of that. Direct your anger where it belongs."

Rowena looked away, her brow furrowed. She raked her curls away from her face, reaching for her bravado, but she couldn't hide the pain in her expression. When she spoke again, it was not of revenge or even Oonagh.

"Move aside," she said, nudging Rose out of the way. "I'll get you this gemstone you are so concerned with." She took a blade from her boot and deftly knocked the gemstone out of the wall. "Easy."

"Rowena," said Rose urgently. "You are loyal to Eana, aren't you?"

"I'm loyal to where I came from. The place. The witches." Rowena rotated the gemstone in her hands, frowning at it. It was small and cloudy. Worthless. Rose was about to press her for a clearer answer— or at least a more reassuring one—when Rowena turned to face her.

Her blue eyes were soft, and for once, Rose didn't feel threatened or hated by the tempest witch. She felt . . . strangely understood. "When Oonagh Starcrest comes to Anadawn, I'll slingshot this stupid stone at her myself. With any luck, I'll take her eye out."

Rose smiled. "I think it might require more than that."

Rowena smiled back. "Let's see what it takes, then."

WREN

While Rose spent the day with Rowena in the underbelly of Anadawn Palace, Wren had an early dinner with Tor and Alarik in the dining room. Cam had prepared a cut of beef so tender it melted in Wren's mouth. To accompany it, the cook served buttered greens and glazed carrots, crispy potatoes drizzled in gravy, and enough plummy wine to fill a barrel. But Wren was too tired to eat very much of it. She fed half of her beef to Elske under the table, which roused a conspiratorial smile from Tor, who appeared to be doing the very same thing.

Chapman arrived after dinner, spiriting the Gevrans away to a suite of guest bedrooms that had been prepared in the east wing of the palace. Wren wondered if the steward had purposely stationed them as far away from her as possible but thought better than to ask. She didn't want anyone at Anadawn to get the wrong idea about her and the king of Gevra.

By the time she returned to her bedroom after dinner, she was already half asleep. She collapsed onto her bed with her shoes still on, passing the rest of the night, for once, in dreamless slumber. Wren awoke at dawn the following morning and dressed as the sun rose over the distant hills, and then she brushed her hair in the mirror. Her hands trembled with anticipation, her throat so dry she went at once to the kitchens for a cup of peppermint tea. Something to settle her nerves and steel her for the journey ahead.

She tried not to think too much about the long and winding road north, or the fact that she would be wedged between two Gevran men who had both, at some point in the last few months, kissed her to the point of breathlessness.

When she emerged from the kitchens, the palace was still sleeping. The tea had not settled Wren's nerves. Rather, it had chased the panic into her limbs and now she found herself restless, pacing. She decided to take an early-morning ride on her new horse, a magnificent desert-born mare that Shen Lo had gifted her for Yulemas. In return, Wren had commissioned a flaming wishing fountain for the Palace of Eternal Sunlight: an impressive stone sculpture that paid tribute to Shen's desert kingdom and burned with enchanted everlights all day and all night.

When she arrived at the stables, she stopped at the sight of a familiar figure wandering along the stalls.

"What are you doing here?"

Tor turned at the sound of her voice. He was not dressed in his official uniform. Instead, he wore a loose white shirt, black trousers, and riding boots. His copper-streaked hair was still tousled from sleep, and though he looked strained, there was no hint of that worry in his voice. "Did you forget I stayed here last night? We had dinner together, remember?"

"I meant *here*," said Wren, coming inside. "In the stables."

"Ah," he said quietly. "I suppose I'm reminiscing."

Her cheeks erupted at the memory of their almost kiss in this very stable, how she had wrapped her legs around him, desperate with desire. It felt like another lifetime now. So much had happened since then. And yet, he was still looking at her the same way—with lightning crackling in his eyes, as if he might take her into an abandoned stall right then and there and finish what they'd started all those months ago.

She swallowed, grasping for composure. "And here I thought you were trying to steal a horse."

He shook his head. "Just inspecting the ones we'll be riding."

Wren looked at him a moment longer, thinking of everything she wished to say to him. About their time in Gevra, how scared and confused she had been in those snow-swept weeks, how many reckless mistakes she had made, how angry she was at herself for them . . . how she had missed him fiercely in the months since. It all crowded together on her tongue, until she could manage only, "It's good to see you again, Tor. After everything. It's been . . ."

"Difficult." His smile was edged with sadness. "I know."

"I've missed you."

"I've missed you, too, Wren."

She swallowed, trying to navigate the sudden tornado of her emotions. She reached for something to say, anything to ease the tension simmering between them. "We won't be riding all the way to the mountains," she said, turning back to the horses. "We'll take a carriage as far north as we can. And anyway, the carriage horses are out in the grazing fields behind the palace. It's a bit of a walk but if you're really curious—"

"I'm not curious about carriage horses, Wren."

"Oh. I thought—"

"I was just hoping I'd run into you," he said, surrendering all sense of pretense. "Alone, preferably."

Wren blinked. "Here?"

"It wouldn't be the first time."

She bit her lip. "Well, no. . . ."

"Forgive me," he said, though he didn't sound sorry. He didn't look it either. He looked . . . hungry. "I don't mean to make you uncomfortable."

Wren smiled. "Yes, you do."

He smiled back, full and radiant. *Stars*. It was like staring into the sun. She blew out a breath. "So, you don't want to meet my magnificent new horse, then."

"I've already met her," he said. "She's beautiful."

Wren frowned. There were twenty-five horses in the royal stables alone, each one as impressive as the next. "How do you know which one I'm talking about?"

He turned and walked to the end of the row, where a dappled silver mare peered out of her stall as if she was listening in on their conversation. He laid his hand against her muzzle. "It's this one."

Wren gaped at him. "How could you possibly know that?"

"Because she's my favorite."

Wren laughed, the weight on her heart easing. Of course, he was right. And really, she didn't know why she was surprised. He was a wrangler, after all. He had a way of reading animals, of sensing their loyalties and personalities.

"You have the same soul."

"Is that so?" said Wren, drifting closer.

He nodded. "Curious. Spirited . . . A little wild."

"I think you mean reckless."

"Only for the right reasons. Or the right person." He turned back to her, a question in his eyes. Wren knew that question. It had stolen her breath more than once. She knew her answer, too. But there were things still unsaid between them. She owed him a confession, and she knew it might change everything. At the reminder of her blizzard kiss with Alarik, something inside her wilted.

Tor came toward her. "What is it?"

She shook her head, trying to find the right words. "It's . . . There's still so much to say, and I don't know where to begin."

Tor lowered himself onto a bale of hay. "Let's start small, then," he said, looking up at her. "Tell me your horse's name?"

Wren was flooded with a curious rush of relief. She could start small, like this. Just talk, the two of them, like old times. The words would build, and eventually she would come to the truth . . . to her guilt. "Didn't you ask her?"

"Contrary to popular belief, I can't speak to animals."

"What?" She feigned a gasp. "How disappointing."

"I know," he said, leaning his head back. "I can only sense the core of their being and divine their entire life's purpose, including but not limited to their greatest desires, their deepest fears. . . ."

Wren stared at him.

He broke into laughter, the sound filling the stables like a song.

She grinned. "I always forget you have a sense of humor."

"You have no idea how wounding that is, Wren."

"Sorry." She perched on the bale beside him. "Back to more serious matters. My horse's name is Breeze."

"Breeze," he said thoughtfully. "Interesting choice."

"I don't know what it is," she confided, "but when I'm near her, when it's just she and I trekking through the woods on a quiet morning in Eshlinn, the storm inside me—my grief and my fear and that insidious little voice that tells me I'm not good enough to be queen, that I'm not good enough to be a witch—all of it just . . . fritters away. And it feels as if I'm back home, standing on the shores of Ortha on a misty spring morning, watching the waves kiss my feet and feeling the sea breeze on my cheeks. And suddenly the world is small again and so am I. All is well. All is peaceful." She looked at her hands, her voice quiet. "She gives that peace to me. So I called her Breeze."

Tor was silent then. Wren was too embarrassed to look at him. When she finally raised her gaze, he was staring at her with such fierceness, her heart began to thunder. "You are more than good enough," he said in a low voice. Angry, but not at her. At the voice in her head. "For this life. For this destiny."

She shook her head. "You're just saying that."

"You of all people should know I don't speak unless there is something worth saying."

Wren smiled. "I suppose you are more of a strong, silent type."

"Only because I like to hear you speak, Wren."

"I can't imagine why."

"Can't you?" he said, leaning into her. His words were a whisper between them, his lips so close Wren couldn't help herself. She raised her chin, brushing her nose against his.

Tor tensed, his eyes going wide then narrowing.

Wren froze, sensing the sudden shift in his mood. "What is it?"

"Smoke," he said, sniffing the air. "Something's burning."

Wren heard the crackle of flames a heartbeat before she saw them. They erupted along the entrance to the stables in whips of amber and gold. And there—just beyond them—a cloaked figure was running. Tor leaped to his feet, grabbing a nearby pail of water. Wren grabbed another, both of them running toward the fire. They managed to douse the barrier of flames and fling themselves through the choking smoke.

Wren stumbled but Tor caught her with one arm, swinging her away from the blaze.

"FIRE!" he roared, turning to fetch more water. "FIRE IN THE STABLES!"

"Wait here!" he called to Wren. Before she could stop him, Tor battled his way back through the smoke to free the horses, who were whinnying and rearing up in alarm. Wren summoned her tempest magic, but the gust was short and sharp, barely feathering the flames. The effort of it nearly knocked her to the ground and sent a searing pain ripping through her scar.

Chaos descended across the stables as the fire grew, devouring the hay and then the wooden beams. Roused by the smoke, soldiers and servants poured out of the palace in droves, rushing to help battle the blaze and to set the animals free.

In the swell of activity, Wren caught sight of the hooded figure again. They were farther away now, far past the north end of the stables and heading for a thicket of trees.

She set off after them, her lungs screaming as she ran. The figure was much faster than her and already leagues ahead. In desperation, she summoned another blast of wind. Her scar burned, her body revolting against the pulse of magic, but the gust found its mark, knocking the figure over.

Wren kept running, pushing through her discomfort to close the gap between them. She was much closer now, but she couldn't risk another burst of magic. The arsonist sprang to their feet and resumed their escape. Despite her best efforts, Wren was losing ground.

Just as the figure reached the tree line, there came a whistle from somewhere overhead. Wren looked up to see a shovel hurtling through the air. It crashed into the figure blade-first, knocking them to the ground. This time, they didn't get up. Wren glanced over her shoulder to find Tor charging after her, like a tiger on the hunt. Impeccable aim. Remarkable speed. She should have guessed.

She reached the figure just as Tor caught up with her. He rolled the arsonist over with his foot, and Wren came to her knees to rip their hood off.

She blinked in utter belief. "FELIX?"

"Nnngh," the Prince of Caro groaned. "My *head*."

"What in the hissing hell are you doing?" Wren shouted, fury filling her.

Felix scrunched his eyes shut as if he was trying to make her disappear.

A shadow fell across Wren and the sharp end of the shovel appeared at Felix's throat. "Speak," growled Tor. "Or I'll bury you alive right here."

Felix whimpered. "Just let me explain. . . ."

"Do it in the next breath," said Wren. "Or my horses will forever trample your shallow grave."

"Can you perhaps remove the shovel from my—"

"No," said Tor and Wren at the same time.

Felix took a shaky breath, and then, to Wren's disgust, he began to weep. "She made me do it," he said, between wracking sobs. "The witch who looks like you."

"Rose?" said Wren, frowning.

He tried to shake his head. "I went to Rose's tower looking for her, but then *she* came to me instead. I saw her in the mirror. She . . . showed me things. She put me under her spell."

Wren stared down at the blathering prince, too horrified to speak.

"I was powerless to resist," he wept. "She promised me my very own magic." His eyes widened, filled even now with a frenzied desire for that power. "All I had to do was play her game, and frighten the queen. Spook the servants and the other witches. Sow terror and discord behind the castle walls . . ." He trailed off. "Make mischief. It was only mischief."

Wren would have laughed if she wasn't burning with fury. Oonagh was toying with them, planting mistrust in the palace, scattering chaos like seeds so that the people closest to them would lose faith, would see them as weak—and all of it was merely a prelude to her bloody return. "You thought burning down the royal stables with *me* inside it was *mischief*?"

Felix chuckled, until he saw the Gevran's face.

"Wrong answer," said Tor, pressing the shovel against his neck. "In

Gevra, if you harm a royal beast, we let them eat you."

Wren stood up, laying a cautionary hand on Tor's arm. "I know it's tempting, but we can't bury the Prince of Caro in a shallow grave. It would be a diplomatic disaster."

"Not for me," said Tor, who was still glaring at the prince.

"Perhaps not," reasoned Wren. "But I'm pretty sure Rose would implode from the stress."

It was precisely at this moment that Rose's voice rang out. "WREN!" she yelled, running barefoot past the smoking stables, dressed only in her nightgown. "What's going on? Are you all right?"

With great reluctance, Tor tossed the shovel aside. "Lucky wretch."

"We'll see," said Wren.

Felix whimpered.

16

ROSE

After Rose failed to find a weapon in the tunnels of Anadawn, she set about planning her imminent trip to the Sunkissed Kingdom. She didn't want to go on her own, and with Wren embarking on her own journey, Rose had decided on the perfect traveling partner.

"Of course I'll come with you!" Celeste squealed when Rose invited her. "I've been dying to see the Palace of Eternal Sunlight since you first told me about it."

It was late evening, and they were meeting in the palace baths, where there was no risk of anyone overhearing them while Rose filled Celeste in on everything that had transpired since Oonagh had crashed into her bedroom at midnight and Wren had returned from her trip to Sharkfin Point. Despite the grim tidings, Rose was glad to be alone with her best friend. It had been far too long since they had sat in this beautiful bathing hall, with its dramatic domed ceiling and mosaicked walls, gossiping and laughing in the steam.

"You should have said something earlier. Shen would have gladly welcomed you as his guest," said Rose as she lowered herself deeper in the water, making sure to wash away all the grime and dust from the tunnels. "You don't need to wait for an excuse to go."

Celeste, who was sitting across from her on the edge of the marbled basin, raised her eyebrows. "It seems as if you were the one waiting for an excuse."

Rose flushed, and it wasn't due to the temperature of the water. "Well, I couldn't exactly abandon my throne to gallivant across the desert just to . . ."

"Romance Shen?" Celeste needled. "Of course you could. You're the queen."

"Which means I have *royal duties*." Rose gave her friend a bashful smile. "And as it happens, now those royal duties necessitate me traveling posthaste to our nearest and, dare I say, *dearest* allies to discuss a very important and highly clandestine piece of news."

"I do love a clandestine mission," said Celeste thoughtfully.

Rose wrung her hands, feeling a sudden swell of nerves. "I just wish I was going with better news. Other than the whole, 'Sorry my evil ancestor is back from the dead and has a vendetta against me, my sister, and our entire country, which she intends to destroy if we don't give it up, which means we're going to war, so I need to borrow one of your deadly witch-made weapons and also your army. Again.'"

Celeste swished her toes in the water. "The Sunkissed Kingdom may be its own sovereign nation, but Shen will fight for you. And so will the witches. You know that."

Rose lay back in the water until she was floating. She gazed up at the mosaic above them, which was, rather fittingly, of a desert sunset.

Being able to swim was still a novelty to her. After her near drowning in the Ortha Sea, Shen had insisted on teaching her how. Rose hadn't wanted anyone to see, so their lessons had taken place in secret over Yulemas when he had come to visit her and Wren at Anadawn.

Every night, they'd sneaked out of the palace and gone down to the Silvertongue River, giggling as they'd picked their way through the reeds. The secrecy of it had been part of the fun. Of course, Rose knew Wren was feigning ignorance about her nightly excursions with Shen, but for that she was grateful.

Rose was grateful to Shen, too, for his kindness and patience. He had been sure to find the gentlest stretch of river, and hadn't once laughed at her fear, only encouraged her to tread deeper as her confidence grew. On the final night of his visit, Rose had been able to swim across the river on her own. Shen had met her on the other side of the riverbank, whooping with pride. Then he slipped right into the water and kissed her deeply under the light of the Yule moon.

In her heart, Rose knew that Shen Lo cared for her, but she didn't know how much she could ask of him. What was even *fair* to ask of him.

"He'd do anything for you," said Celeste, reading the anxiety on her face. "He'll be there, Rose, however you need him to be. We all will."

Rose stared at the golden sun above her and sighed. "I hope so."

Rose woke early the following morning, her heart racing at the thought of her upcoming journey, and the king she would find at the other end of it. She yawned and stretched before going to open the window to welcome the stirring morning breeze.

That's when she saw the smoke.

Her heart leaped into her throat as she realized where it was coming from. The royal stables were on fire.

With a strangled shout, Rose bolted from her room and raced down the tower stairs, caught in such a panic, she didn't even bother to put on her shoes or reach for her dressing gown. By the time she reached the stables, breathless and barefoot, there were soldiers and witches everywhere, and the raging fire was no more.

Through the dissipating smoke, Rose glimpsed her sister and what appeared to be Captain Iversen standing side by side, glaring down at a figure on the grass. Was that . . . Prince Felix?

Rose frowned as she stalked toward them. "What's going on?" she called out. "Is everything all right?"

"It is now," said Wren, stepping back from the quivering prince, who Captain Iversen had pinned to the ground with the sharp end of a shovel. "We've found our arsonist."

"Queen Rose!" Felix croaked. "Mercy! Please! Tell your sister and this Gevran oaf to let me go this instant!"

"No," said Wren, unmoved by the plea. Then she turned to Rose. "Felix just sent our stables up in flames and he claims Oonagh told him to do it."

"She promised me magic!" cried Felix desperately. "I was powerless to resist!"

Rose stared at the Prince of Caro in muted horror. She was about to ask how on earth he had come into contact with their dreadful ancestor when it suddenly occurred to her. "The mirror," she muttered to herself, remembering his furtiveness in the library, that last telltale sapphire winking out.

She raked her hands through her hair. How could she have been so foolish not to put it all together? "This is my fault," she told Wren. "I saw Felix in the library with my mirror, and that very same night, Oonagh rose out of it. He must have been talking to her before I stumbled upon him."

"She came here? In all her glory?" said Felix, sounding like a fanatic. "Did she ask for me? She promised me I would have my own magic!"

"Oh, shut up," said Wren, taking the shovel from Tor and thumping him on the head.

Rose knelt next to the prince. "Felix, you have been used. Oonagh would never grant you power. All you have done today is prove that you are a traitorous wretch. We will send you back to Caro, under armed guard, with a missive to your mother the queen explaining what has happened here. From now on, you are not welcome in Eana. Do you understand? If you step foot on these shores, you will be killed on sight."

"Come to Gevra if you like," said Tor, his voice low and menacing. "We'll show you firsthand what we do to traitors."

Felix grabbed the hem of Rose's nightgown. "Please, Queen Rose, you must forgive me."

Something else occurred to Rose. "Felix, you had something else in your possession that morning. What was that parchment you were clutching?"

"That was simply part of my plan to see you that morning. To woo you." He swallowed thickly. "I went to the mews to find your post so I could take it up to you."

Wren kicked him in the shin. "You weasel."

"You read my royal correspondence?" said Rose, horrified.

"That seems . . . very anticlimactic," said Wren. "Conspiring with our undead ancestor is significantly worse than him reading your letters, Rose."

"It is still rude!" said Rose.

Felix let out another wail. "I just wanted to get to know you better! I had to have you, Rose! You were my only way to bring magic to Caro. And the last thing I needed was you leaving to go to a party. Without me! But then . . . then I saw the mirror . . . and *she* appeared."

"And you fell at her feet like a blundering fool," said Wren.

Rose kicked him away. "Chain him," she cried to the soldiers now swarming at her back. "In chains of iron and chains of magic. And send him back to Caro. His mother can deal with him there."

"Good riddance," said Wren, tossing the shovel aside.

Later, after she had recovered from the shock of Felix's betrayal, scrubbed the smell of smoke from her skin, and got dressed for the day ahead, Rose went to Wren's bedchamber in the west tower, where her sister was packing for her own journey.

"I'm frightened, Wren," she said, closing the door behind her. "Oonagh feels closer every moment. What are we going to do?"

"We're doing everything we can do," said Wren, setting her satchel aside. "I need to be at my strongest to face her, and you need to find a weapon that can kill her."

"I don't like that we'll be apart," said Rose. "It makes me feel uneasy." She let out a humorless laugh. "And we can't even take our magic mirrors with us this time."

Wren took her sister's hand. "Have hope, Rose."

They hugged each other, and Rose desperately prayed her sister was right.

WREN

Not long after saying goodbye to her sister, Wren arrived in the court-yard with her satchel. She was wearing a simple blue dress, a pair of traveling boots, and a long brown cloak, underneath which her hair hung unadorned in loose waves. She took one look at King Alarik dressed in full regalia and Tor standing at attention in his blue-and-silver frock coat and she frowned.

"I told you two to look inconspicuous. We're supposed to be traveling in secret."

Alarik looked down at his shiny silver doublet. "What's wrong with this?"

"You look like a king!"

"Maybe of Eana." He snorted. "In Gevra, this is practically peasant wear."

Wren pinched the bridge of her nose. "Chapman!"

The steward scurried over.

"Please fetch King Alarik something less ostentatious to wear." She turned on Tor. "And you're literally in your uniform. You couldn't look any more Gevran if you tried."

"My other clothes now reek of smoke," he said pointedly.

Wren sighed and then called after Chapman, "And bring something for the captain, too!"

Chapman eyed Elske, who was sitting at Tor's feet. "And, uh, the wolf?"

"Hmm." Wren tapped her chin. "A nice bonnet should do. Something with frills."

"Really?" said the steward.

"No, Chapman, obviously not," said Wren impatiently. "The wolf is fine as she is. She can stay in the carriage until we're far enough north."

Chapman beetled away.

While Tor and Alarik went inside to change, Wren stuck her head inside the carriage. It was a far cry from the golden tour carriage that had ferried them around Eana. This one was plain brown with small windows and two lumpy benches facing one another. Just enough space for three humans and one rather large wolf. The carriage would be pulled by four horses, with two palace guards to serve as coachmen until they reached Glenlock, a town just north of the Ganyeve Desert. It was still about a day's journey from the Mishnick Mountains, but the rest of the route would require them to surrender their carriage entirely.

"*Ahem.*" Wren startled at Chapman's voice, hitting her head on the ceiling of the carriage. His face appeared through the opposite window. "Do remind me why you are gallivanting into the unknown reaches of Eana with a murderous Gevran king and his grumpy-looking soldier?"

"Didn't I mention before?" said Wren. "It's none of your business."

Chapman glowered at her. "As I have told you more times than I care to recall, I am the steward of Anadawn. The queens' business is my business!"

"Not this queen," said Wren, reeling backward. She slammed the carriage door behind her.

Chapman scooted around the back of it. "But—"

"And that *grumpy-looking* soldier just saved all of our royal horses and captured our arsonist," Wren added. "You will treat him with respect."

Chapman folded his arms. "And the murderous king?"

"Treat him however you like," said Wren, with a shrug. "It's your funeral."

He pulled a face. "This all just seems so . . . so reckless."

"Yes. But that's kind of my thing."

Chapman harrumphed. "You will send me into an early grave."

Wren looked him up and down. "How many winters have you passed?" she said, trying to guess. "Forty-nine? Fifty?"

Chapman glowered at her. "I'm only twenty-seven!"

Wren winced. "Have you ever thought about sheep farming, Chapman? A nice, pastoral life somewhere in the south?"

The steward was too furious to answer her. Alarik and Tor returned presently, dressed as soldiers of Eana in frock coats of green and gold.

Wren broke into a grin.

"Don't even start," warned Alarik.

"It suits you."

"What? Poorly tailored trousers?"

"Subservience to me," Wren said brightly.

The king barked a laugh.

Wren shifted her attention to Tor, admiring the way the captain looked in the Eana colors. Somehow, he was even more handsome than before. "Well?" she said, perhaps a little too eagerly. "Do you like it?"

Tor tensed, gripping the icy pommel of his sword. Wren knew she had made a misstep by testing his loyalty in front of his king, but he deftly laughed it off. "If only it came with a shovel."

"I'm sure that can be arranged."

"Nice try, witch," said Alarik as he climbed into the carriage. "Get your own wrangler."

Wren stuck her tongue out at the back of his head as she followed him.

"Well, isn't this cozy," said Alarik sarcastically. "Remind me again why we couldn't go by boat?"

"I told you—the Mishnick Mountains are landlocked," said Wren. "You're familiar with the way water works, aren't you? Just be grateful we don't have to trek through the desert. It would melt all the ice in your veins."

Alarik looked at her strangely. "What if the thaw has already begun?"

Wren was about to ask what he meant when Elske bounded into the carriage. She hopped up beside Wren, taking up the rest of the carriage bench and resting her chin on Wren's lap until the only spare seat left was beside Alarik. Once Tor finished loading the carriage, he climbed inside and settled himself next to the king.

The space was even smaller than Wren had imagined. The air grew warmer, closer.

Tor smiled tightly. "Well. This will be an adventure."

The golden gates of Anadawn groaned as they opened, and the

carriage trundled into motion. Wren flopped back against her seat, listening to the commotion in the courtyard die away. Soon, the comforting rumble of wheels on gravel filled the air, the carriage gently rocking as it gathered speed.

"I hope neither of you gets travel sick," remarked Wren.

"No. But I do get viciously bored." Alarik turned his gaze to the forest outside. "How long will this journey take?"

"A couple of days," said Wren, watching the trees go by. "We'll take the Kerrcal Road north until we reach Glenlock. There are villages along the way where we can rest awhile, get something to eat. After that, we'll ride west into the mountains." She glanced at Alarik. "It will be tough going. Thea says the mountain pass is not for the faint of heart."

"You forget I was trained in the Gevran army," said Alarik, unruffled. "Worry about your own heart."

"Oh, please. I grew up on the knife edge of a cliff," said Wren. "Once a storm blew in and took the roof off my grandmother's hut. I nearly went with it."

Alarik *hmm*ed. "When I was a boy of nine, I fell through the ice in our lake. My father left me down there until I turned blue," he countered, as if they were playing a game. "I couldn't feel my fingers for days. He called it a life lesson."

Wren stared at him in horror. "What was the lesson?"

Alarik smiled but there was no gladness in it. "Watch your feet."

Wren was silent for a moment. "As a child, in the midst of a storm, I threw a dead fish at my grandmother. She was so angry she trapped me in a ring of flames until sunrise."

Now it was Tor's turn to look horrified. "What was the lesson?"

"Watch your tongue," said Wren, with a shrug. "Funny thing is, I think Banba would have forgiven me sooner if my aim had been better."

"It was your recklessness she punished you for, not your tongue," said Alarik.

"For all the good it did me." Wren traced the scar on her wrist absently. "I got worse as I got older."

"My father used to say that recklessness only happens when there is too much bravery to spare," said Tor. "The day I was born, Carrig was caught in the worst blizzard the island had ever seen. He trekked through the night, through ice and hail and snow, just to be at my mother's side."

"Sounds as if she was the braver one that day," said Wren.

"Yes," said Tor fondly. "She is braver, still."

"Which explains where you came from, Iversen," said Alarik. "The first time I ever met Tor, he was wrestling a fully grown ice bear." He laughed at the memory. "You were just a boy then, stalking through that arena as if it belonged to you. My father couldn't tear his eyes off you. I think that's the first time I've ever felt jealousy."

Tor smiled grimly. "I was just as jealous of you, watching from your balcony."

"Now that's a story I wouldn't mind hearing," said Wren.

Tor chuckled. "Very well," he began.

After Tor's story, Alarik offered one of his own, recalling the time he had visited the Sundvik Shore as a child, only to get lost. As he recounted, with great theater, being chased up and down the famous black sand shore by ravenous seagulls, Wren bent double with laughter, eyes streaming with tears. Then it was her turn to offer a tale of woe. She told them of the day she had chased a squirrel into the Weeping Forest, only to get stuck up a tree. Too embarrassed to call for help, Wren had had to wait for Shen to find her. He'd arrived at midnight, scaling the trunk with infuriating ease only to find her curled up in the bough.

This time, Alarik roared with laughter.

"What about the squirrel?" said Tor.

"Must you *always* prioritize the animals?" huffed Wren. "I was the one picking twigs out of my hair for days!"

They all shook with laughter. Wren was glad of the lightness that journeyed north with them, filling the cramped carriage with enough warmth to stave off the evening chill. They traded their tales back and forth, letting the minutes slip seamlessly into hours, until the sun surrendered its fight with the moon and melted from the sky.

They stopped in a small trading town to stretch their legs and fill their bellies. Along with the coachmen, they ate in a tavern half the size of Wren's bedroom, wolfing down rabbit stew with creamy potatoes, carrots, and parsnips, and for dessert—which Wren insisted on—they shared an entire cherry pie. After, Alarik went to freshen up while Wren poached a discarded lamb bone from the kitchen. But when she returned to the carriage, Elske was already munching on one.

Tor, who was leaning against the door, offered her a conspiratorial smile. "Great minds . . ."

Wren tucked the bone into her cloak. "For later, then. You can never have too much of a good thing."

"No," said Tor, holding her gaze. "You can't."

Wren looked up past the carriage, to where the stars were twinkling. There was a chill in the air, but the stew had warmed her. Or perhaps it was the company.

Over dinner, they had decided to travel through the night. Wren knew the road ahead would be rockier than the one behind as they navigated the northern marshes and the surrounding farmland. "We've still got hours to go," she said now, almost apologetically. "I'm sorry it's taking so long."

Tor leaned in. "This time last week I was chasing seven feral snow leopards through the Fovarr Mountains, trying to catch them before they maimed the mountain goats. Now I get to sit across from you in a warm carriage, laughing so hard, I can hardly breathe. Where do you think I'd rather be?"

"Well, you do love your beasts," said Wren. "And your country."

"I love other things, too." He held her gaze, his eyes starlit as the sky. "Other places. Other people."

Wren swallowed thickly. Guilt prickled in her cheeks. The knowledge of what she had done with Alarik in that blizzard—how they had kissed until their breath ran out—was still gnawing at her insides.

Tor's face fell. "Freezing hell, Wren. You don't have to look so frightened."

"It's not that," said Wren quickly. "It's just . . . There's something I need to tell you. About me. And Alarik—"

"What about Alarik?" said Alarik, striding out of the tavern.

Wren spun around. "I was just wondering how long you were going to spend fixing your hair."

"Only half as long as it takes you to tell a story." He winked as he brushed passed her. "Now finish that one about the time you fell into a vat of honey in Ortha. I hear laughter aids digestion."

"Why is it that you favor the stories where bad things happen to me?"

"Because I am a brute, Wren." Alarik flashed a wolfish grin.

"Finally, a bit of self-awareness." Wren clambered in after the king. Tor and Elske followed, and they set off again, traveling into the darkening night. The stew had made Wren sleepy, and with Elske warming her feet, she soon found herself drifting off.

Hours passed, a swath of clouds moving in from the west and snuffing out the stars. Midnight came and went, and then the first brushstrokes of dawn cast their pallid light in the sky. When the carriage hit a rock in the road, Wren was jostled awake. The scar on her wrist was stinging and her head was aching. She couldn't remember her nightmare but she didn't feel rested. She looked down, to where the king's right boot brushed against her knee.

Alarik was fast asleep across from her, with his arms folded over his chest and his head lolling against the side of the carriage. A lock of blond hair curled across his forehead, making him look unkempt. Younger, somehow. The king was smiling in his sleep. It was not a smile Wren had seen before. This one was softer, truer. It whispered of happier times.

Somewhere outside, a nightingale was singing.

Wren was struck by the strange intimacy of this moment, of seeing King Alarik wholly unguarded for the first time.

She looked away, only to catch Tor's eye. He was awake, too.

Watching her watch Alarik.

Rotting carp.

Wren's cheeks burned. "Good morning," she mouthed, a little sheepishly.

"Almost," he whispered. He glanced toward Elske, sprawled fast asleep at their feet.

Wren smiled, patting the empty seat beside her.

Tor raised his eyebrows. Wren knew it was an impossible invitation. For one thing, there wasn't enough space with Alarik's feet kicked up on the bench. And for another, to sit side by side in the semi-darkness would be a test of restraint neither of them would likely pass.

Tor raked a hand across his jaw, considering it. Then he folded his arms, leaning back against the seat.

Wren laid her head against the window, waiting for him to fall asleep first, but the soldier easily outlasted her, and as she drifted off once more, she wondered, idly, if he ever slept at all.

When Wren woke again, the sky was blue, the morning sun flooding the carriage with golden light. She winced as she opened her eyes, trying to get used to the glare.

"Morning," said Alarik. "Did you know you drool a lot in your sleep?"

Wren furiously scrubbed her chin with her sleeve. "Shut up. I do not." She looked to Tor. "Do I?"

Tor stalled. "Define *a lot*."

She flung a cushion at him.

He flopped backward, pretending to be wounded.

Wren thumped on the carriage roof. "Time to stop for breakfast! I'm starving!"

At the next village, they had breakfast in a local tavern. While the coachmen snatched an hour or so of rest, Wren went for a walk in a nearby field, where she threw sticks for Elske. The wolf padded along beside her, watching the flying sticks dispassionately.

Wren looked down at her. "Willful little thing. Don't you play fetch?"

"Not unless you throw a slab of meat," called Tor, who was stalking through the long grass, looking at the wildflowers.

"This is supposed to be fun for her," said Wren.

"Then why don't *you* go and get the stick?" said Alarik, picking up a twig. "I'll even throw it for you."

Wren snatched the stick from him. "Actually, I can think of a better use for this. Why don't I—?"

"Watch your mouth, for once?" said Alarik, before heading back to the carriage. "Didn't your grandmother teach you that?"

"Actually, she taught me to better my aim." Wren fired the stick at him, grinning as it bounced off the back of his head.

Alarik turned to glare at her. "I know you like to pretend to forget, but I am still a king."

"Not in this land," she called after him.

His laughter flew over his shoulder. "In every land, Wren."

By late afternoon, they were finally approaching Glenlock, where spindly wooden houses clustered around a sprawling silver lake, gazing at their reflections. The lake town looked particularly beautiful in the setting sun, like an oil painting come to life.

They peered out of the carriage as they passed, admiring the little town in companionable silence, until at last, the road ran out. Wren climbed out of the carriage and looked to the west, where the Mishnick Mountains skewered the darkening horizon. She circled her scar and, though it ached still, she found she could breathe a little easier. They were almost there.

The coachmen unbridled three of the horses and unloaded their satchels, before heading back to Glenlock, where they would rest for the night before returning to Anadawn.

Tor came to stand beside Wren, surveying the wilderness ahead. "Our journey grows more treacherous."

Wren glanced sidelong at him. "You can ride, can't you?"

Tor smirked. "Beast or horse?"

"Now you're just showing off."

He laughed loudly. The sound found wings and soared across the valleys and Wren burned to follow it. Deep into the mountains, to the magic that awaited them there.

18

ROSE

After ensuring everything at Anadawn was in order, Rose departed the palace the morning after Wren, with Celeste at her side. They reached the edge of the Ganyeve Desert just before sunset. They'd been riding for several hours, and Rose guessed they still had several more to go. Rose thanked the stars that in the previous months, the Sunkissed Kingdom had come to reside closer to Anadawn than ever before, but if she had her way, it would linger right at the edge of the desert, a stone's throw from the Eshlinn woods beyond her palace.

Thankfully, their horses were far from tired. Rose's mare was silver with a moon-white mane and tail. She was a Yulemas gift from Shen, and she had loved the horse at once. Shen had been just as moved by her gift: an intricate sundial inscribed with some of Rose's favorite romantic poetry, where a different line was set aglow at each hour of the day.

She'd christened her horse Starlight, and when Wren had laughed and told her that it sounded like a name a child would pick for a horse, Rose had simply shrugged. "It suits her," she'd insisted, brushing out Starlight's shining mane.

The following morning, Wren had decided to name her horse Breeze, and Rose had smiled, thinking they were not so different after all.

Celeste had taken her own stalwart horse, Lady, and the two women traveled in companionable silence as they crossed into the desert. The horses were sure-footed and quick, and Rose had the feeling that they would find their way back home to the Sunkissed Kingdom even if she wasn't guiding them. For a long time, the only sounds were the gentle *shhh* of their hooves hitting the sand and the occasional melody of the shifting dunes ringing in their ears.

Rose would forever associate the sound with the first time she found herself in the desert with Shen, and even now, hearing the hum of the restless sands made her want to urge Starlight faster so she could be reunited with him all the sooner.

She hadn't told Shen she was coming. With birds dropping from the skies of Eana, she had no way to safely send him such an important message—and if she could, she wouldn't need to take the trip herself. Rose knew she was going to the Sunkissed Kingdom with a mission, and a serious one at that, but she also couldn't deny how much she yearned to see Shen. And this time it would be her surprising him, instead of the other way around. She couldn't help imagining the look on his face when he saw her riding through the ruby gates of the Sunkissed Kingdom. Rose could perfectly picture his eyes lighting up as they landed on her, his grin spreading until his dimple appeared. She would leap from the horse and run to him, and then—

"Stars! How is it still so hot?" Celeste's voice broke through Rose's daydream. "The deeper we go, the worse it gets!"

Rose laughed, remembering how she had felt when she had first awoken in the desert. "It will cool now that the sun is setting. Soon, the moon will rise."

Celeste wiped her brow. "I thought I knew heat. I've spent long summers on the southern seas with Marino. And there, the sun beats down on you from above *and* reflects back up at you from the sea. But *this*? This is simply unreasonable."

To her surprise, Rose found she didn't mind the heat. Not the way she once did. She grinned as she thought about telling Shen how she was adapting to his homeland. She was no longer the sheltered flower she once was—no, she felt that she was now someone who could flourish anywhere she went.

She was stronger than she'd realized.

Stronger than anyone had realized.

And that made her feel as if she could face anything. Even Oonagh Starcrest.

"It is beautiful, though," said Celeste, almost as an afterthought. "Especially now the stars are coming out. I don't know what I imagined but it wasn't this."

Rose knew exactly what she meant. As they rode on, the sky darkened from a riot of pinks and purples into an indigo tapestry dotted with silver-bright stars.

"Surely, we must be nearly there," said Celeste.

"We're close," Rose confirmed, just as the sand began to tremble.

"Rose?" said Celeste, voice rising in a panic. "Is that supposed to happen?"

"Stay on your horse!" said Rose, frantically looking around to see the source of the upheaval. Was it a blood beetle? Some other kind of desert beast?

The dunes in the distance were shaking, sand pouring down their sides, as if something were trying to punch up through the earth. A sickening crack appeared before them, rivers of sand tumbling down inside it.

Then, as quickly as it had come on, the shaking stopped.

"It was an earthquake," breathed Rose, eyeing the chasm that had opened up before them. It was long and jagged but not wide enough to stop them. She hoped. "Come on, Starlight. Jump!"

Rose gripped the reins tight as the horse leaped over the gaping crack in the earth, clearing it with almost a foot to spare. Celeste and Lady landed a heartbeat later, and Rose smiled at her best friend, relief and triumph rushing through her.

They rode on, quicker now.

"Eana has never had an earthquake before," said Celeste, once she had caught her breath. "Or at least not one that I know of."

"Nor I," said Rose uneasily. "I've felt the sands move but never like that."

"Is it . . . ?" Celeste trailed off and Rose knew she was afraid even to say Oonagh's name, as if it would summon her.

Rose would not allow Oonagh to have that power over them.

"If it is Oonagh's doing, we will find out soon enough," she said firmly. "Come. We must hurry!" Her search for a weapon felt more urgent than ever, as if Oonagh herself might rise out of the chasm in the desert and snatch her.

At last, they spied the Sunkissed Kingdom glittering in the distance.

The small but mighty city was entirely contained behind high sandstone walls that shimmered under the rising moon. To Rose's surprise, the towering scarlet gates were flung wide open. Not closed, as she had expected.

Strange.

And stranger still, where moments ago, there had been only the song of the shifting sands, now she could hear music. A low pounding of drums, then the familiar twang of string instruments.

Was the Sunkissed Kingdom having a celebration of some kind? Certainly Rose would have been invited, wouldn't she? Just as Shen had been invited to her own Spring Celebration.

Rose felt a prickle of unease. Well. She supposed it was none of her business what kind of events went on in the Sunkissed Kingdom. And never mind if Shen was having a party—she was here with a purpose.

"Are they expecting us?" said Celeste uncertainly. "Or are the gates usually open?"

"I'm not sure," admitted Rose. "Come, let's investigate."

As they drew closer, Rose saw that there were two footmen at the entrance, both dressed in red-and-black silk tunics. The first approached her and Celeste, bowing low.

Rose thought he must have recognized her as queen of Eana, until he spoke. "Welcome to the Sunkissed Kingdom, ladies. We are glad you found us, and hope the journey here was not too arduous." The speech sounded . . . rehearsed. Rose wanted to interrupt, to tell this oblivious footman that she had, in fact, been to the Sunkissed Kingdom before, that she'd been with Shen and Kai when they'd found it under the sand, for stars' sake, but she let him go on. "Unfortunately, you've missed our formal welcome banquet, but not to worry, there is still plenty of food to be had. We can take your horses for you, and if you hurry, you'll be able to join in the talent display. Everyone has gathered in the square. It's in the heart of the city—just follow the sand statues to the main promenade, and you can't miss it."

Rose frowned. What on earth was he talking about?

"Talent display?" said Celeste, mirroring her confusion. "Whatever for?"

The two footmen exchanged a look. "Of course, a talent is not required," said the other one delicately, as if he was trying to spare her feelings. "If you would rather wait to be presented to King Shen during the ceremonial dancing, that can also be arranged. We need only your names, and of course, your home country."

"*Presented?*" repeated Celeste.

"Our *names?*" Rose choked out. "This must be a joke."

But the footmen were stone-faced.

From somewhere inside the walls, a thunder of applause rang out.

"Name and country," repeated the first footman. "So His Majesty knows who you are."

"Shen knows who I am," said Rose frostily.

"*King* Shen," corrected the other footman. "And of course he does. He invited you here, did he not?" The men chuckled at the very idea of someone appearing uninvited at the gates.

Celeste joined in with their forced laughter. "Yes, of course," she said, summoning a smile. "How else would one be presented if not formally? I am Lady Celeste Pegasi and this is *Queen Rose Valhart.*" She paused meaningfully. "Of Eana. I trust you're both familiar with Eana?"

The footman balked at Rose. "I . . . *Oh* . . ."

The other looked through his scroll, frantically searching for their names.

Celeste deftly batted it away. "Surely, there's no need for such formalities."

There came another burst of raucous applause from deep within the maze of the city walls. "It sounds as if someone is making quite the impression!" said Celeste, sliding off her horse. "We should go and see for ourselves."

Rose followed suit, trying not to show her annoyance as she sashayed past them. "Good evening, gentlemen."

Rose deftly wound her way through the familiar maze of stone paths, drawing ever closer to the commotion in the heart of the city. The streets were utterly deserted, making her feel even more off kilter. Or perhaps it was the conversation with Shen's footmen that had made her uneasy. She had been so confused, she had not even thought to ask them if they had felt the desert quake.

"Are you all right?" asked Celeste, quickening to match her pace.

"Nothing is making any sense!" said Rose. "The footman said that Shen had sent out invitations. But to what, exactly?"

And why did I not receive one? she thought, too embarrassed to voice her hurt aloud.

"I'm sure we'll find out," said Celeste. "Look at those giant sand statues! This must be the path we're meant to take."

They hurried over, and Rose laughed when they reached the first statue. "It looks just like Shen! It even has his dimple!" The statues had clearly been crafted with enchantment magic, each one so detailed they almost appeared to be breathing.

"If that's Shen, then who's *she*?" said Celeste, moving on to the next one.

Rose frowned as she studied the statue. She was a buxom woman with a five-pointed crown on her head and hair so long it nearly reached the ground.

"Strange," she murmured. "She has the crest of Demarre on her dress. And that woman next to her, she's wearing a honey-drop flower on her gown. Isn't that the symbol of Krale?" Rose pointed to another nearby statue, a gasp catching in her throat. "Goodness! Is that Princess Anika?"

"From *Gevra*?" Celeste inspected it. "Stars, I think you're right! I'd recognize that wicked smile anywhere."

"Oh, you would, would you?" said Rose, playfully nudging her friend. Then she frowned as another cheer rang out across the city. "This is all *extremely* puzzling."

"Indeed," said Celeste, still gazing at the sand statue of Anika.

"Stop making eyes at the statue, Celeste. We need to get to the square." Rose pulled her friend along until they reached the end of the path, where they nearly bumped into a young girl who was using her magic to whirl a new statue from a nearby pile of sand. The witch glanced up as they approached. "Oh! Hello!" She beamed. "You must be here for the King's Choice. I'm afraid I don't have time to make your sculpture right now, but if you come back tomorrow morning, I'll add you to the gallery."

Rose didn't like the sound of whatever the "King's Choice" was meant to be, and she was getting impatient. As another cheer rattled through the night, she simply nodded and smiled, hurrying past the witch and into the square.

A large crowd was gathered there, everyone cheering and whooping so loudly, Rose had to stand on her tiptoes to see what they were looking at.

The courtyard was lavishly decorated. Hundreds of red-and-gold lanterns floated over the revelers and trailing garlands hung with glowing flowers were strung across the walls. Long wooden tables covered with what looked to be the leftovers from a decadent feast lined the perimeter of the square, while the crowd clustered around the central dais that held a row of eight golden chairs. On each chair sat a woman, each wearing a crown. Rose frowned, recognizing the women from their sand sculptures.

Her frown deepened at the sound of a familiar laugh. Shen, *her* Shen, was standing in front of this row of preening women, *laughing*.

A loud voice echoed above the din. "From the kingdom of Vask, we welcome Princess Ida." A short woman with pale skin and curly red hair stood and curtsied. She wore a teal velvet gown pinned with hundreds of crystals.

"Vask?" Celeste whispered in Rose's ear. "Vask is beyond even Gevra! How did a princess from the northern continent travel through Eana without us knowing?"

"I have no idea," Rose whispered back. "But I intend to find out."

The Princess of Vask curtsied again, this time toward Shen, who bowed and kissed her hand.

Rose felt her own hand begin to tremble. She was grateful when Celeste took it and squeezed tight.

"The people of Vask were gladdened to hear of the rediscovery of the Sunkissed Kingdom," Princess Ida said, her voice light and airy. "In Vask we, too, appreciate great warriors and fine weaponry. We enjoy the beauty of a good blade, particularly the music it makes when it cuts down an enemy."

"Charming," Celeste muttered.

"In Vask, every child has a blade bestowed upon them at the moment of their birth. As we grow, we learn to master it. To love it. To *become* it." As Princess Ida spoke, her voice grew higher in pitch. Then she stood and unsheathed a long silver sword that was strung across her back. "We do not possess the magic your kingdom has been blessed with, King Shen. But this talent comes from years of disciplined training. It is my honor to present to you the Sword Swallow of Vask."

"The *what* now?" hissed Celeste.

Rose hushed Celeste, her eyes pinned to the Vaskan princess as she began to spin like a top, round and round, her gown fanning out around her as she rose up on her toes. Then there was a flash of silver as she tossed her sword in the air. It flipped once, twice, then plummeted down toward the still-spinning Princess Ida, who tilted her head back and opened her mouth.

The crowd froze as the sword slid into her mouth and down her throat, until all that was visible was the fine black hilt.

Rose's own mouth dropped open at the sight.

With one smooth movement, the Vaskan princess stopped spinning and pulled the sword from her mouth, presenting it to Shen.

The crowd erupted in cheers.

"That was . . . certainly something," muttered Celeste.

Rose was too shocked to say anything at all. She felt as though she had tumbled into some kind of nightmare.

Shen took the sword from the princess, his eyes dancing with mischief. "What a remarkable talent you have, Princess Ida," he said deftly. "Not to mention an iron stomach."

"I've never met a sword I cannot swallow, Your Majesty." The princess winked, and the crowd, drunk on wine and heady from being courted—because Rose was sure now that the entire Sunkissed Kingdom was being courted—cheered even louder.

"I'd like to run her through with a sword," she said under her breath.

"That was the most unsettling thing I've ever seen," remarked Celeste. "And I've seen King Alarik in leather trousers."

Princess Ida returned to her seat, but Rose noticed how her gaze stayed on Shen. "She has some nerve."

Celeste cleared her throat. "Perhaps we should tell Shen we're here before someone swallows a lantern and goes up in flames."

Before Rose could voice her agreement, a horn sounded and the crowd stilled in expectation. "And now, we welcome Queen Adrienne of Krale."

Rose craned her neck to get a good look at the queen, who she knew had been ruling the famously mountainous country of Krale since the tender age of thirteen. The queen of Krale had dark brown skin and large eyes. Her black hair was shorn close to her scalp and her gown was a sheath of pearly white, with a high neckline and long billowing sleeves.

Unlike Princess Ida, Queen Adrienne did not curtsy but stood straight-backed before Shen, presenting her hand for him to kiss. When he did, Rose felt as if she was going to cry.

"I'm afraid in Krale we do not swallow swords," Queen Adrienne said with a soft smile. "Nor are we famed for our fighting. But we do sing." She batted her long lashes. "I have heard it said that the sound of my song is so sweet, it can make even the fiercest warrior lay down their weapon."

Celeste snorted. "I've never heard such a tall tale. I bet she sounds like a constipated duck." Rose's answering giggle was short-lived. When Queen Adrienne began to sing, Rose was sure it was true.

It was the most beautiful sound she'd ever heard, the queen's voice so close to magic, Rose's cheeks began to prickle. The queen of Krale sang in a language Rose didn't understand but she could plainly tell it was a love song. There was longing in her voice, yearning in her eyes, and for the entirety of the song, she kept her gaze locked on Shen, who stared right back at her, entranced.

Rose's heart ached. While she could carry a tune well enough and even play the pianoforte, she knew she would never be able to sing the way the queen of Krale did and mesmerize a man—much less an entire crowd—with such ease.

As Queen Adrienne's song came to a close, the crowd stood silent as if they all shared one lung and were holding the same breath. Shen stood transfixed, too, and when it was over, he took Queen Adrienne's hand and kissed it again.

"Thank you, Queen Adrienne," he said, his voice thick with emotion. "That truly was a gift."

Queen Adrienne grinned as she returned to her seat.

"It wasn't even *that* good," said Celeste.

"Then why are there tears in your eyes?" said Rose.

"Wayward raindrop," mumbled Celeste.

Rose squeezed her hand. "You're a good friend."

Celeste glanced sidelong at her. "Even though I can't swallow a sword?"

Rose giggled. "That only makes me like you more."

The horn sounded again. "We welcome Princess Elladora from Demarre!"

"*That's* her name," said Celeste, with a jolt. "Remember when she came to Anadawn? She was visiting with her parents and she fell into a rosebush and cried." She chuckled at the memory. "She had to sit on a special cushion at dinner."

"Of course," said Rose, brightening at the memory. "I remember now. She certainly looks different."

Princess Elladora stood, her golden hair flowing to the floor. She had light brown skin and pale green eyes that perfectly matched the color of her gown. The dress was cut low at the front, the long train trailing behind her as she took a step toward Shen. Around her waist was a thin belt hung with silver stars.

"Thank you for inviting me to your beautiful kingdom, King Shen." Her voice was low and hypnotic. "When my people heard of its discovery, we released two dozen royal doves and sent them across the sea in celebration. We hope that one may have even reached you here in your desert home."

"I've never heard something so ridiculous," muttered Celeste.

"Thank you, Princess Elladora," said Shen with a gracious smile. "Any emissaries from Demarre, including those with wings, are most welcome here."

Princess Elladora curtsied. "I do not sing nor do I swallow swords. But I have brought my stars. I hope they will please you and your people." She removed four stars from her belt, each of which had sharp, shining edges. "I pride myself on my precision," she said, tossing back her long silky hair. "I must ask you, King Shen, do you agree that trust is the most important element between two countries beginning an alliance?"

"It is," said Shen.

Rose bristled. "Talk about stating the obvious."

"Then please trust me when I ask you to step in front of me and stay perfectly still."

Shen did as he was told, but even at the back of the crowd, Rose didn't miss the tightening of his jaw, the curling of his fists by his sides. He was nervous. And so was Rose.

"Tell me, King Shen," said Princess Elladora, flashing two perfect rows of pearly teeth. "If I impress the crowd, do I win a kiss?"

Rose inhaled sharply.

"Shameless!" cried Celeste.

Shen was nonplussed. "I think they're already more than impressed with what they've seen," he said, returning an easy smile. "It will be hard to impress them further."

"I do like a challenge," said Princess Elladora coyly. She flicked her wrists and the stars flew toward Shen, their sharp edges glinting in the moonlight. Rose gasped as they sliced through Shen's silk shirt. The material fell away from his torso in ruined shreds, leaving him standing bare-chested, but unharmed.

The stars clattered to the floor and the crowd erupted.

Shen chuckled as he surveyed himself. "That *was* impressive," he said, picking up the stars and handing them back to the Princess of Demarre, who returned them to her belt.

She turned to the crowd. "Well?" she called out. "Have I earned my kiss?"

They roared in unison, stamping their feet in support.

Satisfied, Princess Elladora leaned toward Shen, her full lips puckered.

"KISS HER!" screamed someone in the crowd, the chant taking hold almost immediately.

"KISS! KISS! KISS!"

"DON'T YOU DARE!" yelled Celeste, but her voice was lost in the furor.

Shen laughed and gamely kissed the Princess of Demarre on the cheek. She pouted but then winked at him, whispering something that was impossible to hear over the roaring crowd. Whatever it was reddened Shen's cheeks.

Rose felt dizzy at the sight. She squeezed Celeste's hand, drawing strength from her friend, who looked fit to storm the dais and throttle Shen. The horn sounded again, and the minstrels returned to their instruments, the beat of the drum soon echoing through the square.

"And now it's time to dance!" cried the master of ceremonies.

Shen offered his hand to Princess Elladora and escorted her from the dais. They began to dance, and soon the rest of the crowd joined in.

"Ugh." Celeste wrinkled her nose. "What now? Do we go to war with Demarre?"

As Rose watched Shen spin Princess Elladora, she made a quick and crucial decision.

"No. Now we find something suitable to wear so that we may rise like glorious phoenixes from the ashes of this abominable evening and make Shen Lo rue the very moment he decided to take part in this ridiculous display of talent."

"Good," said Celeste, agreeing to the plan. "I've always thought that glamour and revenge go quite well together."

"Precisely." Rose pulled Celeste away from the crowd, making a beeline for the Palace of Eternal Sunlight. "Come. I know just where to go."

19

WREN

Wren had only been trekking for a short while when the ground began to tremble. Tor reacted lightning fast, grabbing both her and Alarik and pulling them to the ground with him.

"Earthquake," he said, frowning into the distance, as if he could see the source of it. The shaking stopped a moment later, and they rose uneasily to their feet.

Wren's throat tightened. "That doesn't usually happen here."

Tor and Alarik exchanged a loaded glance but said no more about it. Wren knew they were all thinking the same thing. Oonagh's power was growing, her reach extending toward Eana. Toward her.

They set off again, but as the afternoon sun arced over the rolling valley, Wren's legs grew heavy. Her head, too. Tor and Alarik walked a ways ahead of her, Elske padding companionably beside her master. While the soldier's footsteps were strong and sure, Wren could see the king was struggling, like her. Alarik had begun to sway from side to side, as if he'd had too much wine, and he kept fiddling with his left sleeve. His scar was bothering him.

Elske looked over her shoulder at Wren, concern shining in her icy-blue eyes.

"Go on ahead, sweetling." Not wanting to make a fuss, Wren shooed the wolf on, then paused to lean against a bolder. She tipped her head back, letting the sun warm her face as she caught her breath.

Tor stopped walking.

"I'm all right," she called. "I just need a minute."

"Good idea," said Alarik, letting himself sag against a nearby boulder. "Let's rest awhile."

Tor looked between them, a furrow appearing between his brows. Then he glanced up at the sun. Wren knew he was calculating how long they had been walking. An hour, maybe two. How long lay ahead of them? The Mishnick Mountains were still a distance away.

"We should have brought the horses," said Tor.

"It's too steep now," said Wren, for the eleventh time. "They'd tire before us."

Tor scrubbed a hand across his jaw, looking doubtful.

"And anyway, it's too late," added Wren.

Alarik laughed mirthlessly. "How pathetic we must look to you, Iversen." He looked as bad as Wren felt, his eyes bloodshot and his cheeks so pale they matched his hair. "Staggering about like a pair of sunstruck children. I think you might have to become our horse."

Wren snorted, but Tor's face was contemplative. She could tell he was calculating the weight of all the satchels and then the people.

"Carry her," said Alarik. "I can walk."

Wren scowled. "So can I."

Tor looked between them. "I should carry both of you."

Elske let out a low whine.

"I think Elske wants to carry me," said Wren.

"Let's not flatten the wolf," remarked Alarik. "We may need her to hunt."

Wren flung a rock at him. He batted it away. "Is that really the best you can do, witch?"

"Next time it will be a bolt of lightning."

He raised his brows. "Now that I would like to see."

"Save your strength," said Tor, removing a water flask from his satchel and tossing it to Wren.

"Tell me about this first witch you named your kingdom after," said Alarik, watching her drink. "Why was she so fascinated with these endless barren mountains?"

"I think you mean our *beautiful sloping hills*," said Wren between gulps.

Alarik snorted. "There's always a lie dancing on your tongue."

Wren tossed him the water flask with unnecessary force. "Eana wasn't just fascinated with these mountains; she made them. She made everything in this country. Every speck of land, every rock and blade of grass, every grain of sand . . ."

Tor and Alarik exchanged a look.

"That sounds far-fetched," said the king.

Now it was Wren's turn to snort. "Wasn't Gevra run by bears for several centuries? You should think about restoring one to the throne. You'd probably be better off."

"I'm sure you'd find some way to make its life a misery, too," said

Alarik. "Tell me more about your precious creator so I can offend her memory just as enthusiastically. How is it that she made this land?"

"She flew here from the stars on the back of a green-tailed hawk," said Wren fondly. "When the hawk touched the ocean, Eana used her magic to turn the creature into land. That's why our kingdom takes the shape of a bird in flight. Everything after that came from her, too. Her magic was boundless; her power was . . . well, extraordinary."

Tor perked up at the mention of the green-tailed hawk. He scoured the skies now, as though he was expecting to see one. "That must have been some bird."

Wren *hmm*ed. "You won't find another in our skies. In any sky. Green-tailed hawks haven't flown in this kingdom for thousands of years."

"A shame," muttered Alarik. "We could use one to get up to those mountains."

On that, they could all agree. Soon, they walked on, but the going was slower than before. After another hour or so, they resolved to stop for a rest, where they shared some apples and cheese from Wren's satchel. After, Wren found enough energy to continue onward, and not wanting to be outdone by her, Alarik did, too. Together, all three of them journeyed deeper into the northern valley, gazing up at the mountains that seemed to grow taller with every step.

Elske led the pack, sniffing her way through the grassy plains, often returning with an unfortunate shrew or a quivering mouse for her master. Tor took them from the wolf with great pride, making sure to scratch behind her ears, before sending her off again. Once, Elske chased a hare so far she disappeared for almost an hour.

"Do you think she'll come back?" said Wren, straining to see her small white blur in the distance.

"She always comes back," said Tor. He looked between them, scanning their drawn faces, their tired gaits. "How are you both bearing up?"

"Great," huffed Alarik.

"Never better," said Wren.

"I could walk ten more miles," added Alarik. "Twenty, even."

Wren rolled her eyes. "You're so immature."

"Something you two have in common," said Tor.

They wandered on. Now that they were in the heart of the valley, the hills seemed to go on forever. There was something strangely soothing about the landscape, as though they were being cradled in the very arms of Eana where no harm could come to them.

"Remarkable," said Tor, tipping his head back to study the towering peaks. "It's like a great rolling ocean has swept us up."

"Iversen the poet," muttered Alarik.

"My kingdom *is* beautiful," said Wren. "It just takes someone with an actual *soul* to recognize that."

"If you ask me, it lacks a certain wildness," mused Alarik. "Although the same can't be said of its queen." He smirked at Wren. "But let's not argue over whose kingdom is better."

"Well, I know which one is safer," she shot back.

"You can have your ancestor back anytime you like, Wren."

"Maybe we should all be silent for a while," suggested Tor. "Save our breath."

In the welcome quiet that followed, Tor hummed to himself, filling the air with the honeyed lilt of his voice. Wren found herself breathing easier, walking just a little farther.

They were in the foothills now, so close Wren swore she could hear the mountain springs tinkling through the valley. But as the sun was sliding from the sky like a golden raindrop, the temperature plummeted. Darkness fell, and Wren's teeth began to chatter.

When they came upon a small clearing, Tor insisted they stop and rest for the night. On one side, they were sheltered by the mountains, and on the other, surrounded by boulders that would protect them from the howling night wind. While Tor went to gather firewood, Wren set down their blankets and pelts to create a makeshift mattress.

Alarik sat on a nearby rock, watching her work. "Didn't it occur to you to bring a tent?"

"I thought we'd make it there by nightfall," said Wren, with a huff of frustration. "And what do you care? Haven't you ever slept outside before?"

"More times than I care to count," he mused. "My father had a penchant for camping in the Fovarr Mountains when I was a child."

"Don't tell me—you once spent the night in an elk carcass?" Wren guessed.

Alarik stared at her. "What is wrong with you?"

"Too many things to list," she muttered, which earned her a laugh from the king. He picked up a blanket and set about helping her.

"Tell me, witch. What's for dinner?"

"Whatever Cam packed for us," said Wren, rummaging about in her satchel. She pulled out a loaf of bread, a cloth filled with sliced chicken, and even a small jar of gravy. It wasn't much but she was suddenly starving, and she knew, once warmed by the fire, the food would taste wonderful.

Tor returned presently with Elske in tow, his arms so full of firewood, Wren couldn't see his face over them. He dropped the logs in the center of the clearing and began piling them up. Wren watched him build their fire, her gaze lingering over his strong arms, how his jaw hardened as he worked.

"Fascinating, isn't it?" needled Alarik.

She shook herself out of her trance. "It looks as if you're building a castle with all that wood," she called out to Tor.

"The more wood, the more warmth," replied Tor, without turning around. "I learned this technique from long winters on Carrig." He glanced up at the cloudless sky, where thousands of stars were twinkling. "The night will get colder still."

After he finished building his tower of wood, Tor sat back on his heels and looked to Wren. "I think this could do with a little magic."

Wren smiled, eager to be of some help. "My speciality."

She stood over the firewood and summoned a wisp of tempest magic, picturing lightning crackling between her fingers. Her magic erupted, setting the wood alight. But it brought with it a familiar shooting pain. She fell to her knees as it tore through her body. She wrapped her arms around her middle to try to bear it.

"Wren?" The anxious rasp of Tor's voice cut through the blackness in her mind.

A groan seeped through Wren's teeth. The pain was already passing, like a shiver rattling down her spine. It had been a warning, not a punishment. A reminder: her magic was tainted, just as she was.

Strong hands gripped her shoulders, pulling her back. Wren realized too late that she had fallen too close to the fire. She opened her eyes as Tor lifted her away from the blaze. Alarik reached out to steady her, his face ashen. "What the hell was that?"

"Nothing." Wren shook them both off. "I'm fine," she said, finding her own footing. "It was just . . . the magic. My magic." She traced the stinging pain in her wrist. "It's painful now. It hurts."

"You should have said something," said Alarik.

"I should have made the fire," said Tor.

"It doesn't matter. It's done now," said Wren, slumping to the ground. Elske came and laid her head on her lap. "Let's eat."

"Good idea," said Alarik. "The sooner we get to those mountains, the sooner this will all seem like a bad dream."

They ate in the glow of the fire with the stars twinkling overhead. Afterward, Wren lay back, searching the sky for starcrests. But the stars never moved, and her lids grew heavy. With Elske curled up beside her, she drifted off, lulled by the muffled chatter of Tor and Alarik, who were lost in tales of their childhoods. Wren was so exhausted, she would have slept the whole night cradled in the foothills of the Mishnick Mountains, between Tor and Alarik, had it not been for the menacing growl that rumbled through their camp sometime after midnight.

Tor was on his feet before Wren even opened her eyes. With the fire burning low, it took her a moment to spot the creature watching them in the dark. She heard the growl again, only it was louder this time. And then she knew. It was a mountain lion. By the outline of its body in the dark, it was far bigger than any she had seen before. And stranger still, its eyes were glowing red.

The mountain lion pounced but Tor dived at the same time, knocking the beast into a boulder. It howled before righting itself again. At closer range, Wren noticed the gleam of its partially exposed skull and the strips of fur hanging off its back. Horror punched through her, stealing her breath. She tried to blink the creature away, to convince herself this was a nightmare, but that awful growl came a third time, shivering all the way down her spine.

"Hissing hell," she cried in a strangled voice. "It's *dead*."

"Not quite." Tor pulled his knife, ready for the next attack. "Stay behind me," he warned Wren, while Elske rounded the creature from the other side, releasing her own terrifying growl.

Alarik stirred at the commotion. Within seconds, he was on his feet, sword swinging.

"Watch it!" said Wren, ducking to avoid the blade.

This time, when the undead mountain lion went for Wren, Tor jumped into its path, grabbing it by the shoulders. Wren had never witnessed such brute force before, or seen a man look so like a beast, but Tor met the creature head on, his teeth bared as he shoved it back. He jerked to avoid its snapping jaws, expertly keeping it at arm's length. They circled each other around the campfire, the wrangler keeping his back to Wren and Alarik and making a shield of his body.

Elske pounced from a nearby boulder, momentarily flattening the mountain lion. But the beast shook the wolf off, its red eyes flashing as it rounded on Wren. The creature wasn't interested in Elske or Tor.

Tongue hanging and bones gleaming, it prowled toward Wren. She had the sudden, sickening suspicion that it could sense her magic. That it wanted to devour it—or perhaps devour her.

Tor was quick to figure out the same thing. He leaped in front of Wren. Alarik flanked her other side, sword raised. "How do we kill a thing that's already dead?" he said.

"Start swinging," said Tor. "We'll work it out along the way."

The lion roared as it jumped at Tor, but this time, he jumped, too, bringing his knife up with a sickening crunch. Wren flinched as it sank between the creature's ribs. She shut her eyes, listening to its last pathetic whimper. Then it slumped at her feet, dead again.

At least for now.

Tor wiped the sweat from his brow as he looked Wren over. Then, satisfied she was unharmed, he removed the blade and cleaned it on his sleeve.

"Now, where did this particular terror come from?" said Alarik, surveying the corpse.

"It's no Gevran beast," said Tor. "The coloring is wrong."

"Wherever it came from, it's one of Oonagh's," said Wren grimly.

Alarik's eyes darted about, his voice turning fearful. "Does that mean she's nearby?"

"She could be anywhere," said Wren, and that was the true horror of her ancestor's dark power. "She moves like a fish when she wants to." She recalled the vision she had once seen of Oonagh falling into the Silvertongue, how she had turned herself into a merrow in the water, with gills slashed into her neck and the long swishing tail of a fish. She could be anything she wanted to be. Anywhere. Wren stared at the mountain lion's decomposing skull. "This creature could be a warning."

"Or a deserter from her army of undead beasts," remarked Alarik.

"Or an attempt on your life," said Tor, his knuckles white around the blade. "It must have scented your magic."

Wren looked at her hands, thinking of the strange smoke writhing inside her. "Or the curse," she said quietly.

Elske padded over to Wren, resuming her post at her side while Tor hoisted the mountain lion onto his shoulder. "I'll burn the corpse. Just in case it decides to reanimate," he said. "Go back to sleep. I'll keep watch until morning."

Though Wren trusted Tor to keep them safe, the attack had left her uneasy. Oonagh could be watching them right now, readying her next ambush. Or perhaps she was simply toying with them, plucking at their fear like strings on a harp. Somehow, that made Wren feel even angrier.

"Don't dwell on it," said Alarik, reading her frown. "It will take more than a half-rotted mountain lion to best Iversen and his wolf." He turned his sword in his hand. "And if it makes you feel better, or indeed envious, I am a remarkable swordsman."

"I don't doubt it." Wren pulled her blanket around her shoulders. "But I don't want to put any of you in danger."

"Then you probably shouldn't have raised my brother from the dead."

Wren turned to scowl at Alarik, only to catch the glint of his smile in the dark. He laughed hoarsely. "It seems to me that whatever curse is inside you is in me, too," he went on. "So we are in this together, Wren. For better. Or for worse."

They stayed awake a while longer, teasing each other to dull the edges of their nerves. When Tor returned with more firewood, they settled into an easy silence. Wren thought she'd never fall asleep again, but before long, she was drifting off. She didn't wake until an hour after dawn when all the birds in the valley were chirping.

Tor was sitting on a boulder, watching the morning mist move across the mountains. His shoulders were tensed and his left hand was tight around the hilt of his dagger. He must have stayed awake all night, guarding them.

She smiled as she threw off her blanket and stood up. "Alarik really should give you a raise."

Tor turned at the sound of her voice, and though his eyes were tired and his face drawn, he managed a smile. "Perhaps you should tell him that."

"*Or* you could come to Anadawn. I'll shower you in diamonds."

Tor chuckled. "I am not so easily bought, Wren."

"Too bad."

Alarik was still sleeping so Wren nudged him with the toe of her boot. His hand shot out, grabbing her ankle. "Do that again and you'll regret it," he murmured, still half asleep.

"Wakey, wakey," said Wren, shaking him off. "I want to reach the mountains by noon."

Alarik groaned as he sat up. Wren looked him over and wondered if she appeared as gray and exhausted as he did. She passed a hand through her hair, tugging at the knots. She desperately needed to bathe.

They packed up their satchels and set off again, walking until the morning sun reached its peak in the sky. The land climbed and they climbed with it, the way ahead growing sparse and rocky.

"There are so many mountains," said Alarik when the wind grew quiet. "How will we know the right one?"

Wren recalled what Thea had told her. *Look for bloom and birdsong, and the opening will reveal itself to you."*

"We'll know it when we see it," Wren said, trusting in the old witch's words.

Fortunately, they soon came true.

Wren spotted the birds before she heard their call.

"Look, there!" she said, pointing ahead, to where the tallest of the Mishnick Mountains jutted up like an arrowhead to pierce the low-hanging clouds. Songbirds swooped and soared around it, calling to each other through the mist.

They stuck to the curve of the mountain as they climbed. Rock face soon turned to flowers, blooming petals of blue and pink and yellow and violet casting a symphony of color all around them until it felt to Wren as if she had strayed into a dream. Somewhere nearby, she heard the sound of tinkling water, and felt a strange calmness come over her.

She exhaled properly for the first time in months.

On either side of her, Tor and Alarik had fallen quiet. Reverent. The birds sang and they listened. They followed the trail of flowers until at last they came upon an archway cut into the mountain face.

Beneath it stood a girl about Wren's age, wearing a dark green robe. She had cornflower-blue eyes, long golden hair, and a placid smile that set Wren's pulse at rest.

"Your Majesty," she said, dropping into a curtsy. "It is our honor to receive you here in the Mishnick Mountains."

Before Wren could respond, Alarik interjected, *"Majesties."*

The girl looked at Alarik then back at Wren. A furrow appeared between her brows, but she swallowed whatever she was about to say and stepped back through the archway. It was only then that Wren noticed the huge cavern behind her and the crystalline waterfall cascading from above.

"Come in," said the girl, her voice soft and lilting. "And be well."

Wren hoped it would be as easy as that.

20

ROSE

Rose strode purposefully through the deserted halls of the Palace of Eternal Sunlight.

"Rose, wait!" hissed Celeste, who was following close behind. "Are you sure we can just . . . be in here like this?"

"Do you think *Shen*—" Rose nearly spat his name—"ever asks himself that when he arrives in Anadawn unannounced?"

"Probably not," said Celeste. "But—and don't take this the wrong way—it isn't exactly your style to go sneaking around like this."

"I can sneak just as well as Wren," said Rose.

"As someone who has caught Wren sneaking around several times, I have to say that your sister is not as good at it as everyone thinks she is," Celeste pointed out. They came to the atrium, where the Forever Fountain was freely flowing, the water lit from within by flickering everlights. "So . . . where exactly are we going?"

"I told you. We need to find something to wear."

Celeste quirked an eyebrow. "I thought we needed to find an ancient weapon."

"Yes, that, too! But first clothes." Rose stole a quick glance at her reflection in the fountain before ushering Celeste away from it. "Shen's hosting a party without me. *Worse* than a party, in fact. We have clearly stumbled upon some kind of suitors' event. And if I am going to confront him—which I will—I need to be looking my best!"

"Of course," said Celeste, marveling at the tapestries on the walls as they entered the west wing of the palace. "So, we're breaking into someone's room and stealing their clothes?"

"Shen stole *me* out of my bedroom when I was fast asleep!" Rose felt compelled to remind her friend. "Surely I can borrow his cousin's clothes for one night." She paused outside Lei Fan's bedroom but then lost her nerve. Celeste was right. This wasn't like her. It was one thing for Lei Fan to lend her a dress; it was another for Rose to simply take one without asking. . . .

Just then, the patter of light footsteps echoed down the hall. Rose and Celeste froze, flattening themselves against the wall like a pair of frightened rabbits.

There came a shadow and then a gasp. "Rose!" Lei Fan's voice rang out. "What are you doing here?"

Shen's cousin looked radiant in an orange silk ensemble. The top had a high neckline but left her shoulders and back exposed. She wore matching silk trousers that brushed against the ground, and her glossy black hair was pulled into a high ponytail that had been wrapped in gold twine.

"Hello, Lei Fan," said Rose curtly, the affection she had for her friend warring with an unpleasant feeling of betrayal. "Surprised to see me?"

"I'm thrilled to see you! I was starting to fear you weren't going to come!"

"What?" said Rose, frowning. "How could I come to something I didn't know about?"

Lei Fan's face fell. "Oh no. We need to go and find Shen."

"Wait!" Rose grabbed her hand. "First, I need your help."

"What is it?" Lei Fan said, stiffening at the panic in Rose's voice. "Is Anadawn in trouble? Is it Wren?"

Rose paused. "Well, yes to both of those things, actually." She batted them away for now. "But that isn't why I want your help. I am severely underdressed. I need to find something to wear."

Lei Fan's brows rose. "Hang on," she said, looking between them. "Were you two about to break into my bedroom?"

"Yeah, pretty much," said Celeste.

"No!" said Rose at the same time. She flushed. "We were actually hoping to bump into you here, and luckily we did!" She laughed, awkwardly. "Oh, sweet fate. How did you know to come here?"

She was answered by a low meow. Shadow, Lei Fan's cat, poked her head out from behind her legs, her wide eyes simmering with suspicion.

"Shadow came to fetch me!" said Lei Fan as though that was an entirely normal thing for a cat to do.

"Oh, you sweet little thing—you must like me more than I thought," cooed Rose, reaching down to scratch behind her ears.

"Or she doesn't like you at all and wanted you to get caught," said Celeste. She waggled her fingers at Lei Fan. "I'm Celeste, by the way. Rose's accomplice."

"My best friend," Rose clarified.

"Of course," said Lei Fan warmly. "I remember you well from the Battle of Anadawn."

"I was just telling Celeste that you have the most magnificent collection of dresses," said Rose.

Lei Fan beamed, delighted by her flattery. "If you were trying to get me on your side, then you have succeeded. Come on, I have new dresses that you haven't seen before!"

"Thank you," said Rose, eagerly following her into the bedroom.

Once inside, Lei Fan skipped across the messy floor and flung open her huge armoire.

"Take your pick," she said. "I personally think the blue silk . . . no, not that one . . . the one behind the yellow one . . . yes, there . . . would make a real statement. It would look incredible on you."

"So, what exactly is going on tonight?" said Rose as she reached for the dark blue dress. It was made of such fine silk, it nearly slipped through her fingers.

Lei Fan hesitated. "You have to understand, it's a Sunkissed Kingdom tradition . . . ," she said almost apologetically. "It's a custom for every new monarch to hold a suitors' ball."

"I knew it!" said Rose as she slipped the delicate blue dress over her head, grappling blindly with the straps.

"But what's unusual about this one is that so many foreign royals were invited," Lei Fan went on. "The King's Choice was once open only to maidens here in the Sunkissed Kingdom. But since we're ready to make our debut to the wider world, it seemed wise to use the event as an opportunity to establish relations with other nations."

"And whose bright idea was it to exclude Rose from the guest list?" said Celeste.

Lei Fan frowned. "I'm afraid I wasn't consulted on the guest list. But

I am certain you would have been invited! There must have been some mix-up. . . . You'll have to ask Shen." Then her eyes lit up. "Although if you ask him wearing *that* dress, he might not be able to form words! Oh, Rose! That is absolutely the dress for you."

"It does seem to fit rather well," Rose admitted as she admired herself in the mirror.

"It looks like it was painted on you." Celeste smirked.

Rose grinned at her reflection. The bodice was formfitting, cut daringly low at her chest and held up by gossamer-thin straps. The silk skirt hugged her hips, and there was one high slit on each side revealing the pale columns of her legs as she walked.

Lei Fan pursed her lips. "It's almost perfect." She rummaged around in a nearby jewelry box and returned with a pair of raindrop diamond earrings, each one the size of an almond. "Here, wear these. And put your hair up like this." She deftly piled Rose's hair on top of her head and secured it with a silver pin, leaving a few artful curls to hang about her face.

She leaned back and assessed her work. "There's something missing. . . . Ah! Good thing I've been practicing my enchantments."

Lei Fan pinched some sand from a jar on her nightstand and set her attention on Rose's gown, whispering a spell under her breath. The dress fluttered, and when Rose looked down, she gasped with joy. Tiny iridescent stars twinkled across the gossamer silk. As she moved, the stars did, too, like tiny starcrests casting her future in real time.

"*Oh*," Rose breathed. "This is the most beautiful dress I've ever worn. And I do own *a lot* of beautiful gowns."

"That is impressive," said Celeste, peering closer. "I can barely enchant the holes in my stockings to mend!" She looked hopefully at Lei Fan. "Do you have anything that will fit me? I know I'm not confronting my lover but—"

"Celeste!" said Rose, blushing.

"Or whatever it is you want to call Shen," she said, rolling her eyes. "But the fact remains. This is my first time in the Sunkissed Kingdom and I'd like to make an entrance, too."

Lei Fan appraised Celeste. "Yellow," she said definitively. "I have a yellow gown that will look ravishing on you."

Lei Fan was right—Celeste did look ravishing in the yellow dress. It had a square neckline and a narrow bodice that tapered in at her waist before cascading into a full skirt. Celeste twirled in the middle of the room, round and round and round, until the dress floated up and whirled around her knees. "If the dress can dance, then so can I," she proclaimed. "It's perfect!"

Rose was having such a good time getting dressed up with Lei Fan and Celeste, she almost didn't want to go back to the party.

But.

She had to see Shen.

No.

Shen had to see her.

Specifically, in *this* dress.

He had to explain himself, and this whole outrageous situation, immediately.

And then Rose needed to find the weapon she had come here for.

"I can't believe Shen Lo thought he could throw a grand party without you knowing," fumed Celeste as they left the palace and returned to the square. "I'll be right here if you need me, Rose. Just let me know if you'd rather me speak to Shen. I certainly have a thing or two I would like to say to him!"

Rose managed a smile. "You go and find Anika. I know you two left things rather unfinished in Gevra. You must have been missing her these past few months."

Celeste sighed. "Of course I would go and fall for a Gevran."

"Well, that's something you and Wren have in common," teased Rose. Thinking of her sister bolstered her now. Wren would be furious with Shen for hosting a party without inviting them. So Rose decided she would be furious, too.

Furious was better than the alternative.

Devastated.

When Rose, Celeste, and Lei Fan arrived back in the courtyard, the dancing was still well underway. Shen was in the middle of the square, spinning Princess Elladora of Demarre, whose head was thrown back in laughter. Mercifully, someone had fetched him a new shirt. For a moment, Rose wanted to pick up her skirts and run as fast as she could out of the Sunkissed Kingdom. Run all the way across the Ganyeve Desert and back to Anadawn. But this was about more than her pride. She needed a witch-made weapon, and she knew she could find one here.

But first, she needed to remind Shen of exactly who she was. And that required an entrance.

"It seems that we have one final arrival to the King's Choice," boomed the master of ceremonies. "But I'm sure we can all agree that a beautiful maiden is better late than never. Especially *this* particular maiden..."

The music stopped. Everyone paused their dancing, craning their necks to see who exactly the enthusiastic announcer was referring to.

"This is going to be fun," whispered Celeste, who was standing behind Rose.

Lei Fan called on the wind. It whistled through the winding streets of the Sunkissed Kingdom and extinguished all the lanterns until only the everlights burned. With a whispered spell and a drop of sand, Celeste extinguished those, too, and then, all was dark.

Except for Rose.

Her dress shone.

She shone.

The wind whooshed through the crowd, pushing it apart, clearing a pathway for Rose that led directly toward Shen. Holding her head high, she proceeded down the path, her dress moving daringly with each measured step. She kept her eyes on Shen and Shen alone. Even in the dark she could trace his outline, but she couldn't see his face. Only the way he stepped away from Princess Elladora and moved, almost spell-struck, toward Rose.

She saw how his arms opened in welcome, and she had to stop herself from running to him. She kept her pace steady, even as she felt the eyes of everyone on her face, her body, heard the rising hush of a thousand whispers.

"Queen Rose Valhart of Eana," cried the master of ceremonies just as Rose reached Shen.

The crowd erupted in cheers but she didn't hear them. There were only she and Shen Lo, the rest of the world falling away into nothing.

"Rose," he breathed, before bowing deep at the waist. He straightened up, caught in the glow of her dress, and she saw his face properly now. He was smiling in disbelief. "I . . . You look . . . beautiful . . . like a dream. . . ." His gaze roamed all the way down her body. He swallowed thickly. "My wildest dream."

Rose didn't smile back. She simply dipped her chin in acknowledgment of his words and then extended her hand.

Shen took it eagerly. As his lips brushed her skin, she felt her heart skip, but she kept her face neutral. Those lips had kissed many hands tonight, and that stung.

The rest of the world crept back in. The crowd grew restless, pushing closer. With a whoosh, the everlights came back on and the lanterns sparked to life. The music started up. Rose recognized the song. It was a popular Eanan dance, where one switched partners throughout. It felt especially apt.

"Aren't you going to say anything?" said Shen as he stepped toward her and raised his palm in invitation. His smile fell, his eyes darting nervously. "This must all seem rather strange to you. . . . It's strange for me, too."

Rose placed her hand against his, her skin tingling at his touch. "On the contrary," she said, trying to keep the hurt from her voice. "You seem quite in your element. Perhaps I should apologize for interrupting."

All around them, other dancers came together and began to spin.

"You're as welcome as the sunrise, Rose," said Shen, his eyes locked on hers. "I'm so glad you're here."

"If that's true, then why didn't you invite me?" Rose's lip trembled and she looked away, embarrassed to be so upset.

Shen blinked in surprise, but before he could reply, the key of the music changed. It was time to swap partners. The queen of Krale stepped forward to take Rose's place. Rose nodded respectfully and saw the Krale queen's eyes light up with recognition. "Your singing was spectacular, Queen Adrienne," said Rose, before turning to the man next to her to carry on the dance.

He had short brown hair and light brown eyes and was so tall Rose had to tip her head back to see his face. Aware that Shen was still watching her—watching them—she gave the man her most dazzling smile. "Good evening," she said coyly. "Shall we dance?"

The man beamed back at her before eagerly taking her hand. "With pleasure, Your Majesty."

He expertly spun her, and when he twirled her back to him, Rose made sure to laugh breathily. "How skilled you are, sir."

She could feel the heat of Shen's gaze on her as she twirled once more, her dress shifting to reveal her legs.

When they next switched partners, Rose found herself dancing with a beautiful witch she recognized from the Battle of Anadawn, who wore a flowing pink gown and a delicate pearl hairband, and after her, a stern-faced dancer from the Krale delegation, before finding herself again in Shen's arms.

"You always drive me to distraction," he said in a low whisper. "I love watching you dance."

"Just not enough to invite me to your ball," Rose said, through a clenched smile.

"Of course I invited you," said Shen, frowning in confusion. "I've been waiting for you all evening."

"You certainly didn't look all that impatient before," said Rose, refusing to be taken in so easily. For all she knew, he was putting on an act to placate her, and she had been made a fool of once already tonight. She glanced around and saw that Celeste had indeed found Anika, and now both girls were dancing, only they weren't following the traditional steps. Instead, they were twirling each other round and round, refusing to switch partners. Celeste was laughing, truly laughing, and the sound of her happiness at least made this evening somewhat bearable. "So, why don't you tell me what the King's Choice is *exactly*?"

Shen's face fell, guilt tugging at his jaw. "It's a silly tradition, Rose. I didn't know exactly what was involved, as I've never been to one." At Rose's unimpressed expression, he went on, desperately trying to explain himself. "My royal council insisted it would be a good idea to throw open our gates and make ourselves known on a grander stage. Not to mention it would be a clever way to establish diplomatic ties. And I trust my advisers, just as my father did."

Rose arched a brow. How ludicrous for a king not to know the goings-on in his own kingdom!

"What *precisely* did you think the King's Choice was?" said Rose icily.

"I thought it would be a party. And I thought you would be here. Since you were invited."

"And what about the performances? The show?"

"That *show* was for my kingdom," said Shen, sweeping a hand through his hair. His cheeks were flushed with embarrassment, and

Rose *almost* believed him. "I'm doing my best not to offend anyone. It's just politics. All of it. You must understand, Rose."

"*You* must understand this, Shen Lo," said Rose, rising to her tiptoes so they were eye to eye. His words might have sounded sincere but she was far too hurt—and worse, embarrassed—to consider them. "You have made a fool of me and I will not stand for it."

Shen's hands tightened on her waist. "Rose, *you* made a fool of *me*. How do you think I felt, waiting all night for you? You never even replied to the invitation!"

"How many times do I need to tell you? I never received one!" Rose said, pressing her hands against his chest to shove him away but instead finding herself caught in his night-dark gaze.

"Well, then it's my word against yours," he said.

"Says the thief."

"Says the king." Shen spun her around and then pulled her back to him, pressing his hand against the small of her back. "Please. I've been waiting all night to dance with you." Suddenly it was all too much for Rose. His hands strong and familiar on her body. His breath soft against the shell of her ear. The hard planes of his chest, the heat of him moving against her. Her silk gown was so thin, it felt as if he was caressing her bare skin.

She ached to feel his hands on her skin, his lips against hers. She ached for all of him alone in a place where they could not be interrupted.

This time, when the key changed, Shen guided Rose away from the dance floor. He led her to a spot at the edge of the courtyard, where they could still see the dancers but nobody could hear them.

"Rose, please listen," he said, his voice ragged. "The Sunkissed Kingdom has its own traditions and I'm still learning them. I only wished to honor what the kings of the past have done." He laughed at the very idea of it. "I'm just relieved Wren didn't show up with you. We both know she would never let me live down this embarrassing spectacle."

"Well, now you'll never know if either of us can swallow a sword."

Shen grinned at her quip, but then his expression grew serious. "All I want is to be a good king, Rose. The kind my mother and father would be proud of." His vulnerability cracked Rose's resolve. She knew it to be true: this desire to make his family proud, this fear that he would fall short.

She raised her hand to his cheek. "Shen, you are a good king. I've never been so certain of anything." Then she dropped her hand, looking away. "Though I am less certain about other things now...."

He frowned. "Like what?"

"Like you and me," she said, stepping back. "I saw how you watched the other women up there. How you applauded their talents and appreciated their beauty. How you gazed longingly at the queen of Krale as she performed her love song!"

"That's because I was thinking of you!" he said, as though it was supposed to be obvious.

Rose folded her arms. "What about the sword lady?"

"That was impressive, you have to admit," he reasoned. "Impossible to look away from, really."

"I suppose it was ... unique," Rose allowed. "But the stars? You certainly seemed enamored with Elladora!"

Shen flashed a dimple. "I was thinking those flying stars would be a clever weapon for *you*. Their grace and delicacy ... they would suit you, Rose. I'm going to have a set made in time for your next—"

"I'm a witch, Shen," Rose said with a huff. "I don't need a weapon." Then she remembered why she was here. "Wait. Actually, now that you mention it—"

"Say that again," Shen interrupted, pulling her close again.

"What?" she said, flustered.

"That you're a witch. I never tire of hearing it." He laid his forehead against hers. "And do you know why?"

She didn't move away. "You are insufferable, that's why."

"Because I love that you know who you are now," he went on. "I love that you have embraced your true soul, Rose. Your true power. You're one of the most incredible witches I've ever encountered."

The word *love* echoed in Rose's ears, and she wished he would say more. Say that he loved *her* so they could at last stop playing this silly game.

"How could you ever doubt my feelings for you?" His voice was stricken, his inky gaze pouring into hers. "When you're here you're the only one I can look at. Everything else—everyone else—falls away."

They gazed at each other, and Rose felt the rest of her resolve crumbling. She wanted to forgive Shen, and more important, she still hadn't told him her real reason for coming. She hadn't told him about Oonagh and—

"Excuse me?"

Rose snapped her head up at the sound of a new voice. Princess Elladora was sidling over to join them, a coy smile on her face. Rose jumped back from Shen as if she'd been burned.

"I'm sorry to interrupt," said Elladora, although she clearly wasn't. "But King Shen and I didn't get to finish our dance." She gave Rose a meaningful look.

"Princess Elladora," said Rose stiffly. "What a long time it has been. You are looking well."

"And you," said Elladora. "Who knew that dear little Rose would grow up to reveal so many . . . surprises?" Her smiled sharpened. "A secret twin! Witches on the throne of Eana! When my father heard, he spat out his soup. We could hardly believe it."

"It has been a time of great change in Eana," said Rose tersely. "But all for the good. We look forward to continuing our strong allyship with Demarre."

"As do we," said Elladora. "And we are keen to build new relations with the Sunkissed Kingdom." Her eyes raked over Shen. "A powerful new ally, to be sure."

Rose's nostrils flared. She had to stop herself from physically stepping in front of Elladora to block her view of Shen.

"Your Majesty, we must continue our dance," said Elladora, holding her hand out to Shen. "Otherwise, it would be a most inauspicious start."

Shen cleared his throat. "Ah . . ."

"You are aware my father boasts a larger navy than even Gevra," said Elladora. "We are a strong ally indeed. As I'm sure you know."

"Seeing as the Sunkissed Kingdom is landlocked, I doubt they have much use for boats," said Rose.

"On the contrary, they will need boats all the more. So that they may rely on more than just Eana to sustain their trade," said Elladora, all too sweetly, ". . . and other pursuits."

Rose bristled. "We also have boats. Many boats. So many boats."

"Not as many as we do."

"Shall we carry on this conversation about boats at another time?" said Shen, stepping into the space between them.

"Once we finish our dance," said Elladora, taking his hand and pulling him away. "Come. I've asked the minstrels to play a traditional Demarre waltz."

"Ah, what a *shame*. I'm afraid I don't know any Demarre dances," said Shen, trying to wriggle free of her grasp.

"It will be my pleasure to instruct you," said Elladora, tugging until he gave way to her.

Rose blinked in surprise as Shen trailed after the triumphant princess. Turning around, he caught Rose's eye. "*I'm sorry*," he mouthed. "*Stay here.*"

Rose glared at the back of his head. She had no intention of waiting around for him. She knew where she could find a weapon. She would simply go and borrow one and return it when she was done. And she didn't need Shen Lo's permission for that.

21

WREN

As Wren entered the mouth of the Mishnick Mountains, she felt as though she were stepping into the heart of Eana itself. She tipped her head back, marveling at the thundering waterfall that gushed down from above. Around her, the walls were hung with the most beautiful tapestries she had ever seen: sweeping landscapes of the surrounding valleys scattered with imagined green-tailed hawks and golden eagles.

There were everlights everywhere. Flames flickered from hundreds of alcoves that climbed up and out of view. Some even burned behind the waterfall, turning the water to a soft, shimmering silver. The cool air smelled like magic. Wren could feel it tingling all around her, like fireflies flitting just out of reach.

She closed her eyes, and beneath the rush of water, heard the faint echo of music. "Someone is singing."

The young healer, who had introduced herself as Maeva, smiled. "Not someone. The mountains are singing."

"Do they always do that?" said Alarik uneasily.

"When they're happy," said Maeva. "So long as there is harmony here, there is music."

"Just like the desert," said Wren, seized by a renewed rush of love for her ancient country.

"Where does the water come from?" asked Tor, running his hand through the silver mist.

Maeva's smile broadened. Wren couldn't help but notice how her gaze lingered on Tor. She ignored the pinch of jealousy in her gut. "The magic here works in mysterious ways," said Maeva. "The water that flows from these mountains is the clearest in the land. It has many healing properties."

"Remarkable," murmured Tor, who was still studying the mist and not the beautiful healer making moon-eyes at him.

At the other end of the cavern, narrow passages branched off in several different directions, tunneling deeper into the mountain. Maeva led them toward the one in the middle, where a young man in matching robes was waiting for them.

He looked a lot like Maeva, with tousled golden hair, round cheeks, and sky-blue eyes. A brother or cousin, perhaps. He bowed to Wren but did not speak. She thought, perhaps, he was too shy.

"Arlo will take you to see the Healer on High," said Maeva. "But first, we must ask you to lay down your weapons."

Tor stiffened.

"No," said Alarik.

Maeva cleared her throat, looking suddenly uncomfortable.

"You see, we are Gevran," Alarik went on. "And an unarmed Gevran is usually a dead one."

Maeva looked to Arlo. The young man pressed his lips together and shook his head. He would not let them pass.

"Is it really necessary?" said Wren. "After what we just encountered in the valley, we'd feel much safer with them in our possession. I can assure you they won't hurt anyone."

Maeva was unmoved. "It is the rule of the mountains, Your Majesty. The Healer on High asks that you lay down your worldly weapons upon entry here. It has been this way since the dawn of Eana. She gestured toward the center of the waterfall. "Look, there. Do you see it?"

Wren squinted. "See what?"

"This is a poor attempt at distraction," said Alarik.

"There's a sword," said Tor, spotting it at once. "It's embedded in the rock behind the waterfall."

Wren's eyes widened. Tor was right. There, behind reams of water, she could just make out the golden hilt of a sword. "Where did that come from?"

Maeva turned on Wren, her brows raised. "Don't you know the story, Your Majesty?"

Wren bristled, cursing herself for not paying more attention to Thea when she spoke of the legends of old. As much as she loved her grandmother's wife, Thea did have a way of prattling on, and Wren always found her mind drifting to other matters: food, adventure, the magic of the here and now. "Of course I know the story," she said archly. "I have just momentarily forgotten the details of it. I've had a lot on my mind lately."

Alarik snorted.

She stamped on his foot.

"*Witch*," he hissed.

"Remind me," Wren urged the healer.

CATHERINE DOYLE & KATHERINE WEBBER

She nodded graciously. "The sword you see behind the falls is called Night's Edge. Legend says it was carved from the underside of the moon and imbued with its ever-glowing light. When the first witch, Eana, left the stars to come to earth, the moon gifted the sword to her. So that it might light the way ahead and help her carve out a new home far beyond the edge of darkness."

Wren couldn't stop staring at the sword hilt. Her fingers itched to trace it, to hoist Night's Edge just as her ancestor once did. This was the closest she had ever come to the first witch, and the nearness of her memory filled Wren with a thrill of excitement.

Maeva went on. "When Eana landed in the ocean on her green-tailed hawk, she used her magic to turn the bird into a land that soon filled with rivers and lakes, forests and flowers. But the winds of our young country were strong and the nights were bitterly cold. In the beginning, Eana was alone. She was lonely. And so, she sought shelter, a place of peace and healing that would help her prepare for her new life.

"She stalked the far reaches of her kingdom, until one day, she heard singing. A sound so pure, it brought tears to her eyes. It was neither bird nor human. The mountains were calling her, and so she came."

Wren glanced sidelong at Tor and Alarik. They were enraptured, leaning into Maeva's tale as though they had never heard a story before. Even Elske had fallen quiet at their feet, her ears pricked up as if she was listening, too.

"For three days and three nights Eana traveled through the Mishnick Mountains, searching for a way in, but there was none."

"But where there's a sword, there's a way," murmured Wren.

Maeva smiled. "Finally, on the third day, Eana raised her sword and with Night's Edge cut an entrance into the mountains. The rock fell away, revealing great caverns that wound deep into the new earth. Her relief was so great that she came to her knees and wept. The tears of Eana gathered and became a waterfall. Ever flowing, ever clear. The mountains became her sanctuary, a sacred place of healing. As a tribute to them and the peace they brought her, Eana left her sword in the rock." Maeva gestured once more to the sword glinting behind the waterfall. "It remains here to this day."

"Impossible," breathed Alarik.

"Every word is true," Maeva insisted. "It is written in our annals."

"Not the magic stuff," he said, swishing his hand. "Trust me, I've seen enough magic to believe in it. What I find impossible to believe is that a sword so powerful has remained there, untouched for so long." He exchanged a knowing look with Tor. "*Surely* someone has thought to take it for themselves?"

"Don't you have any unruly children here?" said Tor.

"Or unruly men?" said Wren.

Maeva's laugh echoed back at them from the cavern walls. "Many have tried to free the sword," she said. "But Night's Edge belongs to the mountain. It is part of the rock. It does not yield."

Tor cracked his knuckles, staring at the sword as if it were an adversary. "I'm sure it would with the right pressure."

"You are welcome to try," said Maeva, with a smirk that implied she had seen many men like Tor try and fail. "But for now, the Healer on High is waiting and she does not suffer lateness." She looked apologetically at Wren. "Even from queens."

Wren shooed the men on. "Let's please keep our priorities in order."

"I would invite you again to stow your weapons," Maeva reminded them. Now that they had heard the story of Eana and her sword, it seemed Tor and Alarik were more receptive to the idea of laying down their own weapons.

Alarik removed his sword and placed it against the cavern wall. "This blade is worth more than your precious mountains," he warned. "If I see so much as a scratch on it there will be trouble."

Tor placed his sword beside it. Then he removed a knife from his boot and a dagger from his inside pocket.

"That wasn't so hard, was it?" said Wren brightly.

Arlo gave her a stern look.

"What?" said Wren.

He pointed at the faint outline of the hilt at Wren's waist.

Tor laughed.

Alarik clucked his tongue. "A queen who doesn't even follow her own rules."

"Oh, shut up." With little ceremony, Wren hiked up her skirts and grappled for her dagger, trying to free it from the band of her dress. Arlo blushed, furiously, averting his gaze.

Alarik watched Wren. "You really are feral."

Tor stepped in front of him, blocking his view.

Wren freed the dagger and chucked it with the others. She refixed her skirts. "Happy now?"

Arlo didn't budge. He pointed at the wolf.

Tor bristled. "The wolf is not a weapon."

"She is my royal adviser," added Wren.

Arlo frowned, then reluctantly turned on his heel. They followed him down an arched tunnel lit by everlights. Every so often, the passage branched off into another smaller cavern, where healers milled about, chatting and laughing among themselves.

At last, they came to an entryway, hung with long drapes. Arlo pushed it aside, bidding them to follow him inside. The chamber was high and domed and roughly the size of Wren's bedroom at Anadawn. The walls were hung with more beautiful artwork while the ground was covered with a decorative rug. The room was lit with so many everlights, it seemed at first to Wren like a place of worship, but there were signs of life here. Several plush chairs were arranged around a wooden table that had been set for tea. The Healer on High stood beside it, teapot in hand. At the sound of their arrival, she set it down gently.

"Your Majesty," she said, dipping her chin. Her voice was low and soothing, like a lullaby. "Welcome to the Mishnick Mountains."

Wren was surprised by how familiar the Healer on High looked. She had light brown skin and warm brown eyes set in a deeply wrinkled face. Her white hair was arranged in long braids that were twisted and pinned, like a crown, to her head. When she smiled she looked just like Thea.

"*Oh*," said Wren.

"The Queensbreath and I are cousins," said the Healer on High, reading the surprise in Wren's eyes. "My name is Willa. Thea and I spent our early years together in these mountains. My seer strand is stronger than I'd hoped. I had a sense you might be coming to visit us." Her gaze flicked to Alarik. She looked him up and down. "Though I did not foresee any Gevrans. Or wolves."

"Don't our ugly green uniforms fool you?" said Alarik mockingly.

Willa snorted. "Perhaps they would if you weren't the spitting image of your father, King Alarik." She gestured at Tor. "And he's built like an ice bear."

"We couldn't risk the truth being intercepted by someone else," said Wren, suddenly unsure of where to begin. "You see . . . uh . . . we've . . . uh . . . got ourselves into a . . . situation."

"*She* got us into a situation," Alarik corrected her. "I was merely an innocent bystander."

Wren rolled her eyes. "*He's* the troublesome one."

"Hmm. Yes. I can sense trouble here." Willa frowned as she looked between them. Her expression soured, as if she could taste something bitter in the air. Then she looked up at Tor, scanning him from head to toe. "You are well," she muttered, more to herself than to them. "Strong heartbeat. Hmm. Yes. Clear soul."

Tor raised his brows. "Er, thank you?"

"No need to gloat," said Alarik.

"You may leave us." Willa dismissed Tor with a flick of her wrist. "Arlo will take you to the dining hall."

Once Tor and Elske had left, the Healer on High turned her attention back to Wren and Alarik. "There is a wrongness here," she said plainly. "A shadow that is not welcome."

Wren looked at Alarik. In his gaze, she saw the reflection of her own fear.

"Let me see what I can find out." Willa took their hands in hers. She turned them over, inspecting their matching scars. Her frown deepened. "What have you two been up to . . . ?"

Wren's cheeks heated in shame.

"Why do I have a feeling you already know?" said Alarik.

Willa didn't answer him. She closed her eyes, her frown sharpening until her brows touched. She began to mutter, speaking so quickly and quietly, it was impossible to make out the words. Wren's wrist started to sting. She ground her teeth, trying to bear the pain, but tears pricked her eyes.

When she looked at Alarik, his jaw was clenched. "Hold your nerve," he said, through his teeth.

But Wren's breath was shallowing in her chest. She could feel the healer prodding at the darkness inside her. Angering it. Black spots swam in the sides of her vision. The pain was taking over. She started to sway.

"Wren," said Alarik. *"Stay."*

Suddenly, Willa snapped her hands away. "A blood spell," she said, with such horror she took a step back. "And not any blood spell. One to raise the dead. What on earth possessed you?"

Wren glared at Alarik.

"Is that relevant?" he said hotly. "It's done now."

"But its shadow remains," said Willa. "It's gnawing at your souls."

Alarik frowned. "That's the first I've heard of having one."

"This is no trifling matter," said Willa. She looked to Wren, who was still swaying on her feet. Willa's face changed from anger to concern. "Sit. Sip. And tell me of the spell."

Wren and Alarik sat down, reaching for cups of tea. Wren sipped, detecting the faint scent of lavender. She felt herself relax. Beside her, Alarik gulped his tea as if he were dying of thirst.

Perhaps he was in more pain than Wren thought.

As they sat and drank their tea, Wren told Willa all about their ill-conceived blood spell. Every time she caught the healer's admonishing glare, she felt like an unruly child who had been found stealing apples from the orchard. Perhaps this was why Wren left out the part about accidentally awakening Oonagh Starcrest in the mountains, and only told Willa about raising Ansel from the dead, which had, of course, turned out to be a colossal disaster.

"So *you* cast a blood spell with *Alarik's* blood," said Willa, once Wren had finished. She sat back in her chair as if she was exhausted from the mere listening to the tale. "That explains the link between you."

"Have you ever heard of something like this happening before?" said Wren.

The healer shook her head. "The witches of Eana have long known what happens when you tamper with blood sacrifice. Therein only evil lies."

"Right. Of course."

"And to even *attempt* such a dangerous spell with a mortal." Willa shook her head. "A *Gevran*. It is unheard of."

"What will it do?" said Alarik, who could no longer hide his anxiety. "This thing inside us."

The healer was silent a moment. "I expect it will kill you."

Wren went rigid in her seat. Hearing the words spoken so plainly and true sent a fissure of alarm through her. "But surely you can help us," she said. "You can heal us, can't you?"

The Healer on High sighed. "Whatever this is, it is beyond even my capabilities."

"No," said Alarik, leaping from the chair. "There must be *something* you can do." He began to pace. "If your mountains can sing and your witches can make waterfalls with their tears, then you can heal this sickness inside us. You're a witch. A *healer*. The best one in Eana by all accounts. This is what you do. So *do* it," he growled.

Willa cocked her head. "Are you finished?"

"That depends. Do you finally have something useful to offer?" he bit back.

"Alarik!" snapped Wren. "This isn't helping!"

Willa drummed her fingers against her teacup, waiting for the king to stop pacing and settle down. Wren tugged his sleeve, urging him to sit on the armrest of her chair. She held her hand on his wrist to keep him there.

Willa went on. "These mountains are the oldest in all of Eana. They possess a magic that far outweighs my own. It is this magic that you both need."

"So, there is a way to heal us?" said Wren hopefully.

"There may yet be. . . ." Willa leaned forward, steepling her hands in front of her lips. "You must journey deep under the mountain to the healing baths. To soak in the waters of the mountains is to bathe in the purest and oldest magic in the land. They are, as you say, Eana's tears." She shot a pointed look at Alarik. "If you are fortunate, the water will dissolve the darkness inside you and unknit the curse you have placed upon yourselves."

"Good. All right," said Alarik, perking up once more. "For how long?"

"Until the water runs black."

Wren frowned. "You want us to *bathe* together?"

Willa crooked a silver brow. "Is that somehow more scandalous to you than colluding with a foreign king to cast a forbidden blood spell that once destroyed the very fabric of the kingdom that you are supposed to protect and rule?"

"Well, not when you put it like that," Wren mumbled into her cup.

Alarik rested his hand on her shoulder, his mood appearing to be much brighter now that Willa had offered them a kernel of hope. "Wren's just unsettled because she's afraid she's going to fall in love with me."

Wren spat out a mouthful of tea.

The king laughed. The sound was a pleasant trill of relief, and despite her deep offense, Wren found herself laughing, too.

"I wouldn't be so confident if I were you," Wren warned him. "You're a Gevran. If you bathe in Eana's tears you might curl up in smoke."

"And you might burst into flames," he shot back.

As the Healer on High watched them bicker, a curious look dawned in her eyes. Wren wondered if Willa could sense something else stirring between them, but she was too afraid to ask.

"Right, then, witch," said Alarik. "Let's get this over with."

ROSE

Rose looked for Celeste in the crowded courtyard but she was nowhere to be seen. Tellingly, neither was Princess Anika. Well, at least Rose knew Celeste would be fine. Rose could look for her after she found the weapon she had come here for. Rose knew that one weapon likely wasn't going to be enough to take down Oonagh, but it would be a start. If Thea said they needed a witch-made weapon to kill an undead witch, then Rose knew they would not be able to kill Oonagh without it.

Now if she could only remember her way to that marvelous armory Shen had shown her the first time she came here. Rose turned on her heel, frowning as she tried to recall which pathway would lead her in the right direction.

A shadow appeared behind her. "Rose? I thought you were waiting for me."

Shen Lo reached for her.

Rose snatched her hand away. "You think a lot of things, Shen Lo. That doesn't make them true."

Shen sighed. "Don't be angry with me for dancing with Elladora," he said, with mounting frustration. "She nearly tugged my arm off. And the last thing I want to do is anger the king of Demarre. You know how notoriously sensitive he is. I thought you'd appreciate that."

She glared at him. "You thought I'd appreciate you leaving me to go and dance with one of your preening admirers?"

"I'm practicing the art of diplomacy." He frowned. "Perhaps I'm not very good at it."

"What you are is dishonest," said Rose. "To call all of those princesses and queens from their homelands and make them think they're making a strategic alliance with you."

"It's not like that," Shen insisted. "I may not be romancing them or intending to ask for their hand in marriage, but I *am* building alliances with them. My kingdom has to trade, Rose. It has to thrive. And for that to happen, the world needs to know about us."

"Then why didn't you just throw a party? Why did it have to be the King's Choice?"

Shen ran his hand through his hair. "You know the title wasn't my idea. It's an ancient tradition. And the truth is, the tradition matters to my people," he went on. "Once I realized what it truly meant, I tried to call it off, but Grandmother Lu counseled me to recognize the importance of the custom even if I don't plan to avail myself of it. During my father's King's Choice, the storm my mother brewed was the most magnificent one anyone had ever seen. She made the lightning dance and the wind sing, creating an entire orchestra out of the elements. As soon as my father saw her, he declared her his queen."

Shen's eyes softened as he recounted his parents' love story.

"Though it might seem silly to me, and to you, it's a way to honor their memory—to honor the ball that has helped sustain this kingdom for hundreds of years."

"And the flirting?" said Rose. "Is that honoring tradition?"

He rubbed the back of his neck. "I was only trying to be welcoming."

Rose snorted.

"Would you have preferred I turned my back on them?"

"Yes," said Rose.

Now Shen snorted. "I hear you've been hosting Prince Felix of Caro," he said pointedly. "How is that any different?"

"It is different because *I* am not giving Prince Felix false hope," she snapped. "I'll have you know I have been rebuffing his advances, as easily and as often as swatting fruit flies in summer! And thank goodness, because Prince Felix has turned out to be a truly terrible palace guest." She stiffened as she remembered his confession about how he had gone through her post. And then there was that crumpled paper in his fist . . . Oh! Shen had invited her after all. *Oh, dear.* Well, there were more important things to discuss with Shen now; she didn't need to tell him right at this moment that she had been in the wrong.

Shen bristled. "What do you mean? Has he threatened you? Hurt you?"

"I'm fine," said Rose. "But he lit the stables on fire this morning."

"He did *what?*"

"I handled it. Well. Along with Wren. And Captain Iversen."

"The Gevran? What's he doing at Anadawn?" Shen's frown deepened. "Rose. What else aren't you telling me?"

"That is why I'm here!" said Rose exasperatedly. "I've come to tell you everything!" She glanced around. "But not here. Is there some-where more private we can go?"

Shen raised a suggestive brow.

Rose whacked him on the arm. "Shen! This is serious!"

"I'm being serious," he said. Then he took her by the hand, and this time, she let him. "This way," he said. "I know just the place. I've been meaning to show it to you."

Rose knew she should be asking Shen to take her to the armory straightaway, but her curiosity was piqued. A part of her wanted to stay in this moment with Shen a little while longer, and pretend that disaster wasn't knocking at their door. Once she told him about Oonagh, well, that would make it real. And she wasn't quite ready for that. She'd tell him once they were in private together, she reasoned with herself. Surely ten minutes wouldn't make a difference.

"How did you manage to get away from Elladora?" said Rose as they walked.

"I thanked her for the dance and told her I looked forward to our kingdoms trading together," said Shen. "Then I ran like the wind before she could catch me again."

Rose bit back her smile.

Shen slipped between two overhanging hedges and pushed open a creaking gate, leading Rose down a path she'd never seen before. Soon, they arrived at a low glass building that seemed to go on forever. It was filled with thousands of plants that sprawled and pressed against the windows, as if they were peering out at them.

"Is this a greenhouse?" said Rose.

"Of sorts," said Shen, leading her inside, where the air was warm and humid. "I've been learning more about the Sunkissed Kingdom. About our treasures. Our history. To me, this place is the most magical in the entire city. It's because of this place that my kingdom was able to grow food beneath the desert. Despite not having a true sun, they were able to create life here. To sustain it." Shen gestured to an endless row of orange and lemon trees. "The plants here have thrived, despite adversity. The same is true of my people."

"It's extraordinary." Rose marveled at the troughs of vegetables and the trees hanging overhead. She spied bright red chili peppers and bulbs of garlic and onions.

They followed the citrus trees deeper into the greenhouse. Far above the trees, beyond the glass, the stars looked bigger than ever, their brightness magnified by the arched roof.

"The last time I was in Anadawn I stole something from you."

"Spoken like a true bandit." Rose glanced sidelong at him, surprised to see that he was serious. "What did you take?"

He smiled then. "A rose clipping from your garden."

"You stole from the royal gardens of Anadawn?" She clucked her tongue. "Chapman would be very displeased."

"And you? Are you angry at me?"

"For stealing a flower? No." Her face fell as she thought of her beloved rose garden that had been ruined by Oonagh. They turned a corner and Rose stopped in her tracks. A towering rosebush stood before her, covered in crimson blooms. "Oh," she whispered, her eyes misting. "It's beautiful."

"That's part of the magic of this place," said Shen. "We can grow anything in any season and quickly, too, with the right care. When I became king, there were no roses in this entire kingdom, and I wanted something to remind me of you."

Rose trailed her finger against the soft petals. "I love it."

Shen turned to her, his gaze full of longing. She let him brush a strand of hair behind her ear, her heart fluttering as he traced her jaw with his thumb. "Now it's the second-most beautiful thing in this greenhouse."

As he gazed at her with those night-dark eyes, Rose felt like a melting candle. Burning bright but still soft and pliable, as if he could mold her in his hands if he wanted.

Shen traced her bottom lip, gently tugging her mouth open. She closed her eyes as he leaned in, pressing his mouth to hers. She sighed with pleasure as their tongues met, losing herself in the heat of his kiss. She ran her hands up his arms, reveling in the feel of their strength as they tightened around her waist.

"I'm still angry at you," she whispered against his lips. "Don't think that because I'm kissing you that I forgive you."

"I would never assume such a thing," he said, kissing her again. "But I will say, if this is how you act when you're angry at me, I can't wait to see what you do when you're happy with me."

"Maybe you should try harder to make me happy, then." Rose smiled as he planted a trail of kisses along her neck. As their tongues met once more, Shen pulled her closer, groaning as he lifted her off her feet and pressed her up against the glass. Rose swung her legs out behind him, accidentally toppling a flowerpot. It fell with a crash, startling them from their kiss.

"Stars!" she cried as the world filtered back in. "We're in a glass house! Anyone could walk by and see us!"

"And?" Shen appeared unmoved. "Perhaps I want someone to see us. Perhaps I want the entire kingdom to see us. Then everyone will know who I choose."

Rose stilled, her heart thundering in her chest. "Don't jest, Shen."

He gently set her down. "I've never been more serious about anything," he said, taking her hands in his. "I choose you, Rose. I chose you the moment you leaped off Storm in the desert, ready to fight me with nothing but a fistful of sand. I chose you when you healed me in Balor's Eye, without even knowing that you could. I chose you when you climbed down the Whisperwind Cliffs, even though you were terrified. I chose you when you found love in your heart for the sister you never knew, when you opened yourself up to the witches and welcomed the truth of who you truly are." He drew a shuddering breath. "I chose you when you saved me here in my own kingdom, when I was too pigheaded and stubborn to see the truth of my uncle's betrayal."

He squeezed her hands. "I choose you, Rose Valhart, and I will never stop choosing you. I promise you that. And this: I will do whatever I can in my power to bring you happiness, to keep you safe, and to make you mine."

Rose's eyes prickled, her heart so full, she feared it might burst. In all the time she had known Shen, she'd never heard him speak with such conviction. She hadn't realized how much she had been yearning to hear him say these things, how badly she'd wanted to know how much she meant to him.

He cupped her face, laying his forehead against hers. "This place might be my kingdom but you are my world, Rose. I love you."

"Oh, Shen!" Rose threw her arms around him and kissed him hungrily, as if she could swallow the words he was saying and keep them inside her forever.

After a moment, he pulled back, breaking the kiss. He gazed down at her, his eyes molten with lust. "'Oh, Shen'?" he said, grinning. "That's all I get?"

"Oh . . . I . . . well . . . I . . ." The words Rose longed to say suddenly felt trapped in her throat. The air in here was warm and heady with the scent of desert roses. Everything felt like a dream, as if time was slowing down around them. There was nothing to fear. Only the truth of her feelings, and once she realized there was nothing scary about that, the words came pouring out. "I love you, Shen Lo. More than I ever thought I could love anyone. I didn't even know I could feel like this. That my heart could feel so full and still hunger for more of you."

"It will get even better," Shen whispered in her ear. "I promise you that."

Rose wished they could stay like this forever, just the two of them secreted away in their glass bubble, but anxiety stirred in the pit of her stomach. The nearness of Shen's desert roses was a constant reminder of what had happened to Rose's own just a few days ago. How Oonagh had ripped through the royal gardens like a cruel winter storm, destroying the flowers and all the life that thrived there. Rose could ignore it no longer—she had come here with a purpose, and it was time to reveal it.

"I need to tell you why I'm here," she said, pulling away from Shen. Her voice grew cold, her body, too. "About why Felix tried to burn down the stables. About Wren. Oh, Shen, there's so much you need to know."

Shen's entire body was coiled with tension. "You're scaring me."

"Good. You should be afraid. We all should," said Rose. "Oonagh Starcrest is back, and she wants war. She's coming back to Eana, to Anadawn. She has already been once." She brushed the tendrils of hair from her shoulder to reveal the marks on her neck.

Shen stilled, rage flashing in his eyes. "She did this to you?"

His voice was low, dangerous.

Rose nodded. "Yes."

He stared at her. "And you waited until *now* to tell me?"

"Well, when I arrived you were a little busy watching women swallow swords and such. . . ." She trailed off. She knew how petulant she sounded. How ridiculous she was acting, but she couldn't help it. "And then Elladora wanted her waltz."

"This is serious, Rose. You've been hurt." He traced his thumb along the marks, his gentle touch at odds with the murder in his eyes. He bit off a curse. "I'll kill her," he said, more to himself than to Rose. "I swear I'll kill her."

Rose caught his hand to keep him from punching a window. "I was hoping you'd say that."

"Tell me everything," he said.

And so she did. Rose told Shen about Oonagh's visitation, and the threat she had made about returning to snatch her throne back. About Wren's curse and Alarik's visit, including their trip to the Mishnick Mountains. She told him that their undead ancestor was out there, raising an army of her own. That Oonagh intended to fight for the throne. That they would need every willing witch and soldier to defeat her, but more important than even that, they would need a witch-made weapon to kill her. That without the blow from a witch-made weapon, Oonagh could never truly die.

When she was finished, Shen slumped to the floor and took a moment to weather the news.

Rose wrung her hands, waiting for him to say something. Anything. When he didn't, she attempted to lighten the mood. "If you do this for me—for Eana—if you pledge to help us find and defeat Oonagh once and for all, then I promise I will forgive you for this horrendously insensitive celebration."

He looked up at her. "How can you joke at a time like this?"

Rose bit her lip. "Well . . . what's the alternative?"

He shook his head, a reluctant smile coming to his lips. "Of course I'm going to help you." He stood. "I'd never let you do this alone. If my heart is going to war, then so am I."

Rose wrapped her arms around him. "Thank you," she whispered.

"But I'll take your forgiveness all the same," he said, pressing a kiss to the crown of her head.

She smiled against his chest. "Don't forget—I also need a weapon."

"We'll go straight to the armory."

There was a loud creak as the door to the greenhouse swung open.

"Leave us!" called Shen.

"Absolutely not." Rose turned around at the sound of Celeste's voice. "We've been looking all over for you two!"

"Did you stop to consider that perhaps we were hiding for a reason?" called Shen as Celeste came into view with Anika right behind her.

Rose frantically fixed her skirts and smoothed her hair, but she could do little for her flushed cheeks.

"Shen Lo, you are shameless," crowed Anika, looking between them. "Making us all perform our little tricks for you and then hiding in the greenhouse with the true object of your affection."

"Hello, Anika," said Rose politely. "It's good to see you, even in these circumstances." And it was good. Rose felt strangely bolstered by the sight of the red-haired Gevran princess, knowing that they were at least united on two counts: their love for Celeste and their disdain for Oonagh.

"It's always good to see me," said Anika, tossing her hair. "Unless you're one of my many enemies, of course."

"I must ask," said Rose. "What was your talent?"

"Oh, the best one." Anika smiled coyly. "My darling fox did a little dance—and then I stood on a horse as it leaped over a wall."

"It was very impressive," admitted Shen.

"Not good enough to win the King's Choice, clearly," said Anika, with a wink. "Never mind. You're not my type anyway—no offense. Now. Enough pleasantries." Anika turned on Rose. "Celeste says you intend to fight your wretched undead ancestor."

Rose nodded. "Once I find the weapon I need."

Anika's lip curled. "That destructive creature has been terrorizing my country for months. We've tried to kill her, with no luck."

"Don't worry," said Shen, leading the way to the armory. "We're about to change that."

23

WREN

The Healer on High rang a bell on the side table, and Maeva returned to collect Wren and Alarik. Wren's stomach knotted as she led them deeper into the mountains, down a winding tunnel that seemed to go on forever. It got darker and warmer until the humid air curled the wayward strands around Wren's face.

Alarik walked alongside her, silent as stone. She watched him from the corner of her eye, trying to read his face in the dimness. His jaw was tight, and his fists were clenched. He must be nervous, too. After all, they were as far from Gevra as they had ever been and Alarik was placing his life—his *fate*—in the hands of witches he knew next to nothing about. A small part of Wren admired him for that.

At last, they reached the end of the tunnel, which spilled out into a cavern that contained a large crystalline pool. The everlights here refracted off hundreds of precious crystals embedded in the rock. They looked like stars, casting the pool in a soft, silvery glow.

Alarik walked along the edge of the bath, running his hand through the steam. "At least it's warm," he said, breaking the strange tension that had followed them under the mountain.

"And healing," Maeva reminded him. "These are Eana's tears, after all."

"So you've said." He turned to look at Wren. "It's not like you to be so quiet."

"I'm just . . . taking it all in," said Wren uncertainly. Now that the reality of what they were about to do was dawning on her, she was feeling squeamish. The cavern was completely empty, save for the three of them, and though the steam was thick, she would still be able to see Alarik through it. Without a shirt. And he would be able to see her, too.

"You're blushing," said Alarik.

Wren scowled at him. "It's hot, that's all. I *don't* blush."

"My mistake." He turned away but not before Wren caught the edge of his smirk.

Arrogant ass.

Maeva cleared her throat. "I'll leave you both. There's a chamber to the side where you can change," she said to Wren. "I'll send someone to come and collect your clothes so that they may be washed and cleaned."

"Thank you," said Wren. "I'm sure you've noticed that the king smells like dung."

"Not unlike the kind that comes out of your queen's mouth," added Alarik. "Perhaps you should wash that, too."

Maeva bit her lip, unsure of where to look. Wren could tell their banter was making her uncomfortable.

"You may go," she said, doing the girl a kindness. "I'm afraid Alarik's only going to get worse in these acoustics. He loves the echo of his own voice."

Maeva shuffled away from them. "Willa says to soak until the water turns black. With any luck, you'll be up in time for dinner."

"Thank you, Maeva," said Alarik, with unusual politeness. "In the meantime, you might see to my Captain of the Guard. I'm sure he would quite enjoy some company."

At the mention of Tor, Maeva flushed bright red. Wren wanted to shove Alarik straight into the water but instead turned around and stomped off toward the side chamber, trying to ignore the irritating echo of his laughter.

Wren peeled off her dress and unbraided her hair, running her fingers through the tangles. Then she kicked off her shoes and socks. She resolved to keep on her underwear and chemise, lest the king get any wrong ideas. The very thought of it brought back the memory of their blizzard kiss.

"*Stop it,*" Wren scolded herself. That was the last thing she needed to be thinking about right now. She hadn't come here to bathe with the king. She had come here to get rid of the curse she had accidentally cast the day they raised Ansel from the dead.

Any thoughts of kissing were unhelpful and distracting and—

"Have you fallen down a crevasse over there?" called Alarik.

"I'm changing," Wren called back. "Mind your business!"

"You are my business, Wren."

Wren grabbed a towel, covering herself on the short walk back across the cavern. Thankfully, the steam was so thick, she could barely see a foot in front of her own face.

She could tell by the sound of rippling water that Alarik was already immersed in the bath. "Well? How is it?"

"Wet."

"Thanks for that." Wren dropped her towel and found the stone steps, following them down into the water. The first flush of heat stole up her legs, wrenching a sigh from her. *"Oh."*

Wren didn't realize how weary she was until the water was lapping at her skin. First her calves and then her knees. Another step, and it was at her hips, and then her stomach. She pushed off the edge, letting the water come up to her neck. She tipped her head back, immersing herself fully.

Salt crystals kissed her skin as she kicked her legs up, floating like a fallen leaf. She sighed again, long and languid.

Alarik stilled in the water. "What are you doing?"

Wren had almost forgotten he was there. "Enjoying the silence. Don't ruin it."

His laugh found her through the steam. She could tell he was close by, but she couldn't see him.

She closed her eyes. "How do you feel?"

"Damp."

"Be serious."

"I don't know." He was farther away now. "Not terrible, I suppose."

Wren turned around, searching for him in the curling mist. She followed his voice, wading toward a ledge at the back of the cavern, until the bath got so deep she had to walk on her tiptoes. Alarik was sitting at the edge of the pool. The water was at his chest, his arms splayed out along the rock behind him. Silver crystals clustered around his head like a crown. His hair was wet and slicked back from his face, revealing the exquisite lines of his bone structure.

"Stop staring at me," he said.

"I'm staring *past* you."

"Whatever you say, witch."

Wren tried to stick her tongue out but she swallowed a mouthful of water. She spluttered, trying to balance on her toes, but the water was so close to her mouth it lapped at her bottom lip.

Alarik smirked as he watched her. "The primary objective is not to drown."

"I'm an incredible swimmer."

"Not from where I'm sitting." He patted the space beside him. "Come."

Wren swam over to the ledge, not because he told her to but because her limbs were beginning to tire. The burst of euphoria she had felt upon entering the baths was fading and she was starting to ache. The water didn't seem to be healing her; in fact she felt as if it was prodding at the curse inside her, waking it. Her head was beginning to spin.

She dragged herself onto the ledge.

It was hotter here, the water deeper. The steam between them thickened.

"Why are you sitting all the way back here?" she asked as she wrung the water from her hair.

Alarik watched her through the mist, tracing the rivulets as they fell across her shoulders. "For privacy."

"From *me?*"

He shook his head. "For us."

Wren's hands stilled. She looked at Alarik and felt a strange calmness come over her. Perhaps it was the steam, but she could suddenly feel the steady thud of her heart in her chest. She exhaled, long and deep and slow. "What do you mean?"

He dropped his voice. "I was feeling lightheaded just now. I thought you might be, too."

Wren frowned. "I felt good at first. But then, I don't know. . . . I felt as if the water was making me feel worse."

Alarik nodded. "And now?"

Wren ran her hands through her hair. "I'm doing better now. My wrist is stinging but not as much as before. And my head has stopped spinning."

"Mine, too."

Wren looked around herself. The water was still clear. "Do you think it's working?"

"I don't know," said Alarik. "Maybe. I don't feel as wretched as I did a moment ago."

Wren looked at him more closely. The shadows in his cheeks didn't look as pronounced, and his eyes seemed brighter somehow. Almost silver, like the everlights above them.

"Now you really are staring at me," he said.

"Now I really am," she admitted. "You look better than before."

"I was just thinking the same thing about you."

"Was I really that bad?"

"Yes," he said at once. "Your eyes . . . they had lost their . . ." He frowned, searching for the right word. "Light."

Wren snorted.

"And you weren't being half as annoying as usual," he added quickly. "I was coming to miss your irritating smugness."

Wren splashed him. "*You* are the smug one!"

"*Me?*" he said, drenching her back. "I was merely trying to match you."

She laughed and he joined in, the sound echoing around them.

Alarik leaned back, looking at the ceiling. "Tell me a story. You're good at that."

"I used all my best stories on the way up here."

"That can't be true. You're bursting with stories."

"How do you know?"

He shrugged. "Because you've lived wildly. You weren't raised as a princess. You were raised by the elements."

"And my grandmother," Wren reminded him.

"Who was something of an element herself."

Wren smiled. "It *was* a bit like growing up in a storm."

"Tell me more about the storm, Wren."

So Wren did. For an hour or more, they sat side by side, letting the steam lick their skin clean as they talked about their childhoods. Alarik's spent in the Fovarr Mountains, hunting, trekking, watching his father rule with an iron fist. Wren spoke of Ortha, of the cliffs that roughened her palms by the time she was five years old. He asked to see them and she held them up. On and on they went, trundling through the stories that made them who they were: guarded, clever, careful. The people who raised them. The people they had lost.

All the while, the water stayed clear around them, and yet in all these long months, Wren had never felt so far from the pain inside her. She began to hope that perhaps the healing bath was working. That even though they couldn't see it, the curse was dissolving.

"Now that you've told me about all the beasts that have tried to eat you over the years, tell me something nice," said Wren, after a while. "Such as where you managed to get that *tiny* sliver of charm from."

He wagged his finger at her. "Careful, witch. You're in grave danger of being nice to me."

She flicked water at him.

He slipped into another tale. Without meaning to, Wren leaned in to listen. "In the spring, when I was a boy, my mother and I would get up before sunrise to skate together. She used to twirl like a dancer across the lake. It was mesmerizing." He smiled at the memory. "I would try to match her only to fail miserably every time. I've never eaten so much ice." He raised his chin, drawing closer until Wren could see the thin white scar on the underside of his chin. "Of all my scars, this one is my favorite."

"What a thing to say," murmured Wren.

He looked at her, his lowered lashes casting shadows along his cheeks. The moment stretched, silent, loaded, the steam so thick, it felt as if it was pressing in on them.

Wren hinged backward. "Banba always hated when I slept past sunrise," she said, breathless. "Once, she tried to spook me out of bed by pretending to be a ghoul. She wore this huge black cloak over her head and stuck giant branches down her sleeves to make her arms look far longer than they really were."

Wren rose out of the water, sticking her hands above her head to try to convey the shape of the monster. "She stomped through the hut and kicked the door open until she filled the doorway." She waved her hands about, mimicking what Banba had done. Alarik broke into laughter and Wren joined in until tears rolled down her cheeks. "I've never screamed so much in my life. Thea came running. She thought I was being murdered."

She slumped onto the edge of the bath, enjoying the cool air on her face. She didn't realize how hot the water was until she was half out of it again.

Alarik stopped laughing. She looked down at him. His eyes fell, from her face to the column of her neck, and then to her white chemise, which was plastered to her chest. And completely see-through. "Wren," he said, the word hoarse.

Wren slinked back into the water. Now it was nowhere near as hot as her cheeks. Embarrassment roared in her ears. She had not come here for this. She had come to seek respite from the pain of the curse, and even though the water ran clear around her, it had been working. Hadn't it?

Alarik swallowed hard. "We're not here to do that again," he said, echoing her thoughts.

She rounded on him. "Do *what* again?"

He lowered his chin, meeting her gaze. "Let's not play this game."

"If you're referring to the blizzard, that was *your* fault," said Wren.

He crooked a brow. "You're the one who kissed *me*."

Wren swallowed her retort. She supposed it didn't matter. The truth was she had kissed the king in a maelstrom of fear and grief. She recalled the endless horror of that day, how she had reached for Alarik in a rush of terror, finding comfort in his arms. But the king was not made to comfort others, to comfort her. He had the same jagged heart as Wren, and while those pieces might recognize each other, they were not made to fit together.

All Wren and Alarik knew together was pain. And now, here they were again, in misery, hoping to find release from a terrible thing they had done together. As far as Wren was concerned, that kiss—and this awful curse—were bound together. Somehow.

"It was a mistake," she said, pushing off the ledge.

"Then why are you still thinking about it?" Alarik challenged. "Every time you look at me your cheeks turn bright red."

"That must mean you're thinking about it, too."

"I never said I wasn't," he said with a shrug.

"This is not helping." Wren sighed. She paddled water, putting as much distance between them as possible.

Her head began to pound again, her limbs so heavy she could hardly swim at all. Suddenly, she felt as if she had climbed ten mountains in a row. Her breath shallowed and stars pinwheeled in the sides of her vision. She could practically feel the thing inside her—the shadowy curse—stretching through her bones.

She scrambled for footing but the water had deepened without her realizing it. She flailed, trying to swim, but her arms were too heavy. It was hard to move, to *think*. "Alarik!"

He was there in the next heartbeat, curling his arm around her waist and dragging her through the water. "Calm down. Breathe."

He pulled her back to the ledge, and she grabbed it with both hands, letting her head slump onto the edge of the pool. "I don't know what happened," she mumbled into the rock. "I felt . . . I feel . . ."

He came to her side, resting his head on his elbows until they were both slumped over the side of the pool, looking at each other. Alarik took a deep breath, and Wren did the same. *In and out, in and out,* until they fell into sync with each other.

He reached over, peeling a strip of wet hair from her eyes. "How do you feel now?"

Gingerly, Wren lifted her head. "A little better." She frowned. "A lot better. I don't understand." Was the water making her sick? But, no. If that were true, she would still be ill now, and she wasn't. It was only when she tried to swim away from Alarik that she began to weaken.

"I think I understand." Alarik sat up, looking stronger now. "Come here." He reached for her and Wren went to him, clambering across the ledge. He took her wrist in his hand, brushing his fingers over her scar. "Can you feel that?"

She looked at his fingers. "It doesn't hurt anymore."

"No," he said quietly. "Not while we're together."

Tears pricked Wren's eyes as understanding dawned on her. The curse was not broken. It was just sleeping. The pool aggravated it, but when they were close together, it wasn't so bad. It was the water that stretched it, prodded it, making them aware of it. But the water wasn't working either. It was still clear. This thing—made of curse and shadow—was still inside her. Inside him.

Wren closed her eyes, sadness and fear guttering through her. "We're still broken."

Wordlessly, Alarik took her in his arms, folding her body into his own until they were skin to skin, and she felt weightless. She sighed as the tension uncoiled from her body. He laid his chin against the top of her head. "But not like this."

His sigh feathered her cheek. It occurred to Wren that he must feel that same weightlessness, too. She turned her face into him, resting her head in the crook of his neck. Soon, she was so relaxed she thought she might fall asleep. He trailed his fingers through her hair, absently stroking it.

"What is this?" whispered Wren.

"Peace," he whispered back. "Just for a moment."

She smiled, then. "Blessed peace."

The moment did not last long. There came the sudden sound of footsteps, and then a familiar voice, shooting through the center of Wren's heart like a lightning bolt.

"Is it broken, yet?" asked Tor.

Wren looked up and flinched at the expression on his face. He looked as if he had been run through with a cutlass.

Alarik gestured at the clear water, a new bite in his voice. "Does it look broken, Iversen?"

"It certainly doesn't look right to me," said Tor, without taking his eyes off Wren, and she found that she couldn't meet his gaze.

24

ROSE

As Shen led them through the Palace of Eternal Sunlight, Rose couldn't help but marvel at the beauty around her. The pale marble floors, the red-and-gold gilded walls, the intricate carvings of suns and moons across the ceilings. And it wasn't just the palace that stole her breath. She couldn't stop looking at Shen. She loved seeing him walk with such purpose, with such a sense of place in his own palace, his own kingdom.

"This way," he said, guiding them back outside into another, smaller courtyard that was hemmed in by the palace itself. He paused at a wall of feather grass, pushing it aside to reveal a narrow wooden door, and ushered all three of them inside.

The armory was even more spectacular than Rose remembered. It was lit by everlights, and the weapons shone in the flickering light. Overhead, axes and swords hung from the ceiling. Whips and staffs lined the walls, and there was an entire section for bows and arrows. In the center of the room was a large table displaying impressive daggers of varying sizes.

Rose knew from her previous visit that the drawers under the table held smaller, more discreet weapons that were no less deadly.

"Oh, I like this room," said Anika, gazing at a mace with a shimmering diamond head. "A *lot*."

"I remember Lei Fan saying that the blacksmiths of the Sunkissed Kingdom take great pride in their work," said Rose. "They believe that in battle, as in death, there must always be respect."

Shen caught Rose's gaze. "I'm surprised you remember that."

"I remember everything I've learned about your kingdom," said Rose softly.

"Did you learn precisely what kind of weapon can take down an undead evil witch?" asked Anika.

"The older the better, I'd guess," said Celeste, tracing the golden hilt of a dagger. "Looks as if we'll have no shortage of choice."

"Then let's take as many as we can carry," said Anika, eyes gleaming.

"It certainly won't hurt our chances," said Rose. She gazed at the table full of beautifully crafted weapons. Which would be the one to destroy Oonagh?

In the flickering everlights, one blade seemed to shine brighter than the rest. A medium-sized dagger with a glimmering golden blade and a ruby-encrusted handle. Rose felt drawn to it in a way she couldn't explain.

"May I?" she asked Shen, gesturing at the dagger.

He smiled at her. "Please."

Rose reverently picked it up, and as she did she felt the magic thrumming inside it. "Oh!" she breathed.

The sharp end glinted in the light, and she knew that it could pierce anything.

Even the heart of Oonagh Starcrest.

"You've chosen well," said Shen, his smile growing. "That dagger is called Daybreak."

"Daybreak," Rose repeated, and the hilt buzzed in her hand in answer.

"Grandmother Lu showed me this dagger when I first returned to the Sunkissed Kingdom," said Shen. "It belonged to my mother. My father gifted it to her, as his father had given it to his mother. Legend says it was forged by the Sun himself and left behind as a gift for Eana, his greatest love, so that she would think of him and be strengthened, even in battle."

Their gazes locked.

"I think my mother would want you to have it," he said quietly.

"It would be my honor." Rose looked down at the dagger, at Daybreak, and she felt with a sudden surety that she had found the weapon she was looking for.

Rose turned her gaze back to Shen. "Thank you," she said. "For this. For everything."

The moment around them seemed to swell, and then Anika cleared her throat.

"Our turn to choose! Celeste, come and look at the archery section with me," she said, slipping her arm through Celeste's and leading her away. "I think you'd look very fetching with a bow and arrow."

Celeste laughed. "I do have excellent aim."

Shen glanced sidelong at Rose. "Seems like Celeste is smitten."

"So it does," said Rose, watching her friend laugh with Anika. "I'm pleased for her."

"How do you think they'll make that work?" he pondered. "It's a long way from Eana to Gevra."

"Celeste will find a way, I'm sure of it," said Rose, hoping it would be true. "I've never seen her so bewitched. If Anika wasn't Gevran, I'd swear she had cast a spell on Celeste."

"Well, it seems Anika is just as taken with Celeste," said Shen, his smile twitching. "Love is certainly in the air tonight." Rose blushed as he caught her hand and kissed it. "If Celeste and Anika can find a way to be together, then surely you and I can figure something out," he went on. "After all, the desert is not so far from Anadawn."

"I wish it were closer. I wish . . ." She sighed. "Oh, never mind." There weren't enough hours left in the night to unpick her desires, her dreams for the future. And even if there were, it was not the right time. "Let's focus on the bigger problem for now. Perhaps after Oonagh is no longer a threat, we can find a way for us."

"To be . . . what?"

Rose gave him a smile. "To be together, of course."

Shen's eyes danced, and Rose suddenly wished that it were just the two of them. Alone. And that they had only each other to think about, not worrying about finding weapons and preparing for war. She imagined Shen clearing the table of daggers, laying her down upon it and—

Suddenly a scream of pure terror rang out, followed quickly by another. Shen whipped his head around, as an entire chorus of shouts erupted. They were coming from the main courtyard. "Something's wrong."

And then the very ground itself began to shake.

Celeste and Anika stumbled from the shadows of the archery cabinet, eyes wide with fear.

"What's going on?" said Celeste, who was clutching a beautifully carved bow and had a quiver of arrows slung on her back.

"I don't know. But we need to find out," said Shen. "Grab your weapons."

Anika hoisted a slim battle-axe over her shoulder. "I'm glad we came via the armory."

Rose slipped Daybreak into its sheath and ran toward the screams.

Rose had seen her fair share of horrors. But as they rounded the corner on their way back to the courtyard, she skidded to a stop, gasping as she beheld the monstrosity that stood before her.

It was a creature of bone and shadow. At first glance, it looked like a horse, but it was something else entirely. Smoke poured from the gaping holes of its long white skull, and it possessed a wide mouth full of needlelike teeth. The rest of its body was made of jutting bones and writhing darkness, and its hooves were thick and smoldering.

Rose's heart thundered as she snapped her chin up. There were hundreds of them stampeding through the courtyard and down the alleyways. They looked like smoke, but Rose felt the ground tremble. She saw how they were knocking down anything and anyone in their way, kicking up dust and sand as they went. These creatures were smoke made flesh.

Nightmares made real.

While Shen scanned the stampede in mounting horror, a creature bolted from a nearby alley and careened straight for him. Rose pulled him out of harm's way and all four of them flattened themselves against the wall, narrowly avoiding another hundred or so that went thundering past.

Revelers screamed as they ran, taking cover wherever they could. Those that couldn't reach the palace in time scaled the walls instead, finding refuge on the roofs. Others dived into the bushes and trees, hoping the branches would protect them.

And still the creatures came.

Once he caught his breath, Shen drew his weapons and jumped into their path, his daggers slicing through the air, but the blades found no mark on the creatures. It was as if he were cutting smoke.

Anika pulled Celeste into a nearby alcove while Rose summoned a gust of wind, hoping she could blow them back, but it only seemed to enrage the beasts further. When some of them broke off from the herd and came for her, she had to clamber up a nearby trellis to safety.

"Let them pass!" cried a hoarse voice. Rose looked up to find Grandmother Lu shouting down from a nearby roof. "Let them pass!"

And so they did. The creatures thundered through the Sunkissed Kingdom, leaving a cloud of destruction in their wake, and then, as swiftly as they had arrived, they were gone.

The ground stopped trembling, and at last, silence fell.

With remarkable speed, Shen scaled a nearby wall and stared into the distance. "They're gone," he said. "Toward the east."

Rose's legs shook as she climbed down from the trellis. Shen went to help her.

"What were those awful things?" said Celeste, stepping out of the alcove. All around them, people were peering out of windows, checking to see if it was safe to come out. The palace attendants emerged one by one, stepping over cracked tiles and broken statues as they surveyed the damage.

"Wraith horses!" Grandmother Lu's voice rang out as she hopped down from the roof, landing easily next to them. "They come from the sands. They're a warning from the desert itself."

"That didn't feel like a warning," said Anika, shaking the dust out of her gown as she joined them. "It felt like attempted murder."

Shen's brow furrowed. "I never believed such a creature even existed. A silly superstition, surely . . ." He trailed off. "And I've certainly never heard of an entire stampede of them."

Grandmother Lu clucked as she leaned on her cane. "A wraith horse appears when death is near." She turned her sharp gaze on Rose. "It is no coincidence that they showed up just after you arrived."

"And not just one," said Celeste uneasily.

"What could that mean?" said Rose.

"Grave danger," said Grandmother Lu darkly. "Death is coming to Eana."

"You're not wrong, Grandmother Lu," said Shen, dropping his voice. "Eana *is* in grave danger." The old woman leaned in as he told her about Oonagh Starcrest.

When it was done, the old woman's voice hardened, and in it, Rose heard the words of a seasoned warrior. "You must not wait for death to come to you, Queen Rose. You must meet this danger head-on and fight it with all of your might."

"We will," said Rose and Shen together.

"Too much time has already passed. Find Oonagh and face her," said Grandmother Lu. "These wraith horses are a warning to us. A gift, not a curse."

"Tell that to your broken cobblestones," muttered Anika.

"Hush now," Grandmother Lu scolded her. "They are telling you to act. To strike while you can."

"I want to," said Rose, gripping her new dagger so hard, her hand ached. "But we don't know where Oonagh is. . . ."

"Then look to the skies," said Grandmother Lu, waving her cane upward. "It appears the wraith horses are not our only visitor tonight."

When Rose looked up, the sky was full of starcrests. The flock was so large, the birds lit up the night, casting their glimmering silver light over the ransacked streets of the Sunkissed Kingdom.

"This is no coincidence," said Shen, marveling at the sight.

"No," whispered Rose, who was grateful to see so many after the skies of Anadawn had been empty of them. Even if she couldn't divine the message they carried.

For Rose, the seer gift remained the most elusive of the five strands of magic. She had imagined that once the witches' curse had been broken and she had gained all five elements of her power, she would simply be able to look up at the starcrest birds at night and see entire visions in their movements, her future at last made clear. But whenever she watched the starcrests, scouring their patterns for clues, she ever experienced only a faint pull toward a certain idea. Sometimes, despite her best efforts, she felt nothing at all.

"I've never seen so many starcrests," muttered Celeste, her eyes glazing as she watched them. Unlike Rose, Celeste had been a seer her whole life, even if she hadn't quite known it. When she watched the starcrests, she said it was like falling into a trance—that one moment she saw birds and the next the sky danced with images, showing all kinds of future possibilities.

"What do you see?" Rose asked her now.

"Danger," she said slowly. "There is danger ahead. . . ."

"We know that!" said Rose, trying not to be frustrated.

"Could they be a little more specific?" said Shen.

"Shh," said Celeste, who was still watching the sky. The birds were flocking, making a new shape. Rose bristled, feeling a sudden coldness prickling in her cheeks.

Shen frowned. "Why does it suddenly feel like winter to me?"

Celeste pulled her arms around herself. "What is that?" she murmured. "It's right on the edge of my mind. . . ."

"I KNOW WHAT IT IS!" screeched Anika, startling them all. "I recognize that shape! It's a place!" She burst into laughter. "It's Carrig!"

"Carrig?" Rose repeated. "Anika, you're not even a witch. You can't just—"

"See how the northeast curves like a snow leopard's tail?" she went on triumphantly. "And there, the southern peninsulas look just like the jutting fangs of a wolf!" Anika clapped her hands, delighting in their confusion. "Carrig is a remote island off the coast of Gevra. More beasts than men roam there. It's where Captain Iversen hails from!"

There was a stretch of stunned silence.

Shen was the first to break it. "Well, that *would* explain the sudden chill in my toes."

"Are you *sure?*" said Rose dubiously. "The starcrests aren't usually so . . . well, *literal.*"

"Surer than sure." Anika flashed her teeth. "My father made my brothers and me study maps every evening when we were children. He said every great leader should know their own land and those of their enemies. The shape in the sky is Carrig. I would wager my best tiara on it."

"She's right," murmured Celeste, who was on her feet now and tracing the birds' movements with her finger.

"Clever girl," said Grandmother Lu, gently bopping Anika on the head with her cane.

Anika glowered at her, but remarkably, held her tongue.

Celeste went on. "But there is a warning in these skies, too. Blood. Bones. Death." She looked to Rose. "I don't know if it's a good idea to traipse across the sea to search for Oonagh in a land we do not know."

"It's better than waiting here," said Rose, recalling all too well the terror of seeing Oonagh in her own bedroom. "We must attack her while we have the advantage, Celeste. If we wait for her to return at full strength, with an entire army of undead beasts, we will be at her mercy. But if we sneak up on her when she's not expecting us, then we can catch her off guard."

"Rose is right," said Shen, joining her side. "In war, the strongest weapon is the element of surprise."

"Now you sound like the king of the Sunkissed Kingdom," said Grandmother Lu proudly. "A true warrior and a true leader."

"I know Carrig," said Anika eagerly. "I visited it many times as a child. My father had a great interest in the wranglers who live there. I imagine it is not much changed. It's the kind of place where time stands still—this little land of beasts and hills."

"And Oonagh," added Shen darkly.

"We must go now," said Rose.

Shen gripped his daggers, squaring himself to the task. "Grandmother Lu, I'm trusting you and Lei Fan to watch over the Sunkissed Kingdom in my absence. Can you do—?"

She tsked and bopped him on the head. "Of course I can." Then she shooed him. "Now go, before another stampede comes and destroys my herb garden!"

"What about Wren?" said Celeste. "Won't she want to join in the capture of Oonagh?"

Rose shook her head. "Wren is too weak. She would want us to go on." Even as she said the words, she knew her sister wouldn't want her to leave Eana without her, but Wren had left Rose behind plenty of times before. She would understand. The sooner they stopped Oonagh, the sooner Wren could recover in peace, and then the sisters could finally focus on ruling together. The way they were always meant to.

As the last of the starcrests scattered into the night, Rose smoothed her gown. She realized that it had stopped glowing at some point in the evening but she couldn't quite remember when. Magic could be unpredictable like that. She sighed. The dagger, witch-made though it was, might not be enough.

If they were going to face Oonagh, might for might, they needed another seasoned warrior on their side. And Rose knew who the best one was.

"Shen," she said. "Is that cousin of yours still in the dungeon?"

25

WREN

Wren stood up abruptly, rivulets of water cascading from her sopping underclothes as she stepped away from Alarik and climbed out of the bath.

"Please call for Maeva," she said, looking everywhere but at Tor. "The healing water isn't working. We need to try something else."

"Oh, stop glowering, Iversen," said Alarik, with a chuckle. "We were improvising. Trying to make these waters do their job."

Tor said nothing at all.

Wren scurried off to the side chamber, all too aware of the soldier's eyes on her as she went. She couldn't shake the look of betrayal on his face. Her cheeks burned as she waited for Maeva to return. Her *heart* burned. What had she been thinking, curling up with Alarik like that? As if they were lovers, indulging in a secret embrace.

She paced back and forth, waiting for her heart to stop rioting. But the pounding only got worse. It was in her head, too. She was getting dizzy again. She knew it would pass—or at least pause—if she returned to Alarik's side, but she couldn't bear to see the hurt on Tor's face again.

She had to explain what happened.

She *would* explain.

This thing inside her—this curse—was clearly more twisted than she thought.

After what seemed like an eternity, Maeva arrived with a fresh set of green robes and matching slippers for Wren.

The young witch looked her up and down. "You don't look well, Your Majesty."

"I'm not well." Wren snatched the robes from her and got dressed in a hurry. "I need to see Willa." She flung a hand out to steady herself against the wall. "And tea," she added. "I'll need some more of that lavender tea."

Willa was waiting for them in her chamber, where a platter of sandwiches and a fresh pot of herbal tea had been laid out. She took one look at Wren and Alarik as they shuffled inside and she sighed. "Oh dear. You'd better sit down."

Wren slumped onto the couch, and Alarik collapsed beside her, sitting so close their legs were brushing.

Tor hovered in the doorway, his hands curled into white-knuckled fists. Willa crooked her brow as though she was reading the cloud of tension in the air, but she made no more of it. "You may remain, soldier. If you so choose."

He dipped his chin but did not come inside.

"The water made it worse," said Wren quickly. "It's like it aggravated the curse."

Willa sipped her tea. "I was afraid of that."

"Then why did you send us down there in the first place?" demanded Alarik.

"Because you asked for my help," she said calmly. "Sometimes the water does not heal. But it does bring clarity." She looked between them. "I can see the bond more clearly now."

"Then break it," said Wren.

Willa considered them a moment, her eyes wide above the rim of her mug. "If the water cannot heal you, then we must use the flame."

Alarik quailed. "Gevrans do not do well in heat."

Willa smiled tightly. "Nor do curses."

After an awkward lunch, Willa led them to a small room in the very pit of the mountain. There was no water down here. In fact, there was no sound at all. The space was barely big enough for all four of them to fit. Thankfully, Tor had left Elske back up in the dining quarters, where she was being fawned over by every healer in the mountain.

In the middle of the room, a silver everlight flickered in a tall earthen bowl. It was a bonfire all on its own, the flame so bright it stung tears in Wren's eyes. She passed her hand over it and felt her fingers tingle. There was magic here. Ancient, rippling magic.

"What is this place?" she whispered.

Willa moved to the other side of the everlight, her face flickering through the flame. "This was once Eana's sanctuary." She raised her hand, making the flame dance. Wren recognized the enchantment magic at once. The healer was good at it, too, easily turning the fire into her puppet. Each sliver of flame a string to manipulate. "When Eana first came to the Mishnick Mountains, she made a home for herself here. She sought shelter from the bitter cold and howling winds, and in the darkness of this mountain, she cast this very flame. It warmed her on the darkest nights and reminded her of all the light that lay ahead of her. It became a beacon of hope, a symbol of the thriving kingdom that this land would one day come to be."

The flame took on the outline of a woman. She was kneeling, her face tipped back to the sky. Wren looked down, half expecting to see her ancestor kneeling on the ground beside her. But there was only the edge of Alarik's slipper and the stone beneath.

She looked back at the flame. "This is Eana's everlight?" she said in disbelief. "The very same?"

Willa nodded. "It has burned here for thousands of years."

Wren closed her eyes, feeling for the presence of her ancestor. Here was Eana's magic. Her firelight. It had burned for eons, through war and death and suffering, through the banishment of the witches and the restoration of its queens. It had seen a great kingdom rise and fall, and still it remained. The thought filled Wren with such a sense of hope, she smiled.

A laugh bubbled out of her.

"What's so funny?" said Alarik.

"Eana will save us," said Wren, feeling sure of it in her bones. "Eana will cure us."

When Wren looked at Willa, the Healer on High was smiling, too. Hope danced in the air between them, as high and bright as the flame.

"So, what now?" said Alarik impatiently. "Do we hurl ourselves into the flame to see if we burn?"

"Your scars will do," said Willa, gesturing for them to hold hands.

Alarik took Wren's without hesitation, his fingers threading through hers with such sureness it sent a ripple of warmth up Wren's spine.

Tor cleared his throat, the sound echoing in the little cavern, and took a step back.

"The fire will chase the darkness inside you," said Willa. "It will drag the curse into the light." She reached into the pouch at her waist and cast a handful of salt crystals into the flames. She began to mutter under her breath. The fire hissed as it grew.

Willa reached through the flame as though it were nothing but air and took their hands in hers. She pulled them into the middle of the blaze and they stood—all three of them—at the mouth of Eana's fire, watching the silver flames lick their skin.

At first, Wren felt nothing. Just a slight tingling around her wrist. Then the pain came hot and lancing through her bones, and a blood-curdling scream filled the chamber. It took her a moment to realize it was her own.

She tried to jerk backward but Willa held her hand to the flame. The healer's words grew harsher, as though she was calling to the thing inside Wren. Then the black smoke came, just as before. Alarik shouted in fear but he was rooted to the flame, too. He watched as the curse poured out of the wound in Wren's skin.

Wren screamed again.

"Release her!" shouted Tor.

But Willa was determined. They had come too far to stop now. Her grip on Wren tightened as Alarik leaped backward, breaking away from her. He slumped against the wall.

Willa kept her gaze on the gathering smoke. "SHOW YOURSELF!"

Wren screamed as another plume of smoke ripped out of her. Her legs buckled but Tor lunged, catching her before she hit the ground. He wrapped his arms around her middle as the smoke formed a face before them. At first Wren thought it was Eana, the first witch, but the longer she stared at the gathering smoke, the more familiar it became.

The face was just like her own. Its mouth opened in laughter, the piercing sound rattling around the cavern.

"Oonagh Starcrest," breathed Willa in shock. "This curse is ancient."

Wren tried to recoil from her ancestor. It was no use. Somehow, Oonagh had buried a part of herself—of her curse—in Wren. She had left her shadow behind, and it was that which haunted Wren. *Harmed* Wren.

She began to tremble violently. The smoke was inside her body, too. It filled her lungs, pouring from her mouth and her nose. She was choking. But Willa wouldn't let go. The healer's brown eyes had turned white, her irises rolling back in her head. She was foaming at the mouth, stuck in a trance. Wren had the horrible thought that the curse was trying to claim her, too.

"Help!" Wren screamed. "Make it stop!"

With a hard tug, Tor yanked her away from Willa, breaking the connection. The healer reeled backward, collapsing in a heap against the wall. The flames lashed out, whipping Tor's cheek as he curled his body around Wren. But he couldn't protect her from the smoke rushing back inside her.

Wren collapsed against him, grasping feebly at the lapels of his shirt. He slid his hand through her hair, holding her head up. She opened her eyes to see the storm in his gaze.

"It's all right," he said, low and calm. "I've got you."

She opened her mouth, searching for words, but a strangled moan seeped out. The everlight was dangerously low, the chamber half-choked with smoke. Wren squeezed her eyes closed, trying to shut out her fear. The smoke was making her lids heavy.

Tor touched his forehead against hers. "It's over," he whispered. "Rest now."

As she drifted off, his words lifted her above the tide of her panic, even though, deep down, Wren knew they weren't true. It wasn't over. The curse was still inside her, writhing, laughing.

The darkness had only just begun.

When Wren came to, she was back in Willa's chamber. She opened her eyes to a dark ceiling and the muffled sounds of voices. She sat up and became immediately aware of her headache.

She flinched. "Ugh."

"You're awake." Tor was sitting in the chair across from her, with Elske at his feet. They were both watching her with the same look of concern. There was a fresh gash along Tor's cheek, the cut bright red against the paleness of his skin.

"You're hurt," said Wren in horror.

"It's only a scratch."

"Iversen's seen far worse. Believe me," said Alarik, who was sitting at the other end of the couch, sipping a cup of lavender tea.

Wren reached for her own cup. "How long was I unconscious for?"

"A couple of hours," said Alarik, handing it to her. "Iversen carried you back."

"Thank you," said Wren.

"It was nothing," he muttered.

"Untold pain and suffering," Alarik said, between sips. "No creepy black smoke, though. Still, whatever that healing spell was . . . I could hardly stand it."

"I'm afraid none of us could stand it," said Willa, who returned presently. Perhaps it was Wren's imagination, but she swore she could trace new crevices in the healer's face, and the hair around her temples looked whiter than before. "When you told me about your blood spell this morning, you never mentioned Oonagh Starcrest."

Wren bit her lip. "Didn't I?"

Willa shot her an admonishing look. "You really didn't think it was pertinent to reveal that your long-dead, famously cursed ancestor was reawakened by your ill-advised blood spell in the wilds of Gevra?"

Wren looked at her hands. "I don't even know how it happened. . . . We weren't trying to find Oonagh. It was almost as if . . ."

"She found us," said Alarik.

Willa grimaced. "This curse is more ancient than any I have seen." She shook her head, as if she was still trying to make sense of it. "The day you cast that blood spell to awaken Prince Ansel, you woke some-one else, too. Someone who had long been waiting for a whisper of magic to find her in those icy mountains."

"Bad luck," muttered Alarik.

"Or fate," said Willa darkly.

Wren tried not to squirm. "Oonagh was right there all along. Waiting."

"She must have sensed the blood spell and found a way to attach herself to it," said Willa, confirming Wren's worst fear. "She used your magic like a rope to pull herself back to life. She anchored herself to your spell. To *you*."

Wren and Alarik looked at each other. Half of Wren wanted to reach for his hand and squeeze it, to say sorry for her part in the blood spell. The other half wanted to punch him for dragging her into this mess in the first place. By the strained look on his face, Wren guessed the king was probably experiencing a similar internal conflict.

The Healer on High leaned toward them, and the rest of the world faded away and all Wren could see was the warning in her eyes. "The curse binds both of you to Oonagh Starcrest just as it binds you to each other. The longer is survives, the stronger it will become. It will kill you, eventually." She looked at Wren. "It is already killing your magic."

Wren pinched the back of her hand to keep from crying, but there was a rock in her throat, and her breath was coming short and sharp. "What can we do?"

"Break the link," said Willa. "Before it destroys you."

"How?" said Wren, Tor, and Alarik, all at the same time.

Willa pulled back, hesitating.

Alarik read her silence. "Ah. You mean for us to kill each other. Or rather, you mean for your queen to kill the interloper. *Me*. To cut her losses, so to speak."

Wren slammed her cup down. "Don't be so dramatic. That's not at all what she's saying."

Willa pressed her lips together. "Your Majesty," she said in a low voice. "Perhaps we should speak—"

"Don't bother," said Alarik. "Your meaning is quite clear. It seems I am in more danger here than I thought."

Tor's hand flew to his waist, grasping for the hilt of his sword. But he was weaponless, just like Alarik. He jerked his head, watching the doorway as if he was expecting an army to come rushing in. Sensing the change in his mood, Elske rose to her haunches.

"Calm down, both of you," said Wren. She turned back to Willa. "This can't be the only way to survive this."

"There is only one other way."

"Tell us," said Alarik, a growl in his voice.

Willa shifted in her seat. "Oonagh Starcrest walks this earth just as she did over a thousand years ago. Your ancestor's curse lives inside you because *she* lives. You woke her up. To break the curse and set things right, you must kill her."

"Fine," said Wren at once. "I was going to do that anyway."

"We have to find her first," said Alarik.

"And best her," said Willa grimly.

"With pleasure." Tor cracked his knuckles, readying himself for the task.

Willa rose from her seat, looking down on each one of them in turn. "There is your cure, though the cost is great. If Oonagh dies, for good this time, the blood debt will be repaid and the curse will shatter."

Wren frowned as something else occurred to her. The healer's promise reminded her of another—a prophecy once uttered by a dying seer called Glenna. "'Break the ice to free the curse,'" she recalled. "'Kill one twin to save another. . . .'"

They all looked at her.

A wash of understanding came over Wren. The day Oonagh

Starcrest broke out of her icy tomb in Gevra, her curse was freed, too. That much was certain. But Wren had been grappling with the second part of the prophecy ever since. *Kill one twin to save another.* "It was never about me and Rose," she said, more to herself than to the others. "It's Oonagh who must die. She is Ortha's sister, one of the original twin queens of Eana." She clapped her hands together, a laugh springing from her before she could stop it. "Rose will live and so will I! Once we kill Oonagh, all will be well again."

Alarik regarded her as though she had just sprouted horns. "Have you forgotten we have no idea where your wayward ancestor is? Or indeed how to kill her?"

Wren batted his concern away, the flood of her relief momentarily buoying her spirits. "So we'll look for her. And sooner or later, we'll find her."

"How simple you make it sound," mused Alarik.

"Well, it's a lot simpler than killing each other. Don't you think?"

He offered the ghost of a smile. "I want to know what Iversen thinks."

Tor was already on his feet. "I think it's time to go hunting."

26

ROSE

The last time Rose had seen Shen's cousin Kai Lo, he had been knocked out by Grandmother Lu.

Along with his father, Shen's Uncle Feng, Kai had attempted to murder Shen, and when that plan had been foiled by Rose, he had come after her with a vengeance. He had caught up with her in the desert, and Rose had truly thought he was going to kill her—until Grandmother Lu appeared with her cane. After that, he had been arrested and placed under guard in the Sunkissed Kingdom.

This is why Rose was expecting Shen to lead them to a heavily guarded dungeon hidden somewhere deep beneath the sands. Instead, he brought them to a small squat building not too far from the stables. Though it was surrounded by guards, the sloping red roof, ivy-covered walls, and flickering everlights made it look remarkably . . . pleasant.

"*This* is the dungeon?" Rose said, frowning.

"In a matter of speaking," said Shen, nodding at one of the guards, who unlocked the heavy wooden doors and handed Shen the set of keys.

They made their way down a lavishly decorated hallway with

polished tiles and a vaulted ceiling. Shen paused in front of another thicker wooden door that was bolt-locked from the outside.

"Are you sure you're ready to see Kai?" he said, turning to Rose. "I can go in without you, if you'd prefer."

Rose straightened her skirts and her spine. "Shen, I am a queen. I can face a prisoner, you know. And it is a favor for me, after all. Oonagh Starcrest is my problem."

Shen caught her hand and raised it to his lips. "You know as well as I do that any problem of yours is one that I will gladly take on."

"Me, too," said Celeste, who was standing just behind them. "You aren't facing Oonagh alone, Rose."

Anika let out a dramatic sigh. "I suppose this is the part where you all expect me to make a declaration of my loyalty to Rose." She swept her hair from her face, fixing her tiara. "I will remind you that I am the princess of a different nation." She paused meaningfully. "But for the good of Gevra and your country, I will stand by you in your fight against Oonagh." She glanced uncertainly at the locked door. "I'll admit I am curious why we are coming to fetch what sounds like a deliciously dangerous man, though."

"Because he's the best fighter I've ever seen," said Rose grimly. "And I know we'll have a better chance of killing Oonagh with him on board."

"Better than King Shen?" said Anika. "Truly?"

"Only just," said Shen begrudgingly. Then he sighed. "Rose is right. My cousin is the strongest warrior witch in my entire kingdom."

Anika arched a brow. "I'm not sure I can stand another moment of suspense."

"Let's just get this over with," said Celeste.

Shen unbolted the door and turned the key in the lock. It yielded with a keening groan, and he stepped inside, ushering the others to follow.

To Rose's complete and utter surprise, the room didn't look like a cell at all. In fact, it looked very similar to the other luxurious bedrooms she had seen inside the Palace of Eternal Sunlight.

"Hello, Queenie," came a smug voice that Rose recognized all too well. In the middle of the room, lounging on a low sofa, was Kai Lo himself. "Did you miss me?"

Rose gaped at Shen's cousin. His hands were wreathed in golden chains, but he was clearly more than comfortable in here. "This is not a dungeon! This . . . this . . . this is luxury!" she fumed.

"These bedsheets are finer than my own," remarked Anika, who was taking a tour around the room.

"And why does he need more than one pair of boots?" said Celeste, peering into the wardrobe.

"Shen!" said Rose. "Explain at once!"

"He *is* my cousin," said Shen, rubbing his brows. "And Lei Fan's brother. He spent some time in the sand dungeons, but he's been upgraded. For good behavior."

"Good behavior!" Rose exclaimed. "Shen, he tried to kill you!"

"It was your idea to ask for his help," he reminded her.

"My help, huh?" Kai perked up. "I see how it is. Lock me up when I misbehave a little bit—"

"Misbehave!" Rose's voice cracked. "That is certainly an understatement!"

Kai steepled his hands in front of his mouth. "Listen, Queenie. I'll level with you. Did I attack Shen? Yes. Did I then try to attack you? Also, yes. But these past few months in the dungeons, I've had a lot of time to think about what I did, and you have to see that it was all because of my father. . . ." His eyes darkened, the truth casting gravel in his voice. "He was manipulating me all along."

"Feng admitted as much in the sand dungeons," said Shen. "Where he will be staying for a long, long time."

"Fine by me," said Kai bitterly. "This was all his idea to begin with."

"And what?" said Celeste, with a snort. "You were easily led?"

"I can be very impressionable." Kai flashed a flirtatious smile. "*And I can make quite the impression.*"

"Not on me," said Celeste with another snort.

"Stars save us from the arrogance of burly men," muttered Anika.

"Enough small talk," said Kai, sinking back into the sofa. "Did you just come here to insult me or do you actually need my help with something?"

"I'm afraid so," Rose relented, deciding to come right out with it. They had wasted enough time already. "My undead ancestor Oonagh Starcrest has returned and is building an army. I want you to help me kill her before she sets foot in Eana and tries to seize the throne."

Kai blinked. "Well," he said, scrubbing his jaw. "That's quite a predicament, Queenie."

"No greater than your own, cousin." Shen crossed his arms as he looked down on him. "Do you want your freedom or not? This is your chance to prove your loyalty."

"Of course I want my freedom." He looked at Rose, his brows hunching. "Give me the chance to earn it."

Rose locked eyes with Kai and remembered all the terrible things he had done to her, to Shen. For a moment, she wanted to march out of this room and throw away the key.

Freeing him felt dangerous, not to mention utterly reckless.

But these were dangerous times. Reckless times. And Rose wanted every possible advantage over Oonagh. The other warrior witches would have to stay behind to defend the Sunkissed Kingdom, but given that he was a prisoner here, she knew Kai would not be missed.

Still, Rose hesitated, trying to decide if it was really worth the risk of freeing Kai. Anika relinquished her snooping and jostled in front of her. "A big beefy warrior like you would get along just fine in my brother's army. If this one"—she jerked her head toward Shen—"doesn't want to keep you around, you can certainly come and try your luck in Gevra. Our morals are much looser. Although if you betrayed the crown, we would have to feed you to our beasts." She pulled a face. "We don't believe in forgiveness. Or redemption."

Kai snorted. "Sounds like paradise."

"I think abruptly switching allegiances to a foreign nation at this moment would probably worsen Kai's case," said Shen pointedly. "Not to mention call his loyalty to me into question. Again."

"Yes, yes, King Shen . . . All hail King Shen," said Kai in a bored voice. "Blah, blah, blah . . . I get it." He raised his hands, jangling the chains around his wrists. "Well, Queenie? What will it be?"

Rose blew out a breath, choosing to trust her instincts. "Get ready to sail the Sunless Sea, Kai Lo. But know this, I'll be watching you. And at the first hint of misbehavior, I'll throw you into the sea myself."

"You've gotten much better at threats," said Kai, with a wide grin.

"And that one is especially effective as I don't know how to swim." Then he frowned. "Wait. Why are we going on a boat?"

Shen clapped his cousin on the back. "I'll fill you in." Then he glanced at Rose. "Grab your things and meet me in the stables in ten minutes." He kissed her, then, right there in front of the others, his lips brushing against hers for only a moment, but Rose felt the urgency behind it. As if he was worried if he didn't kiss her now, there would be no other chance.

She knew then that he was truly afraid of what was to come.

"Carrig is frightfully cold, even by my standards," said Anika as they made their way back to the palace. "You two will need furs. Luckily for you, I always overpack. Come with me."

Anika, along with her nine trunks, had been installed in one of the many guest rooms in the palace. Rose noted the room was nicely decorated, with pale blue drapes along the four-poster bed and gold suns spiraling across the walls.

Anika pointed at her trunks. "I suppose I can't bring them all if we're riding back to Wishbone Bay on horseback, can I?"

"You know you can't," said Celeste. "Choose your most practical outfit."

"And what am I meant to tell my valet?" Anika lamented. "I didn't just magically appear here, you know. I came with staff."

"Leave a note instructing them to follow tomorrow, and swiftly," said Celeste, opening one of the trunks and pulling out a purple cloak trimmed in silver fur. "Oh, this is *divine*."

"Take it," said Anika breezily. "I have a dozen like it."

"And you can wear this one," she said to Rose, pulling out a thick red cloak lined with white fur. Rose and Celeste quickly changed back into their traveling dresses and went to meet Shen and Kai in the stables.

Kai, now unchained, leaped up on his horse in one smooth movement, his whip slung around his waist. He caught Rose looking at it and gave her a wolfish grin. "You hardly expect me to take down your evil ancestor with my bare hands, do you?"

Rose gave him a tight smile as she mounted her own horse, desperately hoping she'd made the right decision. As they rode east, toward Wishbone Bay, the desert air thrummed with a sound she would never forget—the thunder of a thousand wraith horses galloping across the sands.

A warning to them all.

27

WREN

When Wren left Willa's chamber, it was late in the evening. She was too exhausted and much too hungry to think about where Oonagh Starcrest was at that precise moment or how they might go about tracking her down. Alarik wasn't faring much better, and so, on the advice of the Healer on High, they decided to spend the night in the mountain.

They retired to the dining hall, where three bowls of hearty venison stew sweetened with carrots and parsnips were waiting for them. There was crusty bread slathered in butter and generous carafes of pomegranate wine. Dessert was a pear-and-almond pie heaped with fresh cream, and for Elske, a huge meaty bone.

Despite the feast, Wren ate mostly in silence. She didn't have the stomach for polite conversation. Every time she looked at Tor and saw that angry red cut on his cheek, she felt an awful twinge of guilt. She couldn't seem to keep from hurting him, one way or another. In the dining hall under the mountain, healers milled around them. Wren could feel their eyes on her as she ate. Wondering, no doubt, what a queen of Eana was doing in the Mishnick Mountains with the fearsome king of Gevra and his towering captain still dressed as a soldier of Anadawn.

Wren's thoughts soon turned to Rose. She hoped her sister had made it safely to the Sunkissed Kingdom. Wren wished she could tell her what Willa had discovered about the curse and just how pressing their search for Oonagh had suddenly become.

When Wren finished eating, she excused herself from the table. She left the Gevrans to talk strategy—both of them expertly pretending as if that awkward moment in the baths earlier had never happened, that it hadn't cut through Tor like a knife—and Maeva led Wren to a vacant bedchamber up near the mouth of the mountain. The room was small but cozy. A single bed was piled with furs and cushions, lit up by an everlight that hung from the low ceiling. There was a basin in the corner alongside fresh towels, a nightgown, and some fragrant soap. Wren's satchel and traveling clothes were there, too, clean and neatly folded for the morning.

"It's not quite fit for a queen," said Maeva apologetically. "But it's been many years since we received a visitor in these mountains."

"It's perfect," said Wren, already sagging at the sight of the bed. "I'm so tired I could probably sleep standing up."

Maeva smiled. "Ring the bell if you need anything, Your Majesty."

"Thank you, Maeva. I'm sure I'll be just fine."

The healer hesitated.

"Is there something else?" asked Wren.

Maeva looked at her sandals, her cheeks turning even rosier. "I was wondering about the soldier you arrived with. He was so kind to me before when you were in the baths. I wanted to know whether he might—"

"He's Gevran," said Wren, a touch too sharply. "He's loyal to Gevra. He'll soon return home."

"Oh." Maeva looked crestfallen.

Wren felt bad for bristling at the girl's question. She was only human, after all. And Tor was mouthwateringly handsome. Not to mention brave and strong and—

"Pardon me, Your Majesty. I shouldn't have said anything."

"No, pardon *me*. I didn't mean to snap," said Wren. "I'm just . . . well, exhausted."

And jealous.

"Of course. You must rest." Maeva dipped her chin as she backed out of the room, leaving her alone. Wren ran her hands through her hair, her face heating in shame. It was no business of hers what Tor did or didn't do in this mountain, or in his own life.

She had forfeited that right the day she'd kissed Alarik. And in her silence about it since then. She didn't deserve Tor's affection. And if he truly had been cozying up to Maeva earlier then he had obviously come to realize that, too.

Wren slumped onto her bed, deflated. Everything felt wrong. Inside her. Outside her. All too quickly, she drifted off to sleep, but when the darkness swept in, she heard Oonagh's laugh, haunting her from one nightmare to the next.

Several hours before sunrise, Wren woke with a jolt. She swore she could hear singing. She sat up, blinking into the dimness. It took her a moment to remember where she was. The everlights flickered companionably, reminding her that she was safe. She flopped back against her pillow, measuring her breaths until her lids grew heavy.

There were hours to go until morning.

Hours of sleep yet to claim.

Then she heard that sound again—a distant melody echoing through the mountains. She slipped out of bed and then her room, following the strange hum. Out in the tunnel, everlights illuminated the darkness. She followed them back toward the mouth of the mountain until she came upon the gushing waterfall. Eana's Tears.

The sound of tinkling water echoed around the cavern, making a strange melody. The song was a balm to Wren's soul. She drifted toward the waterfall, running her hands underneath the streaming water. She closed her eyes.

"Eana, help me," she whispered. "I need your guidance now more than ever."

The water hummed. A rogue breeze tickled her cheeks. When she opened her eyes, Wren saw the hilt of Eana's sword flickering behind the waterfall. Night's Edge was glowing. Wren wondered how she hadn't noticed it before now. It was so bright, it made the water around it sparkle.

Take it, whispered a voice in the wind. Or perhaps it was in Wren's head. *It is yours to claim.*

Wren looked around, searching the darkness, but she was alone up here. There was nothing but the gentle fall of water and the faraway howl of the night wind. And there, only a stone's throw away, was the very weapon she needed to fell her wicked ancestor. To fell the curse that lived inside her.

Wren kicked off her slippers and hiked up her nightgown, stepping into the pool. It was much cooler than the baths, and she waded through it, quickly, even as her scar began to sting and her bones grew heavy.

The hilt winked, urging her on. The singing swelled. Wren ducked under the waterfall, letting it drench her from head to toe. It plastered her hair to her face and her nightgown to her skin, but she hardly noticed. There was magic in here. Ancient, rippling magic. And it was hers for the taking.

If Wren couldn't wield her own magic against Oonagh Starcrest, then she would slay her ancestor with a sword. And not just any sword. The strongest, most powerful weapon in all of Eana.

After all, Night's Edge *was* Eana.

Wren grabbed the hilt and tugged. Nothing happened. She gritted her teeth, using all her strength. The rock groaned but didn't yield. The water was starting to hurt. The curse inside her was waking up. And it was angry. It didn't want to be here. It didn't want *her* here.

"Come on," Wren pleaded with the sword. "I *need* you."

The rush of the falls grew louder, and for a terrifying heartbeat, Wren swore it would drown her.

The pain in her head grew to an almost unbearable pitch. She was about to give up entirely when the hilt warmed in her hand. Wren blinked, sure she was imagining it. But this time when she pulled, the rock began to crumble. She could see the blade now, bright and gleaming as the moon. Another tug and it slid from the rock. Night's Edge was halfway out.

The mountain was yielding to Wren. The sword was hers to claim. Almost. There came a swear from behind her. Wren startled, releasing the hilt as she spun on her heel. Alarik was stumbling through the water toward her. He must have caught his foot on the edge of the pool.

"What are you doing?" said Wren.

His eyes blazed. "I could ask you the same thing, witch."

He lunged, shoving Wren back toward the wall. She cried out as her head slammed against the rock. Alarik sealed the space between them, pinning her with his body. The waterfall made a veil behind him, sealing them in.

She struggled against him. "Have you lost your mind?"

Wren caught a flash of silver as he raised a knife to her throat. "I knew you'd go for that sword," Alarik spat. "You always meant to kill me."

"You're being paranoid." Wren raised her chin to stop the knife from biting into her skin. It felt dull. A butter knife, she guessed. "I came up here because I couldn't sleep."

"Don't lie to me," he hissed. "You made me believe we were friends. You made me believe we were in this together."

"We are," Wren gritted out. "Just get off me."

"So you can kill me?" His eyes were wide and bloodshot, and he looked like a man possessed.

"Alarik, I promise I'm not going to kill you," she said calmly. "Although . . . I might slap you for this."

"I don't believe you," he said, but this time his voice wavered. His grip slackened. Wren brought her hands to his chest, curling her fingers in the collar of his nightshirt. "Alarik," she said, gently pulling him close. "Look at me. I promise I won't hurt you."

He swallowed. "I just . . . I thought . . ." He glanced at the sword, jutting out of the rock. "I saw it move."

Wren grabbed his chin, pulling his gaze back to hers. "The edge of that blade is not meant for you," she said. "It is meant for Oonagh."

"Oonagh," he said in a whisper.

Wren nodded. "Only Oonagh."

Alarik dropped his head, and then the knife.

His face fell, and he sagged against her. "I'm so tired, Wren. So very tired."

Wren gripped his shoulders, steadying him. "I know you are," she breathed. "So am I."

Alarik raised his head, but the words never came. He grunted as something knocked into the back of his head. It took Wren a second to realize it was a fist.

Tor caught Alarik before he fell. He lifted him up, cradling his body as though he were no heavier than a sack of grain. He frowned at Wren, looking her up and down. "Are you all right?"

She nodded dumbly. "Did you just knock—?"

"Yes," he said, jaw tensed.

Wren almost laughed from shock. "You could hang for that."

"That's tomorrow's problem." Tor turned around and carried Alarik out of the pool. Wren followed him, wringing the water from her nightgown.

"Wait," she called after him. "Will you come back?"

Tor looked at her over his shoulder. "What for?"

Her face fell. She wrapped her arms around herself. "I just thought… Well, to talk?"

He must have noticed her embarrassment or perhaps took pity on her standing in the middle of the cavern like a half-drowned rat because he relented with a sigh. "Wait here."

Wren sat at the edge of the waterfall, her ancestor's sword momentarily forgotten as she waited for the soldier to return. True to his word, Tor came back a few moments later. It was only then that Wren noticed his white nightshirt was plastered to his skin, revealing the hard planes of his chest, and the ridges of his stomach muscles. His hair was damp, too. He raked it away from his face. "What do you want, Wren?"

Wren swallowed, searching for something to thaw this ice between them. "Why did you do that to Alarik just now?"

"He was threatening you," said Tor, casually rolling his sleeves to his elbows. "I saw him pocket a knife at dinner. I was afraid of what he might do with it in his addled state."

"Oh. Right." Wren looked at her hands. "I just didn't want you to think there was anything . . . that we were . . . or that he was trying to kiss me."

"I would have knocked him out for that, too." Wren looked up, struck by the storm in his eyes. He had surrendered his stony facade, and now she see could the pain beneath it. The betrayal. The *anger.* "I should have knocked him out in the baths for touching you as if you were his."

Wren's breath shallowed. "We didn't kiss in the baths."

"Just the blizzard, then." The waterfall roared in the sudden silence. Wren stared at Tor. He stared back, letting her see the accusation in his gaze. Stars, he *knew.* He had known all this time.

Wren opened her mouth, closed it. She couldn't find the words, or the breath.

"Anika told me when I returned from Carrig some months ago," he went on. "I should have turned around and rode home right then." He laughed mirthlessly. "But like a fool, I stayed, hoping I would somehow see you again. Hoping that the fates would draw us back together." He shook his head, his smile rueful. "But it seems, fate has no interest in me. Only you and him."

"That isn't fate, Tor. It's a curse."

"Yes, it is, Wren. All of it."

He turned to go.

"Wait!" She leaped to her feet. "You can't just turn around and leave."

He stilled, eyes flashing. "You can't command me."

"I can in this mountain," she shot back. "In this land. And I'm not done speaking."

He came toward her, his voice a growl. "So, speak, Wren."

Wren swallowed the sudden dryness in her throat. Tor was more beast in this place than she had ever known him to be, and yet the sight of him seething and practically shirtless stirred in her a desperate need to be closer to him. To stand in the headiness of his alpine scent and meet him, glare for glare.

She stared up at him, so tall and broad and immovable in his anger, and gave voice to her own feelings, messy as they were. "It's true that I kissed Alarik in that blizzard. We kissed each other," she admitted. "But it was no fairy tale. It wasn't some stolen moment written in the stars. It was a storm of pain and grief and fear and confusion."

Tor weathered the confession in stony silence, though a muscle flickered in his jaw.

"My grandmother was dead. Oonagh killed her right in front of me and smiled when it was done. Then the world came crumbling down around me." Wren's eyes welled at the memory, her grief catching in her throat. "The pain of that loss was so sudden, so jagged, I swore it was shearing my heart in two. I didn't want to go on, Tor. I didn't want to *live* past that moment."

Wren was crying now, but she didn't care. The words were crowding on the back of her tongue and she had to free them. He had to hear them.

His brow furrowed. He tried to look away from the sight of her pain, but she grabbed his jaw, holding his gaze.

"You weren't there that day. I was alone and out of my mind. I was adrift in this vast sea of maddening grief and Alarik was my life raft. He was the only person I could reach for, and when I flung my hand out, he reached back and caught it. He *saved* me that day. He gave me the strength to go on."

Tor closed his eyes. "So you kissed him."

"Yes," said Wren, her voice ragged. "Hate me if you want. Yell at me. Curse me, for stars' sake! Just please don't walk away from me again. Don't leave it like this." She grabbed the collar of his shirt, shaking him until he opened his eyes to her. "I'd rather have your anger than your silence."

He removed her hands from his shirt, freeing himself from her grasp. "I'm not angry at you, Wren," he said, taking a step back and then another, until he stood before the waterfall, distractingly damp and utterly exasperated. His gaze found hers, a streak of lightning cutting through the storm. "I'm in love with you."

Wren blinked.

"And it's torture." A cold wind rushed in between them, unsettling the strands along his face. He raked them back. "*This* is torture."

Torture. The word echoed back at her from deep inside the mountain.

She had stilled at Tor's confession, her hands still hovering in mid-air, waiting for him to take them. He did not. "And I know torture, Wren. I grew up in the wilds of Gevra. I went to war as a boy. I fought beasts far larger than I was, and buried soldiers much younger."

Wren's eyes filled with tears. How could a confession of love sound so bleak; how could desire taste so sour? How could he compare his feelings for her—their feelings for each other—to the horrors of war? Now here they stood, both shivering and wounded, and neither one of them was the better for it. "What a cruel comparison," she whispered. "How could love ever be torture?"

"Because love is being stuck here in this faraway place, watching you watch him," said Tor. "Watching you *want* him. Watching him caress your hair. Watching him touch your skin. Like—" He stopped short, gazing into the pool at her reflection. "He doesn't deserve you, Wren."

She frowned. "He doesn't have me."

"Are you sure about that?"

"Don't patronize me."

He huffed a humorless laugh. "The truth is bitter."

"*You* are bitter."

"Yes," he said, his voice rueful. "That is another truth."

"I don't want him," said Wren, pressing the point. The silence swelled, and she hated every second of it. "You have no idea what I want."

He cocked his head, looking at her for a long moment as if he was trying to figure out who she truly was. Then he sighed, and it was as if something inside him shifted. Something gave up. "The trouble is, Wren, neither do you."

This time when he turned from her, Wren knew it was over. The sudden fear of losing Tor was like a knife in her gut. She couldn't stand the idea of it, couldn't stomach the sight of his back as he walked away.

"I know what I want!" she called after him.

He kept walking.

She lunged, grabbing his hand. "Did you hear me? I said I know what I want!"

He turned, achingly slow. His gaze found hers, and this time there was a spark of lightning in it. A challenge. Or perhaps, a plea. "Prove it."

Wren grabbed him with the desperation of a drowning woman, ripping the buttons on his shirt as she pulled his body against hers. He yielded, reluctantly, and she raised her chin, claiming his lips with hers. The kiss was short, tentative.

"Please," she whispered against his mouth.

"Are you sure this time?" he whispered back.

She kissed him again, brushing her tongue against his, showing him just how sure she was. "Can't you taste it?"

He groaned into her mouth, his resolve crumbling. Wren rose to her tiptoes and wound her arms around his neck, tugging him closer still. He raked his hands through her hair, holding her still as he lavished her with a kiss so deep and ragged, she lost her breath.

They melted into each other, their soaked bodies pressed together so tightly not even the wind could come between them. The raging heat of their desire chased the chill from their bones, and as the last of their hurt washed away with the water, they both found themselves smiling between kisses.

When the dampness finally seeped into Wren's skin and she began to shiver, they surrendered their embrace. "We should go to bed," she said, between breaths. "We'll catch our deaths out here."

Tor brushed the strands from her eyes. "I'm afraid a head cold is one of the few things I cannot protect you from."

"You seem truly bereft about that," said Wren, taking his hand.

"I am," he said, falling into step with her.

When they reached the door to her bedchamber, she lingered on the threshold. "Stay with me awhile. We can keep each other warm."

He leaned against the doorframe, his teeth winking in the dimness. "Are you frightened of the big bad mountain, Wren?"

"What if Alarik tries to kill me with a soup spoon?"

"It's more likely he'll come for me next," said Tor.

She frowned, recalling the unfortunate circumstances of the king's concussion. "You should probably go and deal with that."

With great reluctance, Tor stepped back into the hall. "Let's hope he's in a forgiving mood."

"Then I really will be worried."

"Good night, Wren."

She waggled her fingers. "Sweet dreams, Captain Iversen."

"Of that I have no doubt." He disappeared into the dimness, the music of his laughter echoing after him. Wren wished she could catch the sound and bottle it, but for now, the memory of their kisses was enough to warm her as she peeled off her sopping nightgown and crawled into bed. She pulled the furs around her, smiling as she dropped into slumber.

28

ROSE

By the time they reached Wishbone Bay, it was just after dawn. The sun peeked out over the horizon, turning the bay a glistening gold. The sea breeze was biting, but Rose welcomed it. She was exhausted from lack of sleep, and with everything that had happened over the last few days, she felt as if she had been awake for weeks. The cool morning air jolted her back to life, to purpose.

"We will take my ship, of course," said Anika, striding toward the imposing Gevran war boat festooned with blue-and-silver flags. "We Gevrans know the Sunless Sea better than any other."

"Wait." Celeste pulled her to a stop. "We should take my brother's ship. I've never known a more skillful captain."

Celeste and Anika stared at each other for a long moment. Celeste set her jaw, and Rose knew no matter how fond Celeste was of Anika, she would never allow anyone to say there was a captain better than her brother.

"Their first lovers' spat," Shen whispered to Rose.

"Who do you think is going to win?" said Kai. "My money's on the redhead."

"I will decide," said Rose, stepping between them. "We will sail on the *Siren's Secret*. Marino Pegasi is a fine captain, but more important, he is a witch. The swifter we sail, the better for all. We will need every gust we can gather."

A short while later, all five of them clambered on to the *Siren's Secret*. There were a handful of shipmates milling about on deck, preparing to sail.

"It's not natural to be floating on water like this," said Kai, glancing uneasily over the edge. "I don't like it."

Shen elbowed him in the side. "Just wait until we're out on the open sea, cousin. Then you'll really hate it."

Celeste tapped the first mate on the shoulder. "Dooley! Where is the captain?"

"He's in his quarters, Lady Celeste. Still sleeping, I imagine." He chuckled awkwardly. "We had a late night, but we'll soon be heading to the southern continent."

"We'll see about that," Celeste muttered under her breath. "Thank you, Dooley." She looked to the others. "This way to the captain's quarters."

"We'll stay up here," said Shen. "Introduce ourselves to the crew."

"As long as Kai doesn't start any fights," warned Rose.

As she followed Celeste belowdecks, trailing her hand along the finely wrought balustrade, she smiled. She knew Marino's ship well, recalling with fondness the day he had first acquired it some years ago, how he had insisted on taking Celeste and Rose on the *Siren's Secret*'s maiden voyage. They had only sailed to the edge of the bay and back, but at the time, it had been the farthest Rose had ever been from

Anadawn. She had stood at the prow with the wind in her hair and the salt spray from the sea kissing her cheeks, marveling at how big the world truly was. Thinking how desperately she wished to explore it.

When she returned, Willem Rathborne had flown into a rage, furious that she'd dared set foot on a ship without his permission. She'd been locked in her tower for a week after that, only seeing her loyal maidservant Agnes when she came to bring up Rose's food. But even that didn't tarnish the memory of Rose's first time on a proper ship, feasting her eyes on the wide-open sea and seeing within it a world of glittering possibilities.

In the captain's quarters, Marino Pegasi was fast asleep. Even with his mouth open and snoring raucously, he was handsome as ever.

Anika let out a delighted squeal. "Oh! He looks just like you!"

Celeste groaned. "That's what everyone says." She thumped her brother on the arm. "Wake up, dunderhead!"

Marino muttered something unintelligible and rolled over, burying his face in his pillow.

Celeste thumped him again. "I said wake up!"

Marino opened one eye, like a cat, and took in the scene before him. He looked at Anika and then Rose, his smile slow and lazy. "Waking up to two beautiful women in my cabin is unexpected but not unwelcome." He cleared his throat as he sat up, and Rose saw he was still in his nightshirt. "To what do I owe this pleasure?" He flicked his gaze to his sister. "And good morning to you as well, Lessie."

"Oh, he's a charmer!" purred Anika. "I should have known!"

Marino's brow furrowed. "Wait. Aren't you Gevran?"

"Which brings us to the matter at hand," said Celeste deftly. "We need you to take us to Gevra. Immediately."

Marino laughed. "Lessie, I'm headed to Caro today. I can't simply take you to Gevra on a whim."

"I told you we should take my boat," said Anika smugly. "Nobody on my boat says no to me."

"Marino, you're taking us to Gevra," said Celeste, scowling at her brother. "I'm afraid it's nonnegotiable."

"I have spices to sell, Lessie. Cloth to trade." Marino threw off the covers and got out of bed, searching for his boots. "Eanan goods have become so popular in Caro that I'm finding myself in great demand. Apparently, they think our very fabric is infused with magic!" He barked a laugh. "Business has been booming ever since Rose and Wren came into power."

"Well, you know what won't help business?" said Celeste, snatching up his boot before he could shrug it on. She waved it in his face. "When all of Eana is ravaged by a power-hungry undead witch!"

Marino frowned. "Wait. What?" He looked to Rose, his brows furrowing at the grim look on her face.

Rose sighed. "Marino, I'm sorry to do this, but as queen of Eana, I order you to take us to the isle of Carrig at once. I'm afraid it is a matter of life and death."

Marino scrubbed a hand across his jaw. "Well, when you put it like that, how could I resist?" He forced a chuckle, striving to lighten the mood. "At this rate, I'm practically already running a ferry service from here to Gevra. I should really start charging."

"You will be well compensated," said Rose.

His face brightened. "I like the sound of that."

Celeste snorted. "Here's something you should know about my brother, Anika. His two favorite things are money and mermaids."

"And great feats of bravery." Marino snatched his boot from his sister and pulled it on. "I love nothing more than the chance to be a hero. Just as long as I don't have to get off my boat. Now," he said, looking up from his laces, "tell me about this undead witch."

Within the hour, they were sailing.

Marino, dressed in his full captain regalia with his plum frock coat billowing behind him in the wind and his tricorn hat set on his head at a jaunty angle, stood at the helm, guiding the ship. Rose and the others gathered nearby, holding on to the railings as they looked to the horizon.

"Next stop—Carrig!" cried Marino, raising his hands and calling down a whip of wind that sent Rose's hair skyward. Celeste and Rose followed his lead, summoning their own strands of wind. They combined in a mighty roar, punching the sails taut. The ship lurched, skipping like a stone across the water.

"Easy there!" yelled Kai, bending to vomit over the side of the ship. "Some of us are still waiting for our sea legs!"

Shen nudged Rose. "Isn't Marino the man you once called the most handsome in all of Eana?"

Marino beamed over his shoulder. "Did you really say that?"

Rose's cheeks flamed. "I *said* that I had seen a lot of women mooning over you."

Kai looked up mid-vomit to assess Marino. "Surely, I'm more handsome," he slurred. "He's just fancy. Put me in a ruffled shirt and I'll look just as good, if not better."

"It takes years of practice to become this dashing," said Marino, tipping his tricorn. "Now then, let me focus on getting us to Gevra as quickly as possible. It sounds as if it's rather urgent." He cast another gust and the ship quickened again.

Kai swayed on his feet, his face taking on a greenish hue. "Please stop," he moaned, before rushing for the railing.

"Here," said Rose, stepping away from Shen and reaching for Kai's hand. "Let me help settle your stomach."

Kai couldn't lift his head but managed to speak. "Aw, Queenie. I didn't know you cared."

"Don't be so flattered," said Rose, releasing a pulse of healing magic. "If you're going to help us kill Oonagh, I need you at your best."

Once they were out on the open sea and had enjoyed a simple breakfast of griddle cakes with jam, Rose found she could barely keep her eyes open. Marino dutifully offered up his own quarters to her, and Celeste quickly decided she and Anika would share the other private cabin on board, which belonged to the first mate.

"What about us?" said Kai, gesturing between himself and Shen. "Are we supposed to sleep in that tiny crow's nest?" He flexed, unnecessarily. "Look at me. I'm far too large."

"You two are more than welcome to avail yourselves of the bunk beds belowdecks," said Marino good-naturedly. "I apologize in advance for the smell."

Shen walked Rose to the captain's cabin then paused at the door. "You know, we aren't in Eana anymore. . . ."

"And?" said Rose, goading him.

"I don't think the same rules of propriety apply," he went on. "Surely ships have their own set of rules."

"I believe you're right," she said, pulling him inside and locking the door.

And then it was only the two of them.

"Well," Shen said, glancing around the small but finely outfitted cabin. "This is far nicer than the crew bunks."

"So you were only trying to talk your way into a more comfortable bed?" Rose teased.

"I wouldn't dare assume I'd be sharing your bed," he said.

"Well, then I insist," said Rose, blushing at her own boldness as she pulled him close, then closer still, until they fell onto the bed together.

Shen brushed a strand of hair from her eyes, gazing down at her as if she was the loveliest creature he'd ever seen. Rose arced up beneath him, wrapping her arms around his neck, before she pressed her lips to his.

Shen kissed her back, hungrily, and she lost herself in him.

Far too soon he pulled away, leaving her lips swollen from his kisses.

"Rose, I don't believe I'm saying this, but we should rest. We'll be at Carrig before we know it. And who knows what we'll find there."

Rose sighed. Thoughts of Oonagh shattered the moment. But still. She was with Shen. And that was what mattered now. She curled into him, bringing his hand around her waist and holding it close to her heart.

Shen nuzzled into her, pressing a gentle kiss to her cheek. The noise from above soon faded until all she could hear was the sound of her breath mingling with his.

When Rose awoke, she was cold and alone. Shen was gone, most likely keeping a watchful eye on Kai. Shivering, she wrapped herself in her borrowed Gevran furs and went to the porthole. The window was covered in frost, the crystals forming intricate shapes on the glass.

She peered out, hoping for a glimpse of Carrig, but all she saw were the eerily still waters of the Sunless Sea glistening under the evening sky. Rose ventured above deck, where Marino was standing with both hands on the wheel, a look of intense concentration on his face.

"Is everything all right?" Rose asked.

"I've never sailed in this part of the Sunless Sea," he said, without tearing his gaze from the water. "I usually make port on the mainland, but this island you're after is so remote, it's caught in its own current. It's best to be on guard."

"Very sensible," said Rose approvingly. "Rare for you."

Marino chuckled. "I am always sensible when it comes to my ship. You know that, Rosie."

"Goodness! Nobody has called me Rosie in years."

He flashed a grin. "You might be Queen Rose now, but you and Celeste will always be Rosie and Lessie to me."

"I suppose I'll allow it," she said, returning his smile.

"I like your Sunkissed king," Marino went on. "I saw him and his cousin playing cards belowdecks with my crew, and he fit right in. A good catch indeed."

Rose let out a burst of laughter. "Catch? He's not a fish!"

Marino gave her a sly look. "He might not be a fish but he is certainly caught. Snared. Whatever you want to call it. Plain as day to anyone who sees the two of you together."

Rose flushed. "He is . . . quite nice," she admitted.

"I'm happy for you," said Marino.

"And what about you? Still looking for that mermaid you saw once upon a time?" Rose said, grinning.

"I'm far too busy for love," said Marino good-naturedly. "The sea is all I need. But I know love when I see it, and you, Rose, have found the real thing."

They sailed on, the sea growing more tempestuous with every passing hour. Rose couldn't shake the feeling that the sea was warning them away. It was as if every wave were pushing them back, trying to send them back to Anadawn. To safety.

Rose clutched Daybreak, holding it close for courage. She would not miss this chance to find Oonagh. To stop her before she came to Eana.

The gray evening quickly turned into a dark night and then a misty morning. Rose wondered if they would ever find Carrig or if they would float forever in the creeping fog, searching for the remote Gevran island.

Finally, Marino called out that he had spotted land. Anika clambered halfway up the rigging and said it was indeed Carrig, that she'd recognize the craggy rock face anywhere.

Rose ran to the prow, eager for her first sighting of the island. The others followed.

She halfway expected to see Oonagh standing on the shore waiting for them. But even from a distance, she could tell that the strand was deserted.

At the sight of the snowy island, Kai made a disdainful grunt, shivering as he pulled his cloak tightly around his shoulders. "I think you brought me here as part of my punishment," he said. "Nobody should ever be this cold."

Rose was about to retort that he was lucky to be there at all, when the ship jolted. There was a deep, rattling thud as it struck something with so much force, she nearly toppled overboard. Kai yanked her back. "Careful, Queenie."

"Marino!" cried Celeste, holding tightly to the railing. "Have we run aground?"

"No!" Marino shouted, his face straining as he wrestled with the wheel. Shen rushed to help him. "We're nowhere near the reef!"

"Something's wrong!" yelled Anika. "The sea is churning! Turn back!"

"We're nearly there!" said Marino, gaining back control of the ship.

But then it jolted again. The deck rattled, and this time, Rose felt it in her teeth. "Marino!"

"HOLD FAST!" he shouted as the water thrashed and churned around them. Out of the depths of the sea shot a huge black tentacle. It lashed through the air before landing on the deck with so much force the entire ship shook.

Rose screamed as she scrambled backward.

Kai leaped in front of her, uncoiling his whip. "Looks as if we've got a live one!"

Another tentacle latched on to the ship, this one even larger than the first. Celeste rolled out of the way before it flattened her while Anika was thrown from the rigging, the mainsail barely cushioning her fall.

The *Siren's Secret* began to list in the water.

"GET THAT THING OFF MY SHIP!" roared Marino. All around him, the crew sprang into action, grabbing every net and rope and cutlass they could find.

As the first tentacle inched toward Rose, Kai struck quick as an adder, his whip slicing clean through it. Thick black blood oozed out.

Anika scrabbled through Rose's feet, narrowly avoiding a third tentacle as it came spearing out of the sea. "It's a kraken!" she screeched. "Cut off its tentacles!"

"I'm trying!" said Kai, whipping at the next one. Shen pounced, striking it with his dagger. The blade sank to the hilt, and he yanked it through, severing the tentacle in half.

From beneath the sea, there came a great watery bellow. The ship creaked as it tilted, and from belowdecks, a frightened shout went up. "Captain! We've sprung a leak!"

"Where's my axe?" yelled Anika.

Celeste spun around to help her search for it just as another tentacle jutted up from the sea.

"Watch out!" Rose leaped, pushing her friend out of the way, just as it came crashing down. They rolled onto their backs, barely catching their breaths before the rest of the terrible kraken emerged, its gargantuan head breaching the surface like an ancient whale.

As the kraken rose from the sea, Rose took one look at its glowing red eyes and knew it was going to sink the ship.

"That's no ordinary kraken!" yelled Anika.

Shen snapped his head up from another severed tentacle, his horrified gaze finding Rose's across the ship. She knew they were thinking the same thing—that this kraken was different because it was undead. And that meant it had come with a purpose.

There was a rush of warm, fetid wind as the kraken opened its humongous mouth, showing its endless rows of needle teeth. Then, to Rose's horror, the creature began to laugh.

It was the laugh of Oonagh Starcrest. The same one that had haunted Rose's dreams.

The kraken's red eyes bored into hers as it cast out another tentacle. Thanks to the combined prowess of Shen and Kai, this tentacle was the last of them. But it was desperate, grasping. Still trembling, Rose unsheathed Daybreak and brandished it at the kraken. She didn't know how Oonagh had managed to enslave this creature, but she could tell by the dark magic throbbing between them that it was linked to her ancestor. That it would keep coming for them if they didn't kill it.

Just as Rose made to strike at the final tentacle, a rising wave crashed into the ship, and she was thrown backward. The kraken lurched, grabbing her by the waist and hoisting her into the air.

"Rose!" Shen's cry rang out, but he was far below her now.

Rose was yanked through the air like a puppet, but her arms were still free, and somehow, she had managed to keep hold of the dagger. The kraken's red eyes flashed as it pulled her toward its gaping maw, its interest in the ship now lost. Rose looked directly into its glowing red eyes as she was dragged close, and closer still, and just as its rotting breath careened over her, she raised her arm and struck, burying the dagger in the fleshy space between its eyes, as deep as it would go. The hilt thrummed as the blade sank true.

The kraken jerked, sliding backward in the water.

Rose slipped from its grip and hit the water just as the thunder of cannon fire filled the air.

"HOLD FIRE!" shouted Shen, but it was already too late. The kraken thrashed weakly as it was pummeled, the glow in its eyes finally fading as it sank lifelessly into the sea.

29

WREN

When Wren woke up the next morning, the mountain was already thrumming with activity. She stretched as she rolled out of bed, recalling the events of last night. Though she did not regret what had happened with Tor, she wasn't exactly looking forward to seeing Alarik this morning.

Her stomach grumbled, adding a more pressing problem. She was starving. She got up and dressed, running a brush through her hair and braiding it down her back. When she arrived at the dining hall, Alarik was sitting by himself, picking at a bowl of berries.

He flung one at her in greeting. "Morning, witch."

"Where's Tor?" she said, catching the berry and devouring it.

"Oh, you mean my midnight assailant?" he sneered. "I've been waiting for Iversen to make an appearance ever since he tried to wake me from my slumber last night. Maybe he's rethought his apology and decided to run off in shame instead."

"I doubt it."

"In any case, it seems I'm in need of a new Captain of the Guard."

She slumped into the chair opposite him. "Don't be so dramatic."

Alarik tapped the purple bruise on his temple. "Tell me, *Queen* Wren, back at Anadawn, do you allow your own soldiers to attack you indiscriminately?"

"You were trying to kill me," she reminded him as a bowl of steaming porridge was set down in front of her. "You're lucky I didn't take it personally."

"Only for a moment." He flushed a little at the memory. "And anyway, that was a misunderstanding."

"Was it?"

"Yes, Wren." He held her gaze, his voice softening. "Forgive me."

"I'll think about it." She drizzled fresh honey on her porridge then added a generous heaping of brown sugar. She eyed the king's bowl of porridge and noted that it was still full, the cooling oats congealing along the sides. "Aren't you going to eat?"

He wrinkled his nose. "I can't seem to muster an appetite."

Wren examined him more closely. In the dimness of the mountain, Alarik looked like hell. Worse than yesterday. The concussion certainly hadn't helped matters. He caught her gaze of concern and offered a wolfish smile. "Your mountains are not so healing after all."

"They're doing their best."

"Their best is not good enough," he said. "Although I did enjoy our trip to the baths yesterday."

Wren's cheeks burned. "That's not funny."

"It's not supposed to be." He sat back in his chair and raked a hand through his hair. "This wretched curse," he muttered. Wren knew exactly how he felt and sensed the same hopelessness and frustration warring inside herself. Even after a full night's sleep, she could still feel exhaustion tugging at her, the curse in her bones demanding attention. "It has burrowed a lot deeper than we feared."

Wren looked to his hand on the table and thought about reaching for it, offering him some measure of comfort. *Taking* some measure of comfort. His fingers twitched as if he was thinking the same thing.

"I'm sorry, Wren." He sighed, looking at her in a way he never had before. With sadness. With contrition. "About all of this. I know it all began with my wishes. My selfishness."

Wren blinked. "Now you're really scaring me."

"What?" he said, brows raised. "We both know it to be true."

"Don't do that." She threw a berry at him. "Don't apologize."

"Why not?"

"Because it's *weird*. It's *decent*," she said, frowning. "And you're . . ."

"A monster?"

"No. You're . . . You're *Alarik*. You're supposed to keep me on my toes," she said, jabbing the air with her spoon. "And I'm supposed to keep you on *your* toes."

"And then when we stop dancing, we both die?" he said, with a dark chuckle.

"I don't know," she murmured. "Maybe."

"I'd much prefer if your ancestor died."

"That makes two of us."

"*Three* of us," said Tor, marching into the dining hall with a face like thunder. Elske, who was padding behind him, looked just as unsettled. Tor was holding a letter. "I've just had word from Carrig."

Wren frowned. Carrig was a small frostbitten island off the coast of Gevra. It was home to wild beasts, snowy forests, and Tor's family.

Alarik was unmoved by the seriousness of Tor's announcement. "I hope it's news of a new outpost, Iversen," he said, tossing him a withering look. "Since you'll soon be finding yourself in need of a different vocation."

Clearly stricken by whatever was written in his letter, Tor barely registered the threat. "My sister Hela sent her nighthawk across the Sunless Sea," he said, slamming the letter on to the table. "It found me while I was taking Elske out for a walk this morning."

"Impressive bird," muttered Wren, while Alarik picked up the letter. "I thought we were well hidden."

Alarik scanned the missive, his frown sharpening with every line.

"Oonagh has ripped through Carrig," said Tor, narrating the tense silence. "She upended the trees and ravaged the farms. She dug up our graveyards and went on a killing spree. Half of our animals are dead."

Wren stiffened in her seat. "Hissing hell."

"And worse," he went on. "When Oonagh left, she wasn't alone."

"What do you mean?" Wren hinged forward, reaching for the letter.

It was Alarik who answered her. "She took the dead beasts with her."

"Her undead army grows by the hour," said Tor grimly.

Wren inhaled sharply. In the silence that followed, she knew they were all thinking of that red-eyed mountain lion from yesterday and how it had come to them in the valley, bearing its rotting flesh and gleaming skull. Oonagh had an entire army of beasts just like that. "She's out of control."

"No," said Tor. "She's preparing for war."

Alarik set down the letter. "The question is, where will she strike first?"

Wren was seized by a sudden sense of urgency. She knew exactly where her ancestor was going. After all, Oonagh had already told them. Rose had gotten marks on her neck to prove it. "I have to get back to Anadawn."

Alarik frowned. "So soon?"

"Yes," said Wren, the truth of it rippling in her bones. She had less time than she'd thought. "We don't have to find our way to Oonagh. She will find her way to us. War is coming to these shores, Alarik."

"Your magic is all but broken," he said, his voice hitching.

Tor wore the same worry on his face. "You can barely hold a sword."

Wren didn't argue with them. "Which is why Rose and I need all the help we can get." She swallowed her pride, fear quickening her words. "Gevra trains the strongest soldiers. It breeds the most fearsome beasts." She looked up at Tor. "Can you spare some?"

"Iversen certainly can't," said Alarik icily. "It's not his decision to make."

Wren turned back to him. "I was asking both of you."

"Ask me, Wren." His eyes sparked as he leaned toward her. "Only me."

She glared at him, sensing his power play and hating her part in it. It was not the place, nor the time. "This isn't a game, Alarik."

"War is Gevra's finest game." He offered her the ghost of a smile. "If I send you an army, what's in it for me?"

Wren knew what he wanted her to say. What he wanted Tor to hear. A part of Alarik was back in that blizzard, still reaching for a moment that was lost to them both.

"Our freedom," she said, leaning toward Alarik until the rest of the mountain fell away. "From illness and pain."

He held her gaze. "And from each other."

Wren sensed the storm in Tor's eyes, noted the tension in his jaw.

"Yes," she said to the king.

Alarik looked away, a shadow falling across his face. "Quite the bargain."

It was not the answer he wanted, but it was the truest one she could give.

"To break the bond, we have to kill Oonagh," she went on, repeating what Willa had told them. "It's the only way we'll survive. If she truly has her own army—"

"Then we must have two," said Alarik, coming to the seriousness of the matter.

Three, thought Wren hopefully. If Shen and the Sunkissed Kingdom witches joined their cause.

"Very well," said Alarik. "If your ancestor wants a fight, then we'll give her one."

Wren could have thrown her arms around him just then, but instead, she smiled, full and bright and truly gracious. "Thank you, Alarik."

The king blinked. "Yes . . . well . . . Our fates are entwined, so it makes sense. . . ."

"It does," said Tor, breaking his silence.

Alarik shot him a warning glance. "That's enough out of you, Iversen. I have yet to deal with your insubordination."

"While you're doing that, I'll gather my things." Wren moved her chair back. "I must ride south to Anadawn to ready our soldiers."

Alarik pushed away his bowl. "And I must prepare to return to Gevra."

"No, you must not." They all looked up at the sound of a new voice. Willa was standing in the doorway to the dining hall. Wren didn't know how long the Healer on High had been lingering there, but by the fearful look on Willa's face, Wren suspected she had heard the contents of the letter. "I'm afraid the king is too weak to make such a long journey. The farther you stray from the mountains, the quicker your condition will deteriorate."

"I can sail well enough," said Alarik.

"Perhaps," reasoned Willa. "But if you leave for Gevra you will not likely return."

"What do you expect me to do?" he demanded. "Bathe under your mountain while I send my country to war?"

"I expect you to do exactly as you like," said Willa, nonplussed. "But the longer you stay in these mountains, the greater chance you will have of fighting in that war when it comes to our shores." She smiled tightly. "It is of course up to Your Majesty."

"Don't be foolish," said Wren, lending her voice to Willa's. "You're not well."

"And what about you?" he returned. "Are we not suffering from the same affliction?"

"Anadawn is a much shorter journey," said Willa. "And Queen Wren is a witch. Though she is ill, she is stronger than you. Her magic still sustains her. For now."

Wren didn't like the sound of those two final words, but she couldn't deny her own weakness either. She was exhausted, but she had no choice. With Rose away, Wren had to get home to Anadawn to defend the seat of their power before Oonagh came to snatch it from their grasp.

Alarik slumped in his chair, coming to the same realization. "So I will stay. And you will go."

"I have to," said Wren, feeling a curious ripple of sadness at having to leave him.

He dragged a hand across his jaw, as if he was trying to scrub the frown from his face. "I know you do."

"Then it is decided," said Willa.

"Not quite yet." Alarik looked to Tor and with unerring calmness said, "Captain Iversen, you are dismissed."

Tor recoiled. "If this is about last night—"

"Forget last night." Alarik waved a hand in dismissal. Despite his harsh words there was no bite in his voice. No anger on his face. There were greater matters at hand now, greater danger. "I'm afraid you'll have to find somewhere else to go. Someone else to guard." Alarik stroked his chin as though a rogue thought had only just occurred to him. "Perhaps you can accompany the queen on her journey back to Anadawn. She's in need of a chaperone. And despite your deficient loyalty, you certainly seem capable of defending *her*."

Tor raised his brows, catching the king's meaning. This was not quite a dismissal—rather it was permission to leave the king and the mountains without guilt. And more than that, it was a move to protect Wren.

"I know what you're doing," she said.

Alarik smiled blandly. "Am I so transparent?"

"Yes," said Wren. "I think it's my favorite thing about you."

"One of many, I'm sure."

"Too many to fathom, Alarik."

"Good luck with this one, Iversen," said Alarik, without taking his eyes off Wren. "I'm sure she will keep you on your toes."

"I welcome the challenge," said Tor.

Alarik gave a mirthless snort.

"Elske will stay here as your guardian while I ride south with the queen," Tor went on.

"Then it truly is settled," said the king. "Everyone wins. Except of course me."

"You will win," said Wren. "We all will."

"We will see," Alarik said distantly.

"*And* you get the wolf. I think we can agree she's the best of all of us."

"Well, she's certainly the least annoying." Alarik pushed his chair back and got to his feet. "I must send word to Anika while I still possess the strength to write."

"Alarik," said Tor, dispensing with his title and speaking to him now not as a king, but an old friend. "Before we leave. May I have a moment?"

"Only if you promise to use your words and not your fists this time."

Tor made a show of tucking his arms behind his back.

"I'll go and get my things," said Wren, leaving the Gevrans to their conversation.

Willa followed her from the dining hall. As Wren left Alarik behind, that feeling of sadness worsened. It bloomed in her chest and prickled behind her eyes. It was the same ache she felt whenever she and Rose parted ways or whenever she thought of her grandmother, now lost to her forever.

She rubbed her chest, trying to banish the discomfort.

"It is the work of the curse, Queen Wren," said Willa, falling into step with her. "It has bound you and the king to each other. That means *all* of you." Her dark eyes were all too knowing, but her words were gentle. "Your pain. Your souls. Your hearts. The bond hurts more when you are apart because it wishes to remind you that it's there."

"Yes," said Wren in a low voice. "It feels as if I'm leaving a part of me behind."

Willa nodded, unsurprised by her revelation. "In a way, you are. The part of you that exists in Alarik. It is, after all, your magic. Twisted as it may be."

Wren frowned. "Does that mean . . . ? What about . . . ?" She trailed off, too embarrassed to say the rest.

"Your feelings?" said Willa.

"I worry about him," Wren admitted. "I feel . . . protective of him. Drawn to him. I don't understand it."

The healer chuckled. "Some things are not meant to be understood. Friendships can bloom in the most unlikely of places. But that *pull* you feel . . ." She looked meaningfully at Wren. "It is, in part, borne of the curse. It runs through the soul. And so it ties you two together."

"So it's not my heart," said Wren quietly.

The Healer on High hesitated, weighing her answer. "Once you break the curse, you will know for sure."

Relief prickled inside Wren. In a few simple words, Willa had made sense of the war inside her, the push and pull of her feelings, the strange closeness she felt to the king, even as she found herself yearning for Tor. If this confusion truly was part of the curse, then it would fritter away once they destroyed it. Wren would have full possession of her heart once more. She hoped.

Wren left Willa and went to gather her things before returning to the cavern aboveground, where the waterfall was full and glistening. A slant of sunlight crept in through the entrance, painting the water gold. It bounced off the handle of Night's Edge, which was still jutting out from the rock.

Wren contemplated wading through the water again, but there were healers milling about now. It would be terribly rude to steal from them. At least in broad daylight. And yet, her fingers itched. It felt as if the sword was calling out to her.

She was going to war, after all. And if she was going to kill her ancestor, she needed a weapon powerful enough to do it.

She jumped at a hand on her wrist. It was Willa.

"From what I've heard, you are not one to do things by halves, Your Majesty." A smile danced across the healer's face, and for a moment, she looked just like Thea. "You may as well finish what you started last night."

Wren flushed. "It was an accident, really. I just . . . I wanted to see if it would budge."

"And after all these years, it finally has." Willa gestured to the glittering hilt. "Eana has spoken. Night's Edge is yours to claim."

Wren set her jaw as she stepped into the pool. Water lapped at her knees, cold and biting. She waded toward the sword, grabbing it with both hands. She closed her eyes, feeling her ancestor's presence in the rush of water and the warmth of the hilt under her fingers.

"Eana, help me," she whispered to the roaring falls. "So I may save this land."

The sword groaned as it loosened, as if the mountain itself were spitting it out. Wren tugged, and as easily as a knife sliding through butter, it yielded to her. She reeled backward, pulling the sword free. And then it was hers.

Wren clutched the sword to her chest and turned around. The healers of the Mishnick Mountains had gathered in the cavern and were watching her now with expressions of awe and wonder. They bowed their heads as she waded toward them, offering respect to their queen and to Eana herself.

Wren spotted Tor standing among them, tall and smiling in his Anadawn uniform. Wren smiled back, the hilt of Night's Edge warm in her hand. She felt stronger already, and more determined than ever. It was time to go to war.

30

ROSE

As the kraken sank beneath the waves, the pull of its current dragged Rose down with it. If she didn't fight it, she would drown here in the icy sea, barely a stone's throw from the island of Carrig. She kicked out, swimming with all her might. Her head pounded and her lungs ached until it felt as if they would burst, but then she spied a glimmer of light above her. She kicked once and then again, straining for the surface.

She rose to meet it, slowly, painfully. And then, there was air. She gasped, gulping in as much of it as she could. Her waterlogged dress was so heavy, it was threatening to pull her back down. She had to swim, to survive. Remembering what Shen had taught her, she kicked her arms and legs out and arched her back, determined to float. She glimpsed Marino's ship listing as it sailed toward her, but the distance was too far to swim. She twisted in the water and saw the shoreline winking through the mist. It was closer than she'd thought—close enough to swim to. Yes, she could do it. She *would* do it.

Rose lay on her back and moved her arms in an arc, first one and then the other. Over and over again. She kicked her legs as she swam, tipping her chin to the sky so she could breathe. Her body was going numb in the water, but she didn't dare slow down.

Don't stop, she told herself. *You're almost there.*

Dimly, she became aware of shouting. Her name floated on the wind—wrought with ragged panic—but she was too far from the voices and too exhausted to call back. Finally, after what felt like an eternity, her hand hit a rock. She turned to find she had floated into a cluster of seaweed. She twisted onto her front, grasping at the shale below her. She had reached the shoreline!

With the last kernel of her energy, Rose dragged herself over the rocks and onto the sand, where she collapsed, utterly and completely spent.

"Rose? Rose!" A familiar voice echoed through the darkness of Rose's mind. "ROSE! Wake up!" A new warmth prickled in her cheeks. "Please wake up." The heat reached her hands, and then her feet. "Why am I such a useless healer?"

Such wonderful warmth. Rose's heart thrummed as it rushed through her, coaxing her awake. She opened her eyes and Shen was there. His hands cupped her cheeks, offering more warmth, as he stared down at her. When their eyes met, he let out a cry of relief.

"There you are. There you are." He leaned closer, touching his forehead against hers. "Rose, I thought I lost you."

Rose tried to speak, but a cough spluttered out instead.

Gently, so gently, as if he thought she might break, Shen helped her sit up. She was still on the shore, the cold water lapping at her feet. "Come here," he said, pulling her into his arms. She sat in his lap and laid her head against his chest. His heart was racing, and he was just as soaked as she was. Rose realized he must have swum to shore after her.

They sat for a moment in silence, his arms tight around her, Rose's head on his chest, both of them thanking the stars for each other.

"What happened?" said Rose. "Where are the others?"

"The ship ran aground," said Shen, jerking his chin to where everyone else was just now clambering off the *Siren's Secret*. "I couldn't wait. As soon as I saw you go under, I dived in. I tried to get to you, Rose, I—" His voice broke. "I was so afraid you—"

"I'm all right," she said, tilting her head up so he could see her face. She smiled. "I swam. Just like you taught me."

Shen took her face in his hands and kissed her deeply. Rose realized he was trembling. She wound her arms around his neck and pressed herself against him, desperate for his warmth. She couldn't get close enough.

Then something occurred to her, and she pulled back. "Shen Lo, did you heal me?"

"I did my best," he said, tucking her hair back. "You were barely breathing. Your lips were blue. . . ."

"Well, whatever you did worked. I'm warmer now."

"Not warm enough." He pressed another kiss to her lips. "We need to make a fire. Or get indoors. And after that, I'm going to murder Marino for firing at that thing when it had you in its grasp. What if he had missed?"

Rose smiled. "It would have been pretty hard to miss the kraken. And anyway, I had managed to slip free." With a violent shudder, she recalled the moments before she had hit the water. How the awful kraken had almost devoured her, and in a fit of desperation, she had buried her dagger between its eyes. "Oh no," she said, jolting upright.

"I lost your mother's dagger. I lost Daybreak. I'm so sorry, Shen. I know how much it meant to you."

"It's nothing compared to what *you* mean to me," he said fiercely. "Forget the dagger, Rose. I'm just glad it saved your life."

But Rose couldn't simply forget it. It was part of Shen's heritage, and a potential key to their own salvation. She covered her face, trying not to cry.

"Looking for this?" Kai's voice wafted across the shoreline. When Rose looked up, he was sauntering toward them, dangling Daybreak by the hilt. He looked Rose up and down. "Good to see you alive and well, Queenie. You certainly wear the ocean well."

"That's enough," warned Shen. "Eyes to yourself."

Rose got to her feet, scarcely able to believe her eyes. "Where did you find that?"

"Embedded in the kraken's face," said Kai, with a booming laugh. "You're not the only thing that washed up on these shores." He moved aside to reveal a beached black mass lying in a heap at the other end of the shoreline. It was indeed the kraken. "Looks like old fish-face here kept your dagger safe for you."

"Thank you for retrieving it." Rose took Daybreak from Kai. It was crusted with black blood, the hilt so dark she couldn't make out the rubies in it.

"What was that giant creepy thing anyway?" said Kai. "Apart from being yet another reason the desert is far superior to the sea."

"No arguments here," said Shen, rolling to his feet to inspect the dagger. "Looks as if we'll need to clean this with spirits."

"We'll worry about that later," said Rose, slipping it into the sheath

at her waist. "That kraken was sent by Oonagh. Didn't you see its glowing red eyes? And it reeked of dark magic."

"She must be here somewhere." Shen turned on his heel, scouring
their surroundings. He stiffened as he spotted something.

"You have missed the creature who has ravaged our island," a new
voice called out.

Rose whipped her head around, just as three women emerged from
the mist beyond the shore.

Kai smirked. "Maybe I like Carrig after all."

The women slowed as they came toward Rose, their eyes widening
as they took in her appearance, noting, no doubt, her uncanny likeness
to Oonagh. They stopped, and the woman in the middle—who Rose
guessed was the eldest—reached for the sword at her waist.

"I'm not her," said Rose, pushing her damp hair back, so they would
see the color in her cheeks, the light in her eyes. "I'm Queen Rose of Eana.
Oonagh Starcrest is my ancestor. A cursed, hateful witch who raises the
dead and uses them to her advantage. I've come here to stop her."

The women hesitated, weighing her words. They were clad in
dark leathers and fur-lined cloaks. By their obvious similarities—
copper-streaked dark hair and pale slender faces, Rose surmised they
must be sisters. In fact, they looked just like Captain Iversen, but where
the Gevran soldier was strapping and broad-shouldered, his sisters
were lithe and slim.

"You are too late," said the eldest, who was taller than her sisters.
Her face was beautiful but stern, her eyes haunted. "The witch who
wears your face is gone."

"She left behind a kraken," said the smallest of the three women, who had a soft voice, and three scars on her left cheek, as though a beast had struck her. "I see you've felled it."

"That was mostly me," said Kai.

Shen shot him a warning look.

Just then, Celeste and Anika came running along the strand. "Thank the stars you're all right, Rose," said Celeste as she threw her arms around her. "Here, I brought you a cloak to warm up." She slung the fur cloak around Rose's shoulders before turning to face the women. "Don't tell me," she said, offering a smile in greeting. "You're Iversens, aren't you?"

The eldest woman dipped her chin. "I'm Hela," she said, finally releasing her sword hilt.

"I'm Greta," said the smallest, who Rose guessed was also the youngest.

"Kindra," said the third as she surveyed the shoreline with a deepening frown. "I hope you haven't brought more trouble to this island."

"They have brought your royal sovereign," said Princess Anika, rolling her shoulders back. "Hello, Greta. Kindra. Hela. It's been many years since I visited this little island, but like Celeste, I can spot an Iversen in even the most crowded marketplace."

The three girls dropped into curtsies so clumsy and unpracticed, Rose almost laughed. There was certainly a wildness about Carrig that held its own charm. She hoped there were fire and food here, too.

"While we Gevrans are not known for our hospitality," said Anika, sharing a smile with the Iversen sisters, "I hope we can make an exception given the circumstances."

WREN

Night's Edge sat securely on Wren's hip as she and Tor left the Mishnick Mountains. Despite its size and heft, the sword made her feel lighter, affording her more energy than she'd had in weeks. She shouldn't have been surprised that an ancient sword that once belonged to Eana herself and that came from the healing waters of her mountains, would possess within it a measure of healing magic, but this latent power had caught her off-guard. She welcomed it gladly. After all, she was going to need every last ounce of strength in the days ahead.

Willa waved them off, her smile tight as she watched them pick their way down the mountain and through the narrow pass, where the northern plains of Eana rolled on in a patchwork of green and gray. The going ahead would be tough but Wren was glad at least of the clear blue sky, and the midmorning sun casting its warmth over them. She carried Eana's sword—though it had only just come into her possession, she could not now imagine herself parting with it—while Tor carried their satchels, one of which had been filled with provisions for the journey home.

Though they set off in good spirits, Wren didn't miss the worried frown that flitted across Tor's face every so often.

"There's no better place for Alarik right now," she said. "He's not well enough to march into war."

Tor's frown only deepened. "For Gevrans, war is often restorative."

Wren burst into laughter, before realizing he was serious. "What could possibly be relaxing about war?"

"It's not the act of war itself but rather what it stands for. And who you stand with." He looked past her, the ghost of old battles flitting behind his eyes. "There's no greater honor than fighting for a cause far beyond yourself, Wren." He gestured toward Night's Edge at her hip. "You'll see soon enough."

Wren gripped the hilt of her sword. "What is this cause?" she said, more to herself than to Tor.

"Peace," he said, without hesitation. "In your country. In yourself."

She nodded. Yes, she liked the sound of that. She could *fight* for that. She looked up at him. "What is the cause for you?"

He smiled. "Don't you know?"

At her look of bewilderment, he chuckled. "You are my cause, Wren."

Wren's cheeks flushed and she stared at her boots, trying to think of something clever to say. But it felt as if her heart was swelling in her chest, and her breath was coming quick and sharp. "Thank you for coming back with me to Anadawn. I don't know what I'd do without you."

It was the truth, as plain as she could say it.

"I'll go with you as far as you want me to, Wren. To the fires of war and beyond that still," he said, and when she looked at him—and saw the storm in his eyes, fierce and unyielding—she knew his words to be true, too. "So long as I don't have to lose you again."

"Never," said Wren. She paused. "Well. Unless I die."

"I'd find you even in the starless afterlife."

Wren's blood roared, heat gathering in her cheeks until she had to look away to weather the sudden swell of her emotions—her happiness at his words, her need to bury them in her soul. They soothed the jagged shards of her heart, filling her with such warmth, she felt as if she could do anything with him by her side. But she couldn't say any of that. All the words, the feelings, crowded together on her tongue, and instead, she let out a soft laugh. "A little overconfident, don't you think?"

He flashed his teeth, seeing easily through her veneer. "Never underestimate a Gevran in love."

She smiled back. "Is this the part where you say your heart is your greatest weapon?"

Now it was Tor's turn to burst into laughter. Wren wrapped herself inside the sound, glad to be near it once more. They wandered on. Despite the ancient magic of the sword at her hip, it was not a true cure for the curse inside her. After a couple of hours, Wren began to tire. Her legs grew leaden, and her head began to spin. She tried not to show her discomfort on her face, but Tor was watching her more closely than she realized.

"Are you all right?"

"Just a little tired."

His brows hunched. "You're pale."

"I'm just—" She stumbled on a wayward rock. He lunged, grabbing her by the waist.

"Let's stop a moment. Drink some water. Have some food."

"I'll be fine," said Wren, stepping out of Tor's embrace. "We're making good progress."

"*Wren*," he said, his voice a growl.

She glared at him over her shoulder. "You can't wrangle me, Captain Iversen."

His eyes flashed, streaks of lightning cutting through the gray. "Care to wager?"

A delicious shiver rippled up Wren's spine. "I like this game."

"Sit," he said, gesturing to a nearby cluster of rocks. "And we can play any game you like."

Wren sat. At Tor's request, she drank some water and ate some bread, along with a thick slice of hard cheese. After, she felt better, if only a little. She rolled to her feet and he leaped up, too, as though he was waiting to catch her.

"I'm all right," she said.

He reached for her cautiously. "Are you sure?"

"I'm sure," she said, touching the hilt of Night's Edge and feeling the warm buzz of its power.

They journeyed on, through the northern plains, talking and laughing as the sun arced over them. Every so often Wren tired. Sometimes, Tor noticed before she did, pulling them off the path and setting up camp somewhere nearby for her to eat something, drink something, rest awhile. As the day wore on, the stops got longer. Wren resorted to sitting on Tor's lap, letting him hold her as she closed her eyes.

By evening, they were still far from the town of Glenlock, where the royal carriage awaited them. The sun had set, and night was falling, casting a chill in the wind. They stopped to eat. Tor built a fire, and after, Wren curled up under a blanket, determined to steal an hour or two of rest. Sleep came swiftly, and when it got its claws into her, it did not easily let go.

When Wren woke, the dawn birds were singing, and the sun was rising over the distant hills. She sat bolt upright to find Tor stoking the dwindling fire.

"You were supposed to wake me!"

"Was I?"

She flung her shoe at him.

He caught it with one hand. "You're cheerful in the morning."

"We're wasting time."

"You were exhausted, Wren."

"I'm always exhausted," she said, throwing the blanket off her. "We have to get on with it."

"We will now that you're awake," he said, coming to his feet. "There are plenty of wild horses nearby. I'll find a couple to wrangle."

Wren stared at him. "You can't be serious."

"I'm as serious as that scowl on your face." He winked, coaxing a reluctant smile from her.

"Come," he said, grabbing their things and stalking ahead. "We're on the hunt."

Wren hurried after him, the sudden spike of adrenaline urging her on until—far sooner than she expected—they came across a herd of horses at the end of the valley.

There were seven of them, grazing on the long grass. Wren was about to ask Tor about his plan when he slowed his pace, raising both hands as if he was surrendering to them. Three of the horses bolted at his approach but the others remained, as though the mere sight of Tor stalking slowly through the grass had lulled them into a trance. He clicked his teeth as he drew closer and then paused, as if he was trying to decide which ones to claim.

To Wren's surprise, two of the horses trotted toward him. The first was a black stallion with a white diamond patch on his muzzle; the other was a smaller brown mare. As Tor approached them with calm and careful strides, the horses bowed their heads, allowing him to place his palms against their muzzles. He whispered something in the space between them, as if he was making a bargain or perhaps he was casting his own kind of spell. In any case, in that moment, the wrangler was a marvel to Wren.

To her astonishment, when Tor turned back to her, the horses followed him.

Soon, they were riding side by side, Tor astride the black stallion while Wren guided the brown mare down the sloping hills and through the rest of the valley, heading east toward the town of Glenlock.

It was midafternoon by the time she spied the silver lake shimmering in the distance, and the narrow houses that huddled along its northern shore.

Wren sat up straighter, buoyed by the sight of civilization. "I'm starving," she said, urging her horse faster. "Let's stop in the first tavern we see and order the entire menu."

"You really do know the way to my heart," said Tor, keeping pace with her.

As they approached the town, Wren narrowed her eyes, searching for the carriage they had left behind a couple of days ago. There was no sign of it anywhere. In fact, there was no sign of anyone. The streets of Glenlock were completely deserted. Even the lake was eerily still. The horses slowed at the edge of the water as though they were afraid to go any farther.

"Wren." Tor's voice was too loud in the silence. "Something's off."

"There's no wind here," she whispered, all too aware of her burning scar. "There's no life at all."

Tor slid from his horse, his hand coming to the hilt of his sword. "Stay here."

"Absolutely not." Wren hopped off after him.

"Wren."

"Don't," she warned.

His nostrils flared. "Fine." He pointed at Night's Edge. "Hoist your sword. And stay behind me."

Wren met him stride for stride. "We go together, or not at all."

"You really are a handful."

"Shush. We're sneaking."

They crept through the town of Glenlock, checking every empty inn and deserted tavern, peering through the windows of silent homes. Several front doors had been left wide open as though the occupants had left in a hurry.

"Where did they all go?" said Wren uneasily.

"The better question is, what chased them away?"

Wren had a horrible feeling she already knew. The longer they spent in Glenlock, the more her scar ached. They were about to turn and leave when they heard a distant wail. Tor jerked his chin up, tracking the sound.

"What the hell was that?" said Wren.

"Let's find out."

The air grew colder as they journeyed farther north, leaving the lakeside for a thicket of trees that marked the town's boundary. For a while, the only sound was the quiet patter of their steps, until something cracked under Wren's foot.

She froze. "Tor."

"Don't look down," he said, but it was too late.

In her hurry, Wren had accidentally trodden on a skull. It stared up at her now, with huge gaping eyes. She stumbled backward, rocked by a sudden rush of nausea. "That's . . . Oh no . . . That's . . ."

"A human skull." Tor bent down to inspect it. "No maggots. It must be long dead."

Wren grimaced. "What the hell is it doing in the middle of the street?" she said, just as another wail rang out. It was closer now, and it didn't sound like a beast. It sounded like a sob. It was coming from somewhere just up ahead, where a line of trees marked the entrance to a graveyard.

"Come on," said Tor, taking her hand in his and gripping his sword with the other.

When they entered the graveyard, Wren had to clap a hand over her mouth to keep from crying out. All of the graves had been disturbed. Headstones lay cracked in two, grass and dirt kicked up and strewn everywhere. Even the trees bent toward the ground as if they were weeping. Nearby, a skeleton had collapsed half out of its grave, as if it was desperately trying to climb out.

Wren swore it jerked its skull to look up at her.

"She's taken all the dead out of Glenlock," she whispered in mounting horror. "These graves held bodies of *people*, Tor." At the sight of another skeleton crushed beneath a shattered headstone, Wren sank to her knees, willing the terror to pass. But it only grew.

And then came that sound again, only this time it was muffled.

Tor tracked it to a nearby tree, where he came to an abrupt halt. He lowered his sword, his voice strained. "Wren . . ."

Wren stumbled after him. When she rounded the tree, she stopped just the same. There, across a small clearing, a boy no older than six sat quivering. He was clutching a sobbing little girl against his chest, begging her to be quiet. She must have been his sister.

"It's all right," said Wren, lowering her sword. "We're here to help you."

When the girl looked up at Wren, she let out a terrified scream. The boy tried to scrabble backward, but he was already wedged against a tree. "Please don't take us," he sobbed. "We don't want to go."

"Hush now," said Wren softly. "We're not going to hurt you."

The girl only wailed harder.

Tor came to his knees, his voice achingly gentle. "Have you seen this woman before?"

The boy looked at Wren and nodded.

Wren's heart sank. Oonagh had terrorized the town of Glenlock and scared the children into the woods. The poor things couldn't even look at her without trembling. "I'm not her," she said, kneeling beside Tor. "I promise you. We just look the same, that's all. I don't want to scare you. I want to help you."

The boy bit his bottom lip, looking between them.

"I'm a soldier, see?" Tor gestured to his Anadawn uniform. The girl looked up, her sob dying in her throat. Wren's likeness to Oonagh might have unsettled the children, but they seemed to be comforted by Tor's presence. "Tell us what you saw."

The boy summoned his courage with a shuddering breath. "The witch woman came up from the river today. She was like a fish first. Then she looked like . . ." He glanced at Wren.

"Like me," she said. "It's all right."

He went on, his words quickening. "There were animals, too. Mountain lions and tigers with scary red eyes and big dripping mouths. Everyone ran away. Some went to the northern mountains. Others headed for the southern road. They took the horses and the carriages, too. Bonnie and I came to hide in the graveyard. But the witch woman came here, too. And then she . . . she . . ." He pointed a trembling hand past their shoulders. "She took the skeletons and made them stand up. She made them go with her."

"*Freezing hell,*" muttered Tor.

Wren fought to control her anger. "And you've been hiding here ever since?"

The boy sniffed. "We're waiting for Papa to come back."

"Come with us," said Wren, standing up. "You can't stay here alone. We'll take you to the next village to find your papa." The children hesitated, fear flitting behind their tired eyes. They could not seem to separate her fully from her ancestor, giving Wren yet another reason to burn with hatred for Oonagh. "Or if you like, you can ride with Captain Iversen?"

The boy nodded. The girl took Tor's hand. He holstered his sword so the boy could take his other hand, and together, all four of them picked their way out of the graveyard and walked back to the horses. Wren walked ahead, with Night's Edge held aloft while Tor spoke with the children about his sword and the kinds of beasts he used to wrangle back on Carrig.

Wren smiled as she listened, trying to put her rage and revulsion aside. They had yet to discuss the full horror of what they had discovered in Glenlock, but with the children among them, they set the issue momentarily to rest and led them safely to the lake, where the horses took them fast and far from the eerie ghost town and the graves Oonagh Starcrest had pillaged there.

ROSE

While the Iversen sisters joined the commotion on the beach, Marino and his sodden crew walked up and down the shoreline, frowning as they inspected the damage the kraken had done to Marino's beloved vessel. Rose didn't know much about merchant ships, but even she could see there was a sizable hole along the left hull, the mast was splintered, and the mainsail had been sheared in two.

"My ship!" lamented Marino as he wrung out his tricorn. "How could that wretched kraken do such a terrible thing to my innocent ship?"

Celeste swatted her brother's arm. "*Priorities*, Marino. We almost died."

"Yes, that was also bad," he added as an afterthought.

"And it wasn't just some angry undead kraken," Shen was compelled to add. "It was Oonagh's doing."

Marino scrubbed a hand across his jaw, making some silent calculation in his head. "The damage appears repairable at least . . . but there's a day or two of work in it before we can even think about setting sail again."

"We don't have much time to spare," said Rose anxiously.

"We will help you. More hands make quick work," said Hela, who had been assessing the vessel herself and was now rising to the challenge with the kind of confidence Rose would expect of an Iversen. "You'll need fresh planks and iron nails. A kit for the mainsail."

Rose smiled at Hela. "You certainly sound as if you know your way around a ship."

"Only the wrecks," she said, with a snort. "We've had more than our fair share wash up here."

"This is no wreck," said Marino with great offense.

"Sure . . . ," said Shen. "It has merely a scratch."

Hela rolled up her sleeves. "Whatever you want to call it, we'd better get to work." She turned to her sisters. "Kindra will fetch our tools and some workers from the village. Greta will take the rest of you up to our cabin. Eat and get warm. It will be cold tonight."

Rose quailed. "Colder than this?"

Greta nodded but didn't quite meet her eyes. "Only when the blizzard sweeps in."

"Great," muttered Shen.

Kai clapped his hand on Marino's shoulder. "I'm not one for carpentry, boat man, but let me know when you need someone to hoist this ship right way up again." He cracked his knuckles. "I'll have it back on the sea in no time."

"Well, thank goodness for overconfident men," said Anika, picking up her damp skirts and making to follow Greta. "Come along, the rest of you, before we all lose our toes to frostbite."

Rose tightened the sheath at her waist as she followed Anika, all five of them traipsing after Greta as she led them into the wilds of Carrig. It occurred to her that both she and Wren were with Iversens. She would have to tell Wren that she'd met Tor's sisters. Oh, she hoped that Wren had safely made it to the Mishnick Mountains and was cured of her own curse. She sent a silent plea up to the sky, a prayer to Eana to keep her sister safe. Even if they were in Gevra now, Rose still believed in the power of Eana, the first witch.

The island of Carrig was covered in snow, marked by pine forests and hills and rugged farmland, and little else as far as Rose could see. Every time she exhaled, her breath clouded in the air. It was the coldest she'd ever been, the chill made worse by the weight of her damp clothes.

Sensing the youngest Iversen girl was uncomfortable in her presence, Rose hurried to walk next to her. "You needn't fear me, Greta," she said gently. "It is merely an unfortunate twist of fate that my sister and I look so much like our ancestor."

Greta huffed a cloudy breath. "It is . . . jarring."

Rose offered her a rueful smile. "I can only imagine what a fright I've given you."

The girl's lips twisted, deepening the furrow between her brows. "We never learned the name of the witch who came here. When she arrived, she came up from the sea like a corpse, bloodless and half dead. With gaping gills slashed into her neck." She shuddered, pulling her arms around herself. "We fled with the other families and hid in the high mountains."

"Her name is Oonagh," said Rose. "And she is as you say—a cursed, undead thing. Tell me—what did she do here?"

"She killed the beasts that came to defend us," said Greta. "In the morning, we found their carcasses at the base of the mountain. Ice bears and snow leopards, wolves and tigers. All of them slain and drained of blood. They died for their bravery." She shook her head, a tear slipping free and glistening against the silver scars along her cheek. "By nightfall, the bodies were gone. But we still heard their howls, their cries."

Rose laid a gentle hand on her shoulder. "I am sorry for your loss."

"That wasn't even the worst of it." Greta came to a stop midway up the hill, turning to a pine forest that clustered around a small graveyard.

"Don't tell me that's what I think it is," said Shen, squinting into the gathering mist.

Even from here, they could see the ground was disturbed. Churned up and spat out, ice and snow scattered like glass.

"Those are grave markers," said Anika, pointing to the wooden stakes that jutted from the snowy earth. "This is a burial ground for—" She stopped short.

"*Stars*," muttered Celeste. "She's not just taking dead beasts."

"She took the bones of our ancestors," said Greta in a hollow voice. "The bodies of our loved ones."

The silence stretched, the wind so cold it felt to Rose as if it was chattering through her bones. She only realized she was swaying on her feet when Shen moved closer to steady her. "It's all right," he said, but it wasn't all right. Oonagh was building an army of dead humans. Rose pictured it in her mind's eye: cursed bones and gaping skulls, the treasured bodies of lost loved ones pulled from their eternal slumber and used like puppets to do Oonagh's bidding.

Rose remembered the vision Oonagh had given her and realized with dawning horror that it was already coming to pass.

"We must stop her," she said, with a bolt of defiance. "Before she grows any stronger."

"Come," said Greta, turning from the empty graveyard and ushering them up the hill. "We're almost there."

Before long, they arrived at a modest log cabin. "We don't have much," said Greta as she showed them inside, where mercifully, a fire was crackling in the hearth. "But what we have we'll share. There's ginger tea and freshly baked bread, and there's rabbit stew, too." She pulled a face. "Though be warned, I'm not much of a cook."

"Good thing you're a looker," said Kai, ripping off his sopping shirt. "Any whiskey?"

Shen punched him in the arm. "Behave."

There were two snow foxes slumbering together by the fire. Greta shooed them into the small kitchen, where a beautiful white owl was perched on the back of a chair, watching them with wide golden eyes.

"Why do I feel as if we're being judged?" said Celeste.

"Forgive Aya's curiosity," said Greta, scratching the bird on her head. "She is not used to the company of men. Apart from my brother, of course."

"No one would blame you for preferring the company of beasts," said Anika, coming to settle in front of the fire. "Frankly, men can be utterly tiresome."

Kai tossed her a withering look. "That is so rude."

Greta's eyes sparked with amusement. "I would rather stroll with an ice bear any day of the winter."

"You know, Greta, I'm something of a desert bear myself," said Kai.

"Please stop," said Shen. "I beg you."

Greta bit back her laughter as she hurried up the stairs. "I'll fetch some blankets and dry clothes."

Rose went to warm herself by the fire and noticed an old gray wolf slumbering underneath the windowsill. Goodness, a wrangler's home really was full of beasts. She thought of Elske and her heart clenched. At least the wolf was with her sister, and they would be taking care of each other.

When Greta returned with dry clothes, Rose took them eagerly, choosing a fur-lined velvet dress for herself. The men divided a small pile of what appeared to be Tor's old clothes, leaving their own clothes to dry out by the fire. After, when they were all dressed and warm, they sat around the rickety wooden table, devouring bowls of rabbit stew. Aya watched them eat, her head swiveling every so often as though she was peering at something outside the window.

"What's Feathers so nosy about?" asked Kai between mouthfuls.

"The weather," said Greta. "There's a blizzard blowing in."

"Poor Marino," said Celeste.

"And his crew," said Rose.

"Should we go and help?" Shen asked.

"Absolutely not," said Kai. "You do what you like, but I am staying right here where it's warm."

After dinner, Greta made a pot of tea. Kai paced back and forth in the small space as if he himself was a trapped Gevran beast, while Celeste and Anika snuggled together under a sheepskin blanket. Rose stared out of the window at the falling snow, wondering where Oonagh could possibly be going next and just how many more graveyards she planned to disturb on her way.

Would she be appearing in Anadawn sooner than she had promised? Or did she have something even more terrible up her sleeve? It unnerved Rose that she didn't know. That she couldn't even guess.

"I'm afraid we're running low on firewood," said Greta, returning from the store in the kitchen. "We've not been able to gather any for fear of running into the witch."

"I'll fetch some," said Shen, rising to his feet. "Kai?"

Kai shook his head. "The snow is no place for a desert-born stud like me."

"Ever gallant," muttered Celeste.

He shot her a blistering look. "I don't see you volunteering, birdwatcher."

"I'm busy," said Celeste, snuggling up next to Anika.

"She is warming the princess of Gevra," said Anika primly. "Which is a task of equal import."

"I'll go with you," said Rose, standing and fetching a cloak from the wall. She passed another to Shen. She was starting to feel antsy inside the little cabin and didn't mind the thought of the snow outside. Perhaps the outdoors would do her some measure of good, and besides, she was always happy to spend more time alone with Shen.

They ventured into the falling snow, hand in hand, looking for firewood. "I have to admit, I think Kai was right about the snow," said Shen, shivering violently.

"Oh, surely you aren't afraid of a little bad weather?" Rose teased.

"I'm not *afraid* of it," he said, gingerly picking his way through a large snowdrift. "I just don't like to lose my footing."

"It snows at Anadawn sometimes," said Rose fondly. "Not like this.

But every couple of winters, the palace will get a light dusting of snow. It makes everything look quite beautiful."

"I suppose we can agree on that," said Shen, gently brushing the snowflakes from her shoulders. "If I have to be out in it, I'm glad I'm with you. We can keep each other warm, at least."

Rose smiled. "I never feel cold when I'm with you."

They carried on until they reached the edge of the wood, where the spindly trunks looked spectral in the darkening night.

"I can break off some of these low branches," said Shen, circling the nearest tree. "They should work for firewood."

"I'll gather the ones on the ground," said Rose. A chill that had nothing to do with the weather stole through her as she knelt in the snow. She could almost sense the shadow of her ancestor stalking alongside her, pulling corpses from the frozen earth. The image was so violent, it stole Rose's breath. She fell back on her heels, gasping for air.

Shen stilled. "Rose?"

"I'm frightened, Shen."

He was beside her in the next heartbeat. "I'm with you. I'm right here."

She turned, laying her forehead against his, and tried to give voice to the great swell of her fear. "I don't want to lose you. I don't want to lose anyone."

"You won't," said Shen. "I promise."

Rose closed her eyes, wishing she could believe him.

When they returned to the cabin with a large bundle of firewood, Kai greeted them at the door. "Welcome back, woodcutters. While you were out smooching in the snow, we came up with a plan."

"What kind of plan?" Rose frowned, looking past him.

"Do you still have Daybreak?"

Rose went to fetch it. When she removed the sheath, the dagger was still coated in the dark blood of the kraken.

Celeste gingerly took it and inspected the bloodied blade. "Since this blade pierced the kraken, and the kraken is linked to Oonagh, Kai thinks we can use it to track her and find out where she's going next."

Shen dropped the firewood by the door and came toward Celeste. "Do you even know how to blood-scry?"

Celeste set Daybreak down. "You never said anything about the *blood*," she said, turning on Kai. "You should know I don't dabble in it. I think we've all learned a valuable lesson from what happened to Wren. Blood magic only leads to trouble."

"I quite agree," said Rose with rising panic. "We can't afford to make things worse than they are."

"Relax, Queenie," Kai scoffed. "Blood-scrying is not blood magic. My mother was an accomplished seer and she often used to scry this way." He picked up the blade and spun it in his hand, catching it by the tip. "Even traces of old blood can hold a link to the person they came from." He wagged the dagger at Celeste. "And since the kraken and Oonagh are linked by blood magic, I reckon we can use this blade to see what your sneaky grave-robbing ancestor is up to." At their sudden silence, he gave a self-satisfied smile. "I bet you're all happy you decided to bring me along now, aren't you?"

Rose turned on Shen. "Will that really work?"

"I've heard of blood-scrying, but I've never seen it done," he admitted.

"That's because you spent your childhood holed up in a stuffy palace," said Kai. "The desert has its own ways."

"We might as well try," said Celeste. "After all, we have nothing to lose."

"And it won't harm Daybreak," said Shen.

"So long as you do it outside," interjected Greta, who had been hovering awkwardly on the edge of their conversation and was now mirroring Aya's look of alarm. "Your magic will frighten my beasts."

Kai glanced at the slumbering gray wolf. Perhaps it was Rose's imagination, but she thought he looked a little scared. "I don't want to get eaten by that wolf," Kai said.

"If it makes you feel better, Lupo would probably just gnaw on you like a meaty chew bone," said Greta brightly. "The poor old thing has lost most of his teeth."

Kai cleared his throat. "Never mind. We'll make the fire outside. When the blood burns, you'll read the answers in the smoke, bird-watcher."

"How simple you make it sound," said Celeste dryly.

Kai puffed his chest up. "Everything is simple when you're brimming with pure unbridled confidence."

"Let's just get on with it," said Celeste, shooing him outside.

"I'm not missing this!" said Anika, wrapping herself in a blanket before rushing to join them.

"Good luck," said Greta, before promptly shutting the door after them and sliding the bolt lock into place.

Rose desperately hoped the plan would work, but after almost being devoured by an undead kraken, it was becoming increasingly difficult to remain optimistic.

Anika looked on curiously while Kai, Shen, Celeste, and Rose cleared a space in the snow behind the wooden cottage. Kai and Shen combined their tempest magic to block the howling wind while Rose and Celeste struck up a small fire that grew quickly under the guidance of their magic.

Kai came to stand beside Celeste then, guiding her with uncharacteristic helpfulness. "Carefully dip the blade into the flames, feeding it as much blood as it will take."

"Don't burn yourself!" said Anika, watching anxiously from the side.

Shen shot her a warning look, raising his finger to his lips.

Celeste blew out a breath, carefully lowering Daybreak into the flames. "Then what?"

"Then, you know . . ." Kai rolled his hand. "Do the seer thing."

Celeste glared sidelong at him. "You said you knew how to do this."

He grinned sheepishly. "I don't have *all* the answers, bird-watcher. Just wait for the smoke."

As the blade heated, the dark blood slickened and slowly dripped into the fire. Then came the smoke, dark and curling and acrid.

Anika began to wheeze. "Oh, what an *awful* smell."

Shen clapped his hand over his mouth, pinching his nose to keep from gagging. Rose held her breath, watching the smoke so closely her eyes began to stream. But there were no shapes to discern, no clues in the gray plumes, only that terrible stench that made her feel sick.

Celeste was faring better than the rest. She began to sway, her gaze clouding as she watched the smoke. Kai laid a hand on her shoulder to keep her from falling into the fire.

"I can see," she murmured after a moment. "I see something." The smoke began to shift, the plumes dancing in shades of white and gray, but still Rose struggled to find the images within. "There are trees here."

Shen frowned. "Can you be a bit more specific?"

"Hush," hissed Anika. "Give her a moment."

"Good," urged Kai. "What else?"

"Hundreds and hundreds of trees," said Celeste dreamily. "With sweeping vines and drooping branches." She shook her head, a furrow appearing between her brows. "It's a forest. So vast I can't see beyond it. It's not a place I've ever been." She closed her eyes, her voice quieting. "But oh, it's beautiful. Beautiful and sad."

"That sounds like the Weeping Forest," murmured Shen. He looked to Rose. "If that vision is true, Oonagh is already back in Eana."

Rose pulled her gaze from the fire. "Then we must hurry."

Once they put out the fire, they returned to the cabin and told Greta what they had found in the smoke. "We'll leave as soon as the ship is repaired," said Rose. She spoke brightly, even as she felt a sense of dread at the thought of going back on the boat.

"In the meantime, you must rest," insisted Greta.

After another cup of warm tea, Rose sat by the fire where the floor had been covered in sheepskin blankets and rough pelts. When her lids grew heavy, she lay down between Celeste and Shen, her hand curled inside his as she drifted off. Even in sleep, Rose drew strength from Shen's nearness and the sureness of her best friend at her other side. All going well, tomorrow, they would return to Eana and ready their armies to face Oonagh. She would not catch them unawares again.

33

WREN

By the time Wren and Tor reached the village of Raddlebrook, just south of Glenlock, the afternoon sun was waning, and the children were fast asleep. They stopped at the first inn they reached, Tor carefully lifting them down from the horse, while Wren went inside to find a caretaker. She was relieved to see that some of the residents of Glenlock had come to shelter in Raddlebrook. Among them was a kindly old woman who said she knew the children's father and would gladly help them reunite.

Once the children were left safely in her care, Wren didn't linger. The mood in Raddlebrook was tense and fearful, and she could not yet offer the people there a measure of comfort. Rather, she owed it to them—and to the rest of her kingdom—to journey home as fast as possible and defend Anadawn from Oonagh's encroaching army.

Despite her growing urgency to get home, the southern road to Anadawn was congested with hundreds more deserters, and Wren's horse was starting to slow.

"Ride with me," said Tor, once they were outside Raddlebrook. "We can cut through the desert and avoid the droves."

Wren perked up at the suggestion. "You Gevrans really do think on your feet."

"It's just like a line in my favorite folk song: 'If you don't think on your feet, you die on your back.'"

"How typically Gevran," said Wren, sliding off her horse and clambering on to his. He pulled her up with one hand, and she settled in front of him.

"You steer," he said, close to her ear. "I'll ride."

"Yes, Captain," said Wren, letting him hold her in place.

They turned west, toward the soft edge of the desert. By the time they reached the Ganyeve, Wren could barely keep her eyes open. Her head lolled, falling against Tor's chest. The heat was so luxurious, so warm, it felt like a blanket curling around her. The thunder of hooves soon lulled her to sleep.

"Burning hell." She jolted awake at the sound of Tor's voice.

"What is it?" she said, sitting up. She looked around, searching the dunes for a stray blood beetle or some other vicious sand creature come to devour them. There was only sand as far as she could see, and a strange and distant rumbling, as though something—or a great many things—was rattling through the desert. But that was not at all what was bothering Tor.

"This heat," he said, adjusting his collar. "I feel as if I'm melting."

Wren glanced at him over her shoulder. His forehead was slick with sweat and his cheeks were redder than she'd ever seen them. "It's because you're Gevran," she said, chuckling. "You're welcome to take off your shirt."

"Won't that make it worse?"

Wren flashed a wicked grin. "Not for me."

"Please don't seduce me right now." He closed his eyes, his face in anguish. "If I get any warmer, I'll burst into flames."

Wren restrained herself. "Don't worry, the sun is setting."

Tor looked pleadingly at the horizon. "I hope I make it until then."

"You will," said Wren, laying her hand on his leg and feeling the muscles tense beneath it. "And then, if you like, we can try to find a hot spring."

Tor let out a groan. "Why would I want to be *more* hot?"

"Poor Gevran," she said, patting his knee. "I'll look after you."

Tor clicked his teeth, and the horse quickened its pace, cutting across the restless sands like a streak of black lightning. The sun soon set in earnest, the last of its light casting streaks of orange and red across the sky. A delightful breeze rippled through the desert.

"Mmm," said Wren as it kissed her cheeks. "This is much better."

"Now I think I could ride like this forever," said Tor.

As they veered east toward the Kerrcal Road, the sky darkened and the stars came out in full force, exploding across the sky in a riot of silver. Wren tipped her head back, watching them twinkle. "Isn't it the most beautiful thing you've ever seen?"

"Almost," he said, smiling down at her.

Wren raised her chin, brushing her lips against his. Tor seized the kiss, sliding his hand through her hair. His tongue brushed against hers, gentle, searching. She melted into him until her entire body began to tingle.

All too soon, she broke away. "We should probably concentrate on the journey."

He smiled against her lips. "As you wish."

Wren turned back to the desert, smiling as he pressed a kiss to her neck. Night swept over the desert, curling them into its velvety embrace as Tor charted the way home, across the rolling dunes and through the sprawling woods, until at last, the white spires of Anadawn Palace rose up in the distance to pierce the dawning sky.

34

ROSE

When Rose woke up, the sky was bright and clear, the sun shimmering across a blanket of fresh snow. Better yet, Marino was knocking at the door of the cottage.

"We were able to mend the hole in the hull," he said when it swung open. His eyes were red-rimmed and tired, but he was chipper. "The *Siren's Secret* is even stronger than she was before. We are ready to depart on your order, Queen Rose."

"The sooner the better," said Rose, getting quickly to her feet. "We must get back to Anadawn as fast as possible, so we can prepare to battle Oonagh. This time we *will* be ready for her."

"We certainly will," said Anika, striding in from the kitchen, where she and Celeste had been having an early breakfast. "Though from here, I will be going my own way." They had all decided that Anika should return to Grinstad to gather the finest of her brother's soldiers before coming to Eana to join the fight against Oonagh. With the combined might of Gevra, Anadawn, and the Sunkissed witches, Rose was certain they could defeat Oonagh. And she had Daybreak now, too.

All they had to do was find Oonagh.

Celeste kissed Anika goodbye, then joined the others as they made their way back down to the strand, where the *Siren's Secret* was already floating offshore. "We made the most of the high tide," said Marino proudly. "We'll have to row out to her."

"Allow me," said Kai, leaping into the rowing boat and nearly toppling it with his weight. He snatched up the oars. "I have the strength of ten men."

Rose and Celeste rolled their eyes but followed his lead, settling themselves at the back of the boat, while Marino clambered into the front.

"Keep your eyes on the water," said Shen, drawing his dagger as he climbed in after them. "We now know Oonagh could be anywhere."

Once aboard the ship, Shen and Celeste insisted that Rose go down to the captain's quarters for safety.

"I am just as capable of either of you!" she protested.

"It's not about being capable," said Celeste. "It is about making sure we get you back to Anadawn in one piece. Eana needs you, Rose. Don't let your pride get in the way of that."

Rose pouted but saw Celeste's point and was glad when her friend came to keep her company throughout the journey.

With the wind on their side and Marino's magic stronger than ever, the voyage passed swiftly, and Rose was grateful for that, too.

When Dooley's voice rang out belowdecks, calling, "Land ahoy!" Rose burst out of the captain's cabin and ran for the stairs, eager to see her beloved Eana once more. She went at once to the prow, reveling in the spray of the sea on her face and the wind in her hair. She could see

Wishbone Bay in the distance, hear the squawk of the seagulls as they soared along the port.

She sighed, long and deep, relieved to be home. Safe in the arms of her kingdom.

Something struck the ship, and she wobbled on her feet. Rose looked down, alerted to a shadow darting by the prow. It became a shimmer, a flash of white in the waves, followed by the swish of a tail. How strange. Rose stared at it for a moment too long, even as her instincts told her to *get back*.

There came a sudden splash as the creature shot up out of the water. Rose gasped, realizing too late what it was. *Who* it was.

In the blink of an eye, Oonagh Starcrest scrambled up the side of the ship, grabbed Rose by the hair, and dragged her into the roiling sea. Rose screamed as she was pulled under, the water so sudden and cold, it shocked the breath from her body.

The last thing Rose saw was Shen leaping from the side of the ship, but by then she was so deep, she knew he would never find her. She kicked and thrashed as Oonagh pulled her down to the seabed, and when there was no air left in Rose's lungs and no fight left in her body, everything went black.

35

WREN

When Wren arrived at Anadawn, the golden gates were already open. Tor stiffened as he surveyed the drawn faces of the guards, the servants lingering in the courtyard and wringing their hands.

Wren sat up straighter. "Something's wrong."

She gripped the hilt of Night's Edge, letting its magic strengthen her. But it could do nothing for her growing feeling of unease. There were far too many people milling about and yet, despite the increase in activity, a strange hush had fallen over the palace. No one was looking at her. In fact, they were looking everywhere *but* at her.

Wren was about to call out to a passing maidservant when Shen Lo appeared, hurrying from the palace with a look of such horror on his face, Wren's heart lurched.

Rose was not with him.

"Wren!" A terrible coldness swept through Wren as Shen sprinted toward her. She threw herself from the horse, stumbling as she landed. He grabbed her shoulders, hoisting her to her feet. "It's Rose." His voice cracked on her name. "I'm sorry, Wren. I'm so sorry." He shook his head, as if he couldn't quite believe what he was saying. "I couldn't save her. It all happened so fast."

"What the hell are you—?"

"I failed her," he said. "I failed you. She's—" He stopped, choking on the word.

"No!" The word burst from Wren like a cry. She shook him off, pushing her way into the palace. "Where's my sister?" she called out. "Rose! Come down, Rose!"

Shen lunged for her hand, pulling her back. "Wren, she's gone."

The coldness in Wren sparked to flame, dread replaced by the white-hot rush of panic. She spun around. "She can't just be gone, Shen. You're talking nonsense." She tried to wrench her hand free. "Get off me. I need to see Rose. I need to see my sister."

"Listen to me, Wren. *Please*," Shen said, refusing to let her go. His voice was as ragged as the look on his face. In all the time Wren had known Shen Lo, she had never seen him look so . . . defeated. The maidservants drifted closer, the soldiers, too. Tor was at her back, a steadying hand braced on her shoulder. It suddenly felt as if the world was crowding in on Wren. And yet for all the faces that surrounded her, she could not find the only one she wished to see. "You all need to get out of my way right now," she said, through her teeth. "Or I swear I'll run you through with this sword."

No one moved.

Shen kept talking. Wren closed her eyes, trying to unhear the words as they burrowed into her mind, painting a story she did not want to know. "We were so close to land. We thought we were safe, that Oonagh had traveled inland, but she was skulking in the water near Wishbone Bay, waiting to strike."

"What does any of this have to do with my sister?" Wren demanded.

"Rose was on the prow when Oonagh came up from the deep. She grabbed hold of Rose. Pulled her down into the water and—"

Wren whirled on Shen, grabbing him by the scruff. "And you let her *go?*"

He let her shake him. "I couldn't get to her in time."

"You were on a boat!" Wren was shouting but she didn't care who heard her. "You're one of the best swimmers I know! Not to mention you trail after Rose every time you're together! And now you're telling me she went overboard and you were nowhere near her!"

"Wren," said Tor, in a low voice. "Take a breath."

But there was no air to breathe. Her fear was smothering her, grief sharpening her temper like a blade.

"I tried to save her," said Shen, his voice hitching with guilt. "I nearly swam to my own death searching for her down there. I did everything I could. I swear it, Wren. I promise—"

"Save your promises," said Wren viciously. She could feel the curse feeding on her pain. It reared up like a dragon, willing to burn anyone who came close to her. "I don't want to hear any more."

This time, when she shook Shen off he let her go. So did Tor, both men falling back as Wren stalked into the palace, looking for answers. Though she knew, just like her sister, she would not find them there.

Rose was not dead, Wren decided in the throne room a short while later. She knew what Shen had told her—a story echoed by a stricken Celeste and an unusually morose Kai—that Rose had been dragged into the deep by Oonagh. But even so, Wren could not bring herself to believe it.

"If Rose were dead, I would feel it," she said as she sat half-slumped in her throne.

Shen had followed Wren to the throne room but he was out on the balcony now, his hands braced on the balustrade, his head dropped as though he could no longer bear to hold it up. Kai was with him, a supportive hand resting on his cousin's shoulder. Tor was standing straight-backed at the doors, guarding Wren's privacy. Though she knew by the concern on his face, he was watching over her, too. Ready to catch her if she fell, to soothe her if she screamed.

Celeste was perched on the arm of Wren's throne, staring vacantly at the floor. She hadn't said much since Wren had arrived, both of them sitting together in the pooling silence, trying to fathom what had happened.

Though the palace was thrumming with activity, it felt strangely empty without Rose, as if even the proud stone walls missed the determined sweep of her skirts, the trill of her voice echoing down the hallways, the sound of her humming as she tended to her roses.

Wren ached for Rose's presence now, hating all the moments she had been short with her sister or acted disinterested in her plans, her dreams. She missed Rose's gentle warmth and clever mind, her unwavering loyalty and clear-eyed optimism. All these months she had taken Rose for granted, sure that she would lead the way, planning their future with the unerring sureness for which Wren had come to trust her.

Ever since their reunion last year, Wren had never even imagined a world where they would not be together, shoulder to shoulder, hand in hand. Ruling. Laughing. Living side by side as their parents would have wished. If Banba had been one half of Wren's heart, Rose was the other, and Wren could not—*would not*—simply go on without her.

No. She refused to believe it.

"She's not dead," she said, even as her voice broke. She scrubbed the tear from her cheek but another one slipped out. And then another. "She *can't* be dead."

Celeste raised her head, revealing her swollen eyes and tear-streaked face. "I saw Rose dragged beneath the waves myself. She didn't surface. We searched for hours, but Oonagh moved so fast, we never had a chance." She raked her hands through her hair, pulling salt crystals from the coils. "She's gone. Nobody can survive that long beneath the water."

"Oonagh can," said Wren, recalling the vision she had once seen of her ancestor. How, following the altercation between Oonagh and Ortha Starcrest on the banks of the Silvertongue, Oonagh had fallen into the river only to enchant gills in her neck and swim as a merrow all the way to Gevra. Everyone thought she was dead, but the truth was Oonagh never died—not really. She simply swam. Not as herself but as a creature made to breathe underwater.

"Oonagh is already dead," said Celeste. "Or undead. The point is, the same rules don't apply to her."

Wren frowned. "She still would have needed a spell." In fact, Wren had cast that very same enchantment herself as a child, swimming in the Ortha Sea for hours until Banba's voice went hoarse trying to call her home. Which meant it was possible—if not wholly plausible—that

Rose had learned that enchantment, too. She had been practicing, after all.

"Rose didn't drown." Wren stood up, and wiped her cheeks again. Steadied her voice. "I would feel it if she did. I know it." She gripped her sword, willing herself to believe it. "I know my sister. She wouldn't have given up so easily." She turned back to Celeste. "Have you seen anything? If not in the sea, then in the starcrests?"

Celeste's brows knitted. "Only the forest I glimpsed in the fire at Carrig." She shook her head. "I saw it before we lost Rose."

"Forest?" said Wren, coming closer. "What kind of forest?"

"One that weeps," said Celeste meaningfully, and Wren knew at once what she meant. The Weeping Forest that bordered the Whisperwind Cliffs. "That's where we thought Oonagh was going when we set sail," Celeste went on. "It's why we left Carrig in such a hurry."

"Of course that's where she's going," muttered Wren as understanding dawned. "Oonagh is taking Rose to the forest of dead witches." At Celeste's frown, she went on. "Oonagh's raising an undead army. And what's better than a single undead witch?" She swallowed thickly. "*Thousands* of dead witches."

"But what does any of that have to do with Rose?" said Celeste.

Wren froze. Suddenly she knew it had everything to do with Rose.

Celeste came to her feet, reading the look on her face. "What is it . . . ?"

"To raise that many witches, Oonagh will need a huge spell. A great sacrifice . . ." And what was more powerful than a queen of the realm? The descendant of not just Eana the first witch but Ortha Starcrest, too. Wren's cheeks began to prickle. Her head spun as her legs started to tremble. The curse devoured her fear, grasping for more. Tor moved like a wolf, catching Wren before she buckled. She steadied herself on his arm, giving voice to her terror. "I think she intends to use Rose."

Celeste's dark eyes widened. "Do you really think Rose is still alive?"

Wren nodded grimly. "If she is, she won't be for long." There wasn't a moment to lose. If Wren's hunch was right, then Rose was in danger, and about as far from help as the country allowed. "We have to go now. We have to hurry." She turned to Tor, grabbing his lapels. "I need you to go to the Captain of the Anadawn Guard at once. Tell him to raise our army. The queen rides at dusk. And we'll need provisions if we're to cut through the desert."

Tor was gone in the next heartbeat, marching purposefully through the halls of Anadawn and carrying her urgency as his own.

"I'll send word to Anika," said Celeste, who was halfway to the door already.

Wren made a beeline for the balcony. She closed the door behind her but Shen didn't raise his head. If he sensed her there, he made no sign of it.

Kai looked at Wren over his shoulder, brows raised.

"I need a moment with Shen."

To her surprise, Kai didn't argue. He stepped away, leaving them alone on the balcony together.

"I'm sorry for shouting at you," said Wren, breaking the stony silence. "What happened to Rose wasn't your fault. The truth is, I'm angry at myself for leaving her in the first place." She bit her lip. "For always leaving her. I haven't been a good sister these past few months."

Shen turned around to face her. "I was there, Wren. And she slipped through my fingers." He bit off a curse. "You were right to yell at me. Hell, you should have skewered me with that fancy new sword of yours. I deserve it."

"No, you don't," said Wren, and she meant it. "You're the only person in this world who loves Rose as much as I do." She grabbed his arms, trying to tug him from his cloud of melancholy. "You have to help me save her, Shen."

He frowned. "But she's gone."

"Not yet," said Wren, hoping she was right. "Oonagh is going to the Weeping Forest. I think she's taking Rose with her."

Shen's mouth was a hard line. "And what if you're wrong?" he said, clearly not wanting to raise his hopes in vain.

"Then we go anyway," said Wren. "Rose would want us to fight, Shen. For Eana. For the witches. For *her*."

Shen's eyes flashed, determination straightening his spine. He looked past Wren, to the sun climbing over the distant trees. "You're right," he said, more to himself than to her. "Let's cut that vicious creature down once and for all. For Rose. For Banba." He returned his gaze to Wren. "For you."

Wren gripped the hilt of her sword, summoning the ghost of a smile. "There's my best friend."

"Always," said Shen, returning it. "Now we fight. And we don't stop until the war is won."

36

ROSE

Rose opened her eyes and knew she had drowned. She was dead. She had to be.

All around her was cold, dark water. The world had turned hazy and slow, and she felt strangely weightless. Numb. She drifted past kelp and seaweed while fish nibbled at her toes.

Her body had fallen deep beneath the waves, far from where anyone would ever see or find her. Far below where she could ever hope to return from. She twisted in the water, noticing the hand curled around her wrist. Something else belatedly occurred to her. She was not alone down here. Oonagh Starcrest was dragging her through the deep and endless waters of her own kingdom.

But the water wasn't choking Rose. She was cold, so cold she couldn't feel her fingers or her toes, but she knew she was breathing. Without opening her mouth, without filling her lungs with air, somehow she could breathe.

But . . . wait. If she was breathing, then maybe she wasn't dead after all?

She blinked, trying to remember how she came to be trapped down here. A memory stirred in the far reaches of her mind. Wishbone Bay glimmering in the distance, the cry of the gulls as they circled the strand . . . Oonagh leaping from the water, dragging her down, down, down. The seabed rising to meet them. Then Oonagh came again, clawing at her neck. Rose remembered the pain, the awful searing in her neck, the burning in her lungs and then the welcome sensation of relief. Of breathing as she was now.

She brushed her fingers along her neck, finding three deep ridges— Oonagh had given her gills when she'd scratched her! That was why the marks had not healed. She looked ahead to find the same markings on her ancestor. She closed her eyes, trying to calm her rioting mind. She was not dead after all. She was living, swimming. No, that wasn't right either. She was being kidnapped! *Again.* Rose ground her teeth in frustration.

It seemed no matter what she did or how determinedly she tried to take control of her own destiny, someone always had other plans for her. And now Oonagh was taking her far from her friends, her people. But she wanted Rose alive. Which meant her ancestor needed something from her. And that scared Rose most of all.

Rose tried to struggle out of Oonagh's vicelike grip but her fingers were a manacle around her wrist. Oonagh didn't even turn around, barely noticing Rose's feeble attempts to flee. She kept her gaze forward, darting onward like a shark.

The water rippled around Rose, alerting her to shadows moving in the deep. There were other creatures down here. Huge terrible things with snapping teeth and grasping claws. Red eyes that shone like blood. Sharks? Whales? Monsters? Rose squinted but couldn't make them out.

Then came a flash of silver up ahead. For a moment, Rose thought she glimpsed a tail and then a mournful face looking back at her. Was that Marino's mermaid, after all? Would she ever see Marino again so she could tell him what she'd glimpsed?

Oonagh turned sharply, tugging Rose away from the haunting creature. "Help me!" Rose tried to cry, but the plea disappeared in a stream of bubbles. She flailed desperately, using her free hand to try wrench herself out of Oonagh's iron grip, but it was no use. Rose might as well have been a piece of driftwood down here.

And still her chest rose and fell, her heart thundering fearfully inside her chest. On and on they went, until time lost all meaning and Rose surrendered her senses. Her body stilled, slowly turning numb, and as hard as she tried to fight her exhaustion, her lids grew heavy until the darkness came to claim her once again.

37

WREN

When the golden gates of Anadawn groaned open once more, Wren was sitting astride her quickest horse and dressed in her fighting leathers, with Night's Edge fastened to her hip.

Shen was riding at her side, a steel-eyed king and a vengeful queen both ready for war.

"Look at us, journeying across the desert to find your sister," he said as they rode out into the wilds of Eana. "Just like the good old days."

Wren chuckled weakly. "At least you haven't lost your sense of humor."

"You know my wit is my sharpest weapon."

Though it had pained Wren to say goodbye to Tor, he had left already, riding north to join Princess Anika in commanding the Gevran army that Alarik had promised to summon to Eana. Wren hoped that promise would hold true and that she would see Tor—and his reinforcements—soon.

Despite her ailing strength, she had insisted on riding without a saddle mate. She hoped the magic in Night's Edge would sustain her strength across the desert. After all, what good was a queen who couldn't lead her own army?

Better than a queen who can't ride at all, Shen had argued, but she had brushed off his concern. Back at the palace, Thea had offered her a modicum of healing, a mere bandage on an open wound, but it was enough to get Wren washed and fed. The nearness of Eana's ancient sword and Wren's own adrenaline had taken care of the rest. So far.

It had been only a handful of hours since Wren's return to Anadawn, the news of her sister's drowning passing through her like a dreadful shiver. Now the entire Anadawn Guard had been assembled, spilling out behind her in their pristine uniforms of green and gold, longswords glimmering at their hips. Celeste rode alongside them, leading the contingent of witches, which included Kai, Bryony, Rowena, and even young Tilda.

Though Thea had volunteered to come and fight, she was of far better use at Anadawn. Wren could not afford to leave their seat of power undefended and Thea was the only one she and Rose trusted to rule in their stead.

"Are you all right?" said Shen as they rode through the trees, setting a course for the Kerrcal Road, and beyond it, the restless sands. By the time they reached the desert, it would be nightfall again. "If you're feeling faint, just give me a signal."

Wren glanced sidelong at him. "The signal will be me falling off my horse and face-planting in the sand."

"Great. Let's see if I can catch you before that."

"Try and salvage my dignity while you're at it."

"Challenge accepted."

They rode on, mostly in silence. Shen's jaw was tensed, every muscle in his body coiled to spring. Wren knew he was thinking about Rose—just as she was. She hoped they had chosen the right direction, and that when they arrived at the Weeping Forest, they would not be too late.

She couldn't help thinking of Alarik either, the weakening king cooped up in the Mishnick Mountains, trying to weather their burrowing curse without Wren there to help soothe his pain. The truth was, Wren wasn't just riding for Rose. She was riding for Alarik, too. And for herself. Willa's warning rang like a bell inside her. She had to kill Oonagh before the curse killed her. All of their fates now balanced on the knife-edge of war.

War with an ancient, powerful being.

"You're starting to sway." Shen's voice cut through Wren's reverie. It was sundown already, and yet she hadn't felt the hours pass. "Do you want us to slow down?"

"No," she said, gripping the reigns tighter. "Every moment is precious."

Shen didn't argue but he didn't set his concerns aside either. "Fix your saddle, Greenrock. Anchor your knees better, so if you do drift off you won't get trampled by the thousand horses behind you."

Wren took his advice, tying herself into the saddle in case she fell asleep. Her shoulders were already aching and her head was spinning. She gripped her sword, uttering a plea to the first witch. "Keep me strong, Eana. Help me fight."

Wren soon drifted off, lulled by the comforting thrum of hoofprints and the sureness of her best friend at her side and charting the way ahead.

Every so often, she became dimly aware of Shen's hand on her shoulder, straightening her in the saddle or his hand on hers, tightening her grip on the reigns, but apart from that, her sleep was deep, feathered only by glimpses of Alarik pacing the dusky halls of the Mishnick Mountains, too wounded even to rest. She saw nothing of Rose, the absence of her sister's presence—even in her thoughts—setting a bone-deep anxiety to work inside her. The curse fed off it, growing greedier by the hour.

Even in sleep, Wren's head pounded mercilessly.

Evening slipped away, turning the sky amber and pink, then a dark velvety blue. When Wren awoke, it was still night and there was a song moving in the wind. The dunes were singing. They had crossed into the desert, the hoofprints behind her dulling to the barest whisper. She groaned, trying to roll the crick from her neck.

A flask appeared in front of her. "Drink," said Shen, keeping his eyes on the shifting sands. "You look like death."

"Thank you for the morale boost." Wren snatched the flask from him and drank deeply. "How far are we from the Sunkissed Kingdom? We could do with another army."

"See for yourself," said Shen, jerking his chin.

Wren's eyes widened as she glanced over her shoulder. Now, instead of one army, there were two traveling behind them. There were at least a thousand more witches from the Sunkissed Kingdom, all dressed in black and armed to the teeth as they galloped across the sand, easily keeping pace with Wren's army. Wren spied Lei Fan grinning among them and Grandmother Lu riding on her haunches, brandishing a glittering gold cane.

Wren's eyes misted, the sight filling her with a rush of strength.

She smiled, suddenly overcome by gratefulness. "I can't believe I slept through their arrival."

"Don't feel bad," said Shen, smiling just the same. "We pride ourselves on our stealth."

"Let's just hope that stealth works on Oonagh."

"It will," he said, and Wren chose to believe it.

"The last time we traveled the desert together, you were an interloper and I was a bandit," he went on. "Now you're a queen and I'm a king. We've come a long way, Greenrock."

"And we still have more to go," said Wren.

"We can tackle any challenge," said Shen, rising up and quickening his horse. "Just make sure you can keep up!"

Wren mirrored him, urging her own horse faster. Night's Edge warmed at her hip, its magic staving off the rising desert chill. Behind them, their armies picked up speed, matching them stride for stride as they rode on into the night.

When the first brushstrokes of dawn feathered the deep blue sky, Wren was already awake. She looked around, searching for landmarks. "We're halfway there," said Shen, who needed no such help. He knew the sands like the lines on his palm. "We should stop to rest awhile," he said, making some silent calculation in his head. "Feed and water the horses before the sun rises in earnest. Your soldiers will need to rest, too." A quick glance over his shoulder made him chuckle. "I didn't think it was possible for anyone to sweat that much."

"Oh, leave them be," chided Wren. "They're doing their best."

The Eanan soldiers were indeed struggling with the sands. Even the Anadawn witches looked exhausted. On Shen's advice, they brought the journey to a halt, seeking respite in a nearby oasis, which was shaded with palm trees. An hour passed and then another while they napped and ate, then stretched their limbs, preparing for the second half of the journey and the unrelenting heat of the rising desert sun.

When they set off again, the air was sweltering. The soldiers began to grumble, their horses slowing in the shifting sand. Wren's head spun, only this time it was from the heat. She rose in her saddle. "Witches, call the wind!"

The witches went to work, brewing a gust that rippled through the ranks of both armies, cooling them as they rode.

"Good idea," said Shen, pushing his hair back from his face. "Now, why didn't I think of that?"

Wren wiped her brow. "Because you aren't melting."

"Ah. True."

The wind was a welcome addition, but it unsettled the sand, turning the air hazy. It was chiefly for this reason that Wren didn't notice the strange shadow gathering in the distance. At least not at first. Then a shout rang out from somewhere near the rear of the troop. It was followed quickly by another.

Wren turned, searching the haze. "What's that shadow?"

Shen stiffened, his gaze on the strange darkness. "It's no shadow," he said uneasily. "It's a flock."

Wren could see it now. There were birds. Thousands of them. They swooped down in droves, shrieking and snapping at the horses. "They're starcrests!" Only, they didn't look quite right to Wren. Their feathers hung in strips of black and silver and their eyes were bright red. She bit off a curse. "They're dead, Shen."

Which meant they belonged to Oonagh.

"They're attacking our riders!" he yelled over the swell of shouting.

Wren's cheeks prickled, the curse yawning inside her at the nearness of her ancestor's army—more dead things come to terrorize them.

She rose in her saddle, hoisting her sword toward the sky. "Soldiers of Eana! Witches of Anadawn and the Sunkissed Kingdom! Hold your nerve!" she cried out. "This wayward flock is no match for our might and speed! Keep your eyes on me and ride hard, as fast as you can."

"Seasoned tempests!" yelled Shen. "Brew your storm and cast it behind you. Make a wall of wind these birds cannot hope to pass. They may possess the element of fear, but we have magic!"

A rallying cry went up. It was followed by a fierce and blazing storm that struck as suddenly as lightning. Lei Fan led the charge, guiding the witches as they stirred a hurricane from the rolling sands.

The birds dived down in a great black cloud, shrieking in anger as the hurricane thundered toward them. It roared like a beast of its own, bringing the sand with it. The air thickened until it blanketed the shadowy swarm and flung them back into the shifting dunes.

The soldiers cheered, relief guttering through the masses as they pulled away from Oonagh's undead creatures. Emboldened by their victory, Wren and Shen turned back to the horizon, chasing it with renewed determination.

Minutes bled to hours, and day once more turned to night. They only stopped to rest when they were certain the birds had fallen away. This time, Wren was so exhausted she fell asleep by her horse with her water flask in her lap. Shen sat at her side, feeding her strips of dried lamb every time she stirred.

"Nearly there, Greenrock," he said, watching her chew slowly, reluctantly. "Can you make it?"

"You know I can," she said, slurring a little.

"Good." He smiled but it didn't reach his eyes. Wren could tell he didn't believe her. She wasn't sure if she believed herself.

The next time they set off, Shen had to help her onto her horse. He tied her into the saddle and secured the sword at her hip, before wrapping the reins around her wrists. Then he hopped up onto his own horse, taking care to ride close as they journeyed on, leading their armies east.

Wren's head lolled, her lids falling with every stride, until at long last, after what felt like an eternity, dawn poured its syrupy light over them. In the distance, Wren spied the climbing branches of the Mother Tree reaching toward the blushing sky. She straightened in her saddle, grabbing the hilt of her sword. It warmed, as if in recognition of this ancient place. This magical tree.

"Hold on, Rose," Wren whispered to the rising wind. "I'm coming."

38

ROSE

Something was stinking. No, *rotting*. Rose wrinkled her nose, trying to make sense of the rancid smell. Her head lolled back and forth as she searched for the light. She struggled to open her eyes, to pull herself from the blackness in her mind.

But that smell. That awful, *putrid* smell ... slowly, it was waking her.

Then she heard a growl. A low, guttural sound that sent a shiver down her spine. Her eyes snapped open. It was dark here, but soft strands of dawn light were filtering through the trees.

Trees. Yes, there were trees. She had made it to dry land. The last thing she remembered was the cold water, gnawing at her bones. That felt like eons ago now. She was dry again, and no longer shivering. Her head was foggy and her mouth was torturously dry. She must have been unconscious for a long time. A rogue vine caressed her cheek, as though trying to rouse her from the dregs of confusion.

She was in a forest. Yes, she could smell that now, too—the damp air was thick with mulch and she glimpsed branches jutting down from above. The trunks that clustered around her were twice her size and larger still.

There came another growl. Closer now. Then a low whine. There were animals here.

Rose blinked furiously. Her eyes adjusted, revealing trailing canopies that hid the sky. She tried to move but her wrists were tied with vines while another snaked around her middle, binding her to a trunk. She had the sudden, sickening feeling of weightlessness. She snapped her chin down to find her ankles were tied, too. Her feet were suspended several inches above the forest bed.

Oh no.

Panic surged through Rose. She was trapped. Pinned to a tree like a moth, with no one to rescue her. No one even knew where she was! Her friends were out in the bay, so far from Rose she could hardly fathom the distance between them. The more she remembered about her abduction, the more frightened she became.

And worse, the growls were getting louder. Shadows flitted between the trees, prowling closer.

"Calm down," she urged herself. "Focus. *Think.*"

Another vine brushed her cheek. Rose looked up, studying the leafy canopies. They seemed to go on and on. And yet there was something strangely familiar about them. Then she glimpsed something else—a single luminous seed floating through the trees.

Rose's heart hitched. She was in the Weeping Forest, the dark sprawling woods near the Whisperwind Cliffs, and just beyond them, the sands of Ortha. The Weeping Forest was a different kind of graveyard entirely. These ancient trees marked the graves of fallen witches from a long-ago battle, and the winds here often keened with their cries.

"Celeste's vision has come true after all," she muttered.

Rose steeled herself, trying to quell the rattle of her fear inside her.

"It's all right," she said, closing her eyes. "I'm not alone. Not really."

She could sense the spirits of her dead ancestors all around her even if she couldn't see them. Their presence gave her strength, made her feel that hope was not yet lost.

But there came that smell again, sweeping through the forest like a rotten wind. And then a growl so close, Rose snapped her eyes open. She cried out as a panther came darting through the trees.

She struggled, furiously, but her hands were bound so tightly, it only made her wrists ache. "Leave me be!"

The panther cocked its head, its red eyes too bright in the dimness. A shudder skipped down Rose's spine as she saw it for what it was: a shell of bones draped in strips of worn skin. Its mouth was full of sharp gnashing teeth. *Stars above.* The panther was half dead.

No. It was *undead.*

Oonagh Starcrest had pulled this rotting creature from its grave and dragged it into the forest.

Another beast came from her left. This one was a decomposing snow tiger, freshly dead. Its entrails trailed along the ground behind it, and maggots squirmed inside its gaping eye sockets. Then came another tiger that was missing half of its skull, and the next was gnawing on its own severed tail. All around Rose, an army of undead beasts moved through the forest, slowly surrounding her. "Go away! Leave me alone!"

Her wrists stung as she desperately tried to pull herself free. She thrashed, wildly, until the vines cut into her skin. The animals growled, scenting fresh blood.

"No!" she cried. "Stay back! All of you!" She snapped her chin up, calling out to the trees. "Witches of Eana, protect me! I am your queen!" But the forest was still, silent. "Please!"

She was answered by a familiar rippling laugh.

Rose froze as Oonagh Starcrest stepped through a break in the trees. "You are no queen," she sneered. "Your time on the throne of Anadawn is at an end."

Oonagh's hair was long and ragged, stained with blood and strewn with twigs. The green of her eyes had turned red, and her cheeks were gravely sunken. She looked like a corpse, so emaciated that Rose couldn't understand how she was moving at all. A pair of undead ice bears stood sentry at Oonagh's side. Their heads were little more than barren white skulls, their mouths filled with huge slabs of crumbling teeth.

"It's not as simple as that!" said Rose, raising her chin to try to show she was not afraid, even as she trembled. "You can't just kill me and be done with it. My sister—"

"Will be along shortly." Oonagh swept closer, her beasts swarming at her back. *Stars.* There were far more than Rose thought, hundreds upon hundreds of undead creatures skulking in the trees. "I suspect she will rise to the challenge of rescuing you. Sisters tend to do that."

Rose's hands twitched. How she wished for her dagger, but she had left Daybreak behind on Marino's ship, leaving her weaponless. *Why* on earth did she keep ending up in this sorry position? Well. She might not have a weapon but she still had her voice. Her courage. She would wield that instead. "This country will *never* bow to you."

"Not without force." Oonagh licked her rotting teeth. "I assure you, fear can be highly effective."

Somewhere in the deep forest, a beast howled.

Rose swallowed. "It will take more than an army of rabid beasts."

Oonagh lunged, closing the space between them until Rose could smell the horrid stench of death on her breath, see the cracks in her teeth. Just how much had Oonagh already sacrificed to raise this army?

"On that we certainly agree," Oonagh said in a growl of her own. "I will need more than beasts to make this country bend the knee." She glanced up at a floating seed. "Which is why I intend to raise my own army of witches." Her lips curled, triumph alighting in her eyes. "They will destroy you all."

Rose almost laughed. "Even you cannot raise the witches! You have given too much already, Oonagh." She looked her up and down, her nose wrinkling. "By the looks of it, there is hardly anything left to give."

Oonagh was unmoved. "Oh, my little trembling rose," she taunted. "This time I won't be sacrificing myself. I will be sacrificing something *far* more valuable."

Rose's breath shallowed in her chest. She searched for air, but terror had snatched it all away. "You can't mean . . ." She trailed off, too frightened to say the words aloud.

Oonagh's triumphant grin was answer enough.

Rose quailed. This wasn't the end of her ancestor's depraved plan. It was only the beginning. "You mean to sacrifice me."

Oonagh traced a sharpened fingernail along her jaw. "Look at all this life inside you. This bleeding heart and valiant soul. Wouldn't it be a shame to simply waste it all?"

Rose squeezed her eyes shut, trying to shake off her horror. She wished more than anything that Wren was here, her sister standing strong and sure at her side. But Rose was utterly alone.

How had it come to this?

She wanted to weep like the forest often did. To scream until she went hoarse. But more than that, Rose realized that she wanted to fight with every breath left in her body. If only she could find a way . . .

When she opened her eyes, Oonagh was already turning from her. A new wind stole through the forest, stirring the vines, and for one impossible moment, Rose swore she heard her sister's voice.

Hold on, Rose. I'm coming.

Oonagh stopped walking, a branch cracking underfoot. "Ah," she said, jerking her chin up. "It seems your sister is right on time."

39

WREN

Wren dismounted her horse at the Mother Tree and sent word to her Captain of the Guard that her soldiers were not to follow her into the forest. Nor were the witches. She had to tread this part of the journey alone.

"Are you sure about this?" said Shen, slipping soundlessly from his own horse. Instinctively, his hands came to his daggers. "If you go into that forest by yourself—"

"I'll attract less attention," said Wren. "We can't attack Oonagh until I've found Rose. We need to get her out safely first."

Shen frowned but didn't argue. They both knew Wren was right. Rose was their first priority. He looked past Wren to the sprawling forest. Today the weeping trees were unusually still, their leafy canopies bent low, as if they were bowing to someone or something.

"Are you feeling up to it?" Shen looked Wren over, his gaze lingering on the shadows beneath her eyes, the paleness in her cheeks.

"I'm going in either way."

"I could—"

"No," she said, firmer now. "It has to be me." She pressed a hand to her heart, feeling her pulse beneath the rattle of her breath. "Rose and I are part of each other. If she's in there, I'll find my way to her."

"I know you will," said Shen quietly. It was the only reason he was letting her go at all.

Wren was glad to have his agreement on the matter. "I'll go in where the trees are thickest," she went on. "When I find Rose, I'll get her out as quickly as I can. In the meantime, surround the forest and be prepared to strike at a moment's notice. The war begins the moment Oonagh catches wind of us." She gripped the hilt of Eana's sword, willing the warm pulse of its magic to strengthen her resolve. "And if you don't hear from me—"

"I'm going after you," said Shen. "And if I bump into Oonagh, it will be all the worse for her."

"Right," said Wren, rolling her shoulders back. "Wish me luck."

Shen pulled her into his arms. "You don't need luck," he said, squeezing her tight. "Just use that fire inside you, Wren. It's as strong as any magic."

She stood back, grabbing him by the shoulders. "You've been the best friend, Shen. I'm so—"

"Don't you dare," he said, clapping a hand over her mouth. "No goodbyes."

Wren peeled his hand away. "Fine. What about 'see you later'?"

He stepped away, clearing the path ahead. "See you soon, Wren."

Wren walked toward the edge of the ancient forest, conscious of the thousands of gazes at her back. And yet, despite the fullness of both armies, the world had fallen silent. Even the wind seemed to have died away, as if it knew what awaited Wren in the trees.

She stopped at the tree line and grabbed a fistful of mulch from the ground. Her magic was all but gone, and the part that remained was deeply wounded, but she would use it one last time, so long as she could. She cast a quick enchantment to dull the sound of her footsteps. The words came easily—after all, she had used this spell on many occasions when she first came to Anadawn to take her sister's place. That all seemed like a lifetime ago now. The mulch shimmered as it fell, before disappearing entirely.

The spell took hold but the effort of it cut through Wren like a knife. She bent double with a painful wheeze, grabbing on to a nearby trunk for balance. She scrunched her eyes shut, swallowing her groan as the curse inside her lashed out. For a moment, Wren swore she was going to vomit, but mercifully, the feeling passed.

She straightened up and stepped over the tree line, silently treading on fallen twigs. Soon, the darkness enfolded her, the damp air thickening with the scent of moss. Wren picked her way through the trees, peeling away hanging vines to try to get her bearings.

"Where are you, Rose?" she whispered to the forest, hoping it might help her. "I know you're in here somewhere. You have to be."

The alternative was too horrifying to consider—that if Rose was not in this forest then she was at the bottom of the sea. Wren scoured the dimness for any sign of her sister, any noise at all. The forest wasn't weeping. It was as silent as her footsteps, as if it was listening just the same.

"Rose," she hissed. "Where *are* you?"

She glimpsed something flickering in the distance. She crept toward it, ducking behind the trunks. It was a luminous seed, floating down from above. An ancient witch spirit. *An ally*, thought Wren. She smiled as she tipped her head back. There were hundreds more drifting down from the canopies.

"Ancestors," she whispered. "Show me the way."

The little seeds did not touch Wren—they kept their memories to themselves—but they did gather together, forming a small silver cloud. Wren gripped the hilt of her sword, feeling its magic pulse against her fingers. It grew warmer, more insistent. The spirit cloud floated westward through the trees, and Wren got the sense that the sword wished for her to follow it, that the glowing seeds would lead her to her sister.

Wren hurried after the cloud, the trees bending backward to clear a pathway for her. Her breath punched out of her, her head spinning from exertion, but she didn't dare slow down. She kept her gaze on the seeds as they floated through the forest, casting their glow along the mossy floor. Just when Wren's legs were threatening to give out and her head felt fit to burst, she heard a rustle up ahead. The branches parted to reveal her sister, stumbling toward her.

Relief rushed through Wren, a sob catching in her throat.

Rose's dress was ragged and filthy, and her hair was a tangled mess, but she was here. She was *alive*.

"Wren!" she cried, stumbling forward. "You found me!"

"Rose!" Wren flung herself through the forest, trying to get to her sister, but the trees crowded in on her, their vines swiping at her arms and legs. She shook them off but they kept coming back, thicker and angrier than before.

"Stop that!" She raised Night's Edge, swinging blindly at the branches, but the sword was oddly heavy now, and the hilt was ice-cold.

Wren froze in the undergrowth. She looked for the silver cloud but it had disappeared deeper into the forest. Still floating. Still searching.

Rose tripped over a branch, falling to her hands and knees. "Help me," she said, with a whimper. "I can't get up."

Wren's heart lurched, the urge to help her sister as strong as ever. But the sword weighed her down, stopping her. Wren was beginning to understand why. She didn't go to her sister, didn't speak another word. She waited for Rose to raise her head, to see if her creeping suspicion was true.

When Rose finally looked up, her eyes were cruel and mocking, her sickly smile far too wide.

"Good," said Wren, staring down at her. "But not quite good enough." She raised Night's Edge. This time, the sword almost floated into position, eager to be wielded. "Hello, Oonagh."

Rose blinked, and the facade fell away, revealing the haunting face beneath. "Little bird." Oonagh smirked as she stood up, her eyes turning as red as the blood on her teeth. "You really are predictable."

Wren's sword glinted menacingly as she stalked toward her ancestor. "Time to die."

"For whom?" Oonagh cocked her head and all around her hundreds of red eyes flashed in the dimness. By the time Wren noticed the beasts, it was too late.

She was already surrounded.

40

ROSE

As Oonagh left the clearing in search of Wren, Rose was overcome by a terrible rising dread. The beasts went, too, their red eyes fading from the shadows as they followed their leader through the trees. Toward Wren.

Rose bit back her scream, growing desperate with panic. Wren wouldn't stand a chance against Oonagh. All those beasts would savage her before she had half a chance to defend herself. No. Rose wouldn't stand for it. She *couldn't*. They had come too far and suffered too much to lose it all now. Rose and Wren had earned their thrones and their kingdom, and Rose refused to let Oonagh snatch them from them at the beginning of their reign.

She steadied her breath. She ignored the sweat dripping down her spine and the tears prickling in her eyes. She had to do something. *Anything*. But despite her determination, her hands were bound behind her back. So, too, were her feet. Rose was stuck. She thrashed and struggled, but the vines only bit into her wrists, drawing more blood.

"Help!" she hissed to the weeping trees. "Please! I have to save my sister!"

The trees stood motionless, watching her struggle. She was alone in this vast place, with no one to help her. Then she glimpsed a glowing seed floating high among the canopies. A new breeze stirred, caressing her cheeks.

"*A witch of Eana is never truly alone,*" it whispered. "*So long as she has her magic.*"

Rose stilled as an idea occurred to her. If she could find a way to cast an enchantment, she could loosen her binds and wriggle free. But she needed earth, dirt, mulch, anything. She twisted her body, scratching feebly at the bark behind her. But the tree was too hard and her fingernails came away without purchase.

"Come on," she muttered, digging into the trunk.

It was no use. She blew out a breath then closed her eyes, tipping her head back until it touched the bark. There were more seeds glowing in the dimness now, and Rose felt her ancestors looking down on her. She sensed they wanted to help her. That perhaps they simply didn't know how.

"Please," she whispered to the spirits of her ancestors. "I just need a little earth. Something to offer for my spell."

At first there was nothing. Just Rose's heart thundering in her chest and the distant thrum of growling beasts. They were getting louder, angrier.

Oh, Wren.

Then there came a faint rustling from above. Rose looked up to see a single leaf floating down from the canopy. It listed like a feather, gentle and slow, until it came to land on her shoulder. Rose twisted her hands behind her back until her palms were facing upward. Her wrists screamed at the unnaturalness of the movement but she pushed the pain away, carefully tilting her body to one side. The leaf tumbled from her shoulder.

It floated toward the ground but Rose jerked just in time, catching it between her forefinger and thumb. She curled it in her fist, eyes streaming with tears of pain and triumph. "Got it," she said, with a sob. *"I got it."*

With the leaf safe in her hand, she closed her eyes, summoning an enchantment. Her voice shook as she whispered it to the forest: *"From earth to dust, I ask these vines, to free me from their wretched binds."*

The leaf warmed in her hand. She released it, casting her offering alongside the spell. The leaf disappeared as it fell. With remarkable quickness, the vines snapped, uncurling from Rose's wrists. She pitched forward, falling on her hands and knees as the vines released her legs. And then, at last, she was unbound.

There wasn't a moment to lose.

Rose grabbed a fistful of dirt from the forest floor and scrambled to her feet. She might not have a weapon to fight Oonagh, but she had her magic and it had not yet failed her. And better still, Rose felt the forest was on her side, too.

She set off in the direction of the growling beasts just as a shadow came darting through the trees toward her. In a panic, Rose fired her handful of mulch.

"Stay back!" she cried.

Shen skidded to a stop. "When did you learn to throw like that?"

"Shen!" Relief surged through Rose as she ran to him. "What are you doing here?"

He scrubbed the dirt from his face. "I came to rescue you."

"Oh." Rose grinned. "Well, I'm afraid you're too late. I've already rescued myself."

He looked her up and down, his frown dissolving into a look of such relief, his eyes shone. "You're alive," he said then, as if he couldn't quite believe it. "Rose, I thought—" He shook his head, unable to say the words. "When you were pulled into that water . . ."

"It's all right, Shen. I'm all right." She pulled him close, and he laid his forehead against hers.

"Rose," he said, suddenly hoarse. "I swear for as long as I live, I'll never let anyone hurt you again." He held her face between his hands as though he was afraid she might disappear from him one more time. "Please forgive me."

"Hush," she said gently. "There's no need to apologize."

"Then let me kiss you instead," he said, pressing his lips against hers with such urgency, Rose lost her breath. She pulled back, breaking the moment.

"There'll be time for this later," she said, reaching for his hand. "Wren's in trouble, Shen. Oonagh's here. And she's not alone."

Shen spun on his heel, a dagger already in his hand. "Come on," he said, leading Rose through the trees, both of them following the noise of growling beasts. "It's time to end this once and for all."

As they wound their way deeper into the forest, Rose became aware of shapes moving in the trees. She whipped her head around, readying a shout, but Shen squeezed her hand. "It's all right," he said in a low voice. "They're with us."

Rose blinked, then stared harder. As the glowing seeds gathered above her, they lit up the other figures. She caught the glint of weapons, heard the determined crunch of boot-steps moving in tandem with them. When she spied Lei Fan in the trees to her left, her heart leaped. She was leading her own battalion of Sunkissed witches. On the other side of the forest, Rose glimpsed Grandmother Lu stalking with Kai Lo, her golden cane swinging as she guided a hundred more witches alongside them.

When Rose glanced behind her, she glimpsed the familiar green and gold edging of her own royal soldiers marching steadfastly at her back. Suddenly, the forest was so full it felt as if it were moving with them, buoyed by a tide of witches and soldiers ready to fight side by side. Ready to win.

A new hope surged in Rose.

Shen caught the smile on her face. "Well. How do you like our odds?"

Rose was about to respond when a ragged howl rang out. The color drained from her face as she thought of Wren, who was still unaccounted for. "We mustn't underestimate Oonagh," she said, quickening her steps.

Finally, they came to a break in the trees. Up ahead, in the middle of a sprawling clearing, Rose spotted Wren and Oonagh standing apart from each other. Wren was holding a sword Rose had never seen before and Oonagh was goading her with that horrid taunting smile.

Rose made to run for her sister but Shen pulled her back. All around them, witches and soldiers had come to an abrupt halt. Rose saw then what she had missed the first time.

The clearing was surrounded by a ring of undead beasts.

High above them, even the glowing seeds had stopped floating, as if they, too, were scared to venture any farther.

"What now?" whispered Rose. She could count fifty or so beasts from their vantage point in the trees, but she was not foolish enough to think that was all of them. There could be ten times as many lurking in the forest or even patrolling its borders. "We can't get to Wren or Oonagh without startling the beasts."

Shen removed another dagger until he held one in each hand. "We'll have to pick them off, one by one." He nodded at Lei Fan and then to Grandmother Lu, giving a covert signal. They each sank into a crouch, readying their assault. "Stay behind me."

"Absolutely not," said Rose. "Give me a dagger." Rose opened her hand expectantly. "I'm a warrior witch now, too, remember? Now please give me a weapon. I know you've got at least five more on your person."

"Including the one you want," said Shen, removing a familiar gilded dagger from his boot. He pressed it into her hand. "You left this behind on Marino's ship."

"Daybreak!" said Rose, feeling the thrum of its magic against her palm. "Oh, am I glad to see this beauty again."

"It might be witch-made, but it doesn't make you invincible. So be careful," Shen said imploringly.

"Oh, please," she said, curling her fingers around the hilt. "When am I ever not careful?"

Shen tossed her a warning look but there was no time to argue the point. He was gone in the next breath, prowling through the trees like a panther.

Rose hurried after him.

Once he reached the edge of the clearing, Shen climbed ten feet up a nearby trunk and leaped soundlessly from above. All across the forest, the witches of the Sunkissed Kingdom struck just the same, descending on the beasts in a blur of black and silver.

Oonagh snapped her chin up, red eyes flashing. "Strike!" she shrieked.

Her beasts sprang into action but for half of them it was already too late. The witches had gained the upper hand. As chaos descended on the clearing, Rose made a beeline for her sister. "Wren!" she cried, swinging Daybreak wildly as she leaped over a snarling fox and nearly tumbled into the mouth of a snow tiger just as Rowena and Bryony toppled it with a combined gust.

"Thank you!" cried Rose, without stopping.

Wren turned at the sound of her sister's voice. "Rose!"

They met at the far edge of the clearing, where Wren swung her sword wildly, fending off the skeleton of a roaring wolf. Rose jumped over its twitching body, flinging her arms around her sister and pulling her close. Wren sagged against Rose, her body shuddering violently as the sword fell to her side. "Rose, you're alive," she said, with a sob. "I knew you were. I *knew* it."

"Hush now, it's all right." Rose struggled to hold her sister up, startled by how ill she looked, how much weaker she had become in the days since they had last seen each other.

Wren hoisted her sword, her body tipping to one side as she tried to run back into the fray. "It's time to end this, Rose. We have to fight."

"You can barely stand, let alone fight," said Rose, tugging her back. "And where did you get that thing?"

"This is Night's Edge. Eana the first witch gave it to me," said Wren. A frown, then. "It's a long story."

"Tell it to me after the battle," said Rose, raising her own dagger to show Wren. "This is Daybreak. It looks as if we've both had some luck with weapons." She glanced over her shoulder to where Oonagh was standing at the other end of the clearing. Even though there were hundreds of witches between them and just as many beasts still snarling and snapping, their ancestor was staring straight at them.

Rose contemplated hurling her dagger at her but thought better of it. What if she missed?

Oonagh's ice bears still stood on either side of her, but the rest of her beasts were falling one by one. Wren swung her sword, barreling her way across the clearing. "We have to do it now!" she shouted. "We have to break the curse."

"Wren! Come back!" cried Rose, but her sister was too determined. Even despite her ailing strength, there was no stopping her.

As the Sunkissed witches and the Anadawn army fought tirelessly against Oonagh's undead beasts, their roars and growls began to die out. Soon, there were barely twenty beasts standing between Oonagh and the twins.

Rose might have felt hopeful—triumphant, even—if it wasn't for the mocking smile that had remained on her ancestor's face. When Wren was almost upon her and the beasts were all but felled, Oonagh uttered a soundless command.

By the time Rose screamed, it was already too late.

The entire forest shook. The trees quivered and the ground trembled as a thousand more bodies burst up from the earth. Rose saw the whites of their bones punching through the mulch before she spied their skulls, toothless and gaping. They were human remains, some so ancient their very skeletons were crumbling, while others were still rotting, their lumbering bodies infested with maggots, their eyes turned red with bloodlust.

They swarmed the clearing in a hail of fresh terror, every bit as vicious and rabid as the beasts that came before them. Only the sudden arrival of Oonagh's reanimated corpses inspired a kind of sickening dread that momentarily brought Rose's entire army to a standstill. It was a mistake that cost them dearly.

As more bodies crawled up from the undergrowth, tearing through soldiers and witches alike, the Weeping Forest echoed with a new chorus of dying screams.

WREN

Rose's scream split the clearing in two. By the time Wren looked up, it was already too late. A rotting corpse leaped from the earth and charged her. Wren landed face-first in the dirt with Night's Edge twisted awkwardly beneath her body.

The undead human screeched, its fetid breath rustling her hair. Wren could sense—rather than see—it unhinge its crumbling jaw. She tried to roll over, but the corpse was too heavy. She cried out but the sound was muffled by dirt, and even if it hadn't been, Wren knew it would have got lost in the horror unfolding around her. Suddenly, everyone was fighting for their lives. Some were now fighting their own ancestors.

Oonagh had outdone her own sickening depravity.

The corpse twisted its skeletal fingers in Wren's hair, wrenching her head back with unimaginable strength. She spied a rusted dagger in its other hand, the blade flashing as it rose. Wren screamed as a fierce wind swept over her. The corpse howled as it was knocked off kilter and then flung farther still, into the dark of the forest, where a pair of soldiers quickly descended on it, retching as they hacked at the cadaver with their swords.

Wren rolled onto her back to find Celeste peering down at her. "Turns out I'm a pretty good tempest," she said, lips trembling.

Wren blew out a breath. "I think I'm going to be sick."

Celeste offered Wren her hand. "Hold your nerve."

"I'm trying," said Wren, taking it. "Thanks, Celeste. I owe you."

Celeste pulled her to her feet just as another corpse lunged at them. This one was a skeleton so ancient all its teeth had fallen away. Wren swung Night's Edge, knocking its skull from its shoulders in one clean strike. It rolled to a stop between them.

"Gross." Celeste swallowed thickly. "But nice sword."

Wren tightened her grip on the hilt, relieved at its lightness in her hand, the ease with which she could swing it and never miss her mark. Then she jerked her chin up, searching the fray. The forest trembled with the clash and clamor of battle, the living and the dead both roaring as blade met bone. She spied Tilda nearby, the young witch hurriedly scaling a tree to outrun a grasping skeleton while Bryony and Rowena ran another through with their swords.

"Where's Rose?" said Wren. "She was right behind me a moment ago."

"She's with Shen," said Celeste, firing another gust to keep a towering, thundering corpse at bay. A Gevran, Wren guessed, by its tattered blue frock coat, the very realization causing her to tremble.

"Stars above, Wren. They keep coming!"

"They won't stop until Oonagh's dead." Wren spied her ancestor at the edge of the clearing watching the entire disturbing spectacle with wry amusement. Wren hated how she was enjoying herself, how all this pain and trauma only seemed to energize her.

Wren held on to the spark of that anger, letting it strengthen her as she slashed and fought her way across the clearing, trying not to look too closely at the corpses she felled, not to study their faded clothing or the jewelry that still clung to their graying skin. She caught glimpses of the battle as she went: Grandmother Lu swinging her golden staff so fast she knocked out three skeletons in one go; Rowena and Bryony brewing a gust so violent, it bent back an entire tree and flung an ice bear into the skies; Shen and Rose back to back fighting a ring of beasts while Kai rolled around nearby wrestling a bear. Then there were the bodies—beasts and humans strewn like leaves across the forest floor and even more scattered through the trees. Some of the soldiers had tried to run, only to be cut down by quicker corpses, wielding unburied weapons. They lay lifeless in the mulch now, their pristine green-and-gold uniforms smeared with dirt.

Everything Wren saw stoked her rage, urging her toward Oonagh and the ice bears that guarded her. Eana's sword buzzed against Wren's fingers as if to say, *I am with you. You are not alone.*

When Wren glanced behind, she saw that Celeste had gone to help Tilda grapple with a leopard twice her size. Now there was only Oonagh in her sights and the screams of her people ringing in her ears. The sooner she felled her ancestor, the sooner they would all be free.

But as Wren fought her way across the clearing, Oonagh disappeared, slipping between the trees as silently as a shadow. Wren hurried after her, squinting into the dimness. In the distance, she spied two lumbering shapes: Oonagh's ice bears. They trailed after their leader as she darted through the forest.

"Coward!" shouted Wren. "Come back and face me!"

But Oonagh kept running.

Wren stumbled as she tried to catch her. Sweat pooled under her shirt and down her spine. The curse was awake inside her, thrashing with each new step. But every time Wren stopped to rest against a tree or bent to catch her breath, Eana's sword glowed, urging her on.

Just a little farther.

You're almost there.

Soon, Wren's eyes streamed from the effort of even walking. She stopped to retch and when she looked up, Oonagh was gone. The forest had fallen eerily silent. Wren looked around, trying to figure out where she was, but the trees all looked the same here, and her head was clouded with exhaustion.

"Where are you?" she hissed. "Come out and face me!"

But there was nothing and no one, just the sound of her own labored breaths. Wren was starting to regret her decision to come after Oonagh. She was all alone in here, weak and in pain, with only a sword to protect her.

"Help me," she called out. "Someone. Anyone."

A familiar breeze swept through the forest and kissed her cheeks. It smelled like seaweed and brine. Like home.

"Ortha." The word poured from Wren like a sigh. Suddenly, she knew exactly where she was. The Whisperwind Cliffs were just up ahead. And beneath them, along a crescent of brassy sand, the place where Wren had grown up, raised by Banba on the wild shores of Eana. It was here that Wren had trained to be a witch, to be a fighter.

A slant of sunlight filtered through the trees, beckoning her onward.

Buoyed by a surge of determination, Wren broke into a run, chasing the edge of the forest just as she used to when she was a child, playing hide-and-seek among these same trees with Shen Lo.

And then the edge of the Weeping Forest was before her, the land flattening as it rolled westward toward the sheer cliffs, and beyond them, Wren's homeland.

Oonagh was standing at the edge of the cliff, waiting for her.

Wren tightened her grip on the hilt of her sword, feeling the spirits of her ancestors gathering at her back. As she stalked toward her ancestor, she felt Banba's presence in the gusting wind. Wren raised her sword, sinking into a fighting stance as Oonagh's ice bears charged. They were huge but clumsy. One veered to the left and Wren struck, skewering the bones in its exposed rib cage. The sword glowed, bright and blinding, and the bear collapsed in a heap, felled by blunt force and ancient magic.

Wren stepped over it.

"Not bad, little bird," taunted Oonagh. "But your strength is fading."

"Not yet," said Wren through gritted teeth. She felled the second bear in four strikes, the sword guiding her hand as she swung.

And then there were just Wren and Oonagh, and the sea wind howling between them. Oonagh raised her hands, summoning her own violent gust. Wren pitched forward, planting her feet to keep from losing her footing. She used her sword as a staff, stabbing the earth as she inched toward Oonagh. It would take more than the wind to stop her now.

"Determined little creature, aren't you?" sneered Oonagh. She raised her hand, pulling a streak of lightning from the cloudless sky.

Wren leaped out of the way just as it struck, burning a hole in the earth. Smoke curled up from the grass, making her wheeze.

But still, she crawled. Little by little, hand over foot. Oonagh cast another bolt and without thinking, Wren raised her sword. She screamed as the lightning bounced off the blade, creating a blinding flash. It ricocheted back at Oonagh. This time, it was she who had to leap away.

Oonagh fell to the ground and Wren seized the moment, lunging at her ancestor. She was on Oonagh in the next heartbeat, her knees pitched either side of her rib cage, the point of Night's Edge at her throat. Oonagh froze, her red eyes going wide. She blinked and they turned green. For a moment, she looked so like Rose that Wren hesitated. But the wind roared, and she remembered Banba and everything else Oonagh had taken from her. Everything she still sought to steal.

She leaned on her sword, drawing blood. "Any last words?"

Oonagh's lips curled. *"Cease."*

Wren froze without meaning to, a sudden terrible coldness sweeping through her body. When Oonagh spoke again, the words echoed in her head: *Stand up.*

To Wren's horror, she stood up. The sword fell slack at her side, as though she had forgotten what to do with it. She tried to fight the voice inside her but it was not hers to command. And neither was her own body.

Oonagh laughed as she rolled to her feet. She came to Wren's side, her bony hand resting heavy on her shoulder. For a distressing moment, Wren thought Oonagh was going to walk her off the cliff and send her plummeting to her death, but instead she turned her around and made her walk back toward the Weeping Forest.

When Rose appeared through the trees, Wren's heart dropped.

"Wren!" she cried with such relief Wren wanted to sob.

"Good puppet," crooned Oonagh as she made Wren raise Night's Edge and angle the point at her sister. "Now the real fun begins."

42

ROSE

When the corpses erupted from the ground, Rose barely had time to leap out of the way. She fell to her knees and rolled over as a bony hand tried to snatch at her. Unscathed and panting, she scrambled to her feet. She whipped her head around, searching frantically for Wren. Her sister had been here just a moment ago, but the forest had swelled and she couldn't hear a thing over the sudden sound of screaming.

Then Rose caught sight of something that made her heart jump into her throat. There, in the middle of the clearing, was Shen. He was lying on his back in the dirt, desperately trying to wrestle the snow tiger that had landed on top of him. The beast was three times his size and its fangs were terrifyingly close to his neck.

"Shen!" Adrenaline flooded Rose and sent her charging into the fray. She hopped over a pair of grappling wolves, then lunged to the left, narrowly avoiding an eyeless corpse. She kept her dagger high and poised to strike, but when a pair of skeletons lunged toward her, she used her tempest magic, sending out a gust so strong it flung them into a nearby tree, sending a crack right up the middle.

When she reached Shen, Rose cast another gust, but a tiger had dug its claws into his shoulders. Shen was losing his fight against the beast. It opened its mighty jaws, releasing a deafening roar as it bored down on him.

Rose leaped onto the tiger's back. Before she could second-guess herself, she brought Daybreak down, skewering the beast between its exposed shoulder blades. She held on tight, squeezing her eyes shut as she pushed the dagger deeper, until finally, she felt the creature shudder underneath her. It released a keening groan as it slumped onto its side.

Rose slid off the beast's back and then, entirely without meaning to be, she was on top of Shen, now straddling him herself.

He stared up at her with wide unblinking eyes. "Rose?" he said breathlessly. "What in stars' name are you doing?"

"Saving your life," she said, with a huff. "Isn't it obvious?"

"I . . . I'm . . ." He blinked, searching for the right word.

"Eternally grateful?" Rose swept the hair from her face, taking a closer look at him. When she spotted the blood seeping through his shirt, her own blood went cold. "You're hurt!"

"I'm all right," said Shen, flinching as he tried to sit up.

Rose gently pushed him back down. "Let me heal you."

"Rose, we're in the middle of a battle! I have to fight."

"First, you need to heal," she said firmly. "Hush now." She closed her eyes, resting her hands against the puncture wounds in his shoulders. They were deeper than she thought, scouring through muscle and bone. But she was a practiced healer, and despite the screams in their midst, she sank into a quiet calmness and set her magic to work. It tingled as it brushed against Shen's.

She heard him groan softly. "That's nice."

Quickly, carefully, Rose knitted his wounds back together. When it was done, she opened her eyes to find her vision was blurry. But even so, she could still see the ice bear that was charging toward them. She screamed, bracing for impact, when a blur shot out from the trees and barreled into the hulking creature, knocking it off course. Kai fell to the ground, punching and kicking the undead bear as they rolled over each other, again and again.

"Kai!" shouted Rose. "You—"

"You're welcome, Queenie!" he shouted back, before ripping the bear's arm clean off.

Shen shot up, holding Rose's shoulders. "You're pale," he said, searching her face. "You shouldn't have—"

"It will pass," said Rose, waving away his concern. "Help me stand, please."

Shen helped her to her feet, anchoring her to him as he fended off what looked like an undead farmer swinging an axe. Mercifully, Rose's head soon stopped spinning, enough that she could withdraw Daybreak from the twitching snow tiger before rushing back to help Shen.

"You need to get out of here," he said as four more corpses came stalking toward them. "Find somewhere safe."

"Like where?" said Rose shrilly. "There are dead things every-where, Shen."

Shen kicked one squarely in the mouth then glanced at Rose. "I can't lose you again, Rose."

"You won't," she said, wincing as she jabbed her dagger through the bones of a gaping rib cage. The skeleton reeled backward, clutching at the phantom wound. "I'm right here. I'm not going anywhere."

"Promise?" Shen pivoted, pressing his back against hers as they slashed and fought in perfect harmony.

"Promise," said Rose.

Time seemed to slow then, until all Rose knew was the sureness of Shen's back against her own and the steady rise and fall of their chests as they battled dead beast and human alike. She wasn't frightened anymore. No, she felt braver than she ever had before. If they survived this—and they *would* survive it because she couldn't allow herself to think any other way—then she would live the rest of her life like this. Bravely.

"Marry me," she said.

"What?" said Shen, cutting down a rampaging cadaver with a single blow.

"Marry me, Shen Lo. I love you. I've always loved you. You stole my heart as a bandit, and you have kept it as a king." Rose paused to cast a gust at an advancing leopard. "And I would marry you even if you weren't a king," she went on between breaths. "Even if you were still a bandit."

Shen laughed. "Is that meant to be romantic?"

"Well, I don't have very much experience when it comes to proposing!" said Rose hotly. "I've never done it before! Just say you'll marry me, Shen."

"I love you, Rose. I'll always love you. But this is a conversation I want to enjoy. To *relish*. And right now, well"—Shen slammed his elbow into a shrieking, red-eyed crone before rounding on another—"we're surrounded by dead people!"

"A fair point," she conceded.

"We need to finish this fight. And if you keep trying to seduce me, we'll never make our way out of here!"

"Proposing to you is not seducing you!"

He barked a laugh. "Trust me, it is."

"You are ridiculous."

"And you love me."

"You are *insufferable*."

"Again, you love me."

Soon, they were both fighting too hard to speak at all. When they had finally managed to battle their way free of their attackers, Rose looked around for Wren but there was still no sign of her anywhere. "I don't think Wren's here," she said, more to herself than Shen. "She must have gone after Oonagh."

Shen scrambled up the nearest tree, climbing ten feet in a single heartbeat. He scanned the battlefield, shouting at the top of his lungs. "WREN!"

Lei Fan sent a warning gust to rattle the tree. Once she got their attention, she pointed toward the other end of the forest. "That way!"

Rose and Shen didn't waste another second. They fought their way across the clearing, tussling with humans and beasts alike, until the trees thickened around them. The dead were everywhere, but the forest was eerily quiet.

Rose whirled around, trying not to look at the bodies on the floor, all these faces of people she had known and loved as their queen. Innocents, sent to fight phantoms and corpses, all to die in a cruel war of Oonagh's making. "This is impossible," she said, her eyes prickling with unshed tears.

Shen squeezed her hand, unable to bring himself to look at the bodies. "It will be over soon."

But Rose had already seen too much. She felt each death like a pinprick in her heart. All these lives wasted and for what? This forest had already endured so much, mourned so many. Rose was starting to fear that no matter how hard they fought, it wouldn't be enough. That Eana would never truly be theirs, that she wouldn't be able to save it.

But then she glimpsed more glowing seeds clustering above her and was reminded of the spirits of her ancestors, and how bravely they had fought here against the Protector's army over one thousand years ago.

It was time for Rose to be brave, too.

She wiped her tears as they walked on into the dimness. "How will we figure out which way she went?"

"There—look," said Shen, pointing west. "Footprints." Rose could make out the outline of Wren's boot-steps in the mulch, but there were other footprints, too—ones much larger and wider than a human's. *Bears*, she realized with a jolt. Oonagh had come this way, too.

Shen followed the trail, pulling Rose with him. "They went west. Toward Ortha."

"They're heading for the cliffs!"

They broke into a run, Rose tucking Daybreak into her bodice and hiking up her dress as Shen darted through the trees, slashing vines and branches out of their way. After what felt like hours, a shaft of sunlight reached them through the trees and a familiar sea wind stung Rose's cheeks.

The edge of the forest was in sight. Rose raced toward the breaking light, overtaking even Shen until she stumbled through the thinning trees and out onto the long grass where Wren was waiting for her.

She almost sobbed with relief when she spotted her sister standing across the grassy plain. "Wren!"

Wren raised her sword and pointed it at Rose.

Rose frowned. "What are you doing?" she said, starting toward her.

Shen grabbed her wrist, tugging her back. "That's not Wren," he said in a low voice. "At least not as she truly is."

It was only then that Rose noticed Oonagh standing at the edge of the cliffs, the sea wind streaming through her dark hair. She mouthed something Rose couldn't hear, but the words weren't meant for her. They were meant for her sister.

When Wren heard them, she charged at Rose.

43

WREN

Dread coursed through Wren as she charged headlong at her sister. She tried to fight her own body, to cast her sword aside and fling herself to the earth to keep from harming Rose, but Oonagh's grip on her mind was too strong. The curse inside Wren was wide awake, listening to its master.

Wren sobbed as she ran, tears streaming from her eyes.

Rose was so startled by the sight, she didn't even move. She just stared at Wren as if she was trying to work out who she was.

Move, Wren wanted to scream. *Get out of the way!*

She was barely ten steps from skewering her sister with the point of her sword when Shen jumped in front of Rose, drawing his dagger. He sank into a protective crouch, his eyes on Wren.

"Don't make me fight you, Greenrock," he said warily. "You know I don't want to."

But Wren couldn't stop. She swung wildly, the sword whistling as it cut through the air. Shen leaped, narrowly avoiding the blade as he landed a spinning kick to her shoulder. Wren was knocked off-kilter,

giving him enough time to catch her right arm and deftly trap it behind
her back.

A scream ripped out of her as he twisted her wrist.

"You have to drop it," he said, close to her ear. "*Try*, Wren."

Wren closed her eyes, willing her body to listen to her and not
Oonagh. But she began to thrash, violently, trying to regain control
of the sword. She knew if Shen dared let go, she would stab him in the
next breath.

Shen seemed to know it, too. He crushed her against him, pinning
her arms to her body. Then he spun her away from Rose. Together,
they faced Oonagh across the long grass. "Just hold on a little longer,"
he whispered. "Help is coming." She jerked and thrashed as he walked
her forward, easily weathering her attempts to flee. "There, Wren. Do
you see the gray sails down in the bay?"

Wren couldn't respond, but her heart gladdened at the sight of the
Gevran warships below them and the fact that, for all her blood-soaked
power, Oonagh Starcrest had not yet spotted them. She was too busy
leering at Wren, enjoying the struggle between her and Shen.

"Isn't one sister enough for you?" Oonagh crowed. "That one
belongs to me."

Shen ignored the taunt. His hand came to the hilt of Night's Edge.
"Can you drop it?"

Wren tried but it was no use. She clenched her teeth, fighting
through the shadows inside her, trying to find a precious kernel of
free will. She knew it was buried in there somewhere, hidden deep
in the recesses of her soul. She crafted her words, pushed them out
onto her tongue, and with all the strength in her body, managed to

eke out a single plea. *"Take it."*

Shen ripped the sword from her grasp and a new scream poured from Wren. She slumped onto the grass, cradling her twisted wrist.

"Wren!" Rose was pacing at the tree line, too frightened to go to her sister, too rooted to turn and run back into the trees. It was just as well because Wren glimpsed a sea of red eyes gathering in the forest, the dead rising again to finish their task. Oonagh's army was back and waiting for her next command.

Shen arced around Wren, angling Night's Edge at Oonagh. "You can't control me," he roared with such anger, Wren hardly recognized him. "Let's finish this!"

Oonagh shrieked in amusement. "Such arrogance!" She brewed a gust between her hands and flung it at him like a boulder, knocking him back. Shen lost ground but kept his footing, coming at her again and again, until Oonagh tired of her own tricks.

The next time she called down the wind, it came like a hurricane, bending the trees as it swept over them. Rose was thrown backward, where she landed in a heap in the long grass. Wren was rolled across the earth, over and over, spitting grass from her mouth. While Shen was the most seasoned warrior among them, he was no match for the ancient power of Oonagh Starcrest. She flicked him like a gnat, sending him back toward the forest, where he lost his grip on Eana's sword and slammed headfirst into a trunk.

When he came to, he crawled through the rising storm to Rose.

"So the desert king has made his choice," said Oonagh as she stopped in the grass beside Wren. She looked down on her, pulling an exaggerated pout. "How sad it is to be rendered second-best, but I have always found it to be a motivation for greatness." She plucked Wren from the grass by her hair and lifted her to her feet. "Or perhaps we should make a martyr of you instead," she said, angling her dagger at her throat. "What do you think, dear puppet?"

"*I* think you're a hateful, soulless creature who has far outlived her welcome on these shores!" Rose burst out. She shook Shen off and started toward Oonagh, clutching Daybreak. This was her chance.

Wren felt the bite of Oonagh's blade as it punctured her skin. "Keep talking," taunted Oonagh. "Every step pushes my blade deeper into your sister. You can kill her yourself."

Rose froze. "What do you want from us?" she shouted.

"Well, now that you mention it, there *is* something I want—" Oonagh stopped suddenly. She snapped her chin up, scenting the wind. At that same moment, Wren felt the curse jerk inside her, as if something— or *someone*—was tugging at her soul.

"*Ah,*" said Oonagh. "My other plaything has arrived."

"I hope I haven't missed the tea party," came Alarik Felsing's unmistakable drawl. "I've been meaning to jab a butter knife in your eye."

Oonagh swung Wren around to find the king of Gevra standing on the edge of the cliff, looking worse than Wren had ever seen him. And that really was saying something. Yet, even despite his weakness, she could tell by the smudges of dirt on his cheeks and the grass stains on his trousers that, somehow, Alarik Felsing had dragged himself up those cliffs.

Wren felt herself smile.

Alarik, for all his suffering, smiled back.

"Oh, my bleeding heart," taunted Oonagh.

"Careful," said Alarik. "You sound jealous."

"*You* be careful, little king," Oonagh shot back. "You are tied to me just as strongly as you are to her."

Alarik cocked his head. "If that's true, then why do I like her and yet find myself wishing for your quick and painful demise?"

Oonagh cast Wren aside, relinquishing her grip on her mind. "You have no business on these shores. Why have you come here?"

Alarik dug his hands into his pockets. "I thought perhaps you might like to kill me."

Wren's heart dropped as Oonagh stilled, intrigued by his offer.

What the hell was Alarik doing?

"I hear you're into that kind of thing," he went on. "Mindless killing. Indiscriminate terror."

"Nothing I do is mindless," said Oonagh, coming toward him.

"I can't say I relate." He flashed a wolfish grin. "But then I am Gevran."

"I've never known a Gevran to go so willingly to their death," said Oonagh, flexing her fingers. Wren felt another gust rising.

"He doesn't mean it!" she yelled, struggling to her feet. "It's just a game!"

"Perhaps I want to play it," said Oonagh, grabbing Alarik by the collar. She pulled him close, until they stood nose to nose along the edge of the cliff. Wren lost her breath. Oonagh could toss him over the cliffs. He wasn't strong enough to stop her, and by the expression on his face, it didn't even seem as if he wanted to.

"Alarik!" Wren screamed, but the king didn't look at her. "Stop this madness!"

She whirled around in a panic and caught sight of Rose and Shen stalking through the long grass, looking for Night's Edge. Shen flicked his gaze to the cliffs, then raised a finger to his lips.

Understanding careened over Wren. She remembered the gray sails floating in the bay, the promise of the Gevran army hovering just out of reach. Until now it hadn't occurred to her to wonder where on earth Alarik had come from or who he might have brought with him. And yet now, here he stood, making a distraction of himself . . . toying with Oonagh just as she liked to toy with them.

Alarik was buying time. He was not strong enough to fight with his sword, but words had never failed him. They were working, even now.

"You do not look frightened." Oonagh scowled at the king. "Is it because I am wearing the face of your beloved?"

Alarik met her hateful gaze with cool indifference. "I'm not afraid, because in all the ways that matter, I am already dead. But you know that. Since this curse in me feeds from you, too."

"How morose you are," she sneered as she lifted him from his feet. "Perhaps I will kill you to put you out of your misery."

To Wren's surprise, Alarik smiled. "Or," he said, as if a new idea was suddenly blooming in his mind, right here on the windswept edge of the world. "If you're feeling ambitious, you could marry me."

Oonagh barked a laugh. "What jest is this?"

Wren was so shocked by the suggestion, she almost laughed, too. From the corner of her eye, she glimpsed a hand appearing at the far edge of the cliffs, noted the cuff of its midnight-blue sleeve trimmed in silver. The Gevrans had breached the cliff-line, and by the way Alarik was talking, he must have known it.

"Gevrans never jest," he went on. "Release me from this wretched curse and I will bow to you, Oonagh Starcrest. I will worship you like no other. You will be my queen and together we will rule the great kingdoms of Gevra and Eana together." He offered her a conspiratorial smile. "And beyond, if you wish it."

"I need no man to rule," said Oonagh, though Wren swore she was wavering a little at the suggestion. Or at the very least, not killing him outright for it. Wren could tell she was tempted, not by the possibility of marriage but by the lure of power it would grant her.

Alarik could sense it, too. "Then you can rule me, as well."

Oonagh peeled her lips back. "Pretty words do not make promises. You are in love with the girl. I can smell it on you. I can sense the longing inside you."

Wren flinched at the words. Alarik made little of them, as though they held no consequence for him.

"You said it yourself," he said smoothly. "You wear the same face as Wren. So what difference is it to me? And you must know I've always admired ambition."

"Lies," said Oonagh, with a hiss.

"Let me go and I'll prove my intention," said Alarik. "Unless you are too frightened to conceive of an even greater future than what you had imagined for yourself."

Oonagh snapped her hand away, dropping him along the cliff edge. For a moment, Alarik teetered on the brink of death. Wren could scarcely breathe. Even though she could sense the army sneaking over the cliffs, she couldn't tear her gaze from the Gevran king. She was rooted in place by the fear of what he might do next.

What Oonagh might do to him.

And then, to her enduring surprise, Alarik knelt in the grass and lowered his head in deference. "My queen."

Oonagh looked down at him, an entirely new smile spreading across her face. For a moment, she looked . . . *triumphant*.

Then a deafening roar shattered the moment.

Oonagh jerked her chin up just as Princess Anika came riding over the cliffs on the back of Borvil, the royal ice bear. The rest of the Gevran army came with her, the soldiers brandishing their swords while their beasts growled through bared teeth.

Oonagh let out her own roar of anger, but by the time she turned back to Alarik, he was already stumbling away from her. She drew her arm back, readying her dagger just as Elske appeared in a blur of white and barreled straight into her. Tor leaped after the wolf, landing on Oonagh with the wild anger of a beast and pinning her to the ground.

Oonagh shrieked as she fell, her command cutting through the air. "STRIKE!"

Behind Wren, the entire forest came to life. Red-eyed bodies shot out from the trees, meeting the charging Gevrans in an almighty clash of brute force. From the skies, a flock of nighthawks descended, trying to pick off Oonagh's army, but there were as many cursed creatures now as there had been in the beginning. As Shen's witches and Wren's soldiers came staggering through the trees, Wren realized with a sinking feeling that they numbered far less than before.

"Wren!" Rose hurtled toward her sister, grabbing her by her shoulders. "Are you all right?"

"I don't know," said Wren, trying to fight the tide of her panic. The

Gevrans had come—refreshed and ready for war—and yet she couldn't shake the thought of all the witches and soldiers lying dead in the forest, felled by corpses that refused to die. "At least I can talk for myself. I can move as I like. So long as Oonagh's distracted I can—" She stopped at the sudden look of horror that came over Rose. "What is it?"

Rose's lips were moving but she couldn't seem to find the words. Wren turned around, following her sister's gaze to the cliff edge, where Tor had been fighting Oonagh only a moment ago.

Now Oonagh was gone. A snow tiger pinned Tor to the earth. And beside the embattled soldier, his beloved Elske lay motionless.

44

ROSE

When Wren spotted Tor and Elske, she screamed. She staggered to her feet then froze midstride.

"Wren?" said Rose anxiously, but Wren said nothing. She had gone perfectly still. Silent. Her eyes were wide with horror and fresh tears were streaming down her cheeks, but she could no longer speak. Rose knew that Oonagh was controlling her sister once more.

Rose whipped her head around, searching the battlefield for her ancestor. It didn't take long to find out where she was. A hand fell heavy on Rose's shoulder, familiar talon-sharp nails digging deep into her skin. She flinched as Oonagh dragged her to her feet then shoved her toward the trees. "*Move*," she hissed in Rose's ear. "Or I'll walk your sister right off that cliff."

With Shen fighting in the fray, Rose had no choice but to obey. While Oonagh steered her into the forest, Wren trailed behind them, caught once more in a trance. Overhead, the Gevran nighthawks screeched and swooped along the cliffs, searching for Oonagh, but she paid them no mind. It seemed to Rose that she had surrendered all interest in the battle entirely.

The world darkened as they passed the tree line, leaving the war behind. Rose turned around, desperately looking for help. She spied Celeste fighting not far from the edge of the forest and for the briefest moment they locked eyes.

Celeste tried to come after Rose, but Oonagh was quicker. She cast a gust so fierce it bent the entire outer ring of the forest inward, crushing the trees together until they formed an impenetrable wall. Their canopies became a dome, blocking out the last of the sunlight and sealing the twins—and their ancestor—inside.

They were well and truly trapped.

In the sudden silence, Rose reached for her sister's hand. It was limp inside her own. Rose hoped Wren could still feel her touch. It was so dark now she could barely see a thing, but Oonagh ripped a branch from a nearby tree and set it alight. She brandished the torch, leading them into the heart of the forest.

Rose tried her best not to look down, knowing the horror she would see, but she couldn't help it. There were bodies everywhere, soldiers and witches lying in pools of their own blood. The farther they went, the more she saw.

Her eyes streamed with fresh grief, her heart aching so badly she could scarcely breathe. When she saw the same tears in her sister's eyes, she squeezed her hand tighter, sharing in her pain. Rose wished more than anything that Wren would squeeze back.

"I warned you not to fight," said Oonagh, kicking aside the body of a girl as though it were merely an exposed tree root. "You should have left your armies at home and surrendered yourselves. Surrendered your thrones. Instead, you chose to waste all these precious lives. These precious witches."

Rose looked down at the girl's body as she edged around it, recognizing the mass of sandy curls. It was Rowena. And there—barely a stone's throw away from her best friend—was Bryony, lying motionless in the mulch. Rose trapped her whimper on the back her hand. Beside her, Wren began to wretch, her very soul revolting at the sight.

Rose was overcome by a burst of anger. "You hateful, wretched monster!" she cried, suddenly remembering the dagger stowed inside her bodice. She reached for Daybreak. "You have made a mockery of this kingdom! Of everything the witches stand for!"

Oonagh turned sharply, backhanding Rose across the face. "Watch your tongue!" she hissed, bringing the torch threateningly close. "This kingdom was mine long before it was yours."

Rose spat out a glob of blood, weathering the sting. Oonagh grabbed her wrist, her nails digging in so Rose could not pull her dagger free. She shouted again, hoping to distract her ancestor before she spotted it glinting under the folds of her dress. "All this pain and suffering is *your* fault!" She wasn't just speaking for herself, but for Wren, who had lost her voice and her magic all because of Oonagh. "No matter what you do to me or my sister, this country will never be yours. Your beasts will tire. Your corpses will rot. Our armies will defeat them and then, when all is said and done, they will come for you, too!"

Oonagh snorted. "You foolish child. Don't you understand? I don't have to win this battle. I have no use for this kingdom's cadavers. My soldiers are already dead. They have but one purpose. And that is to fight for as long as they can. I don't care what happens to them after that."

Rose glowered at her. "If you don't care to win, then what is the point of all of this bloodshed and terror?" she demanded. "Why kill anyone at all?"

"Because a little blood sport is good for the soul." She turned her torch on Wren, who had grown so pale now, she looked like a corpse. "Isn't that right, little bird?"

Wren wasn't able to respond but the glare she gave Oonagh was answer enough. The simple effort of it made Wren stumble on a branch. Rose caught her before she fell. "It's all right," she whispered, even though this was the furthest they had ever been from all right. "I've got you. Lean on me."

When they came upon the battle clearing, Rose found herself wishing for the darkness again. This part of the forest was strewn with so many bodies, she didn't know where to look. It was much brighter here, where thousands of spirit seeds had come together to grieve those that had fallen in battle. They floated above the clearing like a beautiful silver mist, casting their mournful glow upon the dead.

As Oonagh prodded the twins through the clearing, Rose heard weeping. The forest was in pain, the sound so real and haunting, it echoed the grief in her heart and the look on her sister's face. Wren was so stricken by what she saw, she could barely walk, but every time she slowed, Oonagh struck her.

"I'm here," said Rose, pulling her sister close, waiting for the right moment to strike. She only had one chance. "No matter what happens now, at least we're together."

"That's precisely the point," crowed Oonagh, stalking ahead to where the trees clustered around them again. "You see, the simple truth is, only two people must die today." She smirked at them over her shoulder. "Can you guess who those two people might be?"

Rose contemplated flinging Daybreak at the back of her head but she couldn't risk letting go of Wren. Or missing. "Where are you taking us?" she asked instead. The glowing seeds were following them through the trees. Rose sensed they wanted to help but they didn't know how. Neither did she.

"Haven't you figured it out yet?" taunted Oonagh. "We are going back to the very beginning."

Rose frowned, glancing at Wren. She looked just as confused as Rose was. Oonagh called on her magic, dragging a howling wind through the forest. It drowned out the sound of its grief and scattered the glowing seeds. The trees bent backward, clearing a pathway for them and despite Rose's hesitation, the gust quickened her steps, shoving both of them through the forest.

After what felt like forever, light began to filter through the trees. They had reached the other side of the Weeping Forest, where the setting sun painted the canopies amber and gold.

It was only then that Rose realized where they were going. Back to the beginning. Back to the grave of Ortha Starcrest, Oonagh's twin sister. Back to the Mother Tree.

As they left the forest, Rose put her arm around Wren's waist, touching her head lightly against her sister's. Oonagh pushed them on, until all three of them stood before the Mother Tree. Only it didn't look as it had before. Its mighty branches were drooping, its beautiful leaves all but shed as though it had lost the strength to stand. Droplets of what looked like blood dripped from its skeleton and slid down the trunk, pooling on the ground below.

Oonagh tipped her head back, gazing up at the weeping tree. "My sister always had a bleeding heart. Some things never change. Even in death."

Rose's heart sank. Even the Mother Tree looked hopeless. Oonagh's dark magic was destroying it, just as she would destroy Eana. She turned to Wren, seeing the same realization dawning in her sister's eyes.

The Mother Tree was dying.

They had come to the end.

45

WREN

Wren stared up the dying Mother Tree and felt as if her heart was breaking in her chest. Grief was all around them. It rang in the battle cries of their soldiers and allies; it wept through the forest; it bled from the tree that marked Ortha Starcrest's grave. And with it came a feeling of hopelessness that was so complete, Wren couldn't see beyond it.

Even if she could find a measure of optimism or courage in this moment—this ending—she couldn't act on it. Oonagh's grip on her mind was as tight as ever. She had walked her through the forest like a puppet, making her gaze upon the dead—the soldiers who had fought alongside Wren at the Battle of Anadawn, the witches who had played with her on the sands of Ortha as a child. Bryony. Rowena. Elske. More losses than Wren cared to count.

And yet, she knew deep down, with a certain harrowing clarity, that the worst was still to come.

"Don't mourn your fallen friends, little bird." Oonagh's voice cut through Wren's thoughts. She must have been listening in, feasting on her grief. "Once my spell is cast and the sacrifice is made, the witches of the Weeping Forest will rise again and march with me into the new world." She pulled an exaggerated pout. "If you must mourn, save your tears for yourself. And for your sister. Your destiny ends here, just as my own sister's did."

Rose turned on Oonagh, giving voice to Wren's horror. "Do you truly mean to make puppets of our ancestors? To bind them to you like your beasts?"

Oonagh flashed her bloodied teeth as her plan was laid bare in full, grotesque detail. "To garner the most powerful army, you must make the most powerful sacrifice." She looked between them. "And what could be more powerful than one queen?"

Rose refused to answer her, to play into her twisted game.

"Twin queens!" Oonagh cried gleefully. She laid her hand against the bleeding trunk of the Mother Tree, looking up through its bare branches. "And here, upon my own sister's grave, is the perfect place to cast such a spell."

"Of course," said Rose, her voice dripping with disdain. "Why not desecrate the memory of your sister—the kind of selfless and brave queen *you* should have strived to be—along with every other sacred grave you have already disturbed, not to mention the ones that belong to the forest?"

"The witches of this forest will kiss my feet when I drag them from the afterlife," snarled Oonagh. "For too long this country has bent its knee to the will of mortals. Arrogant kings bloated on their own power. Weak-willed queens too frightened to restore this land to what it should have always been: a place of magic. A place for witches." She licked her lips, eager, greedy. "Only when I reclaim the throne of Anadawn will Eana's descendants truly return to power. The pathetic, quivering mortals here will face a swift demise, their bodies cast into everlit bonfires, stoked by witches who bow to me. And it will be my great pleasure to watch them all burn away into nothing."

Oonagh flung her torch at the Mother Tree, the trunk crackling as it burst into flame. The fire stole up the tree, hissing as it devoured its bleeding tears.

Rose brandished her finger, and whether she meant it to happen or not, a gust of wind stirred around her. "You can kill every last innocent person in this land and resurrect as many dead witches as you like, Oonagh, but know this: they will never bow to you. Not truly. You'll go on living your pathetic soulless existence, hated by the very land you claim as your own, reviled by the witches you seek to control, until even the birds fly away from you."

The wind grew, casting Rose's hair skyward. In the spiral of her anger, she pulled a dagger from her bodice and leaped at Oonagh.

Oonagh lunged, catching Rose by the throat before she could make the killing blow. She knocked the knife aside, and it landed in the grass. The wind died out as Rose struggled for air. "Pathetic attempt!" Oonagh spat. "For that, you will be the first to die."

Wren stiffened at the sight of her sister's distress. Oonagh might have rooted her to the spot, but as she watched Rose thrash helplessly in their ancestor's grasp, something sparked inside Wren. A new heat rushed through her veins, rallying against the curse. For a moment, she felt as if her soul was expanding, as though it was reaching through her rib cage toward Rose.

Come on, Wren begged her body, her magic. *Break free.*

"Time to die, little queen." Oonagh dragged Rose kicking and screaming toward the Mother Tree, where an inferno now raged.

Wren began to tremble, her heart pounding so loud she couldn't think straight.

Oonagh slashed her fingernail across Rose's neck, drawing a line of fresh blood.

NO! Wren's little finger twitched. Her left foot moved—an inch and then another. She gritted her teeth, eyes streaming as she tried to break the binds of her curse and free herself from Oonagh's hold. As Rose's blood poured out of her, Wren's anger burned to something brighter, hotter. Wren felt its fierceness and knew it for what it was: love. Blood-borne and bone-deep. A force so powerful and unyielding and *eternal*, even the strongest magic, even the deepest curse could not defeat it.

It flooded Wren, scouring the darkness and breaking apart the chains inside her. She took a step and then another, finding her balance. But time was not on her side.

As Rose's blood fell upon the roots of the Mother Tree and the flames licked her feet, Oonagh cast her spell.

"Blood spilled from a fallen royal, will burn upon this ancient soil, so the heart of Eana may be fed, and its witches returned to me, undead."

Oonagh threw Rose to the ground and raised her hands to the sky, summoning her magic with a guttural cry.

Wren found her voice a heartbeat too late. "NO!"

The sky split in two and from within came a streak of crackling lightning that hurtled straight at Rose.

Wren didn't even think. With all the remaining strength in her body she flung herself through the air, Rose's scream joining with hers as the lightning bolt ripped through Wren's body, sending her spiraling into darkness.

Then came the yawning hollow of death.

And after—nothing at all.

ROSE

Time juddered to a halt as the lightning bolt erupted, cutting through the air in a blinding streak of silver. Rose screamed as it came, but somehow Wren was quicker than the bolt, stronger in that awful interminable moment than the curse that lived inside her. She leaped at Rose, using her body as her shield just as the lightning came crashing down.

Wren shuddered as it tore through her body. For a heartbeat, the entire world turned to bright blinding white where Rose saw nothing—heard nothing—but the sound of her own scream ringing in her ears. Then her sister collapsed on top of her, her spent body crumpling at the bottom of the Mother Tree.

But this spell—this curse—was not yet over. With her heart shearing in two, Rose looked up just in time to see the bolt that had shattered Wren rebound off her broken body and crash into Oonagh. She howled as the light lanced through her, flaring under every inch of skin and bone. With a final, strangled cry, Oonagh Starcrest collapsed.

The flames hissed and thrashed in the sudden silence. They leaped from the trunk of the Mother Tree and made a fiery circle, trapping all three of them inside. Rose wrapped her arms around Wren, bowing her head until her hair fell around her sister like a curtain, shielding her lifeless body from the fire. But the flames that licked Rose's skin did not burn her. They were warm and gentle, and for an absurd, grief-riddled moment, she thought the flames were trying to help them.

It's not too late, she imagined them whispering. *Not yet.*

Rose looked down at her sister's lifeless face and pressed a finger to her throat, feeling for a pulse. There was none. But Rose's magic surged, rising to the challenge. Wren was gone but she was not yet lost.

"Oh, Wren." Rose sobbed as she touched her forehead against her sister's. "Please come back to me."

She closed her eyes, calling on her healing magic. In the quiet of her mind, Rose saw the thread of her own life, shining gold and sure. She reached for it, using the strand as an anchor as she went in search of her sister's life. But there was only darkness ahead, and within it, a simmering sense of foreboding.

Rose ventured a little further, feeling for the familiar thrum of Wren's magic. She was met with silence. There was no power here. No pulse.

Wren! Come back to me! Rose pushed herself further, deeper, until her grip on the world slipped away and her mind grew fuzzy, her thoughts dispersing like ash in the wind. And then at last, she spotted it: the thin brassy strand of Wren's life, slowly sinking into blackness. Rose lunged, grasping for it. Her own thread strained, struggling to bear the distance, but she was so close now, so very *close....*

Snap! Rose felt an awful cleaving inside herself, and then the terrible sensation of falling. Down, down, down she went, the ribbon of her life tumbling with her into the fathomless unknown until Rose had the final fleeting sensation that she was dead, too.

47

WREN

Wren was in the darkness, but she was not all the way dead. She could still hear her sister's sobs, feel the brush of her hair against her skin, smell the roaring fire that surrounded them. But the lightning bolt had rattled her soul loose. One minute Wren was in her body and the next she was above it, peering down on herself from above.

Rose was cradling her, the twins lying together in a heap. The burning branches of the Mother Tree stretched over them, as though in protection. On the other side of the mighty trunk, Oonagh Starcrest lay on her back, staring unseeing at the evening sky. Her eyes were green and glassy, her legs twisted in the dirt. She looked so small and pale now, delicate as a broken doll. Her power had all but drained away, leaving the shell of her body behind.

Behind her, the forest was glowing. The spirits had gathered along the tree line. Wren traced the silvery shapes of her ancestors in the shadows, heard their whispers in the wind.

Loving with your final breath,
And making the sacrifice of death,

Has turned the queen upon herself,
And felled her curse to save yourself.

Wren understood then what she had done. By sacrificing herself for
Rose and bearing the brunt of Oonagh's lightning bolt, she had unwit-
tingly cast a spell far greater than the one her ancestor intended. A
kind of magic so powerful that it rebounded on Oonagh and shattered
the curse that tied Wren to her—the curse that had been feeding her
ancestor's power.

But Oonagh was not yet dead. Her finger twitched, and Wren felt
a distant twinge of panic. The spirits were still whispering but their
voices faded until Wren could no longer hear them. She felt suddenly
trapped, caught in the in-between, suspended somewhere between her
body and soul. She looked up at the Mother Tree.

"Help me," she heard herself say.

The fire surged, and in the whips of amber and gold, Wren saw a
face that looked just like her own. Only it wore a different smile—it was
older, surer. Wren recognized the expression from the royal portraits
at Anadawn, from the tapestry that hung in her bedroom. It belonged
to Ortha Starcrest, the twin sister of Oonagh, who had once ruled the
kingdom of Eana with such bravery and loyalty, she gave her life to
defend it. Ortha's smile grew, her ancient eyes full of love. Not just for
Wren or Rose but for the kingdom they had sworn to watch over.

When the tree spoke, Wren knew Ortha's voice just as surely as
she recognized her own. "Long have you wished for an end to this
darkness, Wren Greenrock. But the weapon you seek has always been
within your grasp, forged by a force far greater than even the oldest of

magic. You and your sister have fought for each other just as bravely as you have fought for this land. Unceasing, undaunted. The love you and Rose share will reshape this kingdom and fill it with new light, if only you find a way to let it."

"I don't know what you mean," said Wren pleadingly. "Show me how."

"Return to your sister and finish what has already begun." Ortha's voice grew quiet, her face fading into flame. "Eana, the first witch, will guide you. As she guides us all, even now."

"Wait!" Wren cried. She wanted to ask how on earth she was supposed to return to her body, but the spirit of Ortha Starcrest had disappeared, leaving only the echo of her words behind. The fire rose with a determined hiss, curling around Wren's spirit and tugging her back down, into the dark.

Wren blinked to find the world had vanished once more. But even in this strange blackness, this place of nothingness, she was not alone. She could see the thread of her life shimmering faintly before her, entangled now with Rose's golden strand. Wren reached out, taking hold of them both. They flared beneath her touch, and slowly, softly, the darkness began to flicker.

Eons passed as Wren followed the promise of light. When the flickering yawned into an amber sky, Wren reached for that, too. She heard the crackle of flame and the faraway whisper of wind rustling through the trees. She pushed on, willing herself back to life. Back to Rose. Until at last, she heard her sister stirring beside her.

"Wren?" Rose murmured. "Are you there?"

Wren opened her eyes to a world of fire and smoke. "I'm here, Rose."

She turned her head, finding her sister's emerald gaze. She looked just as spent as Wren felt, but there was a small smile tugging at her lips.

"Welcome back," whispered Rose.

Wren's smile grew to match her sister's. "Let's finish this."

48

ROSE

Wren's eyes flashed with the same determination that now rushed through Rose. She had plunged into the darkness to find her sister, and somehow, they had returned from the brink together. They were not defeated.

Rose sat up, blinking into the firelight. She didn't know how much time had passed, or how long they had languished together in the darkness, but the sun had set and the moon had risen, scattering a sea of twinkling stars across the sky. The Mother Tree was still burning. The ring of flames was so high now it rested like a crown upon its branches, hiding the forest beyond it. Mercifully, there was no choking smoke or falling ash. Instead of feeling threatened, Rose felt protected, as if the spirit of Ortha Starcrest was wrapping her and Wren in her arms.

On the other side of the mighty trunk, Rose heard Oonagh groan. Their ancestor dragged herself up from the ground, digging her claw-like fingernails into the bark for balance.

Rose jostled her sister, trying to shake her from her daze. "Wren, Oonagh's awake!"

Wren winced as she raised her head. Despite her determination, she was trembling badly. Barely strong enough to keep her eyes open, let alone stand on her own. Rose grabbed Wren by the shoulders, gritting her teeth as she tried to lift her sister to her feet. The effort nearly toppled both of them all over again.

"Sorry," said Wren with a huff. "I'm trying. I'm just so . . ."

"I know," said Rose. "Save your strength."

On the other side of the tree, Oonagh had made it back to her feet, but she was still holding on to the Mother Tree. She closed her eyes and Rose knew she was trying to summon the dregs of her magic.

"Oh no, you don't," muttered Rose.

Wren frowned, steadying herself against the trunk. "We need a weapon."

"She threw my dagger away," said Rose, frantically searching the grass. She flexed her fingers, trying to summon her magic, but she was so exhausted she could barely think straight. And even if she could, what spell could she conjure to kill an ancient undead being? At her heart, Rose was a healer. She did not dabble in murder, and she knew nothing of blood magic.

She crawled over the grass, desperately searching for a glint of gold.

Oonagh began to chant, her body heaving as she tried to cast another spell. The flames drew backward, as though they were cowering from her guttural magic.

"*Rose*," said Wren urgently.

"I'm thinking!" Rose whirled around, searching for something—*anything*—they could use against their ancestor. Something glittered in the side of her vision. The firelight bounced off the golden blade, pulling Rose's attention to where Daybreak lay in the grass. She scrambled toward it as a new wind stirred. The dregs of Oonagh's power rippled around them. Rose looked up at the crackling sky as static plucked at the strands of her hair.

Oonagh was too far from Rose. With the trunk obscuring most of her body, she didn't have a clear shot at her ancestor. But Wren was closer, and steady on her feet. "Wren!"

When her sister turned, Rose tossed the dagger, fast and low.

The sky rumbled, another lightning bolt brewing. Wren snatched up Daybreak, swung herself around the trunk, and charged at their ancestor.

Rose watched in frozen horror as Oonagh twisted out of Wren's grasp. The dagger missed its mark, driving into Oonagh's shoulder instead of her heart. It was not a killing blow, but it was enough to stop the lightning strike. She shrieked in pain as they fell to the ground, grappling with each other in the dirt. Wren slammed her fist into Oonagh's mouth just as Oonagh grabbed Wren by the throat. They rolled over, spitting and choking in the dirt.

Rose was about to leap to help Wren when she heard her name carried on the wind. She turned around, spotting someone moving on the other side of the flames. Her eyes went wide when she saw who it was.

"*Celeste?*" she said with a gasp.

Celeste's clothes were badly torn. Her face was mussed with blood and there were twigs in her hair. She was limping on her left leg, her voice so ragged, Rose had to strain to hear her. "I cut my way through that entire bloody forest," she called out. "To come and give you this!"

Celeste raised her sword as she stumbled toward the fire and Rose knew it at once as Night's Edge.

Wren let out a strangled shout. "Rose! Help!"

Oonagh was on top of her, Daybreak still sticking out of her blood-ied shoulder. One weapon was not enough.

"Throw the sword!" yelled Rose.

Celeste flung Night's Edge through the flames. It landed blade-first in the dirt beside Rose. "Thank you!" she shouted as she pulled it free. The hilt warmed in her grip, the blade so light it lifted like a feather.

Rose took a quick breath. She knew what had to be done, even if it went against every flicker of healing magic inside her. But moral-ity was never black and white. Finding Wren and the rest of the witches—knowing them—after all these years apart had shown her that. Sometimes to save a life—to save a kingdom—you had to take a life. And Oonagh had already lived far longer than most. Her destiny had come and gone, and she had squandered it. It was time for her to die. For good this time.

The sword glowed in Rose's hand as she rushed back to the Mother Tree. Wren had made it onto her feet and was using the dagger embed-ded in Oonagh's shoulder to drive her backward. Their ancestor's teeth were bared, her green eyes blazing with hatred.

Rose raised her sword. "Move," she said to Wren. It was only when Rose's vision began to blur that she realized she was crying. "I'll do it."

"*We'll* do it." Wren released Daybreak, her hand finding Rose's on the hilt of Night's Edge. "Together."

They swung the sword just as Oonagh lunged toward them, impal-ing herself on the blade. They steadied the hilt, driving the blade deeper into her heart until it pinned her to the Mother Tree. Rose's hand shook but she didn't let go, and neither did Wren. They stood shoulder to shoulder, bathed in the soft glow of Night's Edge, willing this nightmare to end.

Oonagh stilled, her final breaths eking out of her. Her face slackened as centuries of anger and hatred left her in a long and final sigh. And then she looked just like Wren. Like Rose. Like her sister, Ortha. As the last vestiges of her cursed magic filtered into the wind, Oonagh's green eyes misted.

"*Oh*," she whispered.

Sensing it was finally over, Rose and Wren released the sword. They stepped back, finding each other's hands.

Oonagh slumped to the ground. She turned her face to the Mother Tree, pressing her cheek against the bark. Rose watched a single tear slide down Oonagh's cheek.

As the fire surged around them, Oonagh closed her eyes and whispered her sister's name. "Ortha, forgive me." It was a spell all its own, a plea. A final offering to the sister she had betrayed and the land she had ravaged in her absence. "Ortha," she murmured as she dropped into darkness, surrendering herself at last to the finality of death.

49

WREN

As Oonagh slumped against the Mother Tree, the tear slipped from her cheek and fell to the earth, disappearing into the soil. The ground thumped as it melted into the roots of the Mother Tree, as though the very heart of Eana were beating beneath them.

All at once, the ring of flames winked out, the fire falling away until only the branches of the great tree burned.

"Look," said Rose, squeezing Wren's hand. Wren tipped her head back, following her sister's gaze. There, in the crown of flames, was the shape of two girls, standing hand in hand. For a heartbeat, Wren thought it was their own fiery reflection gazing back at them, but there was a voice in the inferno that did not belong to Rose or Wren.

No, not one voice. But two.

"As sorrow falls upon the tree,
A broken soul is finally free.
Ashes to ashes, dust to dust,
Our spirits soar on this new gust."

"It's Ortha and Oonagh," said Rose in a whisper. "They found each other." At that, a warm wind stole up from the roots of the Mother Tree, quelling the flames that danced along its branches and scattering the vision of the Starcrest sisters. The wind traveled over the trees then, gathering up the glowing seeds that lingered there and carrying them east toward the sea and the moonlit horizon beyond.

When Wren looked down, the body of Oonagh Starcrest had dissolved into the earth, the ashes of her bones joining her sister's body in the ancient roots of the tree. Only the sword and dagger remained, Night's Edge and Daybreak, so clean, Wren could see her reflection in them.

The Mother Tree sighed, and Wren felt the same relief lifting in her heart. She watched the branches reach up to the sky, growing and twisting as though to touch the moon. The trunk swelled until the enormous tree was almost twice the size as before. It towered over them, bursting into life. New leaves sprouted that were pillowy and green, and within them, tiny flowers of every color bloomed until Wren was sure she had never before seen anything more beautiful or full of magic.

For the first time in her life, she found she could look upon the Mother Tree not with sadness but with joy. With *hope*.

Rose plucked Daybreak from the ground and held it to her chest. "It's finally over, isn't it?" she said as tears ran down her cheeks.

Wren nodded as she picked up Night's Edge. "It's really over, Rose."

"Well. Almost." They both turned around at the sound of Celeste's voice. She was standing where the ring of fire had just been and wearing a look of such sadness, Wren's heart sank all over again. Just behind Celeste, under the soft light of a melancholic moon, the surviving soldiers and witches were coming through the trees, carrying their dead.

50

ROSE

As the trees of the Weeping Forest slowly unfurled, no longer cowering in fear, the sound of weeping filled the air. There was no sign of Oonagh's army.

Rose recognized her own pain in the cries of her soldiers, of the witches, all these people she fiercely loved. She heard their sorrow over those they had lost and their guilt that they had been the ones to survive. And yet, in that pain, there was relief, too. The first to arrive told her what she already suspected: the undead had stopped fighting when Oonagh did, collapsing like windup toys that had taken their last step. The war was over.

But as she studied more and more faces coming through the trees, Rose swayed on her feet, overcome by an old clawing fear that those she loved would not return to her. "Where's Shen?" she said, panic hitching in her voice. "And Lei Fan? And Tilda? And—"

"Just wait," said Wren. But her voice shook just as badly as Rose's did, and Celeste's expression was so grave, she didn't say anything at all. Rose knew she was scouring the tree line for Anika.

As more soldiers spilled out of the forest, wearing torn and bloodied uniforms of green and gold, Rose realized they were looking to her and Wren, waiting for another command or a much-needed measure of comfort.

"We need to take charge," said Rose. "We need to say something."

Wren stepped forward, rising to the task like a true and capable queen. "Warriors of Eana, we have battled together through the darkness and at last emerged into the light. Today marks the end of the war in Eana and the beginning of peace in our land."

"You have all fought valiantly," said Rose, picking up the thread of her sister's speech as easily as if it were her own. "For that we thank you. And we honor those we have lost." Her voice cracked but she went on. "As we mourn them, we will remember their sacrifice and their bravery." She gestured behind her. "Please come and lay your dead beneath the great Mother Tree, where they will find peace in her magnificent shadow."

She rolled her shoulders back, pressing on. "Those who can heal, come to me. Those who can stand, please help those who cannot. We must bring the injured forward so they can be healed."

There was a flurry of movement as soldiers and witches hurried to follow her orders. More broke off and ran back into the forest carrying forth Rose's message.

Rose went to Celeste then, embracing her dearest friend. "You saved us," she said, her voice thick with emotion. "If you hadn't fought your way through the forest to return Night's Edge, I don't know if we would have defeated Oonagh."

"You would have figured something out." Celeste hugged her back tightly. "But that certainly came a lot closer than I would have liked."

"That's an understatement," said Wren, coming to embrace Celeste as well. "Thank you, Celeste. I really owe you."

"Now *that* is the understatement," said Celeste, huffing a tired laugh. She pulled back, glancing around anxiously. "Have either of you seen Anika?"

"Not since we left the cliffs." Rose gave Wren a careful look, her heart aching for her sister. The last time they had seen Tor he'd been pinned beneath a beast, with his beloved wolf collapsed at his side.

As if she was reliving the very same memory, Wren took off toward the tree line, glaring at the forest as if she was willing it to fall away entirely so she could see all the way to the cliffs beyond.

Rose let Wren go. She looked to the trees, too, fear like a fist in her throat, but she was not searching for a telltale glimpse of blue and silver. She was looking for a warrior who moved like the night wind. She was looking for the other half of her heart.

And then she heard a voice that stole her breath. "Rose!"

Shen Lo came tearing through the forest, shirt torn and bloody, but he was *alive*. Alive and running and smiling, and *oh*, his face was the most beautiful thing Rose had ever seen.

Celeste nudged her. "What are you waiting for? Go to him."

Rose hitched up her skirts and ran to Shen, and when she reached him, she flung herself into his arms. He held her tightly, so tightly, as if he couldn't quite believe that she was real.

"Rose," he murmured into her hair. "Rose, Rose, Rose."

Rose laid her head against his chest and listened to the thundering song of his heart. They stood still, holding each other in this moment of sweeping relief, their chests rising and falling in perfect harmony, as the world carried on around them.

"Come with me," said Shen, pulling her into a slip of forest that had been untouched by battle. Even the small white wildflowers that dotted the forest floor were undisturbed.

"You're hurt again," said Rose, gently examining a new puncture wound on his neck.

"I'm fine," said Shen. "It will heal."

"Of course it will. Because *I* will heal it."

"You've already healed me once today."

"I'll heal you as often as I need to. Now hold still."

He brushed her hand away, curling his arms around her waist. "I'll survive," he said, pulling her close. "Leave it for now."

"Stop being so stubborn," said Rose, putting her hands on his chest. "I want to make you feel better!"

"Then kiss me, Rose Valhart." He dipped his chin, brushing his nose against hers. "Please."

"*Oh.*" Suddenly dizzy, Rose went up on her toes, pressing her lips to his. Shen groaned, sliding his tongue into her mouth and deepening the kiss. She kissed him, fiercely, with a hunger that surprised them both. He pulled her closer still, and she pressed herself against him, wrapping her arms around his neck. He groaned again, running his hands down her back as she arched her body against his, losing herself in the heat of his kiss.

When they finally broke away from each other, Rose tilted her head back so she could see his face. He gazed down at her and brushed his thumb across her cheek.

"You, Rose Valhart, are the bravest person I have ever known."

She let out a sound that was part sob, part laugh. "I would quite like to go back to Anadawn and not be brave for a while."

"We can do that."

Rose stilled. "Together?"

Shen's dark eyes sparkled. "Well, I was thinking we could stay at Anadawn for a while, and then perhaps you could come back to the Sunkissed Kingdom with me for a few weeks.... And then after that, we could go back to Anadawn...." He cleared his throat. "And then the Sunkissed Kingdom. And ... Well, you get the idea...." He raised his brows, his voice hopeful. "Don't you?"

"Are you saying what I think you're saying?"

"What? That if anyone here is organized enough to rule two kingdoms, it's you?"

"Shen! Can't you *try* to be romantic?"

He smiled, and it felt as if the sun had come out at night. "I'm saying that I accept your proposal, Rose. That I can't think of anything that would make me happier than to marry you and spend every day of the rest of my life loving you." He held both her hands in his. "I know that falling in love with you took me by surprise. Even now, I'm still reeling from just how much I love you, how lucky I feel whenever you smile at me. I don't know if I'll ever get used to it. I don't think I ever want to get used to it." He raised her hands to his lips and kissed them. "I know how much you love Eana and how deeply you respect the Sunkissed Kingdom, too, and I believe together we will do a fine job of ruling them both."

He grinned and so did Rose. "Perhaps you are a romantic after all, Shen Lo."

"Perhaps you set romance alight in me." Shen glanced through the forest, where the soldiers were still making their way back to the Mother Tree, and his expression sobered. "I nearly lost you twice, Rose. I'll never lose you again. I swear it."

Rose's heart danced as she pressed a kiss to the corner of his mouth. There was just one more matter to settle. "If we are making this official, I'll be expecting a ring."

WREN

Wren hurried down to the tree line, where hundreds of weary survivors were emerging from the Weeping Forest. She met them at the edge of the forest, sharing in their bitter triumph and empathizing with their pain. She was glad of the strength that had returned to her body, relieved that her feelings and actions were her own once more. Instead of despair, hope bloomed inside her. For the first time in months, her limbs felt light, her head clear. She was free. Now that the curse had been broken and Oonagh Starcrest was truly dead, she could be the queen Banba had always believed she could be. She could be the leader her people needed. Wren finally felt equal to the task. And more than that, she was eager for it.

But first, she had to find Tor. Worry lanced through her as she searched the sea of weary soldiers stumbling out of the trees. From the corner of her eye, she watched Rose reunite with Shen, and released a breath of relief at seeing her best friend alive and well, if a little bloodied.

When Rose and Shen slipped into the forest for a quiet moment, Wren continued her desperate search. She stalked back and forth, quietly grieving the bodies of witches and soldiers alike as they were carried out of the woods and laid down beneath the great Mother Tree. There were hundreds of casualties. Wren stilled at the sight of Rowena and Bryony, who had fought side by side and died that way, too. Feeling as if her heart was truly breaking, she knelt beside her friends.

"Rest easy," she sobbed. "You're free now."

The Gevran army arrived after the others. They followed a limping Princess Anika through the trees, carrying their dead brethren and beasts out onto the moonlit plain.

Celeste ran to meet them, shouldering Anika's weight as she guided her up toward the Mother Tree, where Lei Fan and Grandmother Lu had cast a ring of everlights to illuminate the dark. The rest of the witches were here healing the most gravely injured. Wren paid her respects to the fallen Gevrans, terrified of finding two familiar faces lying among the dead, but there was no sign of Tor or Alarik. There was no sign of them anywhere. She turned around, her heart hammering as she searched the masses.

Where the hell are they?

"Don't look so frightened, Queenie," said Kai, who arrived presently without a shirt. "I survived."

"I see your shirt made a worthy sacrifice," said Wren. "Have you seen King Alarik? Captain Iversen?"

"Not for an age," he said, after thinking on it. "But if I had to guess, I'd say the king is at the bottom of the Ortha Sea. And he's not alone down there." His gaze darkened. "Things got pretty ugly once you disappeared."

Wren bit off a curse, refusing to believe it. She had been so attuned to Alarik's pain for so long, surely she would have sensed it, *felt* it, if he'd drowned. But when she looked for the scar on her wrist, she realized it had disappeared. And so, too, had her connection to the king.

But . . . *no.* She would not consider it. Alarik and Tor were safe. They *had* to be safe. The alternative was simply too harrowing to face. There were more everlights burning down by the forest now, illuminating the stragglers coming through the trees. Wren stalked back and forth, waiting, *hoping*. . . .

And then at last, she spotted a familiar figure coming through the trees. She knew Alarik by the silver-branch crown on his head, and how he walked toward her with the ease and confidence of a king. A king who was no longer cursed to die.

Wren broke into a run, buoyed by such relief, she thought she might lift into flight. Alarik was alive. He had survived the battle, survived the curse. They had both fought their way to freedom and won. Alarik stopped when he saw her, but Wren was running too fast to slow down. She barreled into him and they both fell backward, landing in a heap on the ground.

"Oops, sorry," said Wren, clambering off him.

"So much for your queenly grace," said Alarik, laughing in relief.

"What queenly grace?"

"Well, quite."

Wren looked past him, anxiously scanning the dark mouth of the forest. "Where's Tor?"

"I'm here." Tor emerged through the trees and stepped into the moonlight. He was cradling Elske's body, his face so stricken, Wren's heart broke once more. And yet, when he saw Wren sitting unharmed on the ground, his eyes softened. "You're alive," he said, his voice cracking. "Thank the *stars*."

Wren sprang to her feet. "Oh, my sweet girl," she murmured to the wolf. "You beautiful, brave creature."

Elske lay perfectly still in Tor's arms. Her limbs were stiff and cold and her fur was smeared with dried blood. But when Wren laid her hand on her head, Elske's gaze flickered. With great effort, she heaved a shallow breath. "You're still here," whispered Wren.

Tor hugged the wolf close. "She wanted to see you one last time."

"Oh." Wren's eyes filled with tears. As her sadness welled, something flickered to life inside her. A familiar whisper of warmth returned to her bones. Magic. By the way it flared, Wren sensed it was yearning to be used.

"Set her down," she said urgently. "Let me work on her."

Tor hesitated. "But your magic . . . I thought . . ."

"Please," said Wren, kneeling in the dirt. "Let me try."

Tor surrendered his fear and did as he was asked, coming to his knees as he set the wolf down in front of Wren. Elske's eyes flickered, but Wren was not ready to let her go. She had lost too much on the battlefield. She couldn't stand to let another life slip through her fingers.

She laid her hands on Elske's stomach and closed her eyes, willing her magic to obey her. She could feel it blazing inside her, but she had never possessed a healing strand before. She didn't know if she even possessed one now. But time was of the essence, and Wren had to try.

Please help me, she begged her magic. *Let me heal this precious soul.*

The world quieted around Wren, until there was only the weakened patter of Elske's pulse beneath her fingers. In the blackness of her mind, Wren saw a silver thread. It was thin and fraying, the wolf's life force slowly fading to nothing.

Wren reached out to grab it. Her magic lurched, crossing the bridge of their souls until it reached the ailing wolf. It went to work, Wren's fingertips tingling as her magic flooded the gentle creature, knitting her internal wounds back together. Slowly, slowly, Elske's pulse grew stronger. She began to breathe, slow and deep and steady, matching Wren's rhythm.

Wren felt a faint pulling sensation inside her as her magic bottomed out. She began to sway but steady hands came to her shoulders, holding her in place.

"It's working," whispered Alarik. "You're healing her."

Wren felt herself smile. She was so exhausted she could hardly think. She released the thread of Elske's life and watched it glow, bright and sure in the darkness of her mind. Then she let go of her magic entirely and tumbled back into the real world.

Wren opened her eyes to find the wolf staring back at her. Elske blinked, awake, alert. Her tail thumped against the ground, wagging happily as she heaved herself back to her feet. She came to lick Wren's cheek.

Wren giggled. "You're welcome, sweetling."

And then Tor was before her, smiling so broadly Wren could see all of his teeth. "You are a wonder, Wren," he said, pressing a kiss to her hand and then the other. "A beautiful, fearless wonder."

"A *tired* wonder," said Wren, but despite her exhaustion, she couldn't help reveling in her triumph. She was not just a witch but a healer. No longer broken or useless.

"A wonder indeed," muttered Alarik, releasing her shoulders. He stood up, offering his hand to Wren. "If I may have a moment?"

As Tor scooped Elske into his arms and buried his face in her fur, Wren rolled to her feet and followed Alarik a short distance away. Looking at him now in the glow of the everlights, she realized he looked better than he had in weeks. The dark shadows had faded from underneath his eyes and his cheeks were no longer hollow.

His eyes were bright and searing, his wolfish smile coming easily to his face. "You're staring at me again, Wren."

"I can't help it," said Wren. "You look so . . . *alive.*"

He raised a brow. "It's incredible what banishing an ancient corrosive blood curse will do for your self-esteem."

"And your ego."

He barked a laugh. "Thank you, by the way. For taking care of our little problem."

"You're welcome," said Wren. "Though I couldn't have done it without your help."

"My tongue has always been sharper than my sword."

"Yet another thing we have in common."

He *hmm*ed in agreement. "For better or for worse."

"This is better," said Wren. "We're finally free."

His gaze lingered on hers. "I suppose we are."

"What did you want to talk to me about?" said Wren, even though she already had an inkling. Just because the curse between them was broken didn't mean there weren't other things—other feelings—that needed to be addressed.

He scrubbed a hand across his jaw. "Well, I was actually thinking it might be fun to try a new blood spell together."

Wren punched him in the shoulder. "That's not funny."

His eyes danced. "Don't worry, I've seen enough magic to last me a lifetime."

"Then you've learned your lesson at last."

He flashed his teeth. "Who says you can't teach an old wolf new tricks?"

Wren looked at her wrist, tracing the place where the crescent scar had once been. It occurred to her that Alarik's must have faded, too, the last remnants of Oonagh's spell finally leaving their bodies. The king might have seen enough magic for one lifetime, but Wren was pleased to have hers returned to her in full working order. Even now, she relished the familiar hum of it under her skin. "I admit it's nice not to feel broken anymore."

"For what it's worth, Wren, you were never broken to me."

She jerked her chin up.

"Just annoying," he added.

Wren snorted. "Thank you for that modicum of sincerity."

"I'm afraid a modicum is the best I can do."

They were silent then, looking unashamedly at each other as they tried to unpick this strange new closeness that had outlasted the curse. For Wren, her pull toward the king was not the same one she had felt in the mountains. It was softer now, simpler. And yet she could not deny that she felt great affection for the king of Gevra. That the thought of him sailing away from her—from *here*—at daybreak made her feel . . . well, sad.

Alarik turned his wrist over, caressing the spot where his scar had been. "I think I shall miss it, you know," he said quietly. "I suppose I had gotten used to it."

Wren smiled, knowing precisely what he meant. "I think I'll miss mine, too. Stubborn as it was."

"At least it wasn't mouthy," he conceded. "Like mine."

"But you can't deny it made for good company," said Wren.

Alarik didn't deny it. He looked at her, his eyes shining. When he spoke again, his voice was somber. "A good king knows when to fight . . . and when to lay down his weapon." His gaze flitted to Tor and then back to her, and Wren knew then that he understood where her heart truly lay.

Wren nodded slowly. "Sometimes the right thing is to give up. Even for a Gevran."

He offered the ghost of a smile. "I suppose that remains to be seen."

Tor rolled to his feet. He dug his hands in his pockets, waiting. Watching.

Alarik took a step backward. "Well, then . . . Friends?"

"Only if you promise to be nice to me."

"The only promise I'll make is to keep you on your toes." Alarik turned from their conversation to follow Elske up to the Mother Tree, his parting words flying over his shoulder. "You'll have to make do with that."

"In that case, I will gladly make you the same promise," Wren called after him.

His laughter reached her on the wind.

When Wren turned around, Tor was standing before her. His eyes shone silver in the moonlight, and though he was battle-worn and bruised, he looked achingly handsome. Achingly *hers*.

He found her gaze and held it. "Just so there's no confusion, I don't want to be your friend, Wren."

"Good," she said, a little breathless. "I don't want to be your friend either."

Tor opened his arms and she went to him, happily folding herself into his embrace. When he brought his mouth to hers and their tongues met, Wren's magic erupted until she felt as if she was lit from within by the moon itself.

The war was finally over, and though grief hung heavy in the air, love had found Wren again. She reached for it with both hands, swearing to herself that, this time, she would never let it go.

ROSE

Lake Carranam shone like a jewel beneath the sparkling night sky. The reflection of a thousand stars danced across the water, and on the banks, thousands of revelers danced as well. In the middle of it all were Rose and Wren, rejoicing in the merriment, leading the way to peace and prosperity.

A month had passed since the Battle of the Weeping Forest. A month of grieving, and of healing. Tonight, they were remembering those they had lost and celebrating their victory over Oonagh Starcrest.

The Gevrans had returned home shortly after the battle, just as the witches of the Sunkissed Kingdom had. Shen had ridden with his people into the heart of the desert before returning the following day to Anadawn, where, true to his word, he had presented Rose with a beautiful ruby ring. Tomorrow, they would ride east to the Sunkissed Kingdom, to prepare for their wedding and all that would come after.

Shen had made Lei Fan his Kingsbreath, entrusting her to rule while he was away, and after proving himself in battle, Kai was promoted to head of the Sunkissed Kingdom's warriors. Despite the rocky road to their reunion, Shen was happy to have his cousins by his side—to have found his family, at last.

And nobody was as thrilled with Rose and Shen's engagement as Grandmother Lu. Rose thought she knew everything there was to know about throwing a party, but then Grandmother Lu told her that in the Sunkissed Kingdom it was customary for a royal wedding to last an entire week! Not that Rose minded in the least. Especially because Lei Fan was helping her with her wedding wardrobe.

But that was all still to come. Tonight was a celebration of a different kind. A time for Rose and Wren to look to the future of Eana and welcome it with music and dancing.

Cam had truly outdone himself. There was enough food to feed everyone twice over—glazed chickens cooked over open fires, spiced shrimp, candied carrots, roast potatoes—with everything arranged on decadent skewers so they could be devoured between dances.

Dessert was even more mouthwatering. There was a seven-tiered cake of chocolate and vanilla covered in gold-dusted frosting waiting to be sliced and shared.

The wine was flowing freely and so was the music. As Rose and Wren danced among their people celebrating, it felt as if they finally had everything they had ever wanted. Well, almost everything.

Last month, Rose had watched Wren's stricken face as the Gevran ships departed from Ortha. And tonight, in quiet moments when Wren thought no one was looking at her, she wore the same look of longing. Rose knew her sister's heart ached for Tor, but Wren was adamant: her place was at Anadawn by her sister's side.

They twirled together one more time, and then, still laughing, went arm in arm to the edge of the lake.

"Witches, lend us your magic!" Wren called out. "And if you don't have magic, raise an everlight. There's magic in that, too!"

"The spell had better work this time," Rose whispered anxiously.

"It will," Wren assured her. "We're no longer being haunted by our cursed ancestor."

The twins combined their magic, and along with the rest of the witches, conjured a flaming tree in the center of the lake. It grew and grew and didn't stop until, for a moment, Rose feared they were going to lose control of the spell just like before, but then their fire tree settled on the water, shining like a beacon in the night.

The crowd erupted in cheers and the music lifted, soaring triumphantly across the sky.

"What a success!" said Rose, swaying to the music. Her skirts twirled around her, the blushing pink of her dress reminding her of a desert sunrise. It was trimmed in gold lace, with a square neckline and boned corset that cinched her waist before flowing into a lavish tulle skirt. Her long hair was loose and threaded with fine white flowers, and her feet were bare. "I was worried for a moment there."

"You worry too much, Rose." Next to her, Wren looked every bit as resplendent in a gown of midnight blue and silver. Rose suspected her sister had chosen to wear the colors of Gevra to honor her heart, a silent tribute to the man she loved. "I think it's high time to cut that cake!"

Not for the first time that night, Rose marveled at the seven-tiered culinary wonder. "I'm not sure there's a knife big enough."

"Perhaps I should fetch Night's Edge," said Wren. "It's in the carriage."

"Wren! Did you truly bring that sword to our celebration?"

"Well, it did save our lives. I thought it deserved to celebrate, too." She glanced pointedly at the outline of a dagger at Rose's hip. "And don't think I can't see Daybreak hidden under that fancy dress."

Rose bit back her smile. "The point stands. No swords near the cake."

"Very well. We can use our hands instead," teased Wren.

They were interrupted presently by Marino Pegasi, who came ambling over with a wide smile on his handsome face.

"Captain!" said Wren with great delight. "I hardly recognize you without your ship."

"I couldn't miss the celebrations," he said, bowing at the waist. "Well done, my fearless queens. It's good to see you both in such fine spirits."

Rose and Wren both laughed, then kissed him on each cheek.

"You know you are always welcome at Anadawn, Marino," said Rose. "We would certainly like to see more of you."

"I do wonder if it's time for me to reclaim my land legs and settle down," he said thoughtfully. "I have to admit, after what happened out there, I've grown more suspicious of the sea. Who knows what else might come crawling out of it?"

"What about your beloved mermaid?" needled Wren.

Marino sighed. "And how would we be together? Would I live in the sea? Would she live on my boat?" He looked off into the middle distance. "No, majesties, I fear I must find myself a lady with legs."

Rose giggled. "Marino, I think you should be a tad more specific."

"You two can find me someone," he said, turning back to them. "I trust you both implicitly."

"Oh, sure, because we have so much time for matchmaking," said Wren dryly. "Just ask Chapman to put it on the schedule."

"Don't listen to her," said Rose, patting him on the arm. "I *always* have time for love. We'll find the perfect person for you."

"Just make sure Lessie likes her." Marino glanced around. "Where is that troublesome sister of mine, anyway?"

"She's dancing up a storm over there," said Rose, pointing to a circle of witches who were twirling and cartwheeling. Thea was there, too, the old witch dancing just as wildly as the others.

"Marino, I hope you haven't come to steal my bride," said Shen, joining them by the edge of the lake. He gestured to the sparkling ruby ring on Rose's finger. "I'm afraid she's already spoken for."

"I am well aware," said Marino good-naturedly. "That ring is the size of Carrig."

Rose grinned proudly. It really was *quite* a jewel. But nowhere near as treasured as the man who had given it to her.

"It's good to see you," said Shen, clapping Marino on the back.

"And you," said Marino, returning the gesture. "If you ever decide to hang up your crown, there's a place for you on my ship."

"And there's a place for you in my court, if you decide to trade the sea for sand," countered Shen.

Rose cleared her throat. "A place in *our* court."

Shen smiled at her. "Yes, my love. Our court." Then he took Rose by the hand. "I was coming to see if you wanted to dance."

"Why don't we all join Celeste and Thea?" said Rose, turning to

Wren and Marino. "Marino, perhaps we might find you a bride this very night."

"Well, in that case, lead on," he said, falling into step with them.

As they danced by the firelight of the burning tree, Rose looked around at the faces of those she loved most in the world and felt as though her heart would burst with happiness. This past year, she had encountered great darkness, but she had also come to know the true power of love, and she was sure now that whatever obstacles were yet to come, love would see her through.

She dipped her head back to gaze at the stars, whispering a quiet thank-you to Eana the first witch and to Eana the land that had raised her.

Then she hitched up her skirts and carried on dancing.

53

WREN

When Wren returned to her bedroom at Anadawn after the celebration at Lake Carranam, she could hardly feel her feet. Her body ached from dancing, but her magic was wide awake and buzzing with pride for her kingdom. Her people. Her sister. Tonight had been wonderful, a time to remember those brave souls who had given their lives for Eana and to celebrate the victory they had helped Wren and Rose achieve. The darkness was at last behind them. Now was a time of peace and hope for the future.

A future that Wren finally felt truly ready for. As herself. As queen of Eana.

And yet despite the night's merriment, a part of Wren couldn't help but feel sad.

She missed Tor. The Gevran army had set sail not long after the battle, returning to their country with their soldiers and their dead. Though Alarik had officially dismissed Tor from his post during their time in the Mishnick Mountains, the king and his captain had come together in the end, uniting in friendship and victory. Much to Wren's disappointment, Tor had decided to return to Gevra with his army so he could sail on to Carrig to visit his family and help repair the damage

Oonagh had done to his beloved island.

Wren understood why he had to go but it didn't make parting from him any easier. Although a month had passed since she'd last seen him, she still felt the same ache in her heart and resented the icy sea that stretched between them.

Tor had promised Wren he would write to her once his feet touched Gevran soil, and he had kept that promise, sending several missives in the weeks since. Wren had worked up the courage to invite him to the celebrations at Lake Carranam, but she never received a reply, and despite her hopes, Tor hadn't appeared. In fact, she hadn't heard from the Gevran soldier in over a week, and the silence was starting to unnerve her.

She tried not to dwell on it as she kicked off her heels and collapsed on her bed. She was still wearing her magnificent gown, a cinched dress of midnight blue and delicate silver filigree that cascaded into a full layered skirt. She was about to call for a maidservant to help her wriggle out of it when there came a tap at the window.

When Wren saw it was a Gevran nighthawk, she rushed to the window, nearly knocking the poor bird from the sill. She hastily untied the letter from its foot, her heart hitching as she read the familiar scrawl.

> Wren,
> Open the gates.
> Yours,
> Tor

Wren cast the letter aside and raced across the room, forgetting all about her shoes. She hurtled down the tower, taking the steps two at a time and almost crashing into the guards stationed at the bottom.

"Sorry!" she shouted over her shoulder as she continued down the hallway, moving so fast she skidded on the stone. When she reached the bottom floor, she nearly barreled straight into Rose, who was returning from a midnight visit to the kitchens with a pocket stuffed full of what appeared to be chocolate biscuits.

She startled at Wren. "What on earth has got into you?" She frowned then. "You'd better not be running away to Gevra again."

"Never!" said Wren, hurrying past her sister. "This time Gevra has come to me!"

Rose laughed as she watched her go. "Well, it's about time!"

Wren summoned a burst of tempest magic, flinging the palace doors open as she ran. The guards stuck their heads out in alarm but Wren paid them no mind. She thundered into the courtyard, making a beeline for the golden gates.

When she saw Tor standing on the other side, her heart flipped. He was no longer wearing his pristine Gevran uniform but a simple white shirt, black trousers, and leather boots. Moonlight danced along the copper strands of his hair and lit up his eyes as he kept one hand on the trusty hilt of his sword—still battle-ready, even now—and the other curled around the railings as though he wanted to rip the gates from the ground to get to her.

"Open the gates!" Wren yelled to her guards. "Hurry!"

The gates swung open, but before Wren could reach Tor, Elske bounded into the courtyard and pounced on Wren.

Wren laughed as she fell, blinking up at those beautiful icy-blue eyes. "Well, hello to you, too, sweetling."

Elske licked her face in greeting. Then at a word from Tor, the wolf leaped off Wren and ambled into the palace as if the entire place belonged to her.

Tor offered his hand to Wren. "Sorry I'm late."

She grinned as she took it. "You're right on time."

He looked her up and down, his breath catching. "You look . . ."

"Gevran?" said Wren, tracing a swirl of silver thread on her bodice.

"Beautiful." He frowned at her feet. "And barefoot. Why are you barefoot?"

"Because I simply couldn't spend another moment without you."

His face softened. "I know the feeling."

"You're not in your uniform, Captain Iversen," said Wren.

"No. Not anymore."

Wren swallowed, overcome by a sudden rush of desire. If the courtyard hadn't been full of guards, she would have ripped his shirt off right there and then. "You've traveled such a long way," she said coyly. "You must be tired."

He raised his brows. "Now that you mention it, I am exhausted."

She led him into the palace, both of them exchanging giddy glances and bursting into breathless laughter.

They bumped into Rose in the hallway. "A clandestine midnight meeting," she said by way of greeting. "How romantic." She took a bite of a biscuit before leaning down to pet Elske, who was already sitting at her feet. Her lips curled. "You are most welcome back to Anadawn, Captain Iversen."

"It's just Tor now," he said, dipping his chin in thanks.

"I see." Rose grinned, flicking her gaze to Wren. "Well, perhaps you might find yourself a new position soon enough, Tor. In the meantime, I think I'll take dear Elske on a stroll around the palace. It's been far too long since we've seen each other."

"Thank you," said Wren, tugging Tor with her, up one flight of stairs and then another, until they reached the west tower. Wren shut her bedroom door behind them and stood with her back against it, feeling suddenly nervous.

Tor stood across from her in a puddle of moonlight.

"Don't look at me like that," she murmured. "I might melt."

He held her gaze. "I am yours to command, Wren."

"Do you mean it?"

He nodded. "It's been that way long before tonight."

She heaved a breath. "Take off your clothes."

He removed his sword, tossing it aside. And his boots, one and then another.

Wren swallowed. "Don't forget your shirt."

"As you wish."

Wren's breath fluttered as he undid the top button of his shirt. "Wait."

He froze. "What is it?"

"It's you. This. Us." Wren's heartbeat thundered in her ears, but she couldn't go another minute without knowing what he wanted, what lay beyond the promise of tonight. "Why have you come here?"

He blinked in confusion. "Don't you know?"

"I mean, what will you do after tonight?" she said. "Will you leave again?"

He held her gaze. "What would you have me do, Wren?" he said hoarsely.

"Stay," she said. "I would have you stay."

He blew out a breath.

Embarrassment roared in her ears. "Unless you intend to return to Gevra. I don't wish to—"

"I intend to stay." He dropped his hands, leaving his shirt half open. "I won't pretend I didn't come here for you, Wren. That I didn't dream of your face every night this past month, imagining all the things I wanted to say to you, all the things I wanted to do with you. But I'm no fool. I know you're a queen and your kingdom must come first. You have duties that extend far beyond . . ." He trailed off, searching for the right word.

"Love?" said Wren.

He smiled. "I only mean that Elske and I intend to make our own way in this kingdom. You don't owe us anything. We will find our place."

Wren understood then. Tor had come to Eana because he loved her, but he did not wish to burden her with his presence either. Even now, after giving up everything he knew in Gevra, he was putting her needs ahead of his own, slowing his pace to match hers.

But Wren wanted to run headlong into love with Tor. Into forever. And she wanted him to know it.

"What if your place is here at Anadawn?" she said. "With me?"

He drew a breath, hope catching in the air between them.

"You know, there are beasts in Eana, too," she went on. "Great brown bears and hunting wolves. Mountain lions and the most magnificent elk. I was thinking we could start training them. It would do no harm to strengthen our army, especially after the events of the last several months." She bit her lip, suddenly worried that he might rebuff the idea, that she had made a fool of herself for even suggesting it. "That is, of course, if you knew a wrangler that might be—"

"I know a wrangler."

Her cheeks flushed. "I've always thought you looked particularly good in green."

"Didn't you know?" he said, coming toward her. "Green is my favorite color."

"Oh?" she said, looking up at him. "Since when?"

"Since you, Wren."

She smiled, seized by another rush of heat. "I think I'm done talking."

"That makes two of us." Tor was upon her in three strides, grabbing her waist and pressing her back against the door. He seized her mouth, brushing his tongue against hers. She groaned, reluctantly breaking the kiss to hitch his shirt up. He tore it off, flinging it into the fireplace. The flames hissed as they devoured it.

"Oops," he whispered against her lips.

Wren summoned a gust, deftly putting the flames out. "Shirts are overrated," she said, kissing him again.

"So are gowns." His hands found the swell of her breasts then moved impatiently to her corset. He plucked at the laces, ripping them apart one by one. He gave a frustrated huff. "Why must they be so damn complicated?"

Wren rose to her tiptoes to give him better access, trailing kisses along his neck. He stiffened against her, his fingers grappling hopelessly with her corset. "This is torture."

Wren smiled, tracing his earlobe with her tongue. "Isn't that the Gevran way?"

His eyes glinted at her words. "I'll show you the Gevran way." He pulled a dagger from his waistband, his free hand rising to cup the back of her neck. "Don't move," he said as he deftly sliced through the binds of her corset. It fell away in one piece and he groaned again, tossing aside the knife and coming to his knees before her. A growl rumbled in his throat as he tugged the rest of her dress down, pressing a kiss just below her naval. Wren's knees trembled as he stood to unfasten his trousers. The world blurred around them as they came back together, Tor kissing her, wildly, madly, as he lifted her from the puddle of her skirts. Wren wrapped her legs around him as he carried her to the bed.

He set her down gently, taking a moment to drink her in. "My Wren," he murmured as she pulled him down on top of her.

After, when they lay blissfully spent in each other's arms, Tor trailed his fingers through her hair. "After all these years of war, I have finally found my peace," he said. "You are the only cause I will ever need, Wren."

Wren closed her eyes, listening to the steady thrum of his heartbeat. "I love you, Tor. To the end of this life and beyond."

Tor grinned, his hand coming to his chest as if she had shot an arrow through his heart. "Say it again, Wren."

She laughed as she climbed on top of him. "I love you, Tor Iversen." He gazed up at her, lovestruck. "Show me."

"With pleasure," said Wren, leaning down to kiss him.

54

ROSE

Rose Valhart had always loved the kingdom of Eana, even before she had truly known it. As a child, she had spent hours walking among the flowers in her garden, imagining all the others that bloomed across the vast plains of Eana. She knew the mountains in the north were older than most, their proud stony ridges overlooking winding rivers and rolling hills. The valleys in the south were sun-soaked and fertile, home to the finest vineyards. The west coast was wild and rugged, dappled with sea spray and scattered with sands that had kissed the feet of the first witch Eana herself. And in the middle of it all, the desert lay like a golden coin, rich with its own special culture.

The east was vibrant, too, Anadawn Palace standing like a proud soldier overlooking the bustling city of Eshlinn where tavern lanterns flickered long into the night and the air echoed with laughter. Yes, the kingdom of Eana was beautiful—it belonged to Rose, and she to it. But there was another kingdom that had come to possess a part of her heart, and she loved that place just as fiercely.

Just as she loved its king.

As the sun set in the golden heart of the desert, and the Palace of

Eternal Sunlight echoed with birdsong and music, Rose thought to herself that it truly was a beautiful evening to get married.

She *felt* beautiful as she stepped out into the courtyard, dressed in a gauzy ivory gown. The bodice had been embroidered with pearlescent suns to honor the kingdom in which she now stood and roses as a tribute to the land where she had grown up, while the magnificent, tiered skirt cascaded around her like the waves of Ortha. Beneath a finely wrought ruby tiara that perfectly matched her engagement ring, her curls had been adorned with crystals that sparkled like the stars of Eana.

She steadied her breath as the music soared, offering a smile to the king who awaited her at the other end of the aisle.

High on the dais in the courtyard, Shen's molten eyes never left Rose as she drifted toward him with graceful, measured steps. He looked even more handsome than usual, dressed in a red silk shirt, fitted black trousers, and high black boots. His dark hair was swept away from his face by the gold band of his crown, which he wore in honor of the occasion—a lovestruck king finally marrying his starry-eyed queen.

When Rose ascended the steps to the dais, Shen took her hands in his, pressing a kiss to each as the officiant, Daiyu, began the ceremony, speaking poetically about love and commitment. Gazing into Shen's night-dark eyes, Rose found herself daydreaming about everything still to come—the food and the merriment, the music and the dancing, and then, finally, the moment when they would retire to their bedroom and spend their first night together as husband and wife.

Yes, today was already perfect. But Rose knew tomorrow would be even better, and all the days after that, too.

55

WREN

As the sun scattered the last of its rays over the Sunkissed Kingdom, Wren Greenrock sat in the courtyard of the Palace of Eternal Sunlight, watching her sister marry her oldest and dearest friend. She was grinning so hard her cheeks ached. Elske snoozed contentedly at her feet while Tor sat at her side, dabbing his brow with the cuff of his shirtsleeve.

Wren turned to help, opening the button on his collar and then the one beneath it just for good measure. "Hang in there," she whispered. "It will be dark soon."

"You two are shameless," hissed Celeste, who was sitting behind Wren, between Anika and Marino. "Can't you keep your clothes on for two minutes?"

Wren stuck her tongue out. "I don't want my Gevran to melt."

"I can relate," grumbled Anika, desperately fanning herself to no avail. "This heat is *truly* oppressive."

"I did tell you not to wear fur," said Celeste.

"Allow me, Your Highness," said Marino, removing his tricorn and leaning over his sister to fan Anika with it.

She sighed with pleasure. "Oh, that is *divine*."

Celeste batted the tricorn away. "Nice try, brother. Keep your hat to yourself." She flicked her wrist, summoning a cooling breeze. It rippled in the frills of Anika's dress and gently ruffled her hair. "Better?"

"*Bliss*," said Anika, planting a grateful kiss on Celeste's cheek. "Thank you, my love."

Marino sat back with a sigh. "I've never felt so tragically single."

"Don't worry, we'll find you the perfect someone," said Wren.

"I thought you were in love with a mermaid," said Tor.

Marino harrumphed. "Is that really all I'm known for?"

"Yes," said Wren and Celeste as one.

"Hush now, you noisy little parakeets!" scolded Grandmother Lu, who was sitting two seats over. She jabbed Wren with her cane. "Less chatter, more respectful silence."

"Sorry," said Wren, turning back around. But Daiyu hadn't missed a beat. Rose and Shen were still holding hands, gazing at each other so adoringly that Wren doubted either of them would notice if a blood beetle came and devoured their guests.

Tor shifted in his seat, still trying to get comfortable.

Wren followed Celeste's lead, summoning a breeze to cool him.

He closed his eyes, relishing the brief respite. "When we get married, let's do it in a forest. Or on a glacier."

Wren's brows raised. "What do you mean, *when* we get married?"

He opened his eyes, glancing sidelong at her. "One day soon, this will be us."

A delicious thrill stole through Wren. "Will it?" she asked teasingly.

"Won't it?" he said.

Her lips twitched. "Only if you let me swing in from the chandelier."

"My darling Wren," he said, returning her smile, "I wouldn't have it any other way."

They dissolved into muffled laughter, earning them another prodding from Grandmother Lu.

Once the sun had set in earnest, the ceremony came to an end. When Rose and Shen were pronounced husband and wife, they shared a lingering kiss, which prompted the entire courtyard to burst into applause.

Then came an explosion of fireworks. Everyone tipped their heads back, watching enchanted lions and glittering dragons dance across the sky. A great cheer erupted as the people of the Sunkissed Kingdom flooded the streets, rejoicing in their new queen.

56

ROSE

Two blissful weeks after her wedding to Shen Lo, on the night of her return to Anadawn, Rose slipped from her bedroom in the east tower where her new husband slumbered, and clambered out onto the palace roof.

It was good to be home, her face feathered by the river wind and bathed in the starlight of the glittering sky. Her sky. Rose loved every inch of her kingdom, but it was the stars of Eana that most enchanted her. First as a young girl trapped in her tower, peering out at the great wide world, and now as a new queen looking to her future.

She smiled as she lay back on the roof, listening to the palace wind down for the night. The moon was full and bright above her, and Rose blew out a breath, marveling at its immense beauty. How lucky she was to have the sky all to herself. To get to spend the night out here, swaddled in her warmest nightgown with a woolen blanket draped around her shoulders, listening to the song of the nightingale in the trees and the quiet patter of—

"*Hissing seaweed,*" cursed Wren as she clambered out of a nearby window. "It's freezing up here."

Rose sighed. "I did tell you to bring a blanket."

"I got distracted," said Wren as she crawled across the slats in a pair of silk pajamas and sheepskin slippers. Her hair was as messy as a bird's nest and her cheeks were slightly pink. "Tor was teaching me how to—"

"I really don't need the details," said Rose quickly. She lifted the edge of her blanket. "Here. You can share mine."

"Thanks," said Wren, snuggling in beside her sister. She removed a napkin from her pocket and opened it to reveal two crushed yellow macarons. "I brought you a snack."

Rose plucked one from the napkin. "You truly are a good sister," she said, biting it in half and relishing the burst of citrus.

"Almost as good as you," said Wren, nibbling at the edges of the other.

They lay back on the roof, turning their gaze to the stars.

"Our birthday is coming up soon," said Wren.

"Yes," said Rose, who had been discussing it with Celeste earlier that evening. "Don't worry. I've already started planning our party."

Wren snorted. "Of course you have. And here I thought you'd be distracted by your honeymoon."

"A capable queen can handle more than two things at once." Rose smiled coyly as she polished off the rest of her macaron. "Especially when one of those things is *very* enjoyable."

"*I really don't need the details*," said Wren, perfectly mimicking her sister from a moment ago.

Rose's laughter soared, her heart lifting with familiar joy. "Just make sure you get me a good present."

"You mean I have to get you a present for my *own* birthday?" said Wren.

"I'm afraid so," said Rose, starlight refracting off her ruby ring as she dusted the crumbs from her fingers.

Wren blew out a breath. "Very well. But the same goes for you. And I want an elk."

Rose chuckled, entirely unsurprised by the request. Then she turned to her sister, the joviality fading from her voice. Thoughts of their upcoming birthday were making her feel pensive and, more than that, grateful for how far they had come. "It's hard to believe everything that's happened to us these past twelve months. All these years, I thought I had no magic. No family. And now, here you are, like a wish sprung from my wildest dreams."

Wren found Rose's hand beneath the blanket and held it. "Growing up in Ortha, I always thought of myself as unlucky. A witch with no parents, a girl who would have to sneak around and steal her way into a life that didn't truly belong to her. I'm so glad I failed, Rose." She let out a small laugh. "I'm so glad that we decided to do this together. To rule. To fight. To lead. I always thought Anadawn was my destiny, but I see now that it was you all along."

Rose smiled at her sister's words. They warmed her heart, chasing the chill from her toes. "How strange it is to think that this time last year I didn't even know about you," she murmured. "I thought my life was going to turn out entirely differently. I'm so thankful that it didn't. I'm so thankful that you found me."

Wren squeezed her hand. "We found each other."

"At long last," said Rose. "And that's the best gift of all."

Wren perked up. "Does that mean—?"

"You still have to get me a gift," she added hastily.

They pealed with laughter, their breaths making clouds in the air.

"I wonder what the next year will hold for us," said Rose after a while.

"Peace, I hope," said Wren.

"I hope so, too."

They watched the sky awhile, until a flock of starcrests came from the east, soaring over the distant forest and casting silver pinwheels across the sky. Perhaps it was Rose's imagination, but she thought the birds seemed happier than usual, freer.

She studied their shapes in the sky, frowning as she tried to divine their meaning. "What do you suppose they're saying?" she asked Wren. "I can't seem to figure it out."

Wren was smiling at the birds. "That's because they're not prophesizing. They're playing."

"Oh." Rose closed her eyes, overcome by a burgeoning sense of relief. She loved the starcrests of Eana just as she loved all its creatures, but for the first time in her life, she was happy not to know what lay beyond the full moon. For Rose, the future was finally unwritten and she found she liked it that way.

By the serene look on Wren's face, she knew her sister felt the same way. They lay there for another hour, talking and laughing as the starcrests danced above them and the moon bathed the kingdom in its soft and steady glow.

"Do you think we'll still do this when we're old and gray?" said Wren.

"Of course we will," said Rose, feeling the sureness in her bones. "In fact, I think we should do this every full moon, so that no matter what happens in our lives or how they might expand to welcome new love and in time, new family, we'll never stray too far from each other again. What do you think?"

"I think I'd like that," said Wren, with quiet relief. "So long as there are snacks."

"There will be so many snacks," said Rose solemnly.

"Good."

Yes, thought Rose. The plan was good. Their *life* was good.

As the wind stirred and the night grew colder, the starcrests scattered into the west. Exhaustion tugged at Rose. It was approaching midnight and tomorrow she meant to rise at dawn. After all, she had a kingdom to run. Two kingdoms.

Wren yawned as she sat up. "We should head inside."

"Good idea," said Rose, casting off their blanket.

They were just about to crawl back into the palace when a new gust stirred, and a shadow moved in front of the moon. Rose looked up, her breath catching in her throat. There was an enormous bird gliding above them. Each wing was as large as a pear tree, and its feathers were a perfect mix of tawny and gold, aside from its tail, which was a magnificent emerald green.

"Stars above!" she cried, leaping to her feet. "It's a green-tailed hawk!"

Wren stood up to get a better look at the creature. It possessed a magic all its own, like something from a fairy tale or a bedtime story of old. But Rose knew it was even more ancient than that. Long ago, when the earth was young and still unformed, Eana the first witch had left the stars on the back of a green-tailed hawk and come to land in the sea, where the creature changed and grew to become the very country in which they now stood. If Eana was the creator of this kingdom, then her magical green-tailed hawk was the very heart of it.

And now, after thousands of years, another hawk had come.

"It's incredible," said Wren, unable to tear her gaze from the bird. They watched in muted wonder as it came to land on a nearby turret. It turned its head, gazing at them with its large golden eyes. "What do you think this means?"

"It must a sign from Eana, our ancestor," said Rose.

Wren turned back to her, excitement catching in her voice. "Do you think she's smiling down on us?"

Rose nodded, her grin spreading to match her sister's. "Yes, I do."

The two sisters leaned against each other, like mirror images, and watched the hawk lift into flight, soaring through the sky, toward tomorrow.

ACKNOWLEDGMENTS

We are so grateful to have been able to write this trilogy. Thank you to everyone who read *Twin Crowns*, *Cursed Crowns*, and now *Burning Crowns*. We've loved writing these books and hope you've loved reading them.

These books are about sisterhood and strength of community coming together—and we are so lucky to have each other as sisters and our own incredible community. We couldn't have written these books without the support of so many people.

To our amazing agent, Claire Wilson, aka Princess Claire, who is our literary fairy godmother and steadfast champion. Thank you, Claire, for everything!

And to the phenomenal Pete Knapp, aka Prince Pete, at Park & Fine in the US—thank you for being in our corner and coming along for the Twin Crowns ride. More tacos in London soon, please.

We would also like to thank the wider team at RCW, especially Sam Coates for selling the trilogy to many wonderful publishers around the world. Thank you as well to Safae El-Ouahabi at RCW, and to Stuti Telidevara at Park & Fine.

Thank you to our film agents—Michelle Kroes, Berni Barta, and Emily Hayward-Whitlock—for finding us the best partners to continue the Twin Crowns adventure in a new medium.

We will never forget the moment when we sold *Twin Crowns* to

Farshore in the UK and Balzer + Bray in the US—it was such a thrill and we are so grateful to our editors on both sides of the pond for their enthusiasm and excitement for these books. Huge thank-you to Lindsey Heaven and Sarah Levinson at Farshore in the UK, and Kristin Daly Rens at Balzer + Bray in the US, for making the editorial process such a joyous one.

We would also like to thank everyone on the Farshore and Balzer + Bray teams who worked on the trilogy. Special thanks to designers Ryan Hammon in the UK and Chris Kwon in the US for another stunning cover featuring the incomparable Charlie Bowater's art. These covers are so beautiful and bring us so much joy!

We are very grateful to all the retailers and bookshops for their support in the UK, Ireland, the US, and beyond! Thank you to Easons and Waterstones for their stunning special editions. We'd also like to thank all the indies who have supported the series, especially Muswell Hill Children's Books in London, and Books of Wonder in New York City. And we are so grateful to the teams at FairyLoot and LitJoy Crate for supporting the trilogy and creating such beautiful special editions. Special thank you to Anissa de Gomery.

A heartfelt thank-you to our fantastic street team, the Cursed Crowns Crew, for going above and beyond with their support for the book. Abi, Abby, Aina, Alice, Angel, Angelina, Angie, Caitlin, Cassidy, Courtney, Dania, Divya, Elle, Emily, Emma, Gemma, Gigi, Georgia, Haadi, Hannah, Holly, Joanna, Katelin, Katrina, Kayla, Kellie, Kimberly, Lauren, Libby Ann, Macall, Maha, Menna, Pawan, Reka, Rosa, Sam, Sarah, Shobhan, Sofie, Stacey, Stephanie, Tanweer, Victoria Alyesa, and Zhi Ling— thank you all! We have loved getting to know you and are so grateful for everything you have done for the books.

And the biggest thank-you to the readers who have taken Rose and Wren (and Shen and Tor and Alarik and the rest of the gang) into their hearts and shared their love for these characters. It has been so special for us. And we have loved being able to meet so many of you both in real life and online! We hope you love this final book in the trilogy.

And, of course, thank you to all our wonderful friends and family across the globe for their continued support, with extra thanks and love to the Webber, Doyle, and Tsang families. This book is dedicated to a trio of incredible mothers—Grace Doyle, who is Cat's mother; Virginia Webber, who is both Katie's mother and Cat's mother-in-law; and Louisa Tsang, who is Katie's mother-in-law. This trilogy celebrates strong women, and these are three of the most inspiring women we know. We'd also like to thank our fathers, Ciaran Doyle and Rob Webber, as well as our siblings: Colm, Ali, and Conor Doyle and Jack and Janie Webber for their encouragement and enthusiasm. Cat would also like to thank Jack as her husband for his love and support, and Katie thanks her husband, Kevin, for the same.

A special shout-out and lots of love to Katie's daughters, Evie and Mira Tsang, who did not help in the writing in any way but always boosted morale, and Cat's adorable new niece, Ava Doyle. And we can't forget Cat's dog, Cali, who inspired Elske the wolf.

Most of all, we would like to thank each other. This has been such an exciting journey, and it has been so special to experience it together. What a joy to experience the magic of sisterhood and power of friendship in real life. Forever grateful for Twin Crowns, and forever grateful for each other.